Finding You

Jack Whitney

This one is for every person who "didn't make the coffee."
And for all my Chloe's out there.

May you be seen, heard, and then railed backward over the
office desk while wearing a blindfold and getting called a
'good girl.'

Cheers, bitches.

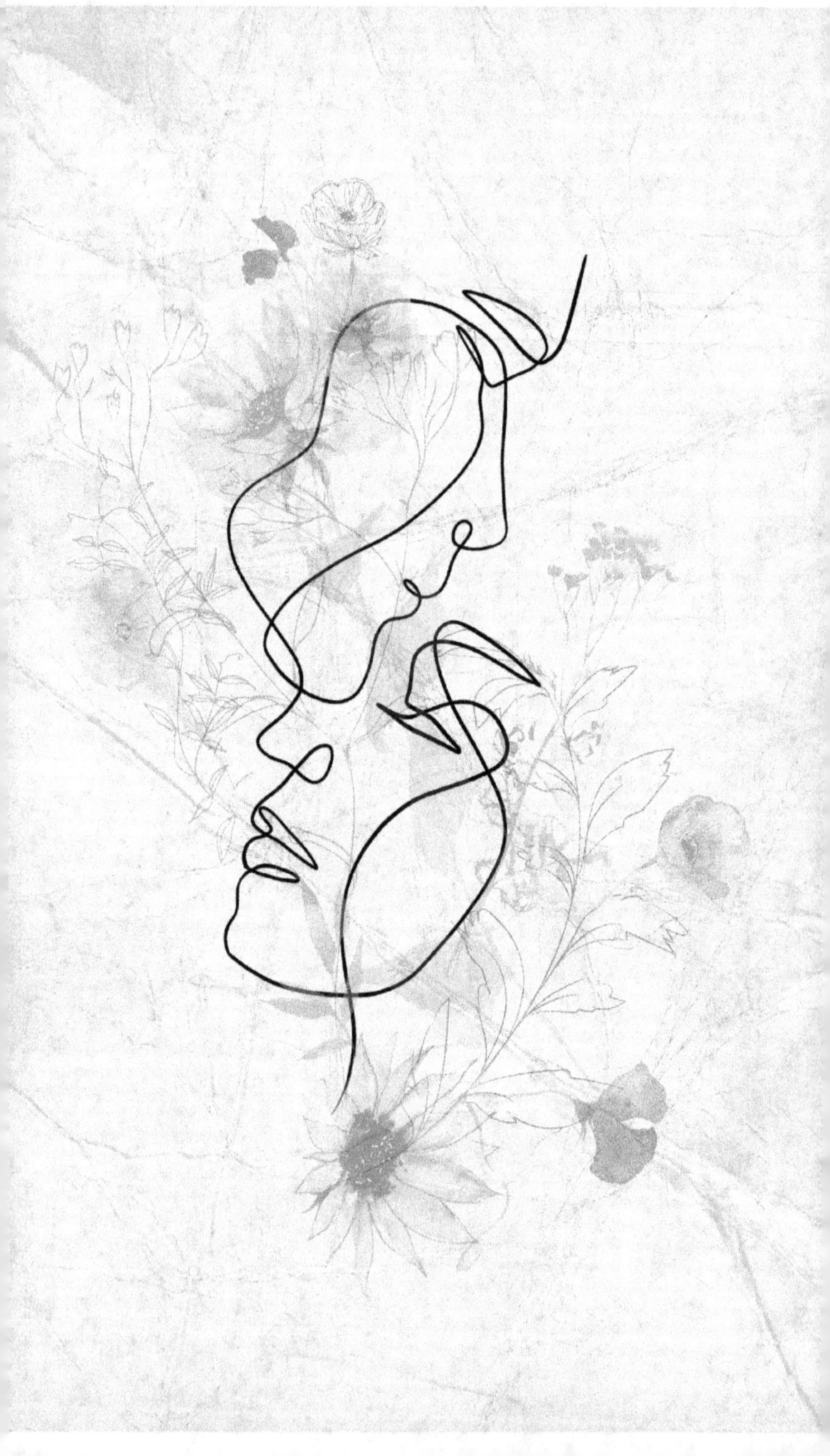

Foreword

While it is not required, it is HIGHLY recommended that you read the short novella, Sweet Girl, before starting this novel.

There are some issues within this novel to be aware of, including some of Chloe's past that she briefly refers to in Sweet Girl.

Here is a list of possible triggers to be aware of within these pages:

Depictions of physical abuse (dreams), and stories of sexual assault, manipulation, and domestic violence. Explicit sex scenes including temperature (wax) play, blindfolding, spanking, and praise.

No acts in this book are in any way meant as a guide to exploring sexual fantasies or to give suggestions. Do not try these acts at home as they are depicted here. Instead, please do your own research if you are curious about the world of BDSM. It is important to learn how to perform these activities safely with your partner. There are a lot of resources out there. Please be safe, and remember aftercare.

Chapter One

Chloe

The quad-shot espresso with oat milk in my hand was not enough coffee to start the day.

It had begun with nearly having an argument with my best friend, and then on the way to work, I'd tripped on three cracks in the sidewalk when my heels got caught, it rained on my walk from the parking garage, and I'd dropped my cell phone in a puddle that looked like it had a layer of oil floating on the top. Not to mention I'd barely been able to sleep due to the weird dreams I'd been having. I kept seeing a hill, golden wings, and feeling shadowed hands touching me. No face, just the shadow. What was most bewildering, though, was the feeling I woke up with every time—butterflies in my stomach, heated cheeks, restlessness in my muscles, an aching heart…

"I think I'm dying," I told my best friend, Lana, on our video chat that morning. Since moving across the country last year, video calls have become our daily ritual. I missed her more than I could express. There was something about Lana that lit up an entire room and made everyone around her feel comfortable. Maybe it was the fact that she was a therapist, or maybe it was just Lana's presence. But I could tell her everything, and she could read me like a book.

"That medical site says I'm dying," I continued.

"You can't trust those sites, babe," Lana said, crossing her legs and leaning her elbow onto the countertop. Her black cat jumped on the barstool beside her, and she pulled the feline into her lap. "You put in a stuffy nose and it comes back with nasal tumors. How did you say you felt again?"

"Hi, Salem," I cooed to the beautiful little cat. "She's getting big."

"Stop stalling," Lana said. "Let's hear it. How did you feel?"

I twisted the bread bag and wrapped the tie around it before throwing two pieces into the toaster. "Racing—no, aching heart. Weak knees. Like… adrenaline? Dopamine? Almost giddy, as if you've had a glass of red wine—"

"I'd like to know what kind of red wine you're drinking," Lana muttered behind the cup of tea at her lips.

I pursed my lips at her, and she chuckled, her spiraled curls falling out of the colorful headband she had wrapped around her head. "Right. Go on. What else?"

"Ah… Warm. My stomach was fluttering almost—"

"Are you sure you didn't eat anything odd?" Lana asked.

"I've had this same dream for a week now. Countless times in the past. I don't think it has anything to do with my eating habits," I replied.

"I mean, you did eat an entire large pepperoni pizza by yourself last night," Lana teased.

My lips twisted as I tried to deny a smile, pressing my palms into the edge of the counter. "Tyler is out of town," I argued. "And it was a Buffalo Chicken pizza—"

"Extra hot sauce, ranch, and a few cider beers," Lana knew. "Did you also have the strawberry ice cream?"

My toast popped up and I took it out to smear red pepper jelly on it. "Pistachio, actually."

Lana laughed softly and took another drink of her tea, her eyes still sleepy from the caffeine not kicking in yet. "Where's

Tyler this week?"

Tyler Drake. My fiancé.

We'd been together three years now, engaged for two of them. I'd had the most challenging time picking a date—to the point that all decisions had been handed over to Tyler's mother and mine. The date, the location, the decor, even my dress.

"Ah… Florida," I said as I sat down at the table with my toast and coffee. "His father wanted to talk to him about the latest investment." I slapped a sarcastic smile on my lips. "It's very exciting."

"Sounds like it," Lana mumbled.

Tyler was—what he liked to call—an entrepreneur. He's had his hands in a few small businesses that he swears will be the next big thing, along with owning a few pieces of real estate. He was always traveling to check on things.

"What about the wedding? Three-month countdown, right?" Lana said.

I nodded and took a bite of toast. "Are you coming next week?" I asked.

"For your dress fitting? Wouldn't miss it. *Especially* since you picked it out without me," Lana replied, batting her lashes and giving me a tight-lipped smile.

"You know I had to do that while my mom was in town—"

"Along with your sisters and Tyler's mom," Lana interjected.

"I'm honestly surprised we found anything. It was the first shop and you know how particular my sisters are," I finished.

"They all made sure you found something while they were there," Lana said. "And I'm still trying to figure out why *they* chose your dress and not you."

I chewed my toast, my stomach knotting. "They've chosen everything else. Why not my dress, too?" I asked softly.

"Because it's your fucking wedding—"

"You know I don't care about those things," I argued. "They do."

"And *why* don't you care about those things?"

Sometimes I hated her.

I sighed and downed the rest of my coffee. "Can we talk about this later?" I said as I stood to clean up the table. "Like… after I've had a few glasses of wine and a big fat steak?"

"Oh, is that what we're having for dinner tonight?"

"It's Friday and Tyler has some fancy dinner with a client, so I won't hear from him until like two in the morning. Therefore, yes. You're my date, and we're ordering a three-courser. Don't worry, I'll order yours too."

"Such a gentleman," Lana said, giving a kissy face to the screen. "Hey, do you think the bridal boutique will also have in my dress to try on?"

"I'll have Tyler call to make sure they do. He can probably pull a few strings."

Lana scoffed. "You mean slap a few hundred dollars in their hands and demand to be taken care of?"

"You're the only person I know that would say that condescendingly."

"It's not a bad thing," Lana shrugged. "He just throws money at any problem he might come across. Including any problem with you."

"Lana…" I said her name in a warning tone, my jaw tightening. It was too early for this conversation, too early to hear her complain about Tyler or bring up any qualms she might have with or about him.

"I'm just saying… Maybe these dreams you're having are part of the universe's way of talking to you," Lana said.

My mouth twisted in annoyance. "What?"

"The things you're describing sound like what it feels like to realize you're in love," she continued. "The warmth. The aching heart, butterflies in your stomach, restless muscles, dopamine, weak knees… Maybe it's your soul reaching out."

"Reaching out for what?" I asked in disbelief.

"For its counterpart," Lana said.

I huffed as I rinsed my cup out. "You're ridiculous."

"Am I, though?" Lana asked.

A heavy sigh left me. I was engaged. I didn't know what she was saying, even as I knew she didn't like Tyler all that much, but this?

"I have to stop by the coffee shop for espresso," I said. "Barely got any sleep."

"Because you were banging that shadow all night," Lana said with a wink. "I'm telling you, babe. The universe is speaking to you. Your soul is crying out and trying to tell you something."

"That I'm dying and having hot flashes?"

Lana scoffed. "You should listen to it."

"Lana…"

"I know, I know—"

"It's not that I don't believe in that kind of thing," I said quickly. "I just… I like where my life is right now. I'm not exactly looking for something to come in and change all of that."

"That's a lovely comfort zone you're treading in," Lana mocked.

"Good*bye*, Lana," I said in a sing-song voice.

She grinned. "Talk to you tonight, babe."

Thank fuck it was Friday.

I'd contemplated everything Lana had said the entire way to my office—which was probably why I'd nearly broken my ankle on the sidewalk.

At least judging by the others in the office elevator, I was not the only person with a shit morning. Everyone was wet and clutching coffees like that was their job, not the ones we were heading to. My new marketing firm was on the thirteenth and fourteenth floors of a large building. I'd founded it with a friend just before meeting Tyler three years ago. We'd started out small, taking on a couple of my clients that I already had and bringing them in for full projects rather than just a few ads like I had been delivering.

Things were going really well, and since moving to California the year before and adding this new office space and a cluster of employees, we'd grown exponentially, even landing a few more prominent clients.

Jasmine, my assistant, met me as the elevator doors opened on the fourteenth floor. I frowned at her standing there looking antsy and excited, a grin on her face and clenching her hands together in front of her.

"Morning, Jasmine," I said upon reaching her.

"Good morning," she replied in a chipper voice.

"What's happening?" I asked. "You never meet me at the doors."

"Did you not get the email this morning?" she asked.

I took a sip of my coffee—my too-hot coffee—and grimaced at the way it burned my mouth. "I've made it a rule never to check my email before the start of a workday," I told her. I'd started too many mornings already stressed out by checking email, and had chosen a few years back to protect my sanity by holding off until logging in.

"Why?" I batted away a heart balloon that someone walking past was carrying. "What did I miss?"

"New client," Jasmine said as she plucked a rose from one of the tables and smelled it. "Ezzie is going around ordering decorations already to celebrate."

Another heart balloon came into my sight line, and I started to realize they were everywhere. And the moment we rounded the corner, I stopped in my tracks.

Hearts—giant red hearts—in balloon form hovered all

around the open workspace. There were pink, white, and red confetti hearts on all the tables, streamers on the doors, pink heart pillows on the community couches, and some of our poufs had been replaced by red floor pillows.

I couldn't stop staring at the audacious decor. "Did someone get engaged?" I asked.

"Ezzie thought it was fitting," Jasmine said.

"It is *May*," I said, wholly flabbergasted that there was heart decor everywhere. "What the actual fuck," I muttered. We continued walking to the back of the room where my office was. "Who is the client?"

The phone on Jasmine's desk rang before she could even respond. She slipped away quickly to answer it, and I strode inside my office, tossing my bag onto the chair by the door. Red roses decorated my desk in a tall white vase, no card or indication as to who they were from. Though the more I thought about it, I realized maybe they were just part of Ezzie's decor.

I wracked my brain trying to figure out who she had landed for her to be changing the office over to red and pink instead of our signature black and green.

There was an email with the subject line 'NEW CLIENT BITCH' at the top of the priorities folder on my computer. I took a moment to settle in my chair before opening it, and when I did, my entire body froze at the logo in the middle of the email.

My heart skipped, heat suddenly beating on my cheeks. I felt like someone was lighting a fire to my entire being. Visions of hands, hearts, snow, and sweating flesh flashed through my mind. Candy hearts on my tongue, a hand across my ass, the moans of cursing to the gods.

"That's my good girl."

The memory of that rasping voice sent a shiver down my spine.

"Oh, fucking hell," I muttered.

Jasmine knocked on the doorframe, making me flinch. "Dani wants to know if you have time to review the Halloween campaign she's working on."

The email had me off-kilter. All noise around me muted.

Cupid's fucking Arrow.

The dating app, Cupid's Arrow, was our newest client.

Fuck. Fuck. *Fuck.*

It continued to be the most popular dating app out there even after the influx of other dating apps trying to emulate their algorithm. Cupid's Arrow had an advantage over the others, however, that no one knew about.

It was founded by the God of Lust himself.

Eros.

He was parading around as a mortal named Gavin Erosin. As for how long he'd been in this disguise, I wasn't sure. I hadn't seen him since that Valentine's Day party five years ago—a night I thought about more often than I should have.

I didn't bother reading the remainder of the project description. All I could think about was Gavin. I hadn't felt that kind of desire, lust, or absolute greed for another person since then. The thought of seeing him again… It knotted and twisted everything in me to the point that I was nauseous.

It wasn't that I didn't want to see him—because fuck, I did.

It was that seeing him scared the shit out of me.

I wondered how I would feel now that I was engaged to someone else. I wondered if that need would still be there. It was only one night, but it had been a night of more than just wild sex. We had truly connected, and by the time the sun rose, I could see myself truly being in a relationship with him. I had felt genuine laughter, want, and happiness that night that I hadn't thought possible with someone with whom I also had an intimate relationship. I'd even opened up with him about my father—something I never did.

We had parted ways and gone back to our normal lives the next day with no way of reaching the other.

I'd often thought about if I'd made a mistake not asking him to change flights the next morning.

"Hello?" Jasmine called. "Earth to Chloe."

I snapped out of my daze, blinking myself back to reality. "Yeah, sorry, what did you ask?"

"Dani wants to know if you have time to look at the project she's working on," Jasmine repeated.

"Ah… Actually—" I gathered my things and started to stand. "Actually, I need to go talk to Ezzie about the email. I'll… Tell Dani to email it to me and I'll look at it today."

"Are you okay?" Jasmine asked.

"Yeah. I'm fine. I'll be back after lunch."

And I left my office without another word.

I had to see Ezzie to find out more details.

As I entered the elevator, I took my phone out and sent a text to Lana.

Make sure you bring vodka to our date tonight. You'll need it, I sent.

It's barely nine and you already need vodka?

We have a new client.

Oh? Tell me more.

You use it on the daily.

Toilet paper?

I snorted. **No. An app. A dating app.**

Three dots strummed at the bottom of my screen for as long as it took me on the elevator and to cross the room to Ezzie's office. I had just closed the phone when Lana's text came through, and I tapped my screen to see it.

You shut your fucking mouth right now!

Ezzie's office was on the thirteenth floor. We had the same office, just one floor apart. The same corner, the same size, but Ezzie was on the business floor while I ran the creative floor.

Ez was pacing back and forth, EarPods in and talking on the phone when I reached her. I knew which client she was talking to without needing an explanation. Ez's negotiating skills were one of the reasons we'd gone into business together. I would handle the creative side, and she could handle the business side.

Although taking on the most popular dating app out there was not exactly what I had in mind.

Babe! I need details! Lana was texting.

Did you see him?

Is he still hot?

I shook my head and crossed my hands in front of me as I waited on Ez. She glanced sideways and finally saw me. Her face lit up, and she held up a finger, signaling me to wait to talk to her.

I looked down at my phone one more time, finding that Lana had sent one more message.

Look at the universe, and there was a wink-face emoji after the words.

I resisted throwing my phone and instead opened it up just as Ez was hanging up her own phone call.

I hate you.

Love youuuu, she said with a kissy-face

"Chloe!" Ezzie said enthusiastically, her arms in the air, and I realized she had finally hung up her phone. I snapped my attention to her and placed my phone in the back pocket of my dark jeans.

Ezzie's beautiful face was glowing. Her short, dark blue hair was curled lightly today, a nude color on her plump lips, and light, simple makeup that accentuated her tan skin. I was envious of her style. Today's outfit consisted of high-waisted black pants with small white stripes and a snug black long-sleeve top that fit her arms, full breasts, and stopped around her ribs, showing off her soft mid-drift.

And barefoot, as she always was around the office.

Ezzie was a tall, plus-size goddess who commanded attention. When she and her girlfriend, Raegan, went to dinner or a bar with Lana and me, it was hard to contain us. Tyler had even made a point in the past to ensure he was out of town to his parents' when Lana and Raegan were visiting.

"Morning, Ez," I said, wishing I could return her enthusiasm.

"Anything you'd like to tell me?" Ezzie grinned, folding her arms over her chest and lifting up her chin. "Anything like 'you're the best' or 'congratulations on nailing that contract, you fucking goddess' or—"

"Great job, you fucking divine," I said with a small clap, chuckling at how proud she was.

She flipped her hair off her shoulders and did a slight bow. "Thank you, thank you. Honestly, it was pretty easy. They contacted us," she said with a laugh.

"Who contacted you?" I asked.

"It was…" Ezzie leaned over her desk and clicked a few times on her computer. "Avril Patel," she finally said. "She's over their marketing department. Says she wants to do a special campaign, including new logos, for their ten-year anniversary, and she's having trouble hiring new staff. So she decided to outsource since it was such a large project."

I let the sentence sink in and took a deep breath, putting on my logical face and ignoring the emotional side that was screaming.

"So, when do we start?" I asked. "Who is our contact? Are we meeting in person or—"

"Are you okay?" Ezzie cut in.

I balked. "Yeah. Why?"

"Your vibe is off," she said. "What's wrong? You're normally excited about new projects, especially large ones with well-known clients."

"I'm excited."

"Tell your face," Ezzie said with a raised brow.

My lips pursed and I looked at the ground. I couldn't hide anything from Ezzie. She always saw through my facade when something was wrong.

"Wedding things," I only halfway lied.

"Ah," Ezzie said, nodding. "Four months out?"

"Lovely August wedding," I said, my tone dripping with sarcasm as I gave her a tight-lipped smile. "I'll be wearing sweat cloths between my thighs."

Ezzie smirked at me. "If I recall, you couldn't choose a date so you let Tyler choose."

I flopped into one of her chairs and sighed. "You sound like Lana," I said.

"Oh, love her. When is she coming?" Ezzie asked.

"She'll be in on Thursday night," I answered. "Remember, I'm taking next week off."

"Perfect timing. I'll try not to bother you. However, we are having a little meet and greet social with some of the team from Cupid's Arrow next Friday. I'd like you to be there to meet everyone."

I nearly hurled on her fluffy white rug, but I knew there was no getting out of it. "Great. Tyler and Lana will be here."

"I'm sure he'll love that," Ezzie teased.

"Yeah," I scoffed. "He will." I slapped the arms of the chair and stood again. "Anything else I should know? I'm going to get a wrap on my other projects before diving into the Cupid's Arrow one."

Or possibly drowning myself in nerves and agony.

Whichever came first.

Chapter Two

Gavin

"No, Mother. I am not coming home next week," I said into the phone.

"Oh, but Eros, it's such a special day," my mother cooed.

My brows narrowed as I reached for my coffee off the shop counter. "What's so special?" I asked. The cute barista caught my eye, and I mouthed a quick 'thank you' to her, winking in response to her leer, before turning on my heel toward the door.

"Because I'll be home too, and what's more special than seeing your own mother?" she replied.

I nearly stopped walking, my face going into a flat expression at her words. "I have work," I said.

"I don't understand *why* you work, love," she said. "It's not like you need to."

"I'm hanging up now," I told her.

"You've done enough mischievous deeds in your life. You could take a step back—"

"So says Aphrodite," I muttered.

"—you don't need the added stress," she continued. "You could come home. Retire. Find a few mortals to bring with—"

"Goodbye, Mother."

I hung up the phone before she could continue. Fucking Styx. I hadn't been home in over a century, and I didn't plan on going any time soon. I enjoyed living a normal life, having a regular job and regular friends. I may have been the God of Lust, but that didn't mean I needed only to surround myself with other gods.

I rounded the corner and pushed the revolving door into Cupid's Arrow's headquarters. What had started out as a few desks in an otherwise empty corner building had turned into five open stories of humming workers. No boring cubicles, but rather couches and private rooms for projects, floor seats and standing desks, treadmills, rest areas, and so much more. I wanted the environment to nourish productivity rather than box it in, and my team had delivered on that.

Of course, the arrows and hearts theme had grown a bit out of control over the years. It was one of the reasons why I'd requested a logo overhaul and rebrand for our ten-year anniversary.

The building was already buzzing as I entered and pushed my shades up atop my head, a few friends greeting me with words or handshakes. I made my way up to the fifth floor with my phone out and checked on numbers. I was consumed with the numbers and loved the gratification of seeing the volume of new users and interactions every day.

For a few hours every day, I toyed with the matches—some for good, some for fun. I checked in on some throughout the week just to see how things were going, and loved it when things went completely sideways or when matches that shouldn't have made it, actually worked out. I'd been to a few of those weddings, carrying an arrow with me just in case things needed a final nudge.

Avril, my marketing director, was waiting for me at the top of the stairs. A middle-aged woman who could run circles around any of the younger techs there. She was my right hand at the company, the go-to person who I could count on to carry out any wild ideas I might have. She was one of the first people I hired in the early days—just arriving from India with her family and looking for work. Her background was in event work and sales, and there was just something about her that I loved. She had become family over the years. I'd lost track of how many holidays I'd spent visiting her house for dinners.

"Good morning, Cupid," she said in her usual teasing tone.

I kissed her cheek as I hit the top step. "Morning, Av. What's new?" I asked, continuing to walk.

Avril joined me. "I had Maddi clear your calendar next Friday evening," she said.

"Why?"

"Social with the company I hired for our ten-year campaign and rebrand."

I paused in my step and looked at her. "We sourced out?"

Avril glanced around us nervously and then nodded to my office. I followed her cue and waited until she had closed the door behind us to continue talking.

"What's up?" I asked.

"Our branding team is short four people," she started. "I hired out because the ones who are left are spread so thin right now with other projects, I didn't want to overwhelm them. Adding this might push some into doing work on their downtime."

"I don't want that," I said. A work-life balance had always been essential to me. I never wanted anyone working more than they should.

"I know you don't," she said. "Which is why I found another firm to handle it. It'll be nice to have fresh eyes on everything, too. They're a younger company, very eager. I think you'll like them."

"What's their company name?"

"Designare Fusion."

I had never heard of it, but I trusted Avril enough to let her do what she thought was best for the company. "Okay," I said, reaching for a licorice rope from my candy vase to chew on. "What else should I know about them?"

"Women-owned," she said. "They haven't had an account as large as ours before. I'm interested to see what they make of it. Both owners will be heading up the project."

"The owners actually know how to do work in their field?" I asked.

"One is a marketing and PR guru who before this company was freelancing in public relations to C-list celebrities and working damage control for a few Twitter fiascos. I think she still does a little of that on the side, so should you ever be involved in some tabloid scandal, we have someone to call," she said with a raise of her brow.

My smirk widened. "I'll try to keep my name out of the tabloids just for you," I said. "What about the design aspect?"

"Their designer also worked in freelance graphic design on her own for small, independent companies. She moved from simple Instagram and Facebook posts to designing entire campaigns within a year of going out on her own. Apparently her load became so much that she reached out to Ezra to partner for their own marketing company."

"Ezra?"

"They call her Ezzie. You'll meet her at the social."

"What's her partner's name?"

"Ah…" Avril strummed her fingers across the back of the chair she leaned against. "I can't remember off the top of my head. I'll try to compile a brief for you this week so you don't look so much like one of those incompetent owners."

"You know that's my favorite look," I said.

Avril cocked a brow, her head tilting sideways. "It's not mine, so we're going with what I think."

"Right," I smiled. "Anything else?"

"These people won't be used to working with you, so I

need you to figure out somehow a way to represent what you're looking for with the rebrand. I know you're used to throwing ideas off of us like pennies, but with this group—"

"I'll try to get my scatterbrain under control," I said, sitting. I gave her a charming smile and leaned back, to which she rolled her eyes and threw a pen at my face.

"Elliot has paperwork for you to sign," she said before turning toward the door. "I'll tell him to bring them in in an hour."

"Thanks, Av. Go ahead and tell Maddi to take the day off since you're doing her job," I teased.

She paused at the door and batted her lashes sarcastically at me. "Just taking care of my favorite dickhead," she said sweetly.

I adjusted in my seat. "Jeez. I thought your husband's dickhead would be your favorite," I grinned.

Avril threw a pillow from the couch at my head, and I dodged it easily. She was still shaking her head when she closed my glass door.

My phone vibrated. I turned it over, finding a message from my mother on the screen, prompting me to press my elbows into the desk and rub my eyes. She'd been on me about going home for a few years now, and I wasn't sure how long I could keep putting it off. Between that and the very little sleep I'd been getting lately, I was exhausted.

I'd started having dreams again—dreams of a feeling and a touch I thought lost forever. In every dream, complete darkness surrounded me and the woman I laid in bed with. I could taste her, smell her, feel her. And every time I had the dream, I only thought of one person: the woman I'd searched for for five years and found nothing on.

Chloe.

The only regret I had in my life was leaving her.

I still think about that night almost every day. It drove me crazy that I'd not changed my flight and taken at least the next day with her. I had no way of knowing where she was any longer. She'd deleted the Cupid's Arrow app almost immediately after that Valentine's night, and I hadn't even been smart enough to remember her last name.

She was a ghost. An apparition that tortured me almost daily. That night had ignited my world again and sent me searching for something that I hadn't felt in centuries—something that was so familiar and yet new.

I'd nearly gone home just to seek the Oracle about finding her, but I knew better than to think Apollo would ever give me an answer after the way we'd ended things.

I smiled at that memory. *Idiot*. A few friends had told me to apologize for humiliating him so long ago, but the rage on his face when we randomly saw each other over the years was much more fun. I'd even played a few more tricks on him with mortals I knew he was lusting after, sending the same blunted arrows after them so they might despise him as Daphne had.

I chuckled and opened the Cupid's Arrow app on my phone. It was really ignorant of him to use my app in the first place, so why not have a little fun?

Maybe I could even dig up a little dirt on anyone from Designare Fusion while I was on it.

Chapter Three

Chloe

Lana's arrival the next Wednesday was a whirlwind of screams and hugs. I hadn't seen her in person in over a year. We'd both been so busy with work that our vacations hadn't lined up. She had already planned our evening—a whiskey distillery, a nice Thai restaurant, and a late-night pajama party that Tyler wasn't invited to. He'd chosen to stay at his parents another day to avoid having to hang around the opposite side of the apartment all night.

"Fuck all, I can't wait for tomorrow," Lana said as she lounged back in the booth we had picked out at the restaurant. "It's going to be epic."

"I think I'll remain wasted the rest of the week," I muttered against my wine glass. "Champagne tomorrow morning at the fitting. Vodka tomorrow night to get through possibly seeing Gavin in the same room as my fiancé—"

"Bloody Mary's Saturday morning for the hangover," Lana interjected.

"—Wine that afternoon for dinner with the in-laws," I added.

"Ugh," Lana grunted, rolling her eyes. "I can't believe you're subjecting me to that torture."

"You can rag on me and complain all you want on Sunday with mimosas at brunch with the girls," I said.

"Fucking, yes," Lana said. "Can't wait to see Ezzie and Raegan so we can all dish about your little conundrum."

"There is no conundrum," I argued. "One look at Gavin will not make me leave Tyler and jump into bed with him," I said.

"Not unless he brings one of his little love arrows," she replied. "Still, filling them in on the details will be fun."

I could only imagine the absolute chaos that would ensue when they found out.

Lana and I laughed and chatted all through our dinner, and by the time we headed home, both of us were on the verge of a drunken stupor, and full of Thai food. We stopped by a late night bakery to fuel our slumber party with cheesecake and chocolate before surrendering back to my apartment.

"—until you see the onesie I found," Lana said as we exited the elevator to my floor. "It's my favorite animal."

"Unicorn or narwhal?" I asked. I fumbled for my keys, almost tripping on the rug down the hallway.

"Aren't they—*oh shit!*" Lana grabbed me to keep from falling—unsuccessfully, and both of us burst into laughter, cursing and sinking to the floor in our dresses.

Our cackles moved down the hall, so loud that one of my neighbors came to their door to check and see if we were okay, which sent us into more boisterous laughter.

I forced myself to my knees and pushed the key into the lock. We fell into the floor when the door opened, and for a few moments, both of us had to lean against the door and the wall to collect ourselves.

"We shouldn't have had that last drink," Lana laughed.

"*You* shouldn't have had that last drink," I joked.

"You're fucking toasted," Lana replied.

"It looks like you both are," came a familiar voice.

My laugh fell so quickly that I started choking.

Tyler was home.

He was standing by the bar, pouring white wine into the three glasses he had sat atop. He only had the amber Edison-style lights on above the counter, shadows from his trimmed, dark brown wavy hair fading over his pale face. He must have cut it while he was seeing his parents—probably his mother said something to him about it looking untidy. He looked so much like a pale version of his father standing there that it nearly threw me off.

A bouquet of roses sat in a clear vase beside the wine glasses, a small box by that.

"Tyler," I managed, gathering my wits and catching my breath. "Tyler, I didn't think you would be home."

His dark brows narrowed slightly, a smirk on his lips. "You sound disappointed," he said.

"What—no." As I stood, I tripped on my heels again, my drunkenness showing in the stammer. "No, I just… I thought you were still in Florida," I said once I'd made it to my feet. I smiled at the look on his face and tried to force myself sober.

Though, failing spectacularly.

"Hey," I said upon reaching him. He wrapped a hand around my waist and kissed me, and I pushed my hand through his wavy hair. A quiet moan sounded from him, and when he pulled back, he gazed at me with narrow eyes.

"You're completely wasted," he said, slight accusation in his tone. "I can taste the vodka on your breath."

I sighed. "I know how much you *love* vodka," I said, knowing it was his least favorite. "Hence why I drank it when I thought you were away."

He chuckled under his breath, his dark eyes moving toward the door. "Hi, Lana," he said, and I could feel his body tense up as he spoke to her.

Lana's happy face had faded, replaced with a fake smile I knew too well. "Tyler," she said upon reaching us. "Fancy seeing you here a day early."

"Couldn't have you stealing my girl away, could I?" he said, hand tightening on me.

"Doubt I'd have to steal her." She grabbed one of the glasses of wine he'd poured. "She'd come willingly."

"Play nice," I said, tapping Tyler's chest. "Both of you," I added with a look at Lana.

She grinned coyly and batted her lashes at Tyler, then looked at me. "Only for you, babe," she said. "So, Tyler, will you be joining our pajama party?"

"I'll pass," he said. "I need to catch up on a couple emails and get to sleep. I've spent most of the day in the airport."

"Oh, you poor thing," Lana mocked with a pout.

I glanced over his shoulder then, truly noticing the roses and the box on the counter. I'd been in such a daze five minutes earlier that I saw it and forgot about it that quickly. "What's this?" I asked.

"Ah…" He released me, and I smelled one of the roses while he pushed the box in my direction. I did enjoy the smell of roses, even if I preferred sunflowers over everything.

"Open it," he said about the gift.

I knew what the long box was before I even opened the lid —a diamond bracelet. I picked it up and held it delicately in my hands.

"My mother said it would go well with your dress. Don't worry, she didn't show it to me," he assured me.

An emptiness settled in my stomach as I stared at it. I wasn't accustomed to expensive and shiny items like this, and I felt awkward wearing such extravagance. I had even been uneasy about the enormous ring he'd given me. I appreciated the gesture more than I could say, only I knew I wouldn't wear expensive jewelry, and spending money on it wasn't something I wanted him to do.

"Wow," Lana said over my shoulder. "Look at that."

Sarcasm dripped in her tone.

"It's beautiful," I forced out. "But you know you didn't have to," I said, meeting his eyes.

"I know. I was told I should wait until our wedding day to give it to you. Something about a gift exchange tradition? I'm not sure. However, I wanted to give it to you now. I've been away a lot this month on this project. I wanted to make it up to you."

Was it horrible that I hadn't noticed that he had hardly been home over the last month?

"It's fine," I said. "I love it."

A lie, except I was too tipsy to get into it then. Especially with Lana there. The argument would have been over the top.

Tyler leaned in and kissed my cheek before taking the box out of my hands. "I'll put this away somewhere safe," he said. "I'm off to bed. Wake me when you come in?"

I nodded, trying to keep the forced-smile on my face. He kissed me again, and then took the box and headed toward the bedroom.

"Night, Lana," he said as he passed.

"We'll try to keep it down," Lana said, her voice dripping with a smart-aleck flare.

The moment he disappeared into the bedroom and we heard the door snap closed, Lana looked at me with an expectant glare.

"Not a word," I said, grabbing my wine.

Lana's lips pressed together thinly, and I could tell it was taking everything in her to bite back the words on her tongue. I knew she wanted to say something about his being there, about the gift he'd brought that even she knew I wouldn't like, and most especially, about my poor attempt to sober up upon seeing him.

"Narwhal," I said firmly.

Lana huffed. "Fine. We can talk about it tomorrow."

Tomorrow.

Fucking hell, *tomorrow.*

I downed my wine at the thought of what might happen the next day. Gavin's face flashed behind my eyes, and my stomach twisted into knots.

One thing at a time, Chloe, I reminded myself.

Chapter Four

Chloe

The following morning, Lana and I woke at the crack of dawn to make it to my dress fitting on time. Tyler was still in bed, exhausted with jet lag, his dark brown hair a mess of loose curls. He had gotten up as I was getting dressed to grab a coffee from the machine, and then got back under the sheets to scroll through his phone.

"What time is this social tonight?" he asked as I looked my outfit over in the mirror.

"Ezzie said eight," I answered. "So we should leave here about fifteen minutes before that."

"I have a meeting across town at six," he said, setting his phone down.

"Is that your way of telling me you're not making it tonight?" I asked.

"No, I'll make it back," he answered. "Any chance to hang out with all of your friends," he added, and I noted the fake smile on his lips.

I almost laughed. "I know we're loud when we get together, but we don't get to see each other all the time."

"What are your plans Sunday?" he asked.

"Ah… it's Lana's last day here, so brunch with the girls and whatever she wants to do—which is probably going to Disneyland," I answered.

"Disneyland?" Tyler repeated.

"Yes," I affirmed, knowing he would probably make fun of us for it and not caring. "Why?"

"Caroline and Matthew invited us to a day on their boat."

"Oh… Ah…" Caroline and Matthew. Ugh. I hated hanging out with them as much as Tyler hated hanging out with Lana. Nevertheless, they were friends Tyler had made in college, and Matthew was now his business partner, so I had to at least put on as much of a smile as I could when I was around them.

They did have a nice boat, in any case.

"Maybe next weekend," I answered. "We—"

"Hey, babe! Let's go!" Lana shouted from the other room. "I know Tyler can't keep his hands off you because he's been away, but Momma needs coffee before this fitting."

I bit my lips together to keep from laughing, and Tyler glanced my way through the mirror, one brow raised. I straightened out my shirt and grabbed my watch. "How can you not love her?" I teased him.

"She's a lot," he replied.

"She is fire and extravagance and complete inappropriateness, and that's why I love her," I countered. I stepped over to the edge of the bed, leaning over to give Tyler a quick kiss. "See you tonight."

Lana was sipping on a glass of orange juice when I emerged, grabbing my purse and giving her a smile. "I love waking up to your shouting," I said.

"I wish I could say the same," she replied. "Though, I didn't hear anything last night or this morning," she added, tilting her head. "So, my conclusion was that he finally used the gag on you."

I chuckled. "Come on. There's a great coffee place next door to the bridal boutique."

When we arrived, my wedding dress was already hanging in one of the fitting rooms in the back. They didn't have Lana's dress in, but she didn't mind. It gave her another excuse to take off work and visit, which also made me happy.

I made her sit outside the fitting room and wait for me as I got into the dress, and when I exited, Lana stopped her pacing and stared at me.

There was no smile on her face, no expression other than a singular raised brow and stern eyes. Nerves threaded through me, and I stepped onto the pedestal for the seamstress to make any final adjustments.

The dress really was beautiful, it was fitted through the torso and hips, sweetheart strapless neckline, mermaid bottom that had a soft slope starting at the hips, not an abrupt angular one. The train behind it was only a few feet, that extra fabric cascading down after the last button on the back.

I pressed my hands to my hips and smoothed the satin fabric, watching myself in the grand, ornate mirror. The seamstress was busy measuring places that needed to be taken in, including the last couple of inches on the flared bottom that needed trimming.

Lana settled on the couch and crossed one long leg over the other, leaning back in the seat as she sipped her champagne. I could practically hear her screaming through the scrutinizing gaze she studied me with. She hadn't spoken a word since I'd come out of that fitting room, remaining completely silent while I spoke to the woman about what I thought needed fixing.

"Can you give us a minute?" I asked once the seamstress

had finished.

The seamstress nodded and left, pulling the door shut when she exited. I watched Lana through the mirror. She twisted one of her caramel spiral curls as she continued looking me up and down. I'd always been jealous of Lana's hair: the caramel and blonde tight spirals that were always perfect to me, no matter how out of control she might complain that they were at times. She'd cut herself bangs over the winter that perfectly framed her slim, angular face.

"Spit it out," I said.

"Spit what out?" Lana replied. "I spit champagne on this couch and I might have to call Tyler to pay for it," she said with a bat of her lashes.

I pressed my lips together thinly. "You know what I mean. I can see it on your face."

"What, that I don't feel like I'm looking at anything my best friend would choose for her wedding day?" Lana stood, flowing black satin tank swaying over her thin frame, bangles jingling on her wrist. Her gaze didn't let up as she came and stood behind me, sinking into one hip and crossing an arm.

"What do you want me to say?" Lana asked.

"The truth," I replied.

"You look like you want to throw yourself in front of a bus," Lana said.

"I meant about the dress," I said. "What do you think of the dress?"

"I think it's pretty," she replied. "It honestly is a beautiful dress, but nothing about this is what you wanted." She began circling around me, checking out every inch of the gown. "It's mermaid style. You've always wanted goddess. It has rhinestones, and you hate sparkle. A gaudy belt? You hate those belts on wedding gowns. Your tits look fantastic, but strapless? You're going to be pulling at it all night—"

"She's putting this sticky fabric on the top so it doesn't

fall," I said.

Lana raised a brow. "This ombre sparkle and tulle on the tail is so heavy that I could put my tiny tits in it and it would still ride down." She sighed with another long perusal over me, and then met my eyes again. "You look stunning, Clo. It hits all your curves, shows off your body, and will be gorgeous at the black tie affair they have planned… It's just not *you*."

I hated how much she was right.

Lana gave me a tight-lipped smile, apparently seeing my crestfallen face. "You asked for my opinion," she said.

"Yeah, yeah," I said, turning and checking out every inch of myself. "Everyone loved it, though," I said. "I know Tyler will think it's pretty."

"He should. His mother helped pick it out," Lana muttered against her glass.

I glared, and she held her hand up. "I know." She sighed heavily before broadening her smile, sympathy almost in her eyes.

Lana topped off my champagne and clinked her glass against mine. "So—" she said, suddenly making her way to the door. "You're a size ten, right?"

"Twelve, sometimes fourteen. Although, in these dresses, I've had to go up a couple of sizes," I replied.

"Perfect. I'll be right back."

I didn't know what she was up to, but I knew there was no point in arguing or even asking.

I turned and stared at myself in the mirror again as she disappeared through the door. She was right. It was nothing that I would ever choose for myself. It was nothing like the dresses I'd poured over in the past.

I gulped back the champagne as the seamstress came back in the room to carefully help me out of it.

Lana appeared twenty minutes later while I threw back my

third glass of champagne and waited for her in a robe. She had another dress in her hands, and my stomach dropped when I saw it.

"What are you—"

"Shut up and try it on," Lana said.

Lana wouldn't let me see much of the dress as I stepped into it. It was only when she guided me out onto the floor and helped me on the pedestal again that I finally got to gaze at the most perfect gown I'd ever seen.

Thin straps of soft lace appliqué that was a V down to my belly button, showing off the sides of my breasts. Cinched in at the waist. High slit on the lace appliqué skirt. A layer of chiffon came over my left breast like one side of a toga, the same chiffon laying delicately around the skirt.

And black.

I ran my fingers over the poppy flower design on the top and the vine-like pattern on the bottom, feeling how supple it was to the touch. But even as soft as it was, it was nothing compared to the buttery feel of that chiffon. It was like holding a dream in my hands.

This was such a bad idea.

Lana came around and stood before me, sinking into one hip as she crossed her arms and peered me over, a small smile on her face.

"Now, that's how finding forever is supposed to look," Lana said.

My heart swelled along with my lungs. Emotion pricked the back of my eyes and behind my nose. I choked out a nervous laugh. "Imagine me showing up in this instead of the other one," I said.

"Scandal of the century," Lana laughed. "Damn, this is beautiful. You know, it's almost *Grecian mountains* beautiful," she added with an expectant raise of her brow.

I scoffed. "I think the dream of being married in the

mountains of Greece has gone out the window," I said. "I know how much you wanted that vacation, though."

"I really did," Lana sighed, then circling the pedestal. "Shame. Where is a Greek god to sweep you off your feet when we need him?" Her grin widened, and I rolled my eyes.

"Stop," I drawled. "You're ridiculous."

She stopped in front of me again, biting her thumbnail and still looking over the dress. "I can't get over this—Hey, Sarah?" She called out for the boutique owner who had been helping us. Sarah popped her head in a second after, her face lit up as she looked at me in the dress.

"Well," Sarah said, coming inside. "I have been wondering what this one looked like on. It looks stunning," she said.

"I agree," Lana said. "How much?"

"That one is seventy-five hundred," Sarah answered.

"Great. Have the seamstress take her measurements while I pay you for it," Lana said.

"What—*Lana!*" She couldn't be serious. Who would—

"I'll take you to a charity gala one day and you can wear it there," she called back as Sarah escorted her to the door.

"Lana, you can't—"

But the door was already closed behind them, and the seamstress was measuring me again.

Chapter Five

Chloe

"I still can't believe you did that," I said to Lana later as we got ready for the social. "You are out of your mind. That dress—"

"It was either I did it then and let that woman measure you on the spot, or I bought it when I came back for my fitting, but you were already naked and in it," she replied.

There was no point in arguing with her. It was done. The gown was bought, and I wondered if I would just end up wearing it around the house on a random Tuesday.

I checked myself in the mirror, thankful that I'd found my high-waist boy-short underwear that would keep my thighs from chafing and go over my stomach to my bra line so there wasn't a crease splitting me in half. The short dress I'd chosen was snug, showing off every curve, dimple, and line I'd once not loved about myself, but now did.

"Are you nervous?" Lana asked.

"About?"

"Seeing your god," she said.

I had tried not to think about the possibility of seeing him all day. I had thought that maybe if I avoided that reality, it might disappear. Only it was staring me in the face, and I couldn't put it off any longer.

"Doesn't matter if he's there," I said. "It was one night.

Nothing more."

"I expect groveling," Lana said as she put on mascara.

"Why?"

"Because he said he would come back for you and it's been five years," she said.

"I'm engaged—"

"And now you're engaged." She slapped her leg. "See. He's late."

I glared, and her teeth bared with the wicked smile on her lips.

"I need a glass of wine," I said as my nerves began to build. "Do you want one?"

"Please. What time is Tyler getting home?"

I left her in the bathroom and went to the fridge where I took out a bottle of white wine to uncork. "Ah… Should be soon. He said he'd be running in—"

The door swung open, and Tyler appeared in a rush through it. "I know, I'm late," he said, removing his tie. "I know. I'll be fast—" He paused and gave me a once over, eyes narrowing at my dress.

"This is new," he noted.

"Yeah. What do you think?" I asked.

"Looks nice," he replied. "Give me five minutes and I'll be ready."

He disappeared into the closet then, nearly running over Lana as she entered the kitchen area. Lana leaned an elbow on the back of the bar chair when she reached me, brow raising.

"Nice?" she asked, lips pursed.

"What's wrong with nice?" I asked.

"Because you look better than nice," she argued. "There's sexy. Fucking hot. Want to pull you into the closet and fuck your brains out before this party—all better lines than 'nice', and more accurate. Did you not see yourself in this dress?"

I gave Lana a sour look, and she took a large gulp of the wine I handed her.

"Okay," she said. "But when you get there and your god shows up and he throws you against a wall to tell you how mesmerizing you are—"

"We're not doing this," I uttered, though my stomach was so full of knots that I wanted to puke.

The thought of seeing Gavin again, with Tyler in the same room… I didn't know how my body would react, what I would say, how I would feel. What do you say to someone who you spent a night with that was only supposed to be about sex, but turned into conversations and feelings for another that you think about daily?

It was just one night.

That was the mantra I was sticking to the rest of the night. Gavin or no Gavin, this was a work event for the largest client we'd ever landed. Things had to go right. I couldn't let my emotions get the better of me.

It was just one night.

So why did it feel like I was about to see someone I'd spent a lifetime with?

A friendly social—that was how Ezzie had described tonight. Not this.

This was a large party.

I thought it would be my team and Ezzie's, our significant others, and a few people we would be communicating with at Cupid's Arrow. But it seemed all persons from both companies had been invited because the entire floor was packed with people, lights were strobing around the dance floor, and a hum of music and conversations filled the room.

"I'll get us drinks," Tyler said before heading off to the bar.

"Ezzie is a liar," I said once he was gone.

"Yeah, this is a bit more than a few," Lana agreed.

"Do you see her?" I asked.

Lana stood on her toes and craned her neck to look around the room, and I listened for Ezzie's laugh. It sounded toward the dance floor, pulling my attention that way, and when I found her, the blood froze throughout my body.

Ezzie was standing at a tall table with her girlfriend and—

Shit.

I know romantics always talk about the room melting away when you see that certain person across the way, how the conversations and music around you turn to white noise, your hands get clammy, and your heart begins to thud in your chest. Face heating, muscles restless, breath shortening… It was that feeling from my dream—that giddy, adrenaline-filled warmth. My face went numb, and I had to swallow the lump of emotion in my throat.

All because I saw *him.*

Gavin.

God, he was even more beautiful than I remembered.

He looked so casual there in his dark jeans and forest green cardigan, a neat white tee beneath it, and the sleeves pushed up to reveal those tattoos and his firm forearms. He was hugging a drink to his chest, his other hand in his pocket, and he was smiling at whatever Ezzie and Raegan were saying to him.

That fucking smile.

His scruff looked just as trim as it had been that night, though his hair looked to be a little longer, a little fluffier.

My hands seemed to remember how soft that hair was, and seeing it so fluffy had my fists opening and closing. His exposed tattoos, the hand wrapped around that cup… fuck, those hands.

And when my gaze moved back up to his face, I forgot how to breathe.

Because he was looking right at me, and I could almost feel the pull of his body from across the room.

His brows narrowed slightly, widened eyes locked on mine like someone had zapped him frozen. I didn't realize I was shaking until I felt my teeth chatter when I swallowed.

I inhaled a too-sharp breath and forced my eyes away from him, almost dizzy as cold sweat broke out on my forehead. How—*how* did just seeing him cause this reaction?

I pinched Lana's elbow. "Hey, I'm going to the bathroom," I told her.

Lana scowled. "Are you okay? What's wrong?"

"Yeah, I'm fine. I just need a minute." My eyes darted back over to where Gavin remained, and Lana's gaze followed.

"Oh, shit," she muttered. "Oh, *fuck*—"

"I have your drink, Chloe," Tyler said as he appeared in front of me. He set the drink on the table and frowned. "Are you okay?"

"Yeah. I'm just going to go to the bathroom. I got dizzy all of a sudden. I think it's the lights." I brushed his cheek comfortingly with my hand, and he kissed my knuckle in response. "Don't worry about me. I'll be right back," I said, removing myself from their sides before either could say anything more.

Fuck.

Chapter Six

Gavin

Avril had lied about the size of this function. She guided me through this throng of people she insisted I needed to meet, most notably the owners, as we would be working closely together for the next few months.

Something felt odd about the party the moment I walked in. The hair on the back of my neck stood, an antsy feeling in my bones. My senses seemed to be on alert. But all that faded when I spotted Avril in the crowd.

"You're late," she said upon seeing me.

"I thought this was supposed to be a small gathering," I said.

Avril smiled. "Some people I want you to meet," she said. She handed me a drink and linked her arm to mine, and I followed her to a table where two women stood. Avril introduced me quickly, and I barely caught their names. I wanted to pay attention to them, only I couldn't for that sensation coming back and taking over, though this time, the same warmth I'd felt during the visions came to the surface.

Eyes were on me. I faked a laugh when everyone else laughed, my abdomen suddenly churning as I searched for the person I knew was staring. People seemed to be in their own conversations, but I noticed someone standing stiffly on the other side of the room. I realized it was them watching me. My gaze focused through the dim amber lights—

Fucking… *what?*

I couldn't function. Breath escaped me. My stomach dropped.

She was there.

It was *her.*

My heart somersaulted at the sight of Chloe. She hadn't changed much, though somehow she was even more beautiful. She was wearing a black, long-sleeve, scoop-neck dress that hugged her full breasts and the curves of her hips, showing off her long legs.

I remembered those legs. I remembered them around my face, my waist, and bent over in front of me. I remembered her softness in my hands, how she tasted, and the noises she made. Fucking gods, those *noises.* I'd replayed them in my head more times than I could count. I'd dreamed of holding her again, and seeing her there… *shit.*

Maybe I could.

But what the fuck was she doing here? Did she work for this company?

I had to know.

A man appeared at her side and handed her a drink. Her friend—Leila? Lisa? Lana? I couldn't remember her name, but she was standing there with them. Had they both moved across the country? Who was the man?

My mind spun. I excused myself from my current conversation, saying I needed to use the restroom, and I stalked around the room, making sure to stay out of her sightline so I could scope things out. The man beside her was just an inch or so taller than her, with dark brown hair and a clean-shaven face. He looked like the investment type— wearing a suit to a casual dinner party. Jealousy twisted my muscles as she brushed her hand on his cheek.

I prayed it was her brother.

She said a few more words, and then Chloe left the group, heading toward the restroom.

I followed.

Waiting outside the door was the longest five minutes of my life.

Chapter Seven

Chloe

In the brief moment Tyler appeared once more with my drink and I tore my eyes away, Gavin had disappeared. I wondered if I'd been wishing to see him so much that my mind had made him up, and it had simply been just some other ginger-haired male.

I headed to the bathroom to take a moment and gather my wits. My cheeks were already red. I braced my arms on the sink and inhaled deeply, counting back from ten and trying to calm my racing heart.

God, if that was him… if I hadn't imagined him…

It was just one night.

I left the bathroom full of fake confidence and told myself he was just another guy, that seeing him was no different from seeing Lana for the first time in months. It was only shock, nothing more—

I was yanked backward, whirled around, and suddenly I found myself pinned against the darkened wall. The familiar heated scent hit me, and I had to dig my heels into the ground to keep my knees from buckling.

All previous thoughts evacuated my numb body.

Gavin hovered there, my navel to his, his forearm flat against the wall above my head. I couldn't hear the music for the sound of my heart thudding violently.

Pain stretched in his eyes. Neither of us knew the words to say. Memories of a night lost—a night I had almost begun to think had been a dream—flashed behind my eyes. Every touch, every smell, every kiss… an intoxication of lust that I hadn't felt since being with him.

Lana's laugh echoed from the ballroom, breaking me from my trance, and I wondered if she'd seen Gavin pull me into the shadowed corner away from the rest of our colleagues and partners.

His grip on my wrist loosened, and he trailed his fingers up my arm. It was a gesture that had me curious if he was as mesmerized and in shock at seeing me as I was at seeing him. I could barely catch my breath, my chest heaving against his. I'd forgotten how consuming his presence was in the five years since we'd seen each other, and once more, I had to remind myself not to fall.

"What are you doing here?" he finally whispered. "What are you…" He started to reach up to my face, like he would swipe my cheek with his thumb, but instead hesitated. His weight shifted from foot to foot, tongue running across his lips. He looked so confused, so torn.

"I didn't think I'd ever see you again," he said, his voice so quiet that it was as though he were only saying it to himself.

Did he not know it was my marketing company he'd hired?

"Hi, Gavin," I managed once I caught my breath.

A smile flinched on his lips. "Hi, Chloe."

God, I'd missed the way he said my name.

I swallowed, unsure of what to do with myself. I was trembling with nerves and adrenaline and pure lust. It was as if my body was crying out for his touch, wondering why he was so close and not caressing every inch of my skin.

"This is weird," I managed, a light, nervous huff of amusement leaving me with my shaking voice.

Gavin didn't let up, but that smile widened, his dimple appearing, and this time he did touch my cheek. "I can't believe you're standing in front of me," he said softly, those fingers trailing on my neck and pushing my hair back. I opened up instinctively, lifting my chin so that his thumb brushed my jaw to the front of my throat. Fuck, his hands…

I think I could have stayed right there in his embrace and not said a word for hours. Just touching him, remembering his body and how it bent and fit to mine.

"Did you not know?" I asked, still in a trance.

"Know what?" he whispered, and I could feel his breath on my cheek.

"That it was my company you hired for the rebrand."

Gavin pulled back, our eyes locking on one another. "Your…" He released me, and the cold absence of his touch burned like cold fire. I wanted him flush to me again. Those few seconds had felt like a long-lost home. I craved it. I craved that warmth, that lingering touch.

"Your marketing company?" he asked.

"Well, I'm co-founder," I corrected.

"That's… Chloe, that's amazing," he said, his face lighting up. "No, I had no idea." A genuine smile lifted to his eyes, making me weak. But that smile fell slightly, and the pain returned to his gaze.

"You moved," he said.

"Yeah, a year ago," I said.

"No, I mean you moved apartments that year," he said, and I shifted on my feet.

"How did you know that?" I asked, knowing I had moved out of that apartment a few months after our night together.

He started to reach for my face again. "Because I went back for you," he whispered.

Oh, fucking hell.

"You…" I didn't know what to say. A lump rose in my

throat. Emotion pricked behind my eyes, and I didn't understand why. "You what?"

"I went back for you that fall," he continued. "To take you on the date we talked about. But you weren't there."

No.

No. No. No. *No.*

"I told you I would," he said, hand back on my cheek. "I thought eight months..." His thumb stroked my cheekbone tenderly, causing me to lean into his touch. I couldn't believe what he was saying.

"Even if you weren't ready for me, I wanted to see you again," he continued. "I couldn't get you out of my head. That night—"

Fuck, I couldn't do this here.

"Gavin, it was one night," I said, and I knew how ridiculous it sounded, knew that while it *was* just one night, it was a fucking great night—a night I'd been waiting for, no, a *person* I'd been waiting for.

"Was it?" Gavin asked. "Because it felt like the start of a lifetime for me."

Shit.

I had to get out of there before the emotion that was trying to surface toppled over. I didn't know why I felt like this, why the mention of him coming back that Fall made me feel like I would cripple into a puddle if I didn't hold onto something.

"I can't," I said, stepping out of his grasp. "I can't do this here. Not now. Not..." I looked down the hall toward the many tables, toward where I knew Tyler was waiting on me, and I took a step sideways.

"Chloe—"

"I can't," I managed. "Not here."

I looked at him one more time, observing his crestfallen shoulders as his grip loosened around my wrist, the broken heart in his eyes, and I forced myself to walk away.

Shit. Shit. *Shit*—

I hadn't moved twenty steps before Lana practically ran into me and sank her arm around mine.

"Okay?" she asked, and I knew I'd been right about her seeing him pull me aside.

"I don't want to talk about it," I said, realizing my voice was cracking. My jaw began to quiver, and Lana's grip tightened. "Lana, I can't—"

God, where had this emotion come from? Why did seeing him make me feel this way?

Lana paused at an empty table and handed me a drink. I downed it quickly, wincing at the alcohol's sting, then picked up her drink and downed it as well.

"Whoa… that well?"

I finally looked at her, and I felt my expression turn to bewilderment.

He had come back for me.

"Let's just get through tonight," I managed. "Where is—"

"There she is!" Ezzie announced as she came up beside us. "Did you just get here? Oh fuck, I love this dress."

I took a deep breath and put on my smiling face as I turned to her.

"Doesn't she look fuckable?" Lana said with a grin.

"Speaking of fuckable—" Ezzie turned to look for someone, her curled hair bouncing. "I need you to meet the CEO of our client. He's so sexy that Raegan invited him to an afterparty. There he is. Hey, Erosin!"

My heart sank, but I pulled myself together as Gavin approached our group. I hated how my body responded to him walking over. I hated the look that he gave me. And I hated that at the very moment he reached us, I spotted Tyler coming up behind him.

"Gavin," Ezzie swung her arm into his. "Gavin, this is the

creative genius I told you about earlier: Chloe Psymer. And this, Chloe, is Gavin Erosin. The owner of Cupid's Arrow."

I was back at that bar on the night of Valentine's Day, standing in front of him, candy hearts in my hands, introducing myself to him for the first time. The memory warmed my cheeks, traveled down to the pit of my stomach, and continued between my thighs.

I hesitated a moment too long before extending my hand, and I was sure Ezzie noticed it, but I tried to recover quickly.

"Nice to meet you, Gavin," I managed, and I wondered if the way I said his name sounded the same way it did in my head.

"Chloe," he replied with a nod, apparently getting my cue not to let on that we knew each other. I knew Ezzie would have had a field day with that, and I wasn't ready. Not yet. Not with everything I was feeling.

A body slid in behind me to my left, lips landing on my cheek. "I lost you, love," Tyler said as he joined us. "Brought your drink over."

Tyler asked something to Lana and Ezzie, but it was all I could do to keep my composure. Gavin was staring at the hand I'd wrapped around my drink—my *left* hand... I avoided meeting his eyes as long as possible, though I was too curious for my own good. I peered up, and my soul crushed beneath the weight of his stare.

Devastation filled every pore on his beautiful face. So hurt, and somehow... somehow the look was familiar. As though I'd seen it on him before... in the light of a candle, darkness surrounding us, an amber glow around him... Perhaps it was an image from a dream I'd once had, or as Lana would put it, an image from a past life. Whatever the case, a void of regret made its way into my chest at the memory, and I didn't understand why.

I pushed the ridiculous thought from my mind when his

gaze pulled away from the engagement ring and moved to my eyes.

Everyone around us was laughing, chatting, and joking, and yet we were in our own universe. He swallowed a gulp of his drink and turned away, suddenly attentive to whatever Ezzie was saying, and before I could break out of my own daze, he excused himself.

"That sounds great," Gavin said to Ezzie. "I'll see you Monday morning for a brief." He nodded and shook everyone's hands in the circle, leaving mine for last. His touch burned me once more, and then he turned to leave.

Breath finally filled my lungs. I inhaled sharply, nearly choking on the sudden wave of oxygen, and took a swig of the drink Tyler had brought over.

"The food at this party is phenomenal," Tyler said. "Have you tried any?"

"I haven't," I managed. "Could you bring me a plate?"

Tyler's gaze narrowed, and he grabbed my waist comfortingly. "Are you sure you're okay? You look a little green."

"Yeah, I'm fine. I just haven't eaten anything except those chips and salsa today," I lied, nervous laughter escaping me.

Tyler didn't look like he was buying it. His hand brushed against my cheek, and just as he opened his mouth to speak, Lana and Ezzie broke out in their usual loud laughter. Tyler shifted uncomfortably, evident that he would do almost anything to get out of this conversation.

"I'll get us some food," he said. "There's an empty table by the bar. I'll wait there for you. I know you want to do some mingling."

Tyler leaned in to kiss me, and as I returned the quick peck, an awkwardness knotted my insides.

It felt… *wrong*.

Oh, fucking hell.

Tyler squeezed my hand and turned to head toward the bar again. I watched him, my heart picking up speed as I remembered why I was so nauseous.

Lana grabbed my arm, her wide eyes on me. "Go," she said, and I knew she meant for me to go after Gavin.

I shook my head. "Lana—"

"Go after him," Lana urged me.

"It's not that easy," I said in a hushed voice.

"And you'll regret it if you don't," she affirmed. "Go."

I swallowed and nodded. I didn't know what I would say or why I even felt the need to follow him. But I knew I had to.

I excused myself from the rest of the team and started toward the door where I knew Gavin had headed. I tried not to appear like I was in a sprint, but I was terrified that he was already gone. A void hollowed out my insides. I was practically skipping through the crowd. Faster and faster. As he left through the front door, I spotted his hair, and I had to catch myself from calling out his name.

Damn his long strides.

"Gavin!" I called out once I was outside. "Gavin!"

Gavin paused, finally hearing me, and he turned around just as I nearly stumbled down the steps.

"Gavin—"

"You're engaged?" he asked.

I stopped just before him and let my breath catch up with me. "Yes," I managed after a couple of seconds.

Gavin took two steps back, apprehension in his eyes as he stared at me. And with a shake of his head and a scoff, he started to turn around again.

"Gavin—"

"I should have known," he practically snapped.

Anger… Angry with me? For moving on with my life? I straightened, my chin thrusting high as I watched him practically storm off. A pulse of rage surged through me, and

I suddenly refused to let him leave like this.

"What exactly did you expect?" I blurted out.

Gavin paused. "What?"

"I mean, what did you expect me to do? Wait around for our paths to somehow cross again?" I asked. "It was one night," and I wasn't sure if I was trying to convince him or myself. "I never thought I would see you again. I didn't think you would *actually* come back."

His angular face softened as he pivoted entirely to face me again. "Of course I came back," he said. "Chloe, you… you woke me up that night. You showed me a reason to want to live life again, not to just go through the motions." He ran a hand through his hair, and then wiped his face. "Do you love him?" he asked.

The question made me want to vomit.

"Excuse me?" I snapped. I had to keep up the facade and ignore the bile rising in my throat.

"Do you love him?" he repeated.

"What kind of question is that?" I said defensively. "We're engaged."

"So, it's an arranged marriage?" he asked.

"What—*no*. We've been dating three years."

"Then it should be an easy question to answer."

There was an edge to his voice, and I wanted to throw my drink in his face or slap him so hard that he fell to his knees.

I stepped back, in complete disbelief at his reaction. The diamond on my finger was a weight dragging me to the depths of hell, but as to answering his question…

"*Fuck you*," I hissed. "That's my answer."

A crooked smile quirked on his lips, showing off that godforsaken dimple and taking me aback. I crossed my arms over my chest, hating what that stupid smile did to me, and the soft laugh that left him didn't help matters.

I turned, intent on leaving him. Unsure of why I'd even

followed him or why I'd thought he needed an explanation. He had been just another fuck. Nothing more.

"Asshole," I grunted as I made my way up the steps.

"What was that?"

I stopped and faced him, five steps up. "I said you're a fucking asshole," I repeated.

"Why?"

"Because you are," I said. "With your stupid smirk and dimple and ridiculous comments on something you know nothing about. I mean, who asks someone that? Especially someone that they haven't seen in years! Not 'congratulations' or—"

"Would that make you feel better? If I congratulated you on an engagement that you can't even tell me you love him?" he asked.

"I—" A loud grunt of frustration left me, my hands curling into open fists like I could pop the air like a balloon if I tried hard enough. "Why—*why*—"

"Why what?"

"Why did it have to be your company?" I asked exasperatedly.

"The Fates have a weird sense of humor," he said.

"Oh, the *Fates*." I rolled my eyes. "Right, Mr. *Eros*." I let out a huff of annoyance, hands on my hips. "You know, I didn't need this. Things were *fine*—"

"Doesn't sound like it—"

"—getting married to a perfectly good man," I continued, ignoring him. "Work was fine. My life was *fine*—"

"You know that word basically means complacent," he interjected.

"—just moved into a new place. Everything in the wedding is planned out—"

"And how is my showing up in your life again derailing any of this?" he asked.

My mouth snapped shut, jaw tightening.

It was a challenge.

He took one step in my direction, hands in his pockets as his eyes cascaded to the floor, then back up to mine, and I stood firm despite the wobble in my knees.

"If it was just one night, why does seeing me, now working with me… why does that change anything?" he asked.

"God, I hate you," I muttered.

Gavin chuckled and moved closer, our faces lining up as he paused at the bottom of the steps. "Do you know what I think?"

I lifted my chin, crossed my arms, and gave him my best glare. "I am afraid to ask, but what?" I questioned.

That crooked smile was back on his perfect lips. "I think yelling at me just now made you feel more alive than the last time you had sex with him. That the reason you hate me isn't because I'm an ass, but because you've thought about me as much as I have you… That seeing me again means you have to come to terms with whether being 'fine' is enough."

His voice was a low rasp, throaty and sinful. I wanted to hit him as much as I wanted him to grab me by the throat and kiss me until neither of us could breathe. His face was so close to mine that one wrong gust of wind could have sent him falling into me.

"And that terrifies you," he finished.

"You think so highly of yourself," I said, voice dripping with the sneer on my face.

"Tell me I'm wrong," he replied.

My heart was pumping wildly. He was right. Arguing with him felt so fucking good. And seeing him… seeing him *was* terrifying.

I couldn't answer, and he fucking knew it.

His tongue darted out over his lips, and he leaned in closer. I stilled, unsure of what he was about to do. But his lips brushed my jaw, his hand grazing mine, and he whispered, "See you on Monday, Chloe."

He kissed my cheek and pulled back, causing my heart to somersault. Those eyes lingered on me a moment, a smirk on his lips, and then he turned to head down the sidewalk.

I was so fucked.

Chapter Eight

Gavin

I don't think I've ever been as happy and then as devastated as I was at the dinner social.

Seeing Chloe again, feeling everything I'd felt for her that night come to the surface. Touching her, seeing her smile, smelling her hair, it all made my insides scream to take her home just to make sure she never disappeared from my sight again.

I was prepared to play whatever game she wanted when she'd acted as though she didn't know me during the introduction from her partner. If she'd wanted to sneak around in her office or not let her colleagues know what had happened between us for the next few weeks, I could deal with that. I could have even handled her not wanting to be with me initially.

But finding out that she was engaged and being touched by another man had nearly made me hurl, nearly made me relapse into the horribly mischievous being I'd once been. I'd never been more jealous of someone or wanted to make them disappear so badly in my life.

But when she came running outside after I left…

That gave me hope.

Our encounter outside, those few minutes, had reminded me of how much I enjoyed being around her. How easy it was to talk and be free to say whatever I wanted. That temper and that cute little way she'd glared at me made me want to throw her over my knees and spank her perfect ass. I wanted her to tell me how much she hated me while I sucked on her clit or I shoved my cock down her throat.

Most of all, though, I wanted to make up for the time we'd missed out on.

I sank my hips against the front of my desk and looked through the papers I'd printed earlier. I liked having documents in my hands when doing research or reading through a contract. These papers, however, were for pleasure, not work.

A knock sounded on my door, and my assistant stuck her head inside. "Gavin, there's a 'Stef' here to see you," she said.

I didn't know a *Stef*.

"Stef? Where from?" I asked.

"Let me in, C," a woman's voice said on the other side of the door.

I may not have known a *Stef*, but I knew that voice. I hadn't heard from her in five years, not since I'd gone to her after that night with Chloe. I had begun having visions of a life I'd forgotten—a life with Psyche, my once wife. I still hadn't figured out how the memories had faded, how I'd somehow forgotten my own fucking wife, but the feelings— her smell, her touch… they were all still there.

I had felt all that again last night when I'd seen Chloe.

I had gone to her to find out what she knew, and at first, she'd been just as bewildered as me, except a week later, she'd shown up on my doorstep with a wild look on her face.

"Someone has been tampering with memory," she said, bursting *through my door.*

"Hello to you too, Seph—"

"No, Eros, you're not hearing me," she said as she rounded on me. "The woman you described, your wife. I told you I didn't

remember you having a wife. I even searched for her in some forgotten texts, only I found nothing. So, I asked Hades, and it was like a bell went off in his head. Like he was remembering something so simple, and he told me everything he could. He beat himself up at the fact that his memory had been tampered with as well" She stepped up to me, her pupils blown. *"Someone erased her,"* she said. *"That's why none of us remember."*

"Let her in, Mads," I said.

Maddi opened the door wider, and in walked the Goddess of Spring herself.

Persephone was wearing high-waisted khaki jogger slacks, combat boots, and a black lace crop top. Her loose pastel pink curls fell softly around her bright face, accentuating her bronze skin, and she was eyeing me with a smirk on her dark plum-stained lips.

Maddi closed the door behind her as she left, and Persephone crossed her arms over her supple breasts.

"Hello, Eros," Persephone said.

I scoffed at her nonchalance. "Stef? Really? What's your husband parading around as these days?"

"Henrik," Persephone said with a grin.

I gaped at her a moment, trying to envision the look on Hades's face when she'd told him that would be his name, and I almost snorted.

"I'm sure he loves that," I said.

"The punishment for putting that name on his license for this century was sound enough," she replied. "I often ask him for it again and again." She ran her tongue along her top lip and rubbed her wrist as if recalling a fond memory.

I chuckled and shook my head. "What do you need, Kore?" I asked as I began flipping through the papers again.

"You know I hate that name," she said.

"I genuinely don't care," I countered. "I'm busy. What do you need?"

Persephone twisted her lips and sighed. "I heard a rumor," she said. "I heard you found her."

I glanced up from the notes, brow raised. "Found who?"

"Psyche."

Chloe's face flashed behind my eyes, but I played it cool. "Where did you hear that?"

"The gods gossip," she said.

"That should be the name of our newspaper," I muttered. "What's your interest?"

"Is it true?" she asked.

I delicately laid the stack of papers on the desk, considering telling her. After all, she was a friend who had helped me with questions and problems I'd had in the past more than once. I knew the only person she would gossip to would be her husband.

And the thought of him gossiping to anyone nearly sent me into a fit of laughter.

"I'm not sure," I finally answered.

Persephone slid into the nearest chair and sat back, bringing her hands up to inspect her nails and crossing one long leg over the other. "Is it the girl from a few years ago?"

"Maybe. Though, if it is Chloe..." My jaw tightened, that same rage rolling through my nerves like a cascade of water over my skin. The image of her fiancé kissing her cheek and touching her arm filled my mind, and my hands clenched on the lip of the desk.

"There's a side of you I haven't seen in a few millennia," Persephone mused delightedly. "I do miss it. All that mindless rage was occasionally sexy." Her head tilted at me, eyes washing over my rigid body as if she were testing to see if the anger was real. "What's wrong?"

"She's engaged," I said as we locked eyes. I crossed my restless arms over my chest. "So, it doesn't matter, does it?"

"Where did you see her?"

"My company hired hers for a rebranding," I explained. "We had a social last night, a kind of 'meet the team' party. She was there, and so was her fiancé."

Persephone's laugh filled the entire room. Her head swayed back, tears nearly springing to her eyes. "Fuck off, are you serious?" she asked between cackles. "The Fates… they have a cruel sense of humor."

"The Fates can forever go fuck themselves," I said.

"The Fates have done you a favor," she argued. "You've searched for this girl for five years with no leads. And now, she's just dropped in your lap. Sure, the engaged thing is a bummer, but are you trying to tell me you're just going to sit back and let that happen? It's Psyche. You're Eros. The two of you are entwined together."

"You don't know that she's Psyche. Maybe she's just Chloe," I argued.

"It has to be her," she said. "The way you described the dreams, how you felt when you were around her that night. You said it was familiar, easy, like your soul recognized her. Did you feel that again last night?"

I shifted the weight on my feet. "I did," I answered.

"Then why are you standing around here on a Saturday looking at—what *are* you looking at?" she asked as she stood, her eyes narrowing at the documents I'd been thumbing through. "Are you—" Her jaw dropped, and she looked up at me wide-eyed. "You're already researching him," she said upon seeing the paper on the top of the stack.

"Wait—"

Persephone snatched up the file and began reading. "Tyler Drake. Thirty-three years of age, from… Florida?" She met my gaze briefly and then looked back down. "Interesting," she muttered. "Parents John and Abigail Drake, also residing in Florida. John is retired from his job in oil—blah, blah, blah —" She skimmed it and flipped a few pages before her brows lifted. "Well, the idiot has money—or rather, *Daddy* does," she drawled. "Though it looks like Tyler squanders it relatively well with some of these business ventures he's financing."

Persephone read on, and I waited patiently for her to finish. I'd read through the file once, but I liked to be thorough, to memorize everything I could about my opponent.

"He sounds like a tool," Persephone decided. She let the stack of papers drop with a thud back onto my desk and gave me a pursed lip glare. "What are you waiting for? Go get her."

I stared at Persephone, chewing on the inside of my mouth, before uncrossing my legs and crossing the opposite in front. "I will not *steal* her away," I began, and Persephone's jaw tightened. I waited for the argument, though when it didn't come, I continued.

"What if it isn't her?" I asked.

"What if it is?" she countered.

I didn't reply, and Persephone stepped closer, leaning in to pick the lint off my shoulder. "Psyche has been missing for centuries," she said. "Though I still don't remember the nature of her disappearance. Neither does Hades. The last thing of significance he could remember about her was her taking the ambrosia to become immortal."

I wracked my brain, trying to remember anything, especially the last night I'd spent with her. But I couldn't. I barely remembered her at all.

"I *forgot* her," I whispered. "Centuries of life, and I *forgot* her… How?"

Pain stretched in Persephone's eyes. "It's not your fault. Someone erased her."

My gaze narrowed at the new information. "How?"

"I don't know," she replied. "But I've been thinking about it for a while now, and I have some ideas about who could have done it."

"Why would anyone go through the trouble of that?"

"You can count your enemies on one hand, Eros," she said. "Take your pick. Start with the one that had the problem last time."

I almost curled the entire stack of papers in my fist, my jaw tightening at the thought of my mother. "Shit," I mumbled. "She has been begging me to come home."

Persephone chuckled. "Oh, I heard that too," she said. "Perfect timing, don't you think?" She brushed my shoulders and straightened my jacket. "The last time you found Psy, she fought for you. This time, you'll fight for her. Remind her of the love you two had, remind her who she is."

I sighed and ran a hand through my hair. "Fall in love. Wake her up—if it is her..." My eyes met Persephone's. "This isn't going to be easy."

She smiled. "True love never is."

Chapter Nine

Chloe

"Hang on," Ezzie said at our brunch date Sunday morning. "The guy that runs Cupid's Arrow is the fantasy man you took home five years ago on Valentine's?" Ezzie's bold laughter filled the room, and she swung her head back with it, blue waves bouncing. "That's fucking amazing."

Lana and I were still hungover from dinner with Tyler's parents the night before, and we were both nursing Bloody Mary's to try and take care of the sting. There had been no dressing up for brunch with Ezzie and Raegan. I had stumbled out of bed and put on leggings, a thin long-sleeve crop top, and Converse shoes, barely spraying my hair with dry shampoo, before meeting Lana in the kitchen and we set off for the brunch restaurant by the wharf.

"It's complicated," I muttered, though Lana was grinning sleepily ear-to-ear.

"I wondered why your energy changed when I introduced you to him," Ezzie said against her drink. She choked suddenly, eyes widening at me again. "You ran after him," she realized. "That's where you disappeared to."

Raegan swung her long black and caramel micro braids back off her shoulder, revealing the shaved design over her multiple-pierced ear, and she grinned teasingly at me. "Oh, you had a little fun already, did you?" she asked.

I eyed Raegan, glowering at the mockery in her sparkling dark brown eyes. Her flawless brown skin seemed to soak in the sunlight, making her positively glow in its warmth.

My cheeks heated, but I hid behind my drink, prompting Raegan's grin to somehow widen.

"Yeah, you did! Get it—" The three began making obscene gestures with their hands, a chorus of "Bow-chicka-wow-wow," sounding from them along with a few more vulgar noises and dances.

I took a large bite of my lox bagel, chewing it like it was the reason for all my frustrations. "I don't know why you're all obsessed with this," I said with a full mouth.

"Because you need a fucking orgasm, that's why," Lana exclaimed.

Raegan choked on the drink she'd just taken a sip of and lunged to her left, spewing the ginger beer and vodka all over the floor from both her mouth and nose. Laughter echoed around the table again, and a few onlookers gave us dirty looks, to which Lana promptly waved at them.

"And I don't mean from your vibrator," Lana continued as Raegan recovered.

"I don't need my vibrator to have an orgasm," I lied. "I have a fiancé."

"That doesn't mean anything," Ezzie said. "Plenty of people marry others who can't give them that on their own. Not in our case, though," she said, sharing a smiling glance with Raegan. She reached over and took her hand, squeezing her fingers. "By the way, we have some news," Ezzie said. "We're engaged!"

Raegan threw her other hand out, and Lana and I jumped to our feet with loud congratulations that we were sure annoyed the rest of the people eating outside, but we didn't care. Our friends were getting married, and I didn't have to hear their plans to know it would be a grand, over-the-top affair in wine country.

"We're thinking a short engagement," Ezzie said once we'd all settled down. "September, October at the latest."

"Wow," Lana said. "My job is not going to like me taking off so much."

"You work for yourself," I argued.

"I have patients who count on me," she said, smirking behind her cup. "But seriously. What are we talking? Wine country? Black tie? Chloe needs to know so she can plan for me."

I raised a brow in agreement. "True," I said, knowing Lana would never have her shit together by herself. "Why a short engagement?" I asked.

"Not all of us take so long to make decisions," Raegan said with a pointed brow.

"To quote one of our favorite movies," Ezzie said, leaning forward. "When you find the person you want to spend the rest of your life with, you want the rest of your life to start as soon as possible."

"I don't think that's the exact quote," Lana said.

"Close enough," Ezzie shrugged.

"I want to watch that movie now," Lana said. She turned to me. "You have that, don't you? When Harry Met Sally?"

"Yeah," I said, halfway in a daze. "Yeah, I have it."

Something about the quote had caused my ears to ring. We'd all loved that quote, sat on video chat and cried over that quote multiple times. I'd always thought that was how I would feel when I eventually found someone I wanted to marry.

"Definitely wine country," Raegan said. "We're not sure yet how formal."

"Ugh," Lana said, signaling the waiter for another drink. "I am jealous of all of you. Where is my other half? You two are perfect for each other," she said with a nod to Ezzie and

Raegan. "You have two men," she said, looking at me. "One of them is a god—do you think he has other gods he can hook me up with?"

"You know who I've always wondered about?" Raegan said as she leaned forward. "Ares."

"Oh, fuck yes," Lana said. "Ares. That's a god I'd like to see."

"I've always liked Poseidon," Ezzie said.

"That's because he's hot in those YA books you and Clo read a long time ago," Lana said. "I've seen the artwork circulating online."

"What about you Clo?" Ezzie said. "Was Eros always your favorite god?"

I glared between the three of them. "I'm unfriending all of you," I said, though I couldn't stop smiling.

As they continued talking about their favorite gods, the only one I could think about was Gavin. My stomach was churning, and I wasn't sure if it was nerves or the amount of alcohol I'd had the last few days. Either way, the thought of what awaited me the next day made me desperate to hang on to today as long as possible.

I was distracted, and nothing anyone did or said could take my mind off how my heart reacted to seeing him again.

Chapter Ten

Chloe

I was a wreck.

My hands were clammy. I hadn't stopped sweating. I'd already put on deodorant three times that morning, and it was barely eight AM. I was running on two hours of sleep. Tyler had asked me multiple times what was wrong throughout the night, had tried to console me thinking it was nerves for the new client or anxiety about the wedding since his sister had come over for dinner and drilled us about details instead of us being able to go out like I'd wanted. Lana had drunk herself silly and passed out before Tyler's sister had even left.

His attempt at making me feel better had left me feeling frustrated and annoyed rather than relaxed. All because the only thing I'd been able to think about while he was pleasuring me was Gavin's stupid face—and not in a good way.

And now, I had to look Gavin in the eyes and pretend as though he hadn't invaded my mind all night.

I put on a neutral face as I forced myself to stop pacing in front of my desk, and I took a deep breath.

Breathe, Chloe, I told myself. *He's just another man. The connection you felt with him was only lust, and just because you had the best sex of your life and can't fuck anyone else without thinking of him doesn't mean anything except that he knows how to use his cock. And his tongue. And his hands. And…*

I didn't realize I had my hand around my throat and my eyes closed as I braced the other against my desk until I heard someone clear their throat.

"Ahem," came a voice toward the now clicking-shut door.

I snapped out of my daze and looked that way, only to find Gavin staring back at me. He had his bag halfway off his shoulder and was eyeing me with quiet curiosity, a smirk looking to be tugging on his lips.

Shit. He wasn't supposed to be there yet. I wasn't ready. I wasn't prepared—not for him, not for the meeting, not for… *anyone.*

"Gavin," I managed, blinking and exhaling my breath. "I… I don't think I realized you would be here so early."

"Okay?" he asked, and the amusement in his tone made my jaw tick.

"Yeah," I said, smoothing out my shirt. "Yeah, fine. I was just setting out some preliminary vision boards on the table here. Ezzie rarely arrives before nine on Monday's so I thought I had time. And usually the client goes to her first, not me." There was a twinge of annoyance in my tone that I couldn't squander. I ambled to the large table in the middle of the room and shifted around some of the papers as Gavin waited patiently to place his own materials down. He sat his bag in one of the chairs and opened the top, pulling out what looked to be a binder.

"What can I help you with?" he asked.

"Ah…" I paused, pushing my hand into my hair. He had caught me off guard, unprepared for dealing with someone and having to talk design before I was ready. I ordinarily had some time to get myself together and ready the room so it was prepared when Ezzie came in with the client. And that was on a typical day.

"I actually just need a minute," I admitted, requiring time to gather my wits.

"Do you want coffee?" he asked.

A hollow sigh left me, my arm swinging downward. "Coffee would be amazing, actually. You can just tell Jas—"

"I'll get it," he said. "I fucked up your routine. Point me toward your coffee area."

I finally looked at him. He was watching me expectantly, his blue sports coat open to reveal a pressed white shirt beneath, three buttons undone at the top and tucked neatly into his belted slim dark khaki pants. The look on his serene face helped me remember to breathe, like his being there and asking to help was calming me down despite the fluster I'd just been in—even the fluster I thought I would be in while in his presence.

"Sorry, what did you ask?" I said.

A smile flinched on his lips. "Are you always this flustered in the mornings?"

"When I'm faced with a man who I just called an asshole two nights ago as a client, and he shows up early before I've had time to gather my wits and have some alone time to figure out my day, yes," I said without thinking.

As a client, Gavin could have balked at my tone and gotten angry or upset. But he didn't seem to mind. In fact, his smile broadened. "Coffee, Chloe," he repeated. "Where can I find it?"

I considered him another moment, my hands on my hips. "Break area is to the right when you walk out of here. Red walls," I answered. "There's an espresso machine, a couple coffee pots made, a pour-over. But you can just tell Jas—"

He headed towards the door as I spoke, and before I could tell him to find Jasmine to make it or even how I liked my coffee, he was gone.

I watched him mingle with my co-workers for a moment,

being his charming self, and I hated the pang of jealousy in my stomach when some of the women smiled as he walked by and spoke to them.

I forced my attention back to the vision boards I needed to organize and started making eight piles: Ezzie, two from her team, three designers from mine, Gavin, and his marketing manager. Organizing helped calm my nerves. It helped me to see it all out—my designs, my team's designs, all the keywords and inspiration photos we'd gathered.

I spotted the binder Gavin had brought in and let my curiosity get the better of me. He was still chatting with a few of the team in the break room, so I had a few minutes to peek. I opened it just enough to glance inside, and found he'd made his own vision boards.

I smiled at that. So cute. The CEO of a major dating app having an inspiration binder. I half expected unicorns or a small Cupid depiction on the outside, though I wondered if he saved that for his phone background.

By the time Gavin started back my way, I was a different person. The room was ready for the meeting, all except for the snacks and the presentation screen, and I inhaled deeply as I took in the beginnings of a new long-term project. I loved this part—all the excitement and possibilities before the wanting to scream and pull my hair out when something eventually goes wrong.

I had just finished setting up the presentation screen when Gavin appeared at the door holding two coffees and a plate of Danish breads. I wondered if the people in the break room had just piled things on once they found out he was bringing them to my office. Everyone knew I could wipe away a plate of danishes like no other.

My heart ached when he smiled my way, butterflies rising in my stomach. I cursed my body for betraying me. I wanted to smile and relax, banter with him as I knew we would.

Nevertheless, the words he'd said Friday night continued to wound me, and I tried my hardest to continue acting annoyed.

"Double-shot blonde roast with cinnamon and oat milk foam, a slight drizzle of caramel on the top," he said.

"Stalker," I said as I took the cup. "How did you know my coffee order?"

"As much as I'd like to say it was intuition, I actually ran into your assistant in the break room," he admitted. "She also told me I should take these in here." He set the plate of pastries on the table. "She was on her way out to grab more snacks for the meeting."

"She's amazing," I said before taking a sip. The warmth pooled in my chest, and I closed my eyes to inhale the cinnamon and coffee smell. So good. I wanted to bathe in that smell.

Gavin was watching me when I opened my eyes, still staring at me with such amusement and delight lighting up his face.

"What's your coffee order?" I asked.

"Why do you want to know?" he asked.

"You can tell a lot about a person from a coffee order," I replied.

"Can you?" One of his hands shoved in his pocket, the other hugging that coffee to him as he started walking around the table. "Black, triple shot with raw sugar," he answered.

I raised a brow. "You're telling me the Valentine's Day god takes his coffee black?" I asked.

Gavin grabbed his chest, feigning hurt. "You wound me, sweet girl," he said, drawing closer. "The Valentine's Day god?"

"I'm sorry, did that hurt your precious ego?"

"A bit, yeah," he said, and the sound of his laugh made my heart tumble. "That's grounds for punishment."

"Oh? Actual punishment or your brand?" I asked without thinking.

"Definitely my brand," he said. "I don't think you had enough last time. I let you off easy."

"I don't think anything about that night was necessarily easy," I said. "I'd say we both worked pretty hard."

Gavin's laugh quieted to a chuckle as he paused before me. He looked like he might touch my face, but instead he picked off a long hair from my shirt, his hand then coming to rest on the chair next to mine. "I can think of one part that was easy," he said, his voice softer.

"Which part?"

"This part," he said. "Us. The back and forth. I'd forgotten just how easy it was."

I swallowed, staring up at him. It was true. Still, it was hard to think of a moment that night that hadn't been.

"I'm still mad at you," I said, hugging my coffee to my lips.

"For the other night?" he asked.

"Yes," I said. "Who says things like that to someone they haven't seen in years?"

"I do," he replied, a sudden sternness in his gaze.

"Why?"

"Because you ran after me."

I froze.

He was right.

The corner of his lips tugged upward, apparently seeing the frustration on my face.

"I forgot how cute you are when you're angry," he teased. "Let's not throw that coffee in my face, though. I need this," he said, signaling his face. "This is the money-maker."

My jaw clenched as I resisted the smile bound to betray me. "I should," I said. "I should ruin your face and shave your head."

"You should," he agreed. "However, if I remember, you

like my hair too much for that."

Images of pulling his hair while he was between my thighs flashed behind my eyes. How soft those strands were, his tongue moving in and out of my center, lips sucking on my clit, my thighs thrown across his shoulders…

One look in his darkened eyes, and I knew he was remembering that too. The smile had slipped, replaced with that sensual seriousness that had once brought me to my knees.

"Let me take you out for drinks," he said.

I blinked out of the daze and cleared my throat. "What?"

"At the brewery downtown," he continued. "You can throw all the drinks you want in my face."

"I would have to drown you to make myself feel better," I muttered. "Why would I go out for drinks with you?"

"So you can tell me what you've been up to these last years," he said, walking backward toward where his binder lay on the table. "You know, I'm happy to see you with your own company. The work is brilliant—"

"Again, stalker," I interjected, feeling a smile tug at my lips. "Have you been searching my portfolio?"

"Part of my research," he said with a shrug. "I'm only sad I missed being there when it happened."

A solemnness swept the grin off my face. "It wasn't that exciting," I said. A lie, of course. I had been a nervous wreck when we'd decided to create our company. I'd saved and printed out mine and Ezzie's first texts back and forth about it, framed our first contract, and even refused to get rid of the first few drafts of our logo.

Gavin stepped back over my way, set his binder on the table, and then reached his hand to mine. My cheeks heated. I looked at our entwined hands, staring at the freckles on his skin as his fingers lay atop my slender ones.

"Liar," he accused, and I scoffed at his blatancy, glancing

back up at him.

"Okay," I said. "So, it was exciting, sure. But not so much that you missed out on something special by not being here."

Our eyes met for a long while, and I could see his curiosity in them.

"Let me take you out for drinks," he repeated.

"You're really pushing this, aren't you?"

"I want to know everything I missed," he said.

Sunlight bounced off the ring on my opposite hand. It was just drinks. *Daytime* drinks. It wasn't dinner. It wasn't going back to his place. It was perfectly innocent drinks. Two friends catching up. That was it.

The way my heart was tumbling over just his hand on mine said otherwise.

"No ulterior motives?" I asked.

His knuckle flicked playfully under my chin, dimple appearing in his smirk. "Not unless you ask for it."

My door opened then, making my heart skip as reality plunged between us. I had forgotten where we were, that there were even other people in the universe.

Ezzie paused in the door, delight and surprise written all over her face. "Well," she said. "I see our client found his way to the meeting after all."

I could only imagine how we looked. Laughing. Our hands entwined. His flicking my chin and standing mere inches from me.

Fucking hell, I'd be hearing it from Ezzie later.

An older woman that I didn't recognize walked in behind Ezzie. "I tried calling you several times, as did Maddi," she said to Gavin. "I thought you'd forgotten."

Gavin turned and smiled at her. "Never," he replied.

I turned away from him and gestured to the room. "I have all the materials set up," I said as Jasmine came running in with refreshments.

"Great," Lindsay, my lead presenter, said. She would be pitching the preliminary ideas from our company to Arrow, not me. I was a shit public speaker, but Lindsay had an ability like no other. I swore she could take your own shit out of the toilet, bag it up, and somehow sell it back to you, and that was why I kept her on the payroll even after she ran away with her ex-boyfriend for a month without telling anyone.

A man came blundering into the room then, long coat swaying behind him.

"Shit," Gavin said under his breath.

The stranger looked so familiar, a handsome, tall man with tan skin and bright brown eyes. Scruff lined his jaw, dark and thick curly hair atop his head only down the middle as the sides were trimmed. A grin split the man's wide mouth as he hugged Avril and made his way around the room, giving everyone hugs and hello's whether he knew them or not.

Gavin turned to me. "I apologize now for anything my friend might say."

I frowned. "Why? Who is—"

But I had been spotted. The man's entire face lit up, beaming my way. He threw his hands up wide in the air. "There she is! The woman of the hour! Give me some—" His long arms swept around me, and this stranger picked me up off of the floor.

"Um… can you put me down?" I asked, giving Gavin a bewildered glance over this man's shoulder.

"I'm sorry," Gavin mouthed to me, an embarrassed smile on his lips.

My feet hit the ground, and the man jumped and clapped his hands together excitedly.

"Oh. Right. I forget we haven't been introduced. I didn't meet you last time, but I heard a lot—and I mean, *a lot*—about you." He winked at me twice and nudged my side. "I'm Zayn," he said as he pushed his hand out toward me.

"Hi…" I said, hesitantly taking his hand.

Gavin was wiping his face nervously behind him, clearly borderline mortified by his friend's behavior.

"Zayn is CFO of Arrow—"

"And his best friend." Zayn turned to Gavin. "I'm hurt you didn't lead with that."

"I was getting to it," Gavin said.

"I think you've scared her enough, Zayn," the older woman said from the other side of the room. "Do you think you can settle down enough for this presentation?"

Shit. I didn't have enough stacks for him, too. I didn't know he was coming.

Gavin gently pinched my elbow and said, "He can share my folder," as if he knew what I was thinking.

A slow breath left me, and I smiled softly. "Thank you."

"If we're all ready—" Lindsay said, clearing her throat at the front of the room. "Let's get started."

Chapter Eleven

Chloe

For two weeks, I hardly saw Gavin.

I was buried in work on his project, barely letting the rest of my team contribute, as I had set such high expectations of the design that I was coddling it like it was my own child.

Each time he came by, I spent more time bouncing ideas off of him than I should have. Ideas that weren't even in my wheelhouse—schemes for dating app events for Halloween, the fall, Christmas, New Year's. To where the day before, I'd told him I needed him to credit me if he ended up using any of them—which he agreed to wholeheartedly.

It was entirely too easy to get caught up in him, entirely too easy to talk to him about whatever popped into my head, and entirely too easy to…

Snap out of it, Chloe.

We still hadn't gone out for that lunch despite his begging. I didn't trust myself, not with the way his eyes seemed to cut through my clothes every time he gazed at me, how every whisper of his hand on mine sent my heart racing out of my chest.

I found myself pacing the office after a few days, my eyes constantly on the elevator doors, waiting for him to come striding through in the casual way he always did.

I noticed I wasn't the only one awaiting his arrival. He had become a celebrity on both floors, and it didn't take much to understand why.

It was after nine that day when Gavin made his entrance. He strode in as usual, hands in the pockets of his dark slim fit jeans, a dark grey sports coat over his Pink Floyd tee. He spoke to a few people who called out his name, stopping to take a moment to chat with each person. Just like every other day, I couldn't stop observing him. When he spotted me staring at him through the frosted panes of my office, his tongue darted out over his lips, his chin rose, and his entire demeanor went from friendly and confident gentleman to god of desire.

Damn him.

I pretended to be hard at work at my desk when he finally got to my office, and this time, he didn't bother knocking.

"Do you know what I don't have?" he asked as he burst into the room.

I settled my elbows on the top of the desk and leaned my chin on my knuckles. "What's that?" I asked.

"I don't have your phone number," he said, stopping before my desk.

"What?"

"Your phone number," he repeated. "I was heading this way and was going to ask if you'd had breakfast, when I realized I didn't have your number."

I quirked a brow, and he handed me his phone.

"Breakfast?" I said. "Sounds like a lie."

"I could have said that I was sitting on my couch with my dick in my hand last night and wanted to see if your fiancé was gone, but I thought you might find that inappropriate for the workplace," he replied.

I eyed the grin on his lips and resisted laughing. "Your presence is inappropriate for the workplace," I said, handing him back his phone with my number inside. "Don't abuse it."

Gavin sat on my desk and leaned over to look at my computer. "What are you working on?"

"Ah… one of my girls came back with a header design. I'm still not sure how I feel about this font. It feels too… rigid, maybe? Your brand is synonymous with fun dating schemes, parties, and the actual arrow, so I'm just not sure this speaks to all of that. What do you think?"

I turned the computer screen so he could see, and he considered it. "You know, I think we should go out for breakfast to chat this over," he said. "I compiled a few notes on the package you sent over yesterday."

It sounded innocent, yet I knew better with the look in his eyes. "I've already had breakfast," I said.

He smiled. "Lunch then," he said.

I huffed a laugh and shook my head. "Gavin—"

Two knocks sounded on my door. We both turned, and I shot up from my seat, my heart dropping so quickly that a wave of nausea washed over me.

"Tyler," I nearly spat. "Hey—I didn't realize you were coming by today."

Gavin tensed, but stood from the desk as I went around to meet Tyler.

"Hey," Tyler said. He kissed me gently, one eye still on Gavin, and wrapped a hand around my waist. "I thought I would come by on my way to the airport." His gaze landed fully on Gavin, giving him a liberal once-over. "Who's this?" he asked, and I noticed the forced politeness in his tone.

"Oh, this is my client. Gavin. CEO and founder of Cupid's Arrow," I said, separating from Tyler's grasp. "You remember him from the social a few weeks ago? Gavin, this is—"

"Tyler," Gavin said, extending a hand. "The fiancé. I remember."

Gavin stood at least six inches taller than Tyler, and somehow he seemed to stand even straighter as Tyler took

Gavin's hand and shook it. A firm handshake, firmer than any normal one should have been.

"Right, I remember now," Tyler said, his chin lifting as if to make himself taller. "You're the one that's keeping my fiancé up late most nights with your project."

"Surprised you know that since every time I ask her about her fiancé, she says you're out of town," Gavin replied. "You travel a lot."

My eyes widened at the snap in his tone, but being his charming self, he relaxed himself on my desk again and smirked at Tyler's tightened face.

"I have my hands in many ventures around the world," Tyler said.

"Yeah? What kind? Anything I might like to invest in?" Gavin asked.

Smug bastard.

I was annoyed that his arrogance and challenge had my thighs tightening. That stupid smirk. I needed to break this apart before they started comparing dicks.

"Ah, well, I can send over some proposals if you like," Tyler said. "I know a few startups that could use the extra cash if you have any lying around."

"I mean, I'm not sure how much you call extra. I have a few duffle bags packed just in case a friend gets kidnapped, maybe a million beneath the mattress in the guest room. I might have some coffee cans buried in the park, too. How much do they need?"

I snorted, and Tyler just stared at Gavin. "You're fucking with me, aren't you?" Tyler asked.

Gavin's cocky smile broadened. "Not completely," he said. "I do actually have some buried in the park for a rainy day."

A quiet laugh left me, and I pulled away from Tyler to walk back to my desk. "He's completely fucking with you now," I said, shaking my head at Gavin. "Ass," I said to him once I'd sat back down.

"Do you two know each other from something else?" Tyler asked, and I realized I hadn't been guarding the look on my face.

Gavin and I exchanged a glance. "We met at a singles party a few years ago," I admitted, turning my focus on Tyler. "You remember that Valentine's that Lana and I talk about? The one I kept the candy hearts from?"

"Oh, that one." Tyler stuffed his hands in his pockets, hesitation written in his wary gaze. "And you two…"

"No," I said, my nervous laughter echoing. I looked at Gavin and gave him a look that read 'help.'

He sighed, but played along. "It wasn't for lack of trying," he said. "I think we mostly talked marketing at the bar that night."

"Did you know this was her company when you hired it?" Tyler asked.

"No," Gavin answered. "No, I truly couldn't place her the other night at the social. It wasn't until that Monday that I realized who she was."

I was so grateful for him playing along that I wanted to pull him into the coat closet and kiss him.

"And how did you two meet?" Gavin asked, leaning back and staring between us.

"Ah…" Tyler looked at me, apparently expecting me to tell the story in full detail, but I sat back in my seat and pointed a hand toward him.

"All yours," I said.

Tyler smiled nervously, hands on his hips. "She nearly ran me over," he replied.

Gavin's brows shot up, and he looked back at me. "What?"

I sighed, deciding to let Tyler off the hook with this one. "I was late for a meeting downtown," I continued. "Distracted on my phone. I barely stopped at a stop sign, and he stepped out onto the road as I turned." I held up my hands and then clapped them together. "Nearly killed him—"

"I told her she could take me out to dinner to make up for it," Tyler said. "She had too much wine. I bought dessert." Tyler's smile lit up to his eyes. "After blowing it with the kiss that night, I thought she'd never want to see me again, but we ran into each other a week later. The rest is history."

I avoided Gavin's gaze, my jaw tightening together. It was a clumsy story. At the time, he'd been the first guy in months to try and flirt with me. I'd been so desperate to feel something that I thought maybe that was it.

I missed how much fun it was in the beginning.

Maybe that was with every relationship, but I thought there would still be some lingering excitement. The occasional heart jump, warm fuzzy feelings with a kiss, truly smiling at him… It had only been three years, after all.

Yet, here we were.

Tyler looked at his watch. "I just came by to let you know I was leaving," he said, and I stood back up, not realizing his visit would be so short.

"Oh," I said as I moved to him again. "Oh, I thought maybe you were staying for lunch."

There was disappointment in my tone. It was surprising that he'd come by. A good surprise, and that sparked something inside me. Hope?

Lana would have told me that I'd set the standards bar literally on the floor.

"Can't," he said, taking my hand.

"You could have just texted me," I said, and I think a simple text would have hurt less.

"You've been so distracted lately that I wasn't sure if you realized my flight was today," he said.

I ran my hand over my face. It was true. I had been in another world since starting this project.

"I'm sorry," I said. "You're right. I'll make it up to you when you get back."

He pushed my hair back, the touch feeling foreign on my skin with Gavin in the room, as if my body was rejecting every brush and contact with him.

And when Tyler kissed me…

It was lingering and more passionate than he'd kissed me in months. And *awkward*—so awkward that I ended up pulling away from him before he wanted to let me go. I wasn't even sure if I'd kissed him back.

Fucking hell.

When we parted, Tyler cupped my face in his hand and gave me a smile. "I love you," he said. "I'll call you when I get off the plane." He glanced past me to Gavin as he started backward, and he nodded in his direction.

"Erosin," he said.

"Drake," Gavin replied with a nod.

I didn't move or look at Gavin as Tyler left the room and strode across the floor, just making it in time for the elevator. Once the elevator door closed, Gavin let out a whistle I knew was meant to mock me.

"Fucking Styx," he muttered. "Someone thinks they need to claim their territory."

"Something tells me if the tables were turned, you would do the same thing," I said, crossing my arms over my chest. "Though probably more to the effect of squeezing my ass or throat."

Gavin scoffed and pushed off the desk, stuffing his hands in his pockets as he strode my way.

"If you were mine, no other being would think they had a chance," he said.

"You think your presence is enough to deter anyone else?"

"No," he said. "But the way you respond to me is."

He hovered an inch from my folded arms, and the absolute

heat radiating off of him made my knees weak, causing a pulsation between my thighs. My jaw went taut at the confidence of his words. I waited for him to continue, refusing to give in.

"He didn't kiss you just now to make me jealous," he continued, a twinge of dominance in his stern tone. "He kissed you to remind you that you're his. That the ring you wear on your finger means your heart, mind, and body belong to him."

"Why would he need to remind me of that?"

"Because he could see the way you look at me. The way your body follows mine," he said, his voice deepening.

My lips pressed together thinly, though the shake in my breath didn't help my case. "Once again, you don't know what you're talking about," I managed.

"Then why didn't you kiss him back?"

My fingers creased on my arms as I tried to push down the frustration suddenly swimming through me.

"You're full of shit," I glared.

He leaned down, and I could see a coy smile on his lips. "Should I see how wet you are from that?" he asked in my ear.

It was hard to stay mad at him, especially when he mocked me and smiled like that. *Cocky bastard.* I bit my mouth to keep from smiling and shoved his chest. He stumbled backward, smirking proudly at me.

"Asshole," I grunted.

"I don't hear you denying it," he mocked.

"Oh, get out," I said, pushing him toward the door.

Gavin laughed, a quiet, devious laugh that embedded itself in my bones. I ignored the chill running down my spine and shoved him again, but he braced his hands on the doorframe and whipped around before I could close my door.

"You didn't answer my question about lunch," he said fast.

My bottom lip sucked behind my teeth, and I tensed my jaw, glancing up at the clock. "Tomorrow. I eat at one."

His face lit up. "I'll take you—"

"You bring sandwiches here," I said before he could finish. "And you look at some designs I have while we eat."

The shock wore off, and his smile softened to one that worked its way into my warming heart. "Okay," he agreed.

Chapter Twelve

Gavin

I leaned against my Jeep and let my thoughts consume me as I waited on the person I had driven across town to meet. My insides still itched uncomfortably from seeing Chloe's fiancé kiss her as he did… it made every possessive bone in my body go into overdrive. I had been jealous, sure, but what I'd said to her was true. Seeing me in the same room as her, perhaps sensing a connection between us, had ignited something within him. I wondered if the idiot had considered changing his flight just to be sure she didn't spend any more time with me.

A motorcycle hummed in the distance, its loud engine revving with every turn up the hill overlooking the valley below. I knew who it was. The god rarely went anywhere without his bike, and I fully expected him to have a six-pack of beer in his bag that he would try to share with me.

A little father-son bonding time, as he would put it. Nonetheless, the way we bonded usually consisted of getting tattoos together, even if he barely had room for more. The big, formidable *God of War*, always trying to prove he could take more pain than his pretty boy son.

He pulled up to the bend, and I pushed off my Jeep where I'd been leaning.

Ares let the motorcycle idle and walked it the last few

yards, then turned it completely off just inches from where I stood. He sat back, his thick shoulders slouching just slightly as he took his sunglasses off and cleaned them with the hem of his white t-shirt. He looked the same as he had for as long as I could remember. Black hair longer on the top, buzzed on the sides, dark salt-and-pepper scruff on his square jaw. He looked as though he'd been hanging out by the beach; his alabaster skin had a sunny glow, the scars on his face and arms standing out in pale glory against it. He had an angry look about him that usually steered most people away.

Everyone except my darling mother, who thought his gruffness endearing.

"I was in Mexico when you texted me," Ares said, his blue eyes meeting mine.

I straightened, pushing my shoulders back. "Hello, Ares."

Ares raised a dark brow and reached back into his bag, pulling out a beer. "What do you need, son?" he said, popping it open with his teeth.

"Cute that you still believe that lie." I loved mocking him about the vagueness of my parentage.

Ares glared, but took a sip of his beer. "Every time..." he muttered. "Where do you think you get your good looks? You think it's all from your mother?" Ares asked. "And that tempter, that jealous thirst. How do you think you once carried out all your mother's schemes without batting an eye at how cruel or devious the plan might have been?" Ares beat on his chest. "All me, kid."

"I'm flattered," I said.

"Who else would it be?"

"There are a few choices. But, I didn't really invite you here to reminisce," I said.

"What'd you invite me for then?" Ares asked as he took a swig of his beer.

"I think I found Psyche."

Liquid sputtered and spat from Ares's mouth. He choked, doubled over, and hit his chest. I watched, unbothered by the show he was putting on, if it was a show. His face was blood red, eyes glazed and bulging.

Maybe it wasn't as much of a scene as I'd initially thought.

When he collected himself enough to look up at me, I still hadn't moved.

"The fuck, kid—"

"You can't tell my mother," I said.

Ares cleared his throat and inhaled deeply. The red tint on his skin dwindled, and he finally straightened up and took a cigarette from the inside of his leather jacket. "I make it a point not to tell your mother things that might upset her," he managed as he lit his cigarette. He pulled his lips taut around the stick and eyed me as he blew out the smoke. "This news… I think that'd upset her, don't you?"

"I love that you'd go to any length to keep her happy," I said, stuffing my hands in my pockets. "It's quite adorable."

"Watch your mouth," he grunted.

My smirk widened.

Ares regarded me again, those questionable eyes moving over my face like he could see my true form sitting behind the glamour, and he wondered if I was fucking with him or not.

"Why are you coming to me?" he finally asked.

"You know as many of my mother's secrets as I do," I said. "This is one she wouldn't share with me if she had something to do with Psyche's disappearance."

"Who says she disappeared?"

"If she hadn't, I'd still be with her," I said. "She had the ambrosia. She was immortal."

"Maybe she got tired of your mother hanging over your shoulder," Ares said.

"Is that what you know?"

"I don't know anything," Ares affirmed.

"But you remember her."

There was something about the way Ares looked at me then that edged my muscles and drew my insides taut. It was a feeling I hadn't felt in centuries, and I wasn't sure I liked what it did to me.

Ares drew another smoke on his cigarette. "Yeah, I remember her," he said solemnly.

"I don't," I said. "Or I barely do."

Ares didn't seem surprised. "There are some things worth forgetting, kid," he said, pushing off his bike. "This is one of them."

"What do you know?" I said, stepping into his path.

A brow raised on Ares's face, but I refused to move. "You don't want to do this," he said.

"I really do," I hissed. "Tell me what you know."

For a long moment, Ares stared at me, and for longer than that, he thumbed the hem of his shirt between his fingers and puffed on his smoke.

"You think you found her?" Ares asked.

I exhaled, relaxing a little as I thought of Chloe's face, and a lump rose in my throat. "Yeah. Yeah, I do."

"Then hang onto her," he said. "Hang onto her and don't let go. You two… you were more than lovers or friends or just another couple. You were *it*, and all of those idiots were jealous of the bond you two had."

Something swelled in my chest. I wanted to remember—I was *desperate* to remember. It was a part of me that felt empty. And hearing Ares say he remembered her, when I didn't, when Persephone didn't…

"What do you mean?"

"I mean if you've found her, then don't worry about what happened all those years ago. Be with her now and enjoy it."

"*Centuries* lost," I managed, almost shaking. "Centuries.

Someone tampered with our history—*erased* her from everything, and you want me to—"

"Let it go, kid," Ares said firmly. "Don't worry over what's long lost." He pushed past me, but I didn't follow or turn.

Long lost… It was bullshit. I looked down at my phone, noticing the time, and then I heard a stream of water hit the ground.

Ares was pissing over the cliff.

"Classy," I muttered, shaking my head. "If you're not going to tell me anything, we're done."

"You want to know what happened, you ask your mother. Not me," Ares said as he zipped up his pants. "I'm not getting in the middle of it."

I glanced at him over my shoulder, seeing him shake his leg as he straightened himself out. My mother… fucking Styx. "That's all I need you for," I said, making my way to the driver's side of my Jeep.

Ares's scoff was a blurt of grunting noises. "Used," he muttered. "As usual."

"Don't take it so personally," I called back.

"When are we going for another tattoo?" Ares asked.

I paused at the door. "Is that your idea of connecting with me?"

"If it is?"

My jaw ticked. "Two weeks," I told him. "Call your guy. We'll get matching unicorns."

"I'm holding you to that."

Chapter Thirteen

Chloe

Are you awake?

My heart jumped. I'd sat up most of the night staring at the television, unable to sleep for the string of thoughts constantly running through my mind. I picked up my phone, thinking maybe it was Tyler, but an unrecognizable number was responsible.

I think blood stopped circulating to my heart. Unknown numbers triggered something deep within me, some level of mistrust that I feared. It wormed its way through my bones and down into my stomach, settling in a pit that made me queasy. I stared at the message and the number, trying to figure out who could be texting me at 2 A.M. or if they even meant to text me as my heart began throbbing in my ears.

I turned away from the phone when the screen went dark and tried to focus on the storyline of the tv show I was watching. Then I began to fidget, scratching the inside of my palm and moving my foot anxiously.

My entire body jumped when the notification went off again.

It's Gavin.

Fucking hell.

I breathed out a long sigh of relief, feeling like a bucket of cold air washed over my sweating skin. It took me a moment to collect my thoughts and calm my heart. I closed my eyes as I repeated back a few numbers, and when the phone came back on with the reminder alert, I finally grabbed it into my hands.

Hey.

Hi.

Can't sleep?

Never, he replied. *I noticed your favorite show was on a marathon. Thought I would see if you were watching.*

I smiled at the screen. We had spent hours that night watching this reality yachting TV show, eating pizza, and making out on the couch.

Actually, I am. I'm surprised you remembered.

Can't watch this show without thinking of you.

I'm not sure if that's sweet or creepy, I said.

Definitely creepy, he replied, and I scoffed at his joke. *Still on for lunch tomorrow?* he asked.

The look on his face when he'd left my office that morning had been ingrained in my mind since.

Yeah, I answered, a warmth spreading over my cheeks. *Though, I should have asked Jasmine if I already had a meeting then.*

I took care of it. She cleared your calendar for me tomorrow.

I reread the text. **When did you have time to do that?**

Before leaving today.

Perks of being the big boss?

Big boss

Owner

Official matchmaker

God, I suggested.

You're the only one I want calling me that

I shook my head at his banter. **So are you picking me up from my office?**

I have a car scheduled to pick you up in the morning.

Something about that statement took me aback. A car… It sounded like something Tyler would do—impersonal and showy. An uncomfortableness washed through me, and I twisted my lip in thought.

Fancy… Could you pick me up instead?

The dots strummed at the bottom of the screen. *It's a nice car.*

I don't need your money, I said. *But time… time would be nice.*

I stared at my phone, waiting on his reply for over a minute.

I'll pick you up at ten, he finally replied.

I thought this was just lunch.

It's an all-day lunch.

I almost laughed. *You don't know where I live.*

Send me your address.

What should I wear? I asked.

Preferably nothing.

Gavin.

Casual, he replied. *Jeans.*

What am I getting myself into exactly?

It's a surprise, he said. *I'll see you in the morning. Goodnight, Chloe.*

A knot wove in my stomach, but I wasn't sure what else to say.

Night

My doorbell rang at ten AM sharp. I took a last look in the

mirror at the front before grasping the doorknob and swinging the door open.

Gavin stood on the other side, glancing down the hall, holding two coffees in his hands. The grey sports jacket he wore had brown pads on the elbows, and he wore a band tee that looked well-worn. His brows were furrowed as he looked to the next apartment.

"Sometimes I forget it's nearing July, but then I see decor like theirs on the door and—" He finally looked at me, and his words trailed.

Those eyes traveled over me so deliberately that I shifted and leaned my weight into my opposite hip, raising a brow at him. I wasn't even dressed in any spectacular fashion.

"—and I… I…" He swallowed and looked at me directly in the eyes. "Hi," he said.

"Morning, Gavin," I said, trying to ignore my ears heating.

The last time he had been at my door, though on the other side of the country, he'd had me pressed against it, his hands beneath my skirt. And judging by the look on his face, he was remembering it too.

His tongue darted out over his lips quickly. "Ah… brought you coffee," he said, extending his right hand to me.

I smiled at the nervousness on his face and took the drink. Our fingers brushed, prompting that feeling to stagger long after our hands had parted. I opened the door a little wider.

"Would you like to come in? I just need to grab my purse," I said.

"Ah… yeah."

I left the door open and walked to the couch where I'd laid my purse. Gavin whistled behind me as the door closed.

"This place is…"

"Cold?" I suggested.

"I was going to be nice and say modern," he said, and I met his gaze over my shoulder.

"*'Nice'* isn't necessarily a word I would use to describe you," I said. I plopped my purse on the bar and looked through it, ensuring I had my wallet and phone charger. "It's okay. You can call it what it is. Tyler isn't a fan of colors in the home, or pretty much any personal interior details. I think he just wants to keep it as close to a model home as possible for when he sells it. You should have seen the look on his face when I tried to put up a photo in the hall there."

"How long have you lived here?" Gavin asked.

"A little over a year. We moved in when Designare Fusion opened up offices and hired employees. This place was one of Tyler's properties that he already had, so it was easy to make the move."

Gavin ran his hand over the top of one of Tyler's tinker toys on the end table. "Where are your things?"

"What things?" I asked.

"Everything from your apartment," he said.

"What, like my blankets and picture frames? They're in storage a few blocks over." I pushed my bag onto my shoulder, and I had to look twice when I saw how he was staring at me.

"What's wrong?"

"Does your fiancé have cameras hidden in every inch of this place?" he asked.

"Um..." I glanced around us, my eyes darting to the corners of the room, to the plants, and then to my open computer. "I don't think so. Why?"

"And he's gone for the week?"

My lips drew into a thin line. "Is there a reason you're asking?" I asked with a tilted head, resisting a smirk.

He scoffed, apparently getting my drift, and shoved his hands in his pockets as he stalked in my direction. My breaths slowed upon his approach, and when he stopped an inch from my chest, he grinned outright down at me.

"Can't be too careful," he said.

I bit the inside of my cheek. "Are you going to be able to keep it in your pants today?"

"Is that what you want?"

"I'm engaged, Gavin."

"And you're making it a habit not to answer my questions," he said. "Seems a little suspicious."

I almost laughed, but ended up just shaking my head. "You're ridiculous." I shoved past him and adjusted my bag further onto my shoulder as I made for the door.

"Where are we going?" I asked.

He reached around me as we hit the threshold, his hand on mine as we both reached for the doorknob, and he twisted it with me. The warmth of that touch blazed through me all the way down to my toes. I hesitated, pivoting my head slightly to look up at him.

"It's just lunch, sweet girl," he said.

I couldn't stop laughing as we sat together at the small, beachside shack, waiting on our food.

"You made out like you had this entire day planned out," I teased him. "Now, who's the liar?"

"I did," he argued. "I had everything. Breakfast on the water, driving to Sequoia Park, picnic, Disneyland, helicopter ride at sunset—"

"Disneyland was an option?" I interjected.

His grin softened as he gazed at me across the table, the morning sun and ocean waves behind him. "I don't think you've been a good enough girl for Disneyland yet," he said.

My mouth twisted, and I swallowed, my eyes fluttering at the sound of him saying those words. Staring at him there against the glow of the sun was one of those moments that made me feel like I was truly looking at a god. His green eyes looked sage in that brilliance, the light coming off his ginger hair creating a flame-like swirl in the strands, and those freckles… fuck, they were cute, popping off his skin like that.

"You know, I would have done all those things," he continued. "But I didn't want you to feel like I was pressuring you into anything or trying to show off."

My lips wrapped around the paper straw in my Bloody Mary, and I sighed. "Thank you," I said, my heart full of relief.

"For what?"

"For not trying to impress me," I replied.

The smile on his lips was small, and he tapped the paper he was fidgeting with on the table as he stared at me. "I didn't know that was something you didn't like."

"It's not really that I don't like it," I said. "It's just that…" My voice trailed, and I looked out at the beach. "It's nothing," I said. I sat up, leaning over the table. "Tell me what's new in the life of Eros."

"Ah… not much really," he answered. "Same job. Same schemes. Same apartment. Nothing nearly as exciting as what's happened with you."

I eyed the smirk on his lips and poured myself a refill of Bloody Mary from the pitcher we'd ordered. "Just because my life has changed dramatically doesn't automatically make it exciting."

"I think a new business counts as exciting," he said.

"I think it counts as terrifying," I said.

"Was it?"

"I don't think I slept for months," I admitted. "A new

business meant not only larger projects, but that I would have to find other designers to delegate to, and I was such a control freak at the time that I thought I would be the worst micromanager in history. When you find the right people, it turns out they make life a little less stressful."

"Did your fiancé invest or help you with startup capital?" he asked.

I scoffed. "No," I said, recalling the conversation. "God, no. I wouldn't let him. He offered, but… It didn't feel right. I mean, what would happen if we broke up? Would he hold that over me?" I shook my head. "I couldn't chance my business on a personal relationship. I learned my lesson a long time ago not to trust money."

"You don't like money?"

"It's not that I don't like money," I said. "I just hate what it does to some people. They get obsessed with it, to the point that they forget what's standing in front of them."

"Isn't that what any obsession does?" he asked. "Fester and eat at you until you can't remember how things were before."

"Sounds like love," I said, smiling.

A quiet chuckle left him. "You're getting married, and you're still anti-love?"

"Love is still tragic," I said with a shrug, repeating the line from our conversation that night.

"And what's tragic about your current relationship that makes you continue to believe that?"

I eyed him. "It sounds like you're drilling holes into the bottom of a perfectly steady boat," I said.

"Sounds like the boat was already sinking."

He stared smugly at me, and before I could say anything, the waitress came around with our food.

There were only the clanks of our silverware hitting the plates for a few minutes, both of us sneaking glances at the other, that coy smile still on his perfect lips. I could hardly eat. I wanted to be mad at him for prying, for calling me out on gaps he could already see. But it was too easy to talk to him and admit the things that maybe I hadn't even admitted to myself. It had been like that previously on that Valentine's night, and it didn't seem to matter how many years had escaped between us.

"You shouldn't smile at me like that," I said as I forcefully swallowed a mouthful of eggs.

"Like what?"

"Like you know all of my secrets."

Gavin's smile widened. He finished the last bite of his food, wiped his mouth, and tossed the napkin on the table. "Want to get out of here?"

"And go where?" I asked.

He shrugged. "It's a beautiful day. Take a walk?"

I almost laughed. "Like a long walk on the beach? Is that your idea of the perfect date?" I asked in a sing-song voice.

Gavin's lips split, showcasing his white teeth as he sat up, pulled his wallet out, and slapped a few large bills on the table. "Baby, if this were a date, I'd have already taken you backwards on the car ride over," he said. "It's been five years. The fact that I haven't touched you yet makes my palms itch."

"You should probably see a doctor about that," I said, taunting him to cover up the sudden throb between my thighs.

He laughed softly, eyes bright when he looked at me again. "Fuck, I missed you," he said.

My smile met his. "It was one night," I said. "Barely enough time to get to know someone enough to miss them."

It was a lie.

Because I had missed him, too.

I wanted to hate him for making me feel this way. But

inwardly, I craved it. I had missed flirting so much. And here he was, the king of flirting, back in my life for two seconds, and acting as though no time had passed.

The way his gaze softened then made me curious about what he was thinking. It was that same look of knowing. I felt as though he could see into my soul, and that notion, that sentiment, made an unfamiliar feeling rise in my chest. A sadness washed over me, and I sat up in my seat.

"How about that walk?" he asked.

I snapped out of my daze and reached for my drink, downing the rest of it back like a shot. Gavin was standing at my side, his hand out, when I was finished.

My fingers slid into his like they were a missing puzzle piece.

Chapter Fourteen

Chloe

The wind coming off the sea billowed my hair back off my face. I hugged Gavin's coat to my body, now and then taking a deep inhale of his scent coming off the cotton. It hadn't changed. It was still just as intoxicating as it had been that night. He'd grabbed it out of his jeep for me before we started out to the sand, and I'd left my shoes there so I didn't get sand in his car. He said he didn't care, but I did. Getting sand out of a car was nearly impossible.

"You know, I've lived near a beach most of my life, on one side of the country or the other, and I think I can count on both hands the number of times I've gone in my adult life," I said, staring out at the glittering waves.

"You need a better beach," he replied. "Then you wouldn't be able to stay away."

Something about the statement suggested that he wasn't talking about the beach.

"I think it's the sand," I said. "It gets everywhere."

Gavin glanced over at me. "Yeah, you can tell you don't get out here much," he said.

My head jerked his way. "Are you calling me pale?"

He chuckled under his breath. "I'm not calling you tan."

"It's nice to know the smartass in you hasn't changed," I said, nudging him.

Fuck, that smile. It was a weakness I couldn't escape. I swallowed in the silence, turning my face away from him and back to the ocean, forcing my legs to move even though they begged to stay in one place.

"Some days I want to jump in the car and just drive," I said. "I feel like there's so much of the world I haven't seen."

"By yourself?"

"Maybe. I'd want it to be a vacation. No work. No meetings. No set schedule or destinations. Just driving and turning onto whatever interstate intrigued me. I'd eat shit gas station food and pick up hitchhikers."

"Beautiful girl driving alone across the country and picking up random strangers on the highway." His brows raised at me. "I think I'd better come along to make sure no one tries to murder you."

"Don't lie. You would come along just for the junk food."

"Imagine all the shit diners we could stop at," he said.

"Mm… I have one request, though," I said.

"Anything."

"We spend my birthday at the Grand Canyon," I told him.

"When's your birthday?"

"February," I answered.

"Fuck," he said, stopping in front of me. "That's five whole birthdays I have to make up for."

I laughed. "Just as long as it's not something extravagant or some expensive gift."

"You've ruined my plans, now."

I laughed. "Sorry," I said.

"Why don't you want any of that?"

"Because…" My laughter faded, an emptiness settling in the bottom of my stomach. "Gifts can't make up for time missed or be a rebuttal for any actions worth needing forgiveness," I said. "Gifts are special. I don't think anyone wants to only feel special when the person they love wants another chance."

Gavin looked me over silently, his smile solemn. "What would you rather have? To forgive someone, I mean."

"A true apology," I replied. "True change. Time together."

"Do you think someone can change?" Gavin asked.

The word struck something in me. I'd heard those words before, seen someone down on their knees and promising things would be different.

"I don't know," I said. "I like to believe it, but in my experience, no."

Gavin didn't speak for some time; the only noises around us were the ocean waves and the seagulls. That serene noise and the smell of the salty air seemed to relax me, and having him in front of me… I don't think my mind had been so at ease in a long while.

It felt good not to guard what I said, to be able to speak whatever came to mind and not be judged for it. Because I knew he wouldn't. I knew there was nothing I could say that he would have balked at, no idea that he would have called outright stupid.

I had longed for that my entire life.

Gavin reached up to my face, his hand landing softly on my cheek. I didn't realize my eyes were closed until I opened them to find him staring at me. My heart skipped, and warmth on my cheeks rose from within, not just from the sun hitting our skin.

Fuck, this feeling. It was hard being near him. It triggered every regretful bone in my body.

"I feel like I should have drunk more alcohol for this conversation," I said, my voice almost shaking with nerves. His smile settled somewhere deep within me, and I had to stop myself from leaning in any further.

"How do you make me feel this way?" I whispered.

"What way?" he asked.

"Like I can be my complete self. Like…"
Like I've known you my entire life and every life before.
I didn't say it, but it felt like an unspoken whisper between us, one that we shared in some repressed bubble that pulled us together again and again until our souls finally took peace in the comfort of the other's embrace.

"I think it's the vodka," he whispered, and I laughed softly, my gaze darting down to the ground and back up. His laughter mingled with mine, that smile slowly faded as he watched me for a long moment, holding my face like if he let me go, I would disappear.

"I tried so long to find you," he whispered.

There was real pain in his eyes, and a lump rose in my throat.

"Don't say things like that," I said, unsure if I could contain myself if he went on.

"You were a ghost," he went on. "You deleted everything."

"I had to," I said.

"Why?"

"Gavin, there are things…" I took a step away from his embrace and turned away. I wasn't ready to talk about why I'd gone dark back then or moved apartments. "There are things you don't know," I finally said, glancing back at him.

He nodded, and I was grateful for his understanding. The gap was closed between us again, and he took my hand in his, his lips pressing to my temple. Chills erupted on my skin.

"Will you tell me one day?" he asked.

I wanted to. It was something I hadn't even told Tyler about. Of course, he'd never asked, and I didn't strictly volunteer to talk about my ex.

Except for that night with Gavin.

I looked up at him, and I squeezed his hand. "Maybe I will. Maybe if you're a good boy," I said, trying to lighten things up.

He reached under my chin and gave it a flick. "That's my line," he said with a wink.

I could have kissed him for not pushing it.

My phone buzzed, and I pulled away to look at the text that had come through. From Ezzie, asking if I'd had a chance to look over the verbiage her team had sent over.

I waved my phone in the air. "Looks like playtime is over," I said.

"Fiancé?" he asked.

"Worse," I said. "Wife."

Gavin scoffed. "Right. Should I take you home or the office?"

"Home."

We walked back to the car in silence, and once there, he opened the door, which I shook my head at and called him a gentleman.

"I'll always be when we're in public, baby," he replied.

"And when we're not?"

His gaze darted to the ring on my finger and then back to my eyes. "Leave the ring in the cupholder and give us five minutes alone. You'll know."

My heart skipped. "Flirt," I forced out, and he closed my door with a grin on his lips.

I was playing with fire.

Gavin zoomed in and out of traffic, and his eyes continued to dart in my direction every chance he got. I found my cheeks blushing every time he smiled my way.

"Keep your eyes on the road," I said.

"I can't," he said.

"I swear if you say something about the last time I was in this Jeep, I'm getting out at the next light."

A quiet chuckle left him. "I was actually going to say I was happy you were back in my life," he said, and my entire body relaxed at the genuine smile on his lips. "Still, now we know whose mind is elsewhere."

I almost rolled my eyes. We were nearing my apartment, but as we turned at the light, a place I hadn't been in months caught my eye.

"Wait," I said, leaning over him. "Stop in here. I want to show you something."

"Here?" he said as he pointed to the storage building.

"Yeah."

The lights inside the hall came on one by one as we moved down it. Gavin didn't say anything, and as we reached my unit, I took my keys out and unlocked the padlock. Gavin helped me lift the gate, and when I flipped on the light, he let out a low whistle.

"Holy fuck."

It was everything I owned. Boxes stacked atop one another, couches and beds and dressers and every other piece of furniture I'd had at my apartment across the country.

I pulled the gate back down behind us—a habit as I didn't like leaving that open for anyone to walk in while I was there alone.

"You brought everything," he said, reaching into a box and taking out a picture frame.

"When I cleaned out the apartment I was in when we met, I put a lot of things in storage. I think I wanted to keep my belongings minimal in the new place just in case..." I paused and opened one of the dresser drawers, finding old clothes there. "But then when Ezzie and I decided to open our offices here and Tyler and I moved, I hired a few people to help me pack and drive over all my things in that unit, too, along with all the things I kept in my apartment. Having a storage place around the corner from our building was convenient. That way all of my things were here when I wanted them."

"You honestly took nothing to your new place?" he realized.

"You've seen my apartment," I said. "None of this would work in it."

I moved to the back of the unit where most of the boxes were stacked up, and I looked for the one that had Lana's name on it. She'd packed it herself—a box with all of our photos and some memorabilia we'd saved over the years. There was a single frame I was looking for, and when I opened up the box, it sat on top.

"Look at this," I said as I took the picture out.

Gavin made his way over and stopped at my back when he reached me. "Is that… is that from that night?" he asked upon seeing the photo.

It was a picture of Lana and me the night of the Valentine's Day event. We were laughing. The flash had been too bright in our faces, but we didn't care. I smiled at the photo as Gavin pushed up behind me, his chest flush to my back. I felt his chuckle in my hair.

"And there's you," I added, pointing to the far corner.

Gavin reached for the frame. He brought it up to his face, squinting at the blurred people in the background.

"In the middle of a crowded room, and all I could see was you," he said. "I'm looking at you here."

"Probably trying to decide which candy heart to put in my belt next," I said. "Speaking of which—" I dug further and brought out a pink shoebox full of things Lana and I had saved from Valentine's and a few other parties she'd dragged me to.

I opened the box, revealing the rest of the photos we'd taken that night, along with concert tickets, some old earrings, the bag of heart candies, the fuzzy red handcuffs, and the note Gavin had left on my pillow.

I'll find you, it had said.

Gavin's hand squeezed my waist. That touch, that simple gesture… it sent my heart into an erratic pace. The way he looked at that note and the things we'd used that night, I wondered what it did to him, if it made his blood rush as much as it made mine.

He reached around me and picked up the note. "I had to search through all of your drawers to find that fucking pen," he said. "I'm surprised I didn't wake you."

"I was so exhausted from… *everything*… you could have made yourself breakfast and I wouldn't have heard you," I said.

"I *did* make myself breakfast," he said, and I laughed, twisting my head to face him.

He had the cutest look of nostalgia in his eyes that warmed my insides.

"You did?" I asked.

"Leftover pizza," he said. "I dug into that snow cream, too."

My entire face lit up at the mention of it. "Did you really?"

"Yeah," he said. "It was good. A lot better than I expected. I actually…" he chuckled at himself, scratching the back of his neck nervously, "I tried to make it a few years later."

"You remembered how?"

"I said I tried," he said. "I think I need another tutorial."

God, he was fucking cute.

As I laughed, he picked up the candy hearts, then the handcuffs. "You have these in storage? Not using them?"

"Tyler isn't exactly so adventurous," I admitted. "And it's hard to look at these without thinking of you."

His smile lapsed as he squeezed my waist. I could see it growing in his eyes then: the hunger for what he knew he couldn't have, the greed for our bodies to be one again, the responses to one another's pleasure. His tongue darted out over his lips as his gaze wandered over my face.

"I like that," he said, and my mouth went dry at the sound of his rasp.

I swiftly turned back to the box, desperate for any distraction to keep my mind from how close he was.

His chest pressed against my back, and I felt him inhale into my hair, his hand moving to rest on the curve of my hip.

"Why did you bring me here?" he asked into my hair.

I cleared my throat, trying to ignore the heat between my thighs. I was trapped between him and those boxes, and I didn't care that I was close to falling into oblivion. I knew he would catch me.

"I don't know," I managed. "I think maybe... maybe I missed my things—"

"Look at me, Chloe," he whispered.

It was a command that went straight to my weak knees. My jaw trembled as I moved, his touch remaining on my waist, guiding me around, and when I was facing him again, I forgot to breathe.

His hand moved from the soft touch he'd had on my waist, his fingers brushing past my stomach, my heaving breasts, my chest... All until his touch whispered on my collar, and he brushed his open palm on my neck. My legs turned liquid at the tension and need my body cried out for right then.

He was so close.

Dangerously close.

"Why did you bring me here?" he asked again.

"I shouldn't have," I muttered.

"Do you know why I think you brought me here?" he asked.

"Why?"

"I think you wanted me to see how much you saved from that night, knowing what it might do to me, and whether you realized it or not, show me that it wasn't just one night to you either. I think you brought me here to see how far you could go. How long you could resist without giving in to how you say I make you feel. But most of all... I think you missed being my good girl," he whispered, his hand enclosing on my throat. "And you crave that praise more than your next breath."

Fuck.

My heart skipped as that fascinating pain spread through me. Gaze fluttering at the sensation—a sensation I hadn't felt in a long while—I realized he was right. I craved this. I craved the push and pull, the secrecy and greed.

"That's not true," I whispered.

"True or false," he rasped against my lips. "If I reached between your thighs, I would find your pussy salivating for my touch."

"You don't know what you're talking about," I barely managed, my voice hoarse and breathless.

He pressed himself closer, so flush I could feel his dick rousing against my abdomen. "Don't I?" he whispered. "True or false, sweet girl."

My chest caved as his other hand creased on my hip. I barely heard my own voice as I answered, "False," on a whimper.

He bent, his nose brushing my jaw, a low chuckle rumbling from his throat. "I love the way you lie," he said. "It gives me all sorts of ideas for how I'll make you regret it." His hand tightened around the outside of my thigh, dangerously close to my ass.

"Gavin..." This was too close. Why had I brought him here? After a long morning of hardly treading above water just being near him, why had I thought this would be a good idea...

My subconscious wanted to betray me. It wanted to sabotage everything around me just to have him one more time. It didn't care who was hurt in the aftermath. *He* was back in my life, and it begged to have him in every way it could.

Traitor.

I thought he would kiss my neck, take me down onto this floor and rail into me until I begged him to stop. Only he hovered over my skin at the brink of driving me into absolute madness instead. My body yearned for his touch, cried out for his lips. I clenched my thighs together at the restless throb aching between them, shivering from trying to hold back.

"I wish you could feel what you do to me," he said as both his hands moved to my hips.

Gavin pulled back and held my eyes as he sank to his knees. A whine caught in my throat. He leaned forward, his lips hovering close to my navel, but he didn't kiss me. His fingers wrapped around the backs of my thighs, massaging my thickness.

"I wish you could feel how much I want you. How much I want to kiss all the places you haven't been kissed these last years." His teeth dragged over my stomach to the waist of my jeans. I held my breath to watch him take that fabric in his mouth and undo the button holding them up.

"How do you know where I've been kissed?" I asked.

"You wouldn't be aching for this if you had," he said before leaning forward to catch the zipper in his teeth. He dragged it downward, exposing the lace panties I was wearing.

Fuckkkk.

I could feel his breath on my abdomen. My neck craned upward as though if I looked away from what he was doing, I could pretend it was all a fantasy in my mind, that the man I'd been dreaming about wasn't on his knees before me, torturing me and taking me to the brink of orgasm without so much as even touching my pussy, that it was all a forbidden dream I could keep secret from the rest of the world.

"You're delusional," I said, while my rocking hips betrayed my words.

"Did you miss the way I tasted you?" he asked as he lifted my leg onto his shoulder. "I bet you hate how I look on my knees before you now, too."

I dared a look down, jaw quivering at the sight of him. Both his hands grabbed onto the waist of my jeans, his forearms against my ass. I thought he might pull my jeans down, was prepared to wake up and maybe slap him for doing so—knowing he would have delighted in that fight and perhaps stopped this tease to take me fully.

But he leaned in, his nose grazing my stomach, teeth tugging at my lace panties. "*Fuck,*" I felt him say against me.

Fuck was right.

I couldn't breathe.

My hips pushed forward and back despite the nagging voice in the back of my head that this wasn't right, that he shouldn't have been touching me like this, kissing me like this. That this was wrong.

Then why did it feel so fucking right?

He nudged lower and lower, his mouth brushing my throbbing cunt through the thick seam on my jeans. A moan left me, and I grasped the edges of the boxes I was nearly sitting on.

"That's it, baby," he whispered. "Dammit, I missed that little moan of yours."

He wasn't even touching me and somehow I could feel my orgasm cresting. I needed that friction so fucking badly, my hips moving up and down as if I were grinding against his face, imagining his tongue teasing my clit and gliding in and out of my soaking cunt.

"You shouldn't say things like that," I said as I closed my eyes.

"I shouldn't say a lot of things," he said. "Except, I don't hear you stopping me."

Because I didn't want him to stop. I was too close to the

first orgasm that hadn't come from a vibrator in five years.

And he didn't even have my pants down.

"Fuck you," I managed.

His chuckle vibrated between my thighs. "I love you like this," he said. "Angry at how much you're enjoying it. I bet that rage gets you soaked, doesn't it?"

"No," I practically whimpered.

"More lies," he said. His mouth pressed to the fabric over my clit, and I jerked, unprepared for that touch. His breath brushed against my abdomen again, face buried there as he tortured me.

"I can still taste you," he said, his forearms pushing my hips closer and trapping me in his embrace. "I can still feel my tongue inside you. In and out. Sucking your clit into my mouth as you begged my name and pulled my hair."

The fantasy spun me. My hips bucked against his face, the pressure of him nuzzling between my thighs making me squirm.

"Gavin…"

"That's it," he whispered. "I want to taste you so badly," he muttered, his teeth biting on that seam again. "The things I would do if I could have you… *Fuck*, baby."

His tone was of yearning and greed, and I needed to know what he meant.

"Tell me," I said against my better judgment. "Tell me what you would do."

He hesitated, and I felt him lean forward again. "I would rip these pants apart just to taste you," he said, kissing at the very edge of my zipper. "I would suck your clit until you couldn't breathe, plunge my fingers in and out of your greedy pussy and spread you wide. You would scream, beg, plead for me to end you. And just when you spilled over, I would bend you back over these boxes and spread your thighs, make you hold your hands behind your back while I pulled your hair and fucked you until you couldn't see anything except the stars. Your pussy would make those beautiful little noises around my cock, too."

He licked my abdomen, bit my jeans, and seemed to pull me tighter after every sentence. My hips were erratic as I envisioned everything he promised. I could feel his mouth on my clit, his cock inside me, his hands in my hair and yanking me backward. Shit, all I needed was for him to touch me and I would collapse in his arms.

I let go of one of the boxes and began to squeeze my tit, grinding my hips on him and laying my head fully back. I succumbed to that fantasy, my eyes rolling.

I barely realized my other hand was in his hair until I felt the softness around my fingers.

"Gods, baby, you're soaking," he hissed. "I can feel you through these jeans. Do you like the idea of me licking you until you cry?"

"Yes," I admitted.

"Squeeze that tit as I would," he said. "That's it. Fuck, baby, yes. You are my good girl, aren't you?"

Fucking hell. A whimper left me, my hips grinding into his face again. "Yes," I cried out, his words and the fantasy sweeping through me. His mouth enclosed on that seam again, and my imagination ran with desire. I was right there on the edge, straining to keep my composure—

"Come for me, Chloe," he said, his hands tightening on my ass. "Let go. I've got you. Fuck, I've got you, baby," he said in a straining voice.

Jaw shaking, I felt my walls coming down, and my release hit me in waves. Both my knees bent up, and I craned my head back, letting that pleasure wash through me over and over. He held one arm tight around me, and I knew he was watching my face as my mouth dropped and I yanked at my own hair. I heard him groan, felt his hand squeeze so tightly on my ass that I knew it would be bruised after.

When that final wave shivered through me, I finally opened my eyes and tried to catch my breath. But the sight that met me caused me to still.

Gavin was still kneeling, one hand still holding my leg over his shoulder, and the other… The other was around his erect cock, cum spilling over his fist.

Our eyes met. Desire locked onto me. He swallowed as his dick finished, his tongue running over his lips. "Do you see what you do to me?" he said in a breathless, desirous voice, pushing to his feet.

My legs dropped to either side of his hips, and I forced my eyes to stay on his. I don't know what came over me, but I reached for his cum-covered hand, and I brought his thumb to my mouth. Stick and salt met my lips, a touch of sweetness. I licked his thumb, reaching for the blanket behind me at the same time, and then I cleaned the rest of his hand with the fleece.

Gavin looked as though he might lose his mind right there.

"That's not fair," he said.

I didn't reply. I couldn't believe what I'd just done, what I'd just allowed. I started buttoning up my pants and straightening my shirt, although I'd gotten no further than pulling up my zipper when I felt Gavin press behind me.

"Next time, I won't respect the ring on your finger until you tell me to stop," he whispered into my hair. "Next time, it'll be my tongue—"

"There won't be a next time," I said, stepping out of his hold. I pressed my hand to my forehead, swallowing and taking a deep breath at the realization of what we had just done. "This can never happen again," I managed.

"What can never happen again?" he asked innocently.

"This," I replied, finally turning and meeting his eyes. "You. Me. Alone. A darkened room. The touching and—"

"The orgasm?" He cocked a coy brow, and I shoved his chest.

"Yes." Even though it was the best orgasm I'd had in years —if he'd actually touched my bare body, I might have combusted completely. Nonetheless, that didn't matter. I had lost control faster than I thought I would.

I cursed under my breath. "Gavin, I can't."

His throat bobbed when I looked back up at him, and the cockiness that had just been in his eyes was slowly fading. "Fuck," he hissed, rubbing his hand over his face. "I didn't—"

"Just take me home," I said softly.

I didn't want to talk about it right then. I had to sort out my feelings and what I needed, what I wanted, and what his coming back into my life really meant.

"Okay."

Chapter Fifteen

Gavin

I avoided Designare Fusion for three weeks.

Chloe sent over a few drafts for me to approve. Nothing more. I had opened and closed my phone multiple times to text her, however I hadn't been able to decide what to say.

It was stupid of me to think it would be that easy. One day alone together, accompanied by worshiping her body and saying wicked things in her ear wasn't enough. It never would be. I could call her 'good girl' and tell her how much I wanted her all day long, but that wasn't what had made me want to find her again all these years—Psyche or not.

It was the ease of conversation, the laughter, and the way she made me feel that made me want to spend all of my time with her. Morning and night. Good days and bad.

And I was an idiot for thinking otherwise.

"You're more distracted than usual today," my mother said in a haughty voice.

I'd convinced her to meet me for breakfast rather than my going home. We sat at a restaurant by the wharf, the noise of seagulls and the smell of salt surrounding us. The only reason I'd agreed was to find out answers about Psyche.

Ares was right. My mother had to know something. She was so overprotective that she would know anything that may have hurt me.

I stared at her opposite me. She'd worn an all-white pantsuit, her strawberry blonde hair pulled back in perfect old Hollywood swirls and waves beneath the wide-brim white sunhat on her head.

Glamorous and proper with a well-crafted smile, that was my mother. All in an attempt to hide her true nature:

A jealous bitch.

"Work," I replied, sitting back in the chair and crossing my ankle over my knee. "We have a large project going on right now."

Aphrodite, or Phoebe as she was calling herself these days when she hosted self-love retreats and yoga-meditation havens for corporate outings, bachelorette parties, or random weekends through the year, whipped off her black cat-eye sunglasses and laid them on the table. She looked apprehensively in my direction, blue eyes appearing icy pale against her porcelain skin in the morning beach light.

"It's more than that," she said. "I'm your mother. I know these things. Is it a girl?"

"Do you genuinely expect me to discuss my love life with you?" I asked before taking a sip of my Bloody Mary.

"You run a dating app, sweetheart. I expect you have quite a few woman problems, and I can't imagine the time it would take to go through all of them," she sighed. "Why are you so hostile? What have I done this time?"

My mouth twisted as I stared at her, remembering my mother's jealousy of Psyche's beauty the first time and the way men turned to worship her instead of Aphrodite. She'd even sent me to 'take care of Psyche' as she'd done with so many things before, and since then.

Of course, that job had backfired in the best way, and I'd ended up finding my soulmate.

She wasn't wrong. I wasn't ordinarily hostile with her. We had actually had an amicable relationship over the last few centuries. But ever since talking to Persephone and realizing that Psyche had been erased from our history, my suspicion of Mother had grown.

Today, I was so bottled up with anticipated rage at what I was about to ask her that I couldn't help myself. I tried to breathe and calm myself before the ugly monster I had once been portrayed as made its way to the surface.

"There's something I want to ask you about," I said.

She blotted her mouth and dropped the napkin. "Here I thought you just missed me," she said with a bat of her lashes. "Fine. What is it? What has you so bent out of shape?"

"What is the last thing you remember about Psyche?"

Aphrodite choked on her mimosa. I didn't say anything as she continued to cough, causing a scene almost as she looked around us and people stared to make sure she was okay. She brushed one man off who stood to check on her, and the man glared at me as though I'd done something wrong by not saying anything as she choked and sputtered.

I knew better.

"Are you finished?" I asked as she fanned her face and smiled at the other patrons, nodding to a few to assure them she was okay.

"My gods," she said with nervous laughter. "Champagne up the nose. Never a good—*are you out of your mind?*"

Her persona changed in a flash. Everyone around us seemed not to hear the snap in her facade, and were suddenly so intrigued by the conversation around them that they forgot they'd just been concerned about her. She was leaning over the table, her voice a hiss, nostrils flared and a wild look in her dilated eyes.

"How dare you bring up that girl now," she snapped. "After all these centuries. I don't care how much she may have proved her love, the fact is she betrayed you. And then she *left* you. And you expect me to do what, exactly?"

"What do you mean she left me?" I asked, sitting up in my seat.

"She ran away," she said. "And I held your bleeding heart for *years* after while you spent every countless hour trying to find her."

My heart began to ache. I didn't remember it. I barely remembered our time together, much less the pain of her disappearance, and if she had actually ran away?

That kind of pain… I should have felt it.

"Why don't I remember?" I asked.

Aphrodite hesitated. She stared at me, her lips pressed into a thin line, and she sat back in her seat. That was a look I knew, and my fists curled at the sight of it.

"Mother…"

"I did what I had to," she seethed. "I did what was needed to protect you from that pain."

"What did you do?"

"You have no idea what it's like to see your child in such agony, Eros," she said. "I won't apologize for helping you the only way I knew how."

"By making me *forget my wife?*" I was shaking. My voice threatened to grow, true form dancing at my fingertips as rage coursed through my veins.

Her chin raised. "It's what was necessary."

It took everything in me not to launch myself across the table, grab her by the throat, and squeeze her long neck until it crushed beneath my grasp. "And my friends? You made them forget her, too?"

"It was better for everyone," she replied.

I couldn't breathe. My own mother…

What she said about her disappearance didn't make sense, not with what I did remember, with what Persephone remembered.

"She wouldn't have just run away," I argued, my voice

softer. "We were happy."

"I don't know what to tell you, son. She left. You became a shell of yourself. I fixed it." Aphrodite snapped up a piece of celery and chewed it loudly. "What is the point in bringing any of this up? She's gone. It's not like you'll ever find her again."

I didn't reply, but I stared at her with such malice that I was surprised I wasn't glowing. I gathered my phone and wallet, and gulped down the last few sips of my drink.

"Goodbye, Mother," I said shortly, standing to my feet.

"Sweetheart—"

But I was gone before she could say more.

Chapter Sixteen

Chloe

I was still red-cheeked when I thought of that storage room.

My ass had had a bruise on it the entire weekend. It was a reminder of the control I'd lost, a reminder not to allow myself to be so alone with him again. Because if it did…

I wasn't sure I'd have the willpower to stop it.

In his absence, I had tried to focus more on work the last few weeks. It had been difficult to look at his logo and not think of him, but I managed a few sketches and sent them over, only getting a few words in reply. I didn't expect anything else, and honestly, I was grateful he hadn't said anymore.

"Have you talked to him yet?" Lana asked on our morning video chat.

"Who?" I asked.

"Gavin."

My eyes darted from her to the bedroom where Tyler was sleeping. He'd been home off and on. When he was home, I tried to focus on him, especially the moments when he was actually with me. He had a habit of planning out his days when he was home—golf, friends for drinks, boat excursions…

"Why would I need to talk to him?" I asked, hoping she got my drift not to talk about this on a video call that Tyler could most likely hear just down the hall.

"For… design things," Lana recovered. "I didn't know! He's never home!" she mouthed.

"He's asleep!" I mouthed back. I straightened up, pulling my toast out of the toaster and glancing to the bedroom to make sure I didn't hear anything. "No, I haven't talked to him. I'll have to figure this out alone," I told her. "It's just font."

"You look tired," Lana said as her cat jumped into her lap. "Up all night working?"

"No," I said. "Tyler's mother started texting me at 3 A.M. about fucking roses. I don't think she realizes there are time zones between us."

"That's why you put that thing on Do Not Disturb, babe."

"Yeah. Well. Damage is already done." I lifted my coffee mug to my lips and took a hesitant sip, unsure of how hot it was. Still too hot to drink. Dammit. I needed coffee.

"When will you be here again?" I asked Lana.

"I'm waiting for a call from the boutique. Most likely next month."

"That's just weeks before the wedding," I said.

"I'm not too worried about it," Lana said. "I think it'll be fine. Mine won't need as many alterations. Did you go back for another fitting?"

"I did. It's hanging in my storage unit. Along with the other one—"

"What other one?"

I jumped, almost spilling my drink all over my computer at the sound of Tyler's voice. "Fucking hell, Tyler," I said, clenching my chest. "I hate it when you do that."

He smiled, wrapped an arm around my waist, and gave me a kiss on the cheek. "Morning," he said softly. "Morning, Lana," he said to her.

"Good morning, Tyler," she replied, and I noted the drip of

sarcasm in her voice. I gave her a look, and she just smiled in return.

"What other dress are we talking about?" Tyler asked, grabbing a mug from the cabinet.

"Just a reception dress," I said.

"The most gorgeous dress there ever was," Lana interjected.

"Sounds like Lana likes it better than the one you already have," Tyler said to me.

"That's because I picked it out," Lana said. "Her *best friend*. Someone who actually knows her."

"I'm sensing some hostility this morning," Tyler said, and I knew his tone would send Lana over the edge.

"Oh, look at the time," I said, wide-eyeing Lana. "I have to get ready and go into work."

Lana grinned behind her mug. "You do that, babe. Have fun," she said with a wink.

I exited the chat and closed the computer before she could say anything else that might incriminate me.

"What was that about?" Tyler asked, leaning his hips against the counter.

"Nothing," I said, grabbing my phone. "She's just getting anxious, I think."

There were five text message notifications, all from the same person, all back-to-back within a span of ten minutes with the last one reading '*???*'.

I almost slammed the phone down.

"Can you please tell your mother to calm down about the state of the roses she's evidently flying in from Ecuador?" I said, unable to contain myself. "Apart from going down there myself and picking them one by one, there's nothing I can do about the shade of red. She's already texted me multiple times this morning and acting as though I'm ignoring her."

"Aren't you?"

"It's barely 7 A.M.," I argued. "Doesn't she know what time zones are?"

"It's an important detail to her," Tyler said with a shrug.

"It's not her wedding," I snapped.

Tyler took a long sip of his coffee, his eyes never leaving mine. "Do you not want roses?" he finally asked.

I sighed and braced my palms on the countertop, closing my eyes as I calmed myself down. I had tossed and turned for most of the night, unable to sleep as the moment Tyler's mother began texting me, all I could think about was the wedding. I kept imagining what that day might be like—all the guests, the black-tie affair, the extravagance that would be so foreign. Thinking about it should have made me excited, I thought. But all it did was weave a never-ending knot through my insides, pulling and tugging and binding me to the decisions that had been made for me.

"The roses are fine," I finally said. "I just refuse to let the shade of them ruin my life."

A soft laugh came from him. "You can tell her yourself this weekend," he replied.

"What's this weekend?" I asked.

"They're coming in for a weekend in the vineyards," he said. "We leave Friday afternoon."

Shit. It was already Wednesday. "When were you going to tell me?" I asked.

"This afternoon," he replied. "I had a surprise for you."

I wasn't sure how many more surprises I could take.

"What kind of surprise?"

He sighed, set his cup down, and came to stand in front of me. I wasn't sure I liked the way he looked at me, like he was about to apologize for whatever was on his mind. He reached out for my forearm and took my hand in his.

"I'm leaving for New York on Monday when we return," he said. "And then the week after, Matthew and I will head to

Tokyo for a couple of weeks."

"You're going to be gone three weeks?" I asked. "The wedding is in six."

"I'm sorry," he said, rubbing my arm. "I know it's a lot, but this deal—" An excited smile had spread on his lips. "This deal will set us up for *years*. I can stop traveling as much. We can buy a house back on the east coast. You will never have to work another day in your life."

Things I didn't want.

"But I like working," I said.

"Not when we have kids running around, you won't," he said as he took a step back, still hanging onto my fingertips. "Four. Five, maybe. You'll have your hands full."

Nausea twisted my stomach. "I thought we were going to travel first," I managed through the queasiness. "Travel a few years and *then* think about kids."

"You're one trip around the sun from thirty, love," he said. "Time to get the factory open."

"And if I don't want kids now?"

He paused amid putting on his coat and frowned at me. "What are you talking about?"

"I mean… I want them, but what if I don't want them *now*? I just got my business running smoothly."

"Something you won't have to worry about once this deal goes through," he said. "You can sell Ezzie your part of the company when we move."

"What is this timeline?" I asked, anxiety swelling inside me.

"If the deal goes like I want… six months. Maybe eight."

Six… *six months?!*

"Tyler, I've barely had my business a year," I said as breath seemed to escape me. "When were you going to tell me all of this? When were you going to run any of it by me?"

Then he just smiled. "I wanted it to be a surprise," he said.

"Getting told you never have to work again, that's a pretty great surprise, don't you think?"

Except I love my job.

He leaned over and kissed my cheek, then grabbed his coffee mug from the counter. "I'll be late tonight. Don't wait up."

I stood flabbergasted in that spot for what felt like hours. Six months.

Six fucking months.

It felt like someone had told me I had six months to live.

I was so frustrated from the argument that I broke a heel going to work when a skateboarder cut in front of me, and I had to walk barefoot from the parking garage.

I didn't bother texting Lana about it yet. I wasn't ready to see the poignant look on her face when I told her what he'd said, and she said 'I told you so.'

"Where are your shoes?" Jasmine said when she caught up with me.

"It's a long story," I muttered. "Do I have anything today?"

"Nothing on the books. Sarah said she had a new design for you to look at for Arrow," Jasmine answered.

"Amazing. Tell her to send it over to me?"

I rushed into my office, late from taking extra time in the shower as I'd put the water as hot as I could stand it in an attempt to drown out the noise in my head. It was almost 10 o'clock already. I was so behind already.

But I stopped at the window, my heart stumbling at seeing who stood outside. Gavin looked so contemplative there, like he was debating whether to come inside. A sharp breath entered my lungs as I thought of the last time we'd seen each other. His leaving me at the elevator, not daring to come anywhere near the apartment after what had happened between us.

I watched him with a soft smile on my face for a long

while, all thought of the issues that had plagued me that morning pressing to the very back of my mind into a little locked corner that I had no intention of visiting while I was at work.

Chapter Seventeen

Gavin

I stood outside Chloe's office building an hour after leaving my brunch with mother, and I stared at Chloe's floor, trying to figure out what I would say to her.

Ran away…

Something didn't feel right about what my mother claimed. Psyche running away wouldn't put her in this century with a new life and identity. That would take memory work, kidnapping, putting her under for years… Someone would have had to dedicate centuries of life to this one cause.

Fucking Styx. I needed my memory back.

I pushed that bit to the back of my mind and focused on the problem at hand. I wondered how Chloe would act toward me after the way we'd left things; if it would be awkward between us or if she would act as though nothing had happened.

I'd never been nervous before. It was new, and I hated that feeling of doubt.

My phone buzzed as I took my last sip of coffee. I looked at the lit screen, and my stomach dropped at the name that came up—Chloe.

Are you coming in or do you plan on staring up at our windows like you're waiting on Rapunzel to let her hair down?

A smile quirked on my lips, and I texted her back. *The good knight usually waits for the damsel to be in distress before rescuing her, doesn't he?*

He does. Except you're not the good knight. You're the evil king. Here to steal the princess away and make her see that villains do it better.

Maybe I'm the dragon the knight has to defeat.

That poor knight.

I laughed softly, and three dots appeared at the bottom of the screen again.

Come upstairs, dragon. I have some things to show you.

My anxiety turned into a full knot around my heart, but I entered the building a little more at ease than I had been minutes before.

Chloe's office had glass walls; the one facing the rest of the room had frosted stripes every two feet. I could see that she was pouring over two prints on blackboards by the exterior wall made entirely of windows when I made it to her floor. I spoke to a few of the people I'd met on my last few visits as I walked across the room to her.

Her eyes lit up when I knocked twice and stepped inside the threshold.

"About time," she said, that beautiful smile on her lips.

It happened then, that feeling of warmth and joy and familiarity. It knotted itself in the pit of my stomach, fluttering my heart and sending my senses into overdrive as it spread out to my extremities. Seeing her smile at me... a smile I hadn't been sure I'd see again after our restrained tumble in the storage locker.

"Come tell me which of these you like better," she said. She held up the two prints, and I swallowed as I joined her in looking at them.

I was *nervous*. Fucking *nervous*.

There were two logo designs on the boards, though neither for Arrow. I leaned over her shoulder, able to smell the rose scent of her shampoo as I did, and I made myself consider the sketches in front of me rather than the magnetism of her body.

"Left," I decided.

"Great. That's the one I was leaning toward as well." She moved to her desk and sat the boards atop it, then turned and leaned her hips against it, arms crossing over her chest. "How have you been?" she asked.

"Heartbroken," I answered, and her lips flinched like she might smile again.

"Poor Cupid alone in his top-floor condo, tiring of the sound of ocean waves in the background?" she bantered.

My chest swelled at the fact that she was joking with me.

Fuck, I was a goner for her.

"It's the bed," I replied. "Too big. Too soft. Too comfortable. Makes it hard to get up in the mornings."

"That's why I usually sleep on the couch," she said. "Something about that middle bar in a decorative couch that hits across your back keeps you awake."

"No idea why, though," I said, smiling.

"None. It's such a mystery," she said with a soft chuckle.

The brightness in her eyes faded just noticeably as I stared at her for a beat, and I realized why they were so bright. They were glistening. Around them was the slightest smudge of mascara, a pink twinge on her nose and eyelids. She had been crying, and the thought of her sobbing alone made my fist curl.

Chloe cleared her throat and pushed off the desk. "One of my designers has a few other examples to show you regarding verbiage placement on the social post templates. How long do you have before you need to return to your office?"

"I can stay as long as you need me," I told her.

She shuffled a couple of papers. "Sarah should be in in a few minutes. She had an appointment this morning, so she's running a little late, if you can stay to look at what she has for you."

I chanced a touch on her elbow, hoping she would talk to me about what was on her mind. "Are you okay?" I asked.

"Ah… yeah," she said, running a hand through her hair. "Yeah, I'm fine." Her eyes closed as she wiped her face, almost like she was trying to wake herself up. "I haven't gotten much sleep the past few weeks."

"Everything alright at home?"

"Why, are you hoping it isn't?" she blurted.

She cursed under her breath the moment the words escaped her, her fingers pinching the bridge of her nose. "Fuck. I'm sorry. You didn't deserve that."

"Yes, I did," I said.

A small smile slipped onto her lips. "Yeah, you did," she said. She glanced toward the elevator then and gave an upward nod to the crowd exiting the doors. "There's Sarah. I'll let Jasmine know you're coming over to look at what she has." Her finger pressed onto the phone on her desk, and Jasmine answered.

"Hey Jasmine, can you let Sarah know Gavin is coming to look at those templates in a few minutes? She just needs to show them to him."

"Will do," Jasmine answered.

The phone clicked, and Chloe looked back up at me. "What are your plans for the day?"

"No plans," he said. "I've already had the hardest part this morning. Wanted to get it over with."

"What was that?"

"Breakfast with my mother," I answered.

"Is that so…" Her voice trailed like she was remembering

something. "Wait, when you say your mother, you mean…" She raised a poignant brow, and I chuckled under my breath.

"Yes," I said.

"Like Aphrodite?" she asked.

"Yes."

Both of her brows elevated this time, and she laughed. "You know, one day, you'll have to show me proof that you indeed are a god."

"I can do that," I said.

"Maybe after, I can meet your mother," she said. "I'd love to know if the stories are true."

"I can honestly say that I don't know if I want you to meet her," I said, thinking of how that would go after this morning's conversation.

Chloe's lips split into a genuine smile. "Ashamed of me?" she asked.

"Terrified of my mother's jealousy," I corrected.

"Why would your mother be jealous of me?"

"Because you're beautiful," I answered.

A twinge of red appeared on her cheeks. "Plenty of people are beautiful," she countered.

"Not like you," I argued.

Her gentle eyes met mine, and just as she opened her mouth to speak, Jasmine buzzed through on the com.

"Sarah is ready for him," Jasmine said.

Chloe leaned back and hit the button. "Sending him now." She jerked her chin toward the door. "When you're done with her, can we take a walk?" she asked.

I regarded her again before answering. "Yeah. I have time for that. Are you sure everything is okay?" I asked.

"No," she admitted. "I just need to clear my head."

"Okay."

Chapter Eighteen

Gavin

She chose the park by the water for our walk. We hadn't stopped talking since I held the door open for her to leave her office. I was beginning to hate the sound of my own voice. She was the only person who could make me converse and smile as she did. My cheeks fucking ached after a day with her, and I loved every second. So much, that it was hard for me to look away from her as we walked. I barely glanced at where we were going.

A skateboarder cut in front of us, making me grab Chloe as she jumped out of his way. Delightful laughter left her lips, but I eyed the skateboarder as he rolled away, something familiar about him snagging my attention. The blonde curly hair beneath the baseball cap, the wing-decorated Converse on his feet, the cut of his gaze back at me.

Uneasiness curled in my veins, but I didn't get a moment to explore further. Chloe was still giggling in my arms, and when she straightened out of my grasp, she peered at me with a questioning gaze.

"What?" I asked, forgetting about the skateboarder.

"I keep thinking about how much my life has changed since that night, and yet when I'm with you, it feels like no time has passed."

We exchanged soft smiles, and I stuffed my hands into my

pockets as we went on. "It feels like that for me, too. Every time you mention your wedding, I have to grasp onto something to ground me back into this reality and remind myself that I didn't wake up with you beside me."

"Reality is a weight right now," she said, her chest heaving with an audible, heavy sigh. "Like it's dragging me further and further toward a life I don't recognize."

I slowed my walk and looked down at her, warmth filling my chest at seeing her beauty against the setting sun. "What do you mean?" I asked.

"I mean, I'd much rather be living in some erotic monster fantasy," she said.

"We've moved on to general monster erotica now?"

"Demons and minotaurs are still my comfort reads, although spiders and orcs are new monsters I'm trying out," she said.

Those were two unexpected genres I hadn't heard of. *Spiders?*

"I don't even know how to respond to that," I said. "How does the spider one work?"

"Maybe one day, I'll read you an excerpt," she said, her eyes shining up at me.

I think my mouth moved into something of a smile, though I wasn't sure as I was trying to envision the spider logistics. Eight legs… were there arms? Pinchers?

A laugh sounded from her, prompting her to clap her hand over her mouth to hide it. "I can see it on your face," she said. "That one threw you."

"I'm really curious now," I admitted.

"I'll show you some artwork," she said.

"That might help," I said, and she continued to snicker at me. I stuffed my hands into my pockets, unable to keep from staring at her as we walked on. "Are you reading any gods smut?" I asked once she'd collected herself.

Her mouth twisted, lashes hitting the lids of her eyes, and the cutest fucking smile split her lips. "Why do I need fictional god erotica when I can just think of you?"

My insides were a warped braid of nerves and desire. Instinct wanted me to kiss her, tell her I was the only god whose name would ever grace her lips, but nerves held me back, and I had to force my gaze forward.

"What does your fiancé think about your reads?" I asked.

"Ah… he's a little confused by them. He just doesn't understand the appeal. I tried to film his reaction to a hot minotaur scene once, but he was so disgusted by it that it turned into an argument instead of a funny bit like I thought it would be."

"Killjoy," I said, and she laughed in agreement. "How are the wedding plans coming along?"

"They're… coming, I guess. Lana is traveling into town again soon to try on her dress," she said. "I'll be glad when it's all over, and I can burn the dress they picked out for me."

"They?"

"Lana is still mad about it. My mother and sisters helped me pick out a dress instead of her. She keeps telling me it isn't what I would have chosen."

The mention of a wedding dress had me spiraling. "And you think she's wrong?" I managed.

"No. She's right," Chloe admitted. "It's beautiful. Long and white, flares out after my hips, strapless… but… I've always envisioned myself in a black wedding dress," she said.

A black wedding dress…

The mention triggered something profound. A memory tugged at the very back of my mind—a memory I couldn't retrieve. It was more frustrating than anything I'd ever experienced. My fists curled in on themselves as I tried to pull more of that to the forefront of my mind.

"Gavin?" she called out for me, and I quickly pushed the feelings far down into the pit of my stomach and kept moving forward.

"Sorry, I'm just trying to envision you in that dress," I said. "So, why didn't you get the black dress?" I asked.

"My sisters wouldn't allow it. They've always told me I was being ridiculous. That I should wear a fitted satin mermaid dress with a simple rhinestone belt around my waist—not that there's anything wrong with that. It's beautiful, but it's just not me."

"It's your wedding," I said.

"Sometimes it doesn't feel like it," she replied. "There are so many voices and opinions to navigate, and I don't want to disappoint anyone. It's almost like—" She paused as if what she was about to say was something she hadn't admitted out loud before and then shook her head. "It's stupid."

"Tell me," I said.

She considered me, those bright brown eyes looking more sincere than I'd seen since she walked back into my life, but the look was fleeting, and she turned back to stare at the sunset.

"It's like something inside me doesn't think it's real," she admitted. "Like a part of me is separated from the entire ordeal, and it's not truly me getting married. And maybe that's why all their decisions haven't affected me."

I forced myself to stay calm at the revelation. "What would you have instead?" I asked.

"If it were up to me, there would be no fancy dinner or long ceremony," she said, looking straight ahead. "There would be no over-the-top table settings, no talking to women I haven't spoken with in years and asking them to be a bridesmaid just to match the number of friends he has for groomsmen. No guest list of people I've never met before. There would only be him and me, in the mountains during a sunset like this one. Maybe a small party the next day or week after we'd had time to enjoy our new life, just to celebrate with family and friends. Nothing fancy. Nothing stressful. Just simply us."

Something about what she said prompted that nagging in the back of my mind again. It was that same feeling like when there's a word on the tip of your tongue, but you just can't think of it.

"What's stopping you?" I asked.

"Expectations," she answered. "Tyler has so many people looking at him because of who he is and his father. He's expected to have this extravagant party. And then there's my family who is so caught up in those expectations that they are being more and more vocal about adding things and creating something excessive and completely unreasonable."

She stopped walking and shook her head, an embarrassed smile on her pink lips. "I'm sorry," she said, rubbing her forehead. "I'm sorry. I'm unloading all of this on you. I don't even know why."

"Sometimes it's easier to talk to someone you don't know as well," I said.

"Maybe," she agreed, beginning to walk again. "Are you sure you want to hear it?"

"Keep talking, baby," I said. "We have another mile before we reach the bar I wanted to take you to."

"The brewery you've been talking about?"

I nodded. "It's just around that corner. You have until then to spill all the details."

"And when we get there?"

"When we get there, I'm buying you a few drinks, and you're going to kick my ass at ski ball."

The smile I'd come to love so much spread across her face and lit up her eyes. "I'd like that."

"I thought you might," I said, my mouth dry at the sight of

her looking at me like that. "Tell me where you're getting married so I can crash it," I managed.

She snickered under her breath and nudged me in the side. "It's the Fairmont Del Mar, I think? I probably have the name wrong. It is gorgeous. I went with him to tour it, at least, though his parents had already booked the date and put down the deposit."

"You didn't choose your own wedding date?" I asked, getting more confused by the second.

"It ended up being just what the venue had available," she answered. "His parents were tired of waiting on us to pick a date, so they surprised us with the venue and date."

"Sorry, what?"

She looked like she might laugh. "I know. It's insane."

"So, none of this. Not the venue, the dress, the decor, even the date… none of this is your choice?"

She looked out at the ocean and then back to me. "Nope."

Fuck, I wanted to sweep her up into my arms and run away so she could have something she truly cared about.

"Where do you *actually* want to get married?"

"If it were my choice, Greece," she said without hesitation. "But when I was asked where I wanted, for some reason saying Greece didn't feel right. I couldn't envision him standing at my side with the mountains around us."

I was on the verge of wringing her neck and telling her to wake up, that she couldn't pick a date because he wasn't who she should be with.

Greece…

She wanted to get married in fucking Greece.

"For as long as I can remember," she continued, "I've had dreams of standing atop a mountain in Greece, beautiful black lace dress, sunflower and poppy bouquet… I don't know how I know it's Greece, but I know that it is. And I know that the shadow standing before me is the person I feel in my dreams, too—"

Blood stopped circulating in my body. "What dreams?"

A quiet scoff left her as she threaded her hand through her hair and pushed it back. "It sounds ridiculous when I say it out loud. But lately, I've had dreams where I wake up, flushed, my heart is pounding, and I feel almost giddy. For the past couple of weeks, there's been a new segment to it. I'm in a completely dark room, all except for the light of a single candle. Every time I see that candle, something tells me not to pick it up. Not to turn it on the shadow behind me. But I do it. Again and again and again. And each time, I wake up before I can see whatever is there."

I froze, completely still at what she'd just described. That night… the candle…

"I know it's the most ridiculous thing ever, but I—Gavin?"

The world around me washed away, and I fell into memory.

Chapter Nineteen

Chloe

I had to do a double-take at the way Gavin was staring at me right then, the way he didn't even seem to be breathing. There was a bewildered look on his face, one that I couldn't figure out. He looked as if he'd seen a ghost, like I'd just said something that prompted him to lose his mind.

"Gavin?"

"You…" he shifted, his hand raising as if he were going to place it on my cheek, but he hesitated. His tongue ran over his lips, throat bobbing as he swallowed. Agony and confusion filled his now glistening eyes. His hands stretched and curled, and I noticed his fingers trembling.

"Gavin?" I reached up for his face, hoping to bring him out of whatever stupor had taken him over. "What's wrong? Are you okay?"

Even his jaw was shaking. I huffed out loud and gave him a nervous smile.

"Gavin, you're scaring me," I managed. "What is it?"

"It *is* you," he breathed, and even though I wasn't sure what he meant, my chest tightened.

"It's me," I said, trying to pull him out of the daze. "It's me, Chloe. Are you okay?"

A tear spilled over his cheek. My stomach dropped. I didn't know what was happening. Had I broken him? How do you break a god?

Shit.

"Please, come back to me," I said, holding his face. "Don't die or go mad or whatever is happening. Do I need to slap you?"

A smile flinched on his lips. He blinked, cursed under his breath, and stepped away from me like he was waking himself up. "Shit," I heard him mutter, his back to me. "Fucking Styx."

"Gavin? Are you okay?"

He finally turned around, tears evacuated, leaving only his widened eyes staring back at me. "Yeah," he said, approaching me again. "Yeah. Just talking about Greece... I haven't been in a while."

He was lying, and I didn't know why.

"Liar," I accused. "What just happened?"

"I thought I saw..." But he shook his head. "It doesn't matter." He reached for my hand and kissed my knuckles, his gaze lingering on me a little longer.

But something changed then, and the look of admiration that had just been in his eyes darkened. His fingers tightened on my own, and his lips pressed into a thin line.

"You know, I think I'm feeling a little lightheaded," he said, his shoulders pushing back. "I think I'm going to have to have a raincheck on the drinks." He let go of my hand so abruptly that it practically fell against my leg, and he started walking in the opposite direction.

"What... Gavin—" I lunged for his arm and pulled him back to me.

Pain stretched in his eyes. Pain and outright rage. I had never seen such emotion in his gaze. I had seen him frustrated, domineering even, but this...

"Are you... are you angry with me?" I asked, my heart beginning to race.

"No," he said, though his tone was exasperated. "No, I'm not… Actually—you know what? Yes, I am, Chloe."

"What? How—"

"Because you settled," he said bluntly.

I stammered, staring at him in disbelief. "I *settled?* What does that even mean?"

"Tyler," and the way he spat out his name was like poison.

"What is wrong with Tyler?" I couldn't believe him. "He's perfectly normal. He's… he's a gentleman and—"

"Your perfect fucking hero," Gavin muttered, hands on his hips.

I balked. "Excuse me?"

"He's the idiot you described the night of the party—"

"Oh, fuck off, Gavin," I snapped. "So what if he is? Is there something wrong with that?"

"He's not good enough for you," he said. "He's not… Chloe, you can't tell me that your love for him is the kind of love you would fight for."

"Why shouldn't I?" I asked. "He's nice. He's honest. He—"

"Are you listing qualities off a menu?" Gavin cut in.

"Is there something wrong with a nice guy?"

"He's boring," Gavin blurted. "Admit it. Does he even challenge you? Does he satisfy you?"

"That's none of your fucking business," I sneered, and the words burned my throat.

He scoffed. "I'll take that as a 'no' then."

I was livid. My jaw quaked with the rage and frustration swelling up inside. "Not everyone can be the god of *lust,*" I finally snapped, barely able to catch my breath. "God, you… you're such a fucking asshole!"

Gavin didn't move, didn't look away, but his chest rose and fell like he was trying to calm himself down. "There's a reason why this wedding doesn't feel right," he said, his voice calmer than it had been a moment before—almost too calm, and the world seemed to dim in its wake.

"A reason that you're letting everyone else make the decisions," he continued.

He had to be fucking kidding me. A choke of a sarcastic laugh left me, and I shook my head at myself for ever trusting that he was just being a good friend and listener.

"I *knew* I shouldn't have admitted that to you," I said. "Fuck my vulnerability. I should have known you'd somehow make this about you. I thought you were different, but you're just another typical guy. I pour my heart out and tell you these things as a friend, and suddenly you think this is about you and me."

"I didn't say that," he argued. "I'm simply saying—"

"*One night,*" I cried out. "One fucking night together, and you think your cock's good enough for me to walk away from an engagement?"

"I think the fact that you don't seem to give two fucks about your own wedding is enough for you to walk away," and the way he said it made me pause. "Gods dammit, Chloe. You just told me that who you envision yourself standing beside at the altar isn't even your own fucking fiancé."

"It was a *dream.*"

But he ignored me.

"And while we're on the subject, yes, I do think that night was enough," he added. "Maybe not enough to declare that you should marry me right now, but enough to ask that you give us a chance."

Tears glistened in my eyes, emotion wrecking my chest and threatening to break down every part of me. I didn't care that people were walking by or that we had onlookers across the street.

I was shaking with rage, hating every word coming out of his mouth. Hating *him.*

"*Don't you fucking dare,*" I seethed through clenched teeth.

He was before me in a second, his chest rising and falling against mine with every labored breath. "I asked you once if you loved him, and you couldn't answer," he hissed. "Answer me now. Do you love him?"

"We are *not* doing this." My voice was shaking.

He took my hands in his, his grip so tight that I couldn't pull away despite my trying. I needed to get away from him. I couldn't do this. Not now. Maybe not ever. Damn him for every word coming from his stupid lips.

"Let me go—"

"Look at me," he said, his grip increasing on my arms. I wrestled again and again, desperate to be free of the truth staring back at me.

"Let me go!"

"Fuck, Chloe, look at me!"

I choked on a sob as I finally met his agony-filled gaze, and my struggling waned.

"I don't mean do you just care for him," he said, his voice softer. "I mean, do you love him as you could love me?"

My shoulders limped, and my heart plummeted into my stomach. Tears spilled out of the corners of my eyes as I struggled to catch my next breath.

"Gavin, don't—"

He yanked me fully into his arms, holding my waist and calming my writhing as his thumb swept across my cheek.

"Tell me to walk away."

My tongue was stuck to the roof of my mouth; my jaw clenched shut.

"Dammit, Chloe, tell me," he practically begged, emotion threading his voice. "Tell me I'm fucking crazy, that I'm losing my mind. Tell me that this, you and me, everything we feel when we're together, isn't worth the vacant days. Tell me this isn't worth the pain I feel without you. Tell me these years were as agonizing for you as they were for me, but that while every day without you felt like forever, that this… here and now… this is everything."

My knees almost gave way. I couldn't see from the tears streaming down my face. Every word was an arrow into my heart, shredding and bleeding the muscle until there was nothing left.

How fucking dare he—*how fucking dare* he make me feel this way?

"Tell me, Chloe," he almost whimpered, and I could see the tears in his eyes, pleading for me to put him out of his misery. "Break my heart," he whispered. "Completely this time."

I couldn't do this.

"I have to go home," I wept, wrenching out of his grasp.

"Chloe—"

"Don't touch me," I snapped as I took a few steps away. "I have to…"

I ran away from him as fast as my Converse would allow.

Away from the pain. Away from the fear. Away from reality.

I couldn't feel my body as the tears continued to fall.

Chapter Twenty

Gavin

A path was wearing on my rug from the pacing I'd been doing since my fight with Chloe.

I kept opening my phone to her text screen and then closing it. I didn't know what to say or where to even begin explaining for my outburst.

Fucking Styx.

I was in agony over hearing what she'd said had been her dream wedding and the person she felt in her dreams. Her words had sparked a memory in the very back of my mind— me sitting in complete darkness, holding Chloe against me, chatting in the middle of the night about secrets and dreams that we'd told no one else. I had seen her standing on that hill in the black dress where her family had left her once—given her up for the monster the oracle had said she was destined to marry.

I was that monster, and she was my wife.

My Psyche.

It had all clicked. The feeling of her, the sound of her laugh, her smell, her taste… I remembered it. And while I may not have remembered what happened when I lost her, I remembered small moments after the trials, when we were finally together, finally *happy*. Fuck, I had wanted to kiss her right then—scoop her into my arms and scream it from the top of my lungs. I could have run off with her and told her everything, demanded to the gods that they restore whatever memory had been taken from us both.

But I didn't.

Instead, I had lashed out at her.

I sank into the chair and pushed my hands into my hair, bracing my elbows on my knees. I was so fucking stupid.

So gods damned stupid.

I was falling for her all over again—Psyche or not.

I wanted that for her, too.

I wanted her to love me of her own accord, because I would love her even if she never remembered who we were. I would love her in every life; no amount of time or tampering by our enemies could change that.

I was determined to live in the now with her as much as she'd let me.

And that started with somehow getting her back into my life.

A knock sounded on my door, making my heart jump, but I settled before I could get my hopes up. Chloe didn't know where I lived. And even if she did, why would she ever come see me after the way I just shouted at her?

I set my phone on the glass coffee table and made my way to the door, the impatient knocking making my ears hurt. I barely had my fingers off the lock when the knob twisted, and Persephone walked in, nearly knocking me off balance.

"Hello to you, too," I muttered as she tossed her bag on the countertop. Her head twisted around as she slowly took her coat off, and I could see the furrow of her brows.

"It's quiet," she said. "Why is it so quiet? You usually have on the television. Did someone die?"

"Just my heart," I said under my breath, closing the door. "Why are you here?"

"Do I require a reason to visit a friend?" she asked.

I stepped over to the bar as I considered her question and took two short glasses out of the top cabinet. "No," I decided. "Whiskey?"

She tossed her coat over the barstool. "Always," she said. "I forgot how nice your apartment is. It feels like a home unlike most of these luxury condos."

"It's the plants and pictures," I said, nodding over to the far wall between two halls, one that led to the master bedroom, the other to two guest rooms and my office. Persephone strode over to it, wrapping her arms around her chest.

"I remember this," she said, pointing to one of her, Hades, and myself. Hades looked as broodish as ever, the smolder on his full lips and in his dark eyes, the flash bouncing off of his dark brown skin. Persephone had sprung the selfie on us in the midst of one of the godly retreats Zeus liked to host every few years. Centuries earlier, I saw the retreat as a great weekend to prank as many gods as possible. It was all in good fun, though I hadn't been to the retreat the last few times he'd held it due to working. I enjoyed my job, and had always enjoyed labor of some sort, whether it was a real job or simply doing my mother's bidding.

"I remember your mother arriving shortly after and having one of her meltdowns," I said, sipping my whiskey and handing her her own.

"He's hosting it this fall, you know," she said. "Another retreat. The beginning of October."

I wasn't sure I could take being around all of them. October... I couldn't think that far ahead. It was barely the second week of July. It was as if I was counting down to the end of my life—August 26th.

Chloe's wedding day.

I ran my hand over my face, nearly squeezing my cheeks and jaw, and I threw back the remainder of my whiskey.

Fucking Styx.

Persephone was saying something about the retreat, listing out the venue and how she was trying to persuade Hades into actually attending with her. However, I stepped back over to the bar and poured another drink.

"Seph, I really don't have the patience for gossip right now," I said. "Why did you come by?"

Persephone stopped talking and raised a brow over her shoulder. "I was just coming by to see if you learned anything from your mother the other morning," she said.

"How do you know about that?" I asked.

"Because your mother doesn't have a poker face, and when I ran into her a few days ago, the mention of you made her go all teary-eyed, and she ran away before I could ask what had happened."

"Don't let those tears fool you," I said, my jaw tightening at hearing she'd not had the gall to tell Persephone what happened herself. "She ran away so she wouldn't have to admit to you what she admitted to me."

"Unexpected," Persephone said. "Go on."

"She's the reason we don't remember Psyche," I said.

Persephone's blank eyes didn't leave mine. She blinked, over and over, and I thought she'd stopped breathing for a moment.

"I'm sorry, what?" she finally asked.

I told her about the breakfast I'd had with Aphrodite, about what she'd said to me about Psyche running away, and how she'd erased the memory and mere mention of her throughout history.

Persephone's hand clenched so tight around the glass that it shattered, and her only reaction to it was another blink. Nostrils flaring, she took a beat of silence as it sank in, and I poured her another drink.

"This is why I should stay in the Underworld all year

long," she muttered under her breath. Her lashes hit her eyelids as she gazed my way. "Something tells me that isn't what you're truly upset about, in any case. This—" she pointed to me and wiggled her hand in a circle "—feels like more rage than just Aphrodite pissing you off."

I didn't say anything as my fingers curled in on themselves.

"Eros, what's really wrong?"

I settled into the chair nearest me, steepled my fingers beneath my chin, and stared into the dead fireplace. "What's wrong is that my wife…" I could hardly get the two words out. The salutation stuck to my tongue and choked in my throat. "My *wife* is marrying another man," I managed. "And I just ruined everything."

Persephone sank into the couch as if if she stood any longer, her knees would give way beneath her.

"It's her?" she asked breathlessly.

I nodded.

"You're sure? You remembered?"

"Nearly everything," I said. "It's like… something she said, a dream she was having triggered my memory, and it all fell into place." Tears burned the backs of my eyes. "Gods, I'm such an idiot."

"I doubt that," she said.

"No, I am," I argued. "I was so fucking mad about how much of herself she was giving up when it came to her wedding that I lost my mind. I started shouting at her in the middle of the fucking park."

"How much did you remember?"

"I remembered seeing her for the first time, those nights together in the dark… I remembered the trials she went through after she betrayed my trust, her visiting you in the Underworld as my mother asked—"

"Jealousy is a fickle thing," Persephone muttered.

"—I even remembered her coming back to me. The ambrosia. But still… the last thing I can see is that final day at Delphi. It's like it just ends. We went for a hike and came back to stay the night near the temple. I remember lying beside her under the stars, holding her to sleep… and then it just… it all fades," I finished.

I did a double-take at the look on her face then—furrowed brows, stern eyes, pursed lips.

"What?"

"I'm trying to figure out why you chose to lash out and not tell her who she is," she said.

I shot back the rest of my drink and stood to my feet. "I'm not doing that," I said.

"Why the fuck not?" she asked, rising to her own. "You say you remember her, and you remember your past with her. Why don't you tell her?"

"Because I don't want to scare her," I said. "And because…"

My voice trailed, my hands bracing against the counter.

"Because I don't want her to love me simply because of who we once were. I want her to love me," I said. "This is a new age. Things aren't the same. I want this to be her choice, not getting left atop a mountain for some monster like the last time. I want to be sure of that before I tell her anything."

"Such a romantic," she cooed.

I picked up a wine cork from my basket and chucked it at her head. "Shut up," I said, glaring.

She smirked as she let the cork zoom past her, and she tucked her elbows into her side, entwining her hands together. "So, what are you going to do about it?"

My eyes moved to her, but I didn't speak, and she went on.

"I mean, you say you fucked up. So, why aren't you out fighting?"

"I am fighting," I snapped. "What, do you want me to

push myself on her?"

"No, I want you to get off your ass and prove to her why she should be with you," Persephone said.

"She's not a fucking trophy."

"No, she's your fucking wife," she affirmed. "Act like it."

My jaw clenched. I couldn't argue.

I stripped off my shirt and headed into the bedroom.

"Something you need to take care of?" she asked.

"No," I said, changing into workout shorts. "I'm going for a run. I'll see where it takes me."

Chapter Twenty-One

Chloe

"He said I've settled," I admitted to Lana when I got home, a twinge of annoyance in my tone. "Can you believe that?"

I had texted Lana on the way home, my eyes blurry behind the tears streaming down my face, nearly wrecking several times. Although with the way I'd felt... that tangle in the pit of my gut, my heart ripped out of my chest, ears still ringing with his words... maybe a car crash would have been an easier feat than facing what Gavin had said to me.

There was a long silence on Lana's end of the video call—long enough that I finished my wine and wiggled the cursor to make sure my computer hadn't frozen.

"Are you still there?" I asked.

Lana avoided my gaze, tucking a curl behind her ear as she stared at the keyboard.

"What?" I asked.

"You're not going to like my answer," Lana muttered.

"What do you mean?" I questioned, preparing to get defensive.

Lana turned up her own drink and gulped the rest of it. "He's right," she said.

"About?"

"You settling."

"What—no, I haven't," I argued. "Tyler is nice, he's funny

he's—"

"Boring," Lana drawled, hanging her head back. She sat up and slapped her thighs, shaking her head. "Fuck, the only thing interesting about him is the fact that he has money, and he doesn't even know how to spend it right," she said. "He's fucking boring. Admit it."

"He is not—"

"He thinks he can fix everything with those gifts when you don't even like shiny things," she continued.

"That's how his parents fixed things—"

"He doesn't even realize you don't *like* shiny things," she added. "Which means he's not paying attention to you."

"It's a nice gesture."

"And he's never home."

"He travels for work."

"He thinks you want some house in the suburbs with the white picket fence and a litter of children."

"Maybe one day, I will."

"And most importantly—"

"I swear, Lana if you bring up sex—"

"—He doesn't make you happy," she finished. "But now that you've brought up your problems in the bedroom, why don't we just add that to the list?"

I glared at her, unable to form words or coherent thoughts in retaliation. She waited for it, too, a smug smile slipping onto her lips the longer it took me to respond.

"I hate you," I grunted.

Lana grinned outright. "Oh my god, do you know who I just realized Tyler is?" she asked, eyes widening.

"Who?"

"He's like the guy you settle for after you've dated a serial killer," Lana said.

If I'd been eating something, I would have choked. "What?"

"I mean, not literally," she said. "That's more than likely a super unhealthy relationship. Him lying to you, pretending to be a different person, probably *great* sex though—"

"What's your point?" I interjected, the talk making me anxious.

Lana scoffed, her smile genuine this time. "What I mean is, Tyler is the safe, mediocre guy you settle for after you've had years of the most thrilling love of your life—after you've dated the guy who gave you butterflies, who turned your world upside down, who made you smile with one look, the one who pushed you to your edge and thrilled your adrenaline every day. The one who made you feel safe and desired, like the most important person in their life—"

"It was *one night*," I repeated for what felt like the thousandth time.

Of course, Lana ignored me.

"—Tyler is the opposite. Sure, he makes you feel loved, and you probably think you love him. There's nothing truly wrong with him, but he's not the person you would fight for."

Every word from her lips made my heart fall further into oblivion.

"He's not the person you expect to tear the world apart to get you back," she continued. "For instance, if you were to get kidnapped, Tyler is the guy who will call the FBI and beg and plead and barter to get you back. He's going to throw whatever money he has at it, and when he does get you back, he'll probably put some sort of protection detail on you. He'll say it's all in your best interest, essentially having you locked down every minute—which is, of course, a terrible idea because then you're going to fall for your bodyguard since most of us have that whole thing for the knight in shining armor and the forced proximity—"

"Lana," I said, drawing her back on track.

"My point is," she circled back, "Tyler isn't the person who will barrel in himself and make you question whether he's actually the hero because of the number of bodies he leaves behind trying to find you."

The talk made my hair stand on end. I began to fidget, my ears burning. The scenario reminded me of one person, but I knew if she had been describing him, it would have been a much darker scene, one that would've had me in the starring role as the victim of the killer, strung up as a mindless shell. No family. No friends. No existence other than his sharp cage of endless manipulation.

I couldn't go there. I wasn't sure I could claw my way out again.

"Babe, he's not Aidan," Lana said then, her voice even as she talked about my ex-boyfriend.

"I'm not thinking about him—"

"I can see it on your face," Lana cut me off. "Aidan was the pressure at the bottom of the Mariana Trench."

"Yeah, and Tyler is the fucking kiddie pool," I said as I dragged my fingers through my hair, pushing it back and to one side. "Maybe that's why I'm hanging onto him."

Her lips pressed into a thin line, and I heard her sigh audibly. "I didn't know you were that scared," she said.

"Of course, I'm fucking scared," I blurted. "I still can't show my face on social media because of that deranged asshole." My hands wiped over my face and behind my neck. "What I feel when I'm with Gavin... that urge to fall head over heels and forget reality just to live in a perfect bubble with him... I don't want to do that again. I don't want to think my only purpose in life is to please him."

"I don't think you will," Lana said.

"Why?"

"Because he won't let you," she said. "You're worked through so much, Clo. You're really doing amazing. Don't let that asshole be the reason you settle for less than you deserve."

Fear wavered through me at simply the mention of that first relationship. A breakdown tickled at the back of my eyes for the second time that day. It moved from my weighted shoulders down my stiff spine to my wiggling toes. The hair on the back of my neck stood.

Being alone that night suddenly made me uneasy.

I glanced toward the door, taking notice of the twisted deadbolt and chain at the top locked through. However, regardless of how secure it looked, I made a mental reminder to shove one of the bar stools beneath the knob.

"I'd be telling you all this whether Gavin had come back into your life or not," Lana said, bringing my attention back to her. "I've tried telling you since you agreed to marry Tyler."

She had.

"And I don't hear you telling me I'm wrong," Lana added.

"I think for a long time, I'd decided this was as good as it could get. Especially after…" My voice trailed, a lump stuck in my throat. I'd thought my relationship with Aidan had been how love was supposed to feel, and I'd been wrong about that too. "Fuck, this is why I shouldn't even be in relationships," I muttered. "I feel like I've gone from one extreme to the other."

"Lucky for you, there's someone in the middle who wants you, too," Lana said. "And who you want as well. Of course, if that doesn't work either, there's nothing that says you can't love yourself. But you never have to settle."

I ran my hands through my hair again, tugging at the roots to the point that it hurt. "Tyler and I are staying with his family at a vineyard this weekend." I clapped my hands in front of me, a sarcastic laugh leaving my mouth. "This is all I'm going to be thinking about."

"Where is Tyler now?" Lana asked.

"He texted about an hour ago and said he was staying with Matthew. He surprised Tyler with a bachelor outing or something like that," I answered.

"Perhaps a weekend with him is what you need. How long has it been since the two of you had time together when one of you wasn't working?" she asked.

"Forever," I said. "I'm not sure this counts as a vacation, as his entire family will be there."

"Don't go with failure on your mind," she said. "Be with him. See if it reminds you why you fell in love with him in the first place. Maybe Gavin and I are wrong. And if things still don't feel right, just make sure you score with Tyler's dad before you break it off."

"Lana," I said, almost rolling my eyes at her obsession with Tyler's father.

"Only joking," she said. "But really, though."

I sighed out the gravity plaguing my restless heart. "What if you and Gavin are right?"

"Then you decide if 'just fine' is good enough for the rest of your life."

I peered toward the door again, my jaw aching from the weight of my clench. "I'm going to try to go to bed," I said, gathering my glass and dinner I'd forgotten to eat.

"He's not in California, Clo," she said, apparently having seen my glance to the door.

"Yeah, well, moving states doesn't exactly cancel out fear," I said.

Lana gave me a solemn look, and I shook my head. "I know. Just… text me later?"

"I will. Love you. Get some rest," Lana said.

"I'll try. Love you, too. Night."

I closed the computer and pressed the heels of my hands on the counter, closing my eyes and counting back from ten to try to calm myself. And when I opened them—

A shadow moved outside my door.

Two feet, like someone was standing in front of it. I couldn't move. Couldn't breathe.

Fucking hell, had I thought about this so fucking hard that it actually came true?

I closed my eyes and rubbed them again, hoping it was just my mind playing tricks. Stars clouded my vision from how hard I had pressed. I looked to the bottom of the door again, finding the shadowed legs still lingering. I couldn't look away or see anything else except the horrifying possibility that it might be him…

It's probably just a drunk neighbor standing outside the wrong door.

I backed up slowly, sure not to make a noise. I grabbed a knife from the counter—

The shadow backed up, and within a blink, it was gone.

A stagnant breath finally left my lungs. The knife clattered loudly to the granite, and I pressed my hands onto the lip again, my head hanging as I collected myself.

All I could think about was how much I wanted to text Gavin to come over.

And maybe that should have told me all I needed to know.

Chapter Twenty-Two

Chloe

I was determined not to set myself up for outright disappointment this weekend. I knew I could get in my head and set my attitude up for failure, but for whatever reason, I wanted Gavin and Lana to be wrong.

I wondered if that was because I was too scared to face what needed to happen if they were right.

I squirmed in the cushy seat of the private jet Tyler had chartered to take us up the coast. He was pacing back and forth on his phone, saying the same phrases repeatedly, or so it seemed. I hoped it wasn't like that the entire weekend. His parents hated when he was on the phone, and they usually looked to me to say something to him about it—which I always failed at.

I sighed back onto the headrest and glanced out the window.

Two days.

It was just two days.

We would return Sunday afternoon, and Tyler would leave again for New York City that evening.

A man appeared through the curtain separating us from the cockpit then. A handsome blonde, mid-forties, tall and lean with flecks of white in the scruff lining his jaw. I realized this was our captain, and Tyler nearly ran into him when he tried to approach me.

"Are we all ready?" the captain asked.

"Ah…" I glanced at Tyler. "Does he have to be in his seat?"

"He does. We don't want anyone falling or getting hurt," he said.

"Shame," I muttered. "That might be fun to watch—Tyler?" I called out, trying to grab his attention. "Hey, Tyler, he's asking if we're ready."

Tyler pulled the phone down and looked between us. "I'm still waiting on some cargo," he said.

"Cargo?" I repeated.

The captain nodded at Tyler before disappearing again to the cockpit. A stewardess offered me a drink, and I gladly accepted it.

It had only been an hour, and I was already looking down at my phone like it might save me. I wasn't sure what I was hoping for—rescue text from Lana, an apology from Gavin, Ezzie texting to say the office had caught fire…

That was what I needed. Someone to run in and yell 'fire' at the top of their lungs to get me out of this misery.

Try harder, Chloe, I reminded myself. *Stay here. Stay in this moment. Don't wander. You haven't even gotten off the ground yet.*

Tyler looked out the window then and pointed like he was seeing a best friend. "There he is. There's my boy!"

A man was striding across the tarmac, pushing a large, unmarked cart. Tyler bolted to the front to speak with the captain.

"As soon as that's on the plane, we're out of here," he said to him.

"What's in the box?" I asked when Tyler finally sat down across from me.

He leaned over before buckling his seatbelt and kissed my cheek. "You're too pretty to worry about things like that."

I gave him a tight-lipped smile. It should have bothered

me more that he was unwilling to tell me the box's contents. Although, as the plane ascended and I took my tablet out to do some work, I decided I frankly didn't care.

"Are you going to put that down this weekend?" Tyler asked thirty minutes into the flight.

"Yeah, I will. I just wanted to wrap up a few things while I could," I answered.

"I'll be glad when you don't have to do that anymore. Won't you?" he asked.

I bit my tongue. "I actually enjoy my job," I said, setting the pen down. "It isn't a burden to me, and it's my dream."

"Graphic design? That's your dream? I thought your dream was staying home and reading," he said.

"I do love those things, but owning my own company and not having to answer to anyone while I make my own money is one of my dreams, too."

"Why do you need to make your own money?"

"Because I was taught not to depend on anyone else—" I held my head, calming my frustration. "Can we not talk about this now?" I asked. "I'm trying hard to keep an open mind about this weekend."

His brows furrowed, hurt in his eyes. "What does that mean?"

I gave him a look. "You know I don't always get along with your parents."

"They're my parents."

"And there's no rule that says I must like them," I argued. "All it says is that I have to like you."

Tyler reached across the table for my hand. "You know I love you," he said.

"I know," I sighed.

"And you know I wouldn't make you do anything you don't want to," he continued. "But I have other things going on this weekend that I need to take care of. My mother and sister have wedding details that they want to finalize with you. My father wants to hear this proposal we're working on… it's a big weekend. Do you think you could try to enjoy it? Or, at the very least, fake it?"

My lips flinched with mild amusement. "As long as there are no more surprises," I said.

"None," he said. "I swear."

Tyler's family greeted us at a vineyard in the hills. It was sunset, and I had to admit how beautiful it was seeing the setting sun going down behind the vast rolling grape fields. Lights were strung up between some of the olive trees in the courtyard. I had Tyler tell me the vineyard's name so I could suggest it to Ezzie and Raegan for their wedding. I took a picture and sent it to her.

Wow, Ezzie replied. *That's gorgeous. How far away?*

Tyler chartered a jet for the weekend. Took us a couple of hours, I replied.

Ooo… traveling the high life this weekend. Look at you, Ezzie teased.

It's all for show, I replied. **Are you two checking out venues?**

We are. I might see if this place has a tour open tomorrow or Sunday.

If you come this way, let me know.

Asking for a rescue already? she asked.

Not yet, but I might be by tomorrow.

"We have a cake tasting tomorrow, my dear," Tyler's mother, Abigail, said as we sat around one of the fire pits. I put my phone face-down on the stone edge and wrapped my lightweight coat tighter.

"The bakery is just twenty minutes away. John has a car picking us up," Abigail continued. "After, Molly wants to shop at some of the local places. Did Tyler have any plans for you?"

Tyler's older sister, Molly, hadn't arrived yet at the vineyard. She had two children and had gotten a divorce from her husband a year after the second one was born. It was a running family joke that she was currently fucking her manny.

I couldn't blame her if she were. Colin was fifteen years younger than her, tall with dark, fluffy hair and glasses, had a fantastic English accent, and spoke four languages. Not to mention how amazing he was with her kids. Fuck, *I* wanted to give him a blowjob after watching him with them.

"Tyler hasn't mentioned anything," I answered. "Said he had some things he needed to take care of himself. He told me there were a few wedding details I needed to help you to wrap up."

"*Quite* a few," Abigail said before gently touching my knee. "We're so happy you were able to join us this weekend. Getting you on the phone during your work week is very difficult."

"I have a lot to do," I said, sipping my wine.

"Here's to hoping this deal of Tyler's is worthwhile so you can put that all behind you," she replied, holding up her glass, her blonde hair bright against the waning sun. "He's had so many deals fail. It would be nice for him to finally land the 'big one,' as he calls it."

"Do you know what it is?" I asked.

She waved me off. "Tyler is just like his father. Secrets, secrets, secrets. Did you have a chance to look over the rose shades I sent pictures of?"

I downed the rest of my drink and picked up the next one, trying to quell the annoyance swelling inside me. I didn't understand *why* I was so annoyed. I should have cared—should have been excited.

Instead, I was fighting back a desperate outburst.

The following day, I found myself awake before everyone else. We were staying at a hilled villa on the vineyard property. I took my coffee outside onto the veranda overlooking the entire estate, wrapping my robe tight against the dry morning air. The view was stunning—rolling hills of grapevines, olive and oak trees surrounding the property. A few trees dotted the landscape and stood in rows to help vegetation and biodiversity.

The entire view was purple with the sunrise, fog lingering around some of the ground. I inhaled the scent of my coffee and sat on one of the cushy couches, pulling my feet up and beneath me as I took out my phone to take a photo, then sent it to Lana.

Bring me back here one day, I texted her.

Bitch. Ez and Rae better be getting married there, she texted back.

I sent her photos yesterday, I said. **She was going to try to get a tour this weekend.**

That would be nice. Why are you up so early?

Wanted a few minutes of peace to enjoy this, I said.

How is it going?

Hard to tell. I'm trying.

I was. I had even tried being intimate with Tyler once we'd settled into bed. I had *really* tried.

But god, it was a desert down there.

I had blamed it on the wine and ended up giving him a hand job instead, then took a long, hot shower to wash his touch off of me. Once more, it had felt so wrong. I was worried he was beginning to notice, curious if he might ask me if something else was going on. But he hadn't.

I know you are, Lana said. *Send me pictures later and let me know what cake we're having.*

I smiled at the phone. **Will do.**

Tell Daddy I said hello, she added with a winky face.

A laugh escaped me. **Sure thing.**

Amber light peeked over a hill as I took another sip of coffee, rays of sun crawling over the ridges in its wake, illuminating the fog in a yellow haze.

It gave me wanderlust.

I had always wanted to travel and had even planned on taking a sabbatical with Tyler to travel in a couple of years. We discussed doing a world tour for our fifth anniversary early on. However, it didn't sound much like that was what he wanted any longer.

I looked down at my phone again, my thumb itching over the screen as I noticed Gavin's name on my messages list, and a boulder grew in my stomach when I looked out at the landscape again. I wanted to send him a photo, tell him simply good morning, maybe compare views and ask if he was up early with his coffee.

But as a light flicked on in the kitchen, and I saw Tyler's father rummaging around for his coffee, reality washed over me.

His father, John, had always been the family's nicest, most normal member. Quiet, reserved, and very handsome. He rocked that salt-and-pepper look better than anyone I'd ever seen. It suited his olive skin and seemed to bring out the wisdom in his grey eyes. Lana had always said that if I was smart, I would have tried to land his dad instead, though I wasn't about to try and bring out the crazy in Abigail.

I heard the sliding door open and looked back to find John heading my way. Tyler looked very much like him, except he'd gotten his pale skin and blue eyes from his mother, and he also didn't have his father's rugged confidence. John cared for himself; his beard was always trimmed neatly, and he still worked out to keep himself in good shape.

As he came toward me, that confident aura seeped into the air like a potion wavering through the fog.

"Morning, Chloe," he said, pausing at the edge of the veranda where I was curled up.

"Morning, Mr. Drake," I replied.

He scoffed. "I've told you before, call me Dad. Especially now that you'll be in the family."

I pressed my cup to my lips as a smile rose, knowing what Lana would have said to that sentence. "How about I just call you 'John' instead? We'll compromise," I said.

"Compromise accepted," he said. He sipped his coffee, staring at the landscape as I was. "I try to tell my wife she should get up early like this to enjoy the moments we all seem to forget," he said. "But sometimes it's nice to have those few minutes to myself."

"Tyler is never up this early unless he has a flight," I said.

"He sleeps like his mother," John said. He sighed audibly and sat down on the nearest couch, facing the vineyard instead of sideways like the one I was on, and he crossed his ankle over his knee. "He tells me he's looking at houses near us."

"That's what he tells me, too," I replied.

"I take it that's not your idea," he said.

"He wants to start our family," I answered with a slight shrug.

It had always been easier to talk to John. His calming presence was open to listening, and while I may not have told him all of my secrets, it was nice to get his opinion on things. I even talked to him when I'd started my business and asked him what he would and wouldn't have done looking back on his endeavors. He'd given me a lot of great advice, and I knew even if Tyler and I were to break up, I could call him anytime, ask him anything, and he'd tell me the truth.

John huffed amusedly and shook his head. "My son is an idiot," he said behind his coffee mug, and I frowned.

"Why's that?"

"Because if I were him, I'd want you to myself as long as possible," he said. "Let things fall into place as you go, not force it."

And this is why you are superior, I thought.

He leaned back on the couch, his arm draped across the back. "You've only had your business for a year, haven't you?" he asked.

"Barely."

"Are you planning on running it from Florida?" he asked.

"I haven't thought that far ahead. I only just found out about his plans on Wednesday," I said.

"I can talk to him if you like," he said. "Tell him to give you more time."

"I don't think he'd like that I ask you for advice sometimes."

"What he doesn't know won't hurt him," he said, and I had to lift my mug to my lips again to hide the blush on my cheeks.

"I hear you're tasting cake and finalizing flowers today," he added.

"With Molly and Abigail. Molly wants to shop after," I said.

"Of course she does," he smiled.

The glass door slid open then, and Abigail appeared in her silk robe with her own cup of tea.

"Do me a favor," he said, angling his body toward mine. "Find out if Molly is sleeping with Colin. I feel as though I should get to know him better."

"Planning on treating him to the good old 'treat my daughter well, or else' talk?" I mocked him.

"Probably worse than that," Abigail said as she joined us. She sat beside John and curled herself into his open arm, laying her head on his shoulder.

A soft smile appeared on her face then that was reserved only for her husband. It usually emerged in the brief moments when she thought no one was looking, or when she hadn't had a chance to stress over what was happening that day, and what she needed to get done. When it was only them.

I was envious of it.

John leaned over and kissed her forehead, and I heard him quietly tell her how beautiful she looked in the sunrise before asking her if she slept well.

My broken heart ached watching them, a fantasy entering my mind of sitting outside at sunrise and being looked at like that, talked to like that. And it wasn't Tyler who I saw seated beside me.

I looked down at my phone, somehow expecting to see a text from Gavin—like I could summon him with just the idea of him. I don't know what I thought he might say. I don't know if I was waiting for an apology or something that told me he still wanted to talk to me. I was so confused about everything.

"—in a couple of hours," I heard Abigail saying. "Chloe?"

I snapped out of the daze, realizing she was talking to me. "Hm, what? Sorry, I zoned out for a minute," I said sheepishly.

"I said we're leaving for the city in a couple of hours," she repeated. "I wanted to give Molly time to get the children up and ensure Colin had everything for their day. He's taking them to some dirt biking trail up the road."

"I might join them," John said. "Sounds fun."

"No, I think your son has a few things he wants to talk to you about before you can play with your grandchildren," Abigail said.

John lolled his head back in a comical manner and groaned. "Fine," he said. "I'll give the second-born attention."

I snickered behind my mug, and John winked my way.

"I'll start getting ready," I said as I finished the last of my coffee.

Chapter Twenty-Three

Chloe

"First, we have our bananas foster cake," the baker, Demi, said as she set the cake slices before us.

We sat outside beneath a vine-covered pergola that looked out onto the sprawling gardens of one of Abigail's friends. She'd paid for the bakery to bring the cake tasting there instead of us going into their shop simply because she wanted her friend's opinion on the selection, seeing as Diana was a food critic.

"The key to these tastings is to spit it out after you've tasted it," Molly said, pushing her straight black hair off her shoulder. She looked much more like her mother than Tyler. However, Molly had inherited their father's olive-toned skin, unlike her brother.

One thing she hadn't inherited from her father was his gentle spirit.

"Exactly right," Diana, Abigail's friend, said.
"That's a great idea," Abigail agreed. "We all want to fit into our dresses, don't we?"

There was a brief glance my way, and I almost laughed. It was cute that they thought they could say something disguised as a basic insult as if I needed reminding that I would be in a custom gown within six weeks and shouldn't overindulge.

I asked for another glass of sparkling Moscato and dug my fork into the bananas foster cake, intending only to make a point to show that I wouldn't be bullied into spitting out a perfectly good bite of cake, but fucking hell. It was so tasty that I wanted to eat the entire piece.

"How many more slices do we have to try?" Molly asked.

"I asked for five flavors," Abigail replied, and I could feel her eyes upon me.

I swallowed my second bite of cake and glanced at Demi as she paused at my side, asking how I liked it.

"Can I box up what we don't eat to go?" I asked her.

She smiled, amusement in her eyes, and she squeezed my shoulder. "Anything the bride wants."

Molly, Abigail, and Diana were all staring at me when I turned back to the table.

My phone buzzed in my pocket as the server brought out the next flavor. I took it out to see the message as Demi began talking about the cake—Dark chocolate with strawberry compote, salted toasted walnuts, whipped vanilla cream in the center, and walnut buttercream on the outside.

God, that one tasted even better.

But the taste of the cake went amiss when I saw the text waiting for me.

Can we talk?

It was from Gavin.

My jaw tightened at seeing his name on the screen. I started to quickly put away the phone, but another text came through.

I've been by your place three times, he said. *But I didn't know if Tyler was home.*

Three times… I pondered if that had been him at the door the other night when I'd nearly panicked.

I couldn't talk to him. Not at that moment, and maybe not even that week. I had too much to think about, too much to figure out.

And it was all his fault.

"Chloe?" Abigail called out. "Everything okay?"

I stuffed my phone into my purse and shoved the bag under the table. "Yeah," I said, grabbing my wine glass again. "Just Lana asking how the weekend is going," I lied.

"Can she go one day without talking to you?" Molly asked. "It seems you two are joined at the hip. Tyler says you video chat morning and night."

"Most of the time," I said. "She's my best friend."

"I think I talk to my best friend once a month," Molly said after spitting out her cake. "Too much work trying to keep up with everyone. Social media is helpful." She glanced at me. "Tyler says you're not on any socials. I thought he was lying to protect you from us, but I couldn't find you either."

The line of questioning made me uneasy. "I, uh, I don't have it. Took myself off a few years ago," I replied. "It was too much for my mental health," I lied. "I would hyper-fixate on it and judge myself based on the attention it brought me."

"Ugh. I know that feeling," Molly said. "Even still, I couldn't cut myself out of it completely. I like knowing what's going on in the world. Oh! I need to get a picture of us before we get too full and bloated on cake," she said as she scooted her chair toward me.

I gave in and sat up, smiling as she took the selfie.

"Perfect. And with this background, it's even more beautiful," she said, and I could see her pulling up another screen with the photo on it.

"Oh, can you not post it?" I asked her.

Molly frowned. "What? Why? I'm not tagging you."

"I know, but can you just not post?" I asked again, my heart rate rising as she continued typing. "I genuinely don't want my face on there."

"Chloe, it's just one photo," she laughed. "Don't be weird.

Are you ashamed to be seen with us?"

"No, I just—"

"Half of our family doesn't even know what you look like," Abigail interjected. "They're all curious."

My hands began to sweat as they continued to talk around me, and Molly resumed writing her caption.

I was one breath away from knocking her phone into her wine glass.

"It's so pretty—" Molly showed the photo to Abigail and Diana, then turned it back around and ignored my pleas. "I'm posting it. Everyone wants to know what Tyler's *mystery* fiancé looks like," she said with a giggle.

I could hear my heartbeat in my ears, my frustration rising. "Please—"

"Oh, good," Abigail spoke over me. "You should get one of us, too—"

"I said *don't post the fucking photo!*" I snapped suddenly.

The three of them stopped talking, and the waitresses paused in the midst of switching out our desserts. Everyone's eyes landed on me, and I forced myself to take a breath.

My hand was curled around the fork like I could snap it in half.

"Please... Do not post any photos of me," I managed in the calmest voice I could control.

Molly slowly set down her phone, the app she had pulled up now closing. "Okay... no need to freak out," she mumbled.

"There is reason to freak out when I asked you nicely twice not to post, and you continued to do it," I snapped before I could stop myself.

"Chloe, it's just a photo," Abigail said. "You don't need to get upset."

"Yeah, what's with you?" Molly asked.

I closed my eyes, counting back from five before

responding. "You know, I'm feeling tired. I think I'll just catch an Uber back to the vineyard." I stood, gathering my things and refusing to respond to their flabbergasted expressions. "Ah… I liked the chocolate one—"

"I can make you a box," Demi said before rushing off.

"Chloe, you don't have to leave," Abigail said.

"I do," I said exasperatedly. "Because when someone asks you not to do something so simple, you don't keep pushing when you don't know their reason behind refusing it."

"Then tell us why you don't want your picture posted. Do you not want us to share wedding photos, either?" Molly scoffed. "That will be hard to tell nearly three hundred people."

"This is uncalled for," Diana said. "Disrespectful. Your mother-in-law arranges all of these things, has dealt with all of these decisions, and you can't even be grateful enough to let her post a photo of you—"

"No, I cannot," I affirmed. "I don't owe you an explanation as to why, either. And while we're on the subject, I never asked her to do any of it. You all were so impatient and ready for your son to be married that you took it upon yourselves to plan it. I am grateful for all of it. I really am. But you don't get to throw it in my face when I never asked."

Demi returned with a bag, and I took it, quickly thanking her. I looked around the table one last time, my gaze landing on Abigail. I gave her a tight-lipped smile, and she nodded slightly in response.

I didn't say anything else as I rushed through the extravagant house, all the way to the front, where I stood alone for the next twenty minutes waiting on my Uber to pick me up.

None of them came to ask me not to leave.

"I hope you like the lemon one," Demi said as she and her team put away some of the tasting boxes. Demi sat a box down in the back of her van and dusted off her hands on her white apron, peering at me over her cat-eye glasses. Her permed, short black hair was smoothed to her head, little pinwheel curls secured to the sides. She reminded me of a 50s pinup model with her hair, the glasses, and the pink dress. Her brown skin was flawless, a shimmer of highlight accentuating her cheekbones and petite face. Something about her smile seemed familiar, but I couldn't place it.

"It's my favorite," she said, and I blinked.

"What?"

"The lemon cake," she explained. "It's a lemon poppyseed cake, lemon curd, and elderflower buttercream between the layers. Candied lemons and sanding sugar on the top. And a light vanilla buttercream on the outside. It's the one I usually do as a sort of naked cake and decorate with flowers. The taste is divine if I do say so myself."

My lips flinched like I might smile. "Sounds delicious," I said. "I'll try it when I get back to the vineyard."

"Which one?" she asked.

"Ah, Wiltons," I answered.

"Oh, that's not far from us. Abigail should have had us bring the cakes there. It would have been less of a drive," she said with a look inside. "You know, I can take you back if you like," she offered.

"That's okay," I said as I looked at my phone, seeing where my driver was. "My car is almost here. Thank you, though."

"You don't remember me, do you?" she asked.

I ogled at her beaming face, the familiar look making me wary. "Should I?"

"It's funny. I didn't remember you until I saw you," she said, a small laugh leaving her. "My daughter mentioned you last week. Still, I didn't know who she was talking about. I remember telling her she'd lost her mind in that gods-awful place she lives half her year in." Her eyes lifted to mine. "But here you are."

"What are you talking about?" I asked as my ears began to ring.

Her smile simply grew wider. "I think you'll know soon," she said, turning back to her van.

"Wait—" I called out. "Who are you? How do you know me?"

Demi was getting in the driver's side of her van by the time she turned around. "I'll see you again soon," she said, closing her door in my face. "I hope you like the cake!"

Dust surrounded me as she drove away, and I was left standing in its cloud as my driver pulled up.

What. The. Fuck.

Chapter Twenty-Four

Chloe

"Today was weird," I said to Lana as I sat outside on the stone wall that separated the villa lawn from the rows of grapevines. I had brought out with me my computer, a glass of their sweetest wine, and the boxes of cake. No one was back yet, and the sun had just begun to set.

"How so?" Lana asked. "Also, you're making me jealous with all this cake."

"It's delicious, too," I said. "I had to Uber back from the tasting before finishing, so the baker put them in boxes for me."

"What? Why?" Lana asked.

"Molly tried to post a photo of me."

"Ah, fuck," Lana muttered. "Did you just leave, or—"

"I lashed out," I said.

"Oh, fun!" Lana said, her face lighting up. "That's my girl. Tell me more. What happened?"

"Hey, Chloe?"

The voice came from the top of the hill, and I looked over my shoulder to find Tyler approaching.

"Busted," Lana said.

"Looks like it," I muttered. I glanced at the computer screen. "Text you later?"

"I'm heading to bed. Call me when you get back

tomorrow. I need the details. Make sure you tell Daddy 'hello' for me," she winked.

I rolled my eyes. "Goodnight, Lana."

I closed my computer just as Tyler made it down the last stretch, hands in the pockets of his grey slacks. I could see the twinge in his jaw, and I knew his sister had texted or called him about what had happened at the cake tasting.

He paused a few feet away and jerked his chin toward the computer. "Lana?" he asked.

"Nightly chat," I shrugged.

"Do you have to tell her everything that happens between us?" he asked, snap in his tone.

My eyes narrowed. "She's my best friend. I don't tell her everything."

"No, but you were about to tell her what happened today, weren't you?"

"Yes. I wanted to make sure I didn't overreact," I said.

"You did," he said. "That's the answer. You did overreact."

I felt my nostrils flare, my lips tighten with the scowl on my face. "Says who?" I asked defensively.

"Says everyone I've talked to. You yelled at my mother," he said, more of a statement than a question.

"I did not yell at your mother," I snapped. "If anything, she was the one I was the least upset with."

"You ruined her afternoon with one of her oldest friends. Now, Diana thinks you're a spoiled bitch, and she told my mother she should call all her wedding contacts and cancel everything."

"Well, maybe she should."

The words left my mouth before I realized I was saying them.

Tyler's eyes widened, and I swallowed as I took a deep breath, thinking of any way to reconcile the blunt verbiage without an all-out fight on the lawn.

"What I mean," I recovered slowly, "is that if she feels that way, she should. She doesn't have to take on planning this out on her own. I never asked her to do this—I never *expected* her to do this. She can cancel everything, and I'll deal with it over time. It'll just be a while before we get married."

And I'll have time to figure this all out.

"I didn't mean to lash at them," I said. "I really didn't. But they just kept pushing."

"Chloe, it was one photo," he argued. "What was one photo going to hurt?"

A fucking lot was what I wanted to say.

"You know how I feel about social media," I said instead.

"I thought you said you would try."

"Tyler, I am trying," I said. "I am. What do you want me to do? Give in to every request they have?"

"Yes," he said flatly.

"That's not trying. That's rolling over," I argued. "That's getting walked on, and I've done that before. It only makes you resentful."

Tyler sighed and ran a hand through his hair. "You weren't always like this," he muttered, our eyes meeting. "Something's changed within the last few months."

My teeth gritted together, but I didn't move from my place on the wall.

"Is it the wedding?" he asked. "Are you anxious about it, about getting married?"

"I just have a lot going on," I said, and it wasn't a complete lie. "We have the biggest client we've ever had at work. Everything with the wedding… I honestly think it might be harder not knowing what's going on. And then, this whole six to eight months before moving to Florida threw me this week."

He hung his head for a silent moment, and I wondered

what he was thinking—if he thought I was lying, if he had any idea about my affair with Gavin, or that I was seriously pulling away from him more and more every day.

I was curious if he had even noticed.

"I'm leaving from here tomorrow," he said then. "A car will take us to the airport around lunch, but the jet will take you home. I think you need to figure out what's going on with you. Fuck, Chloe, I'll book you the next three weeks at a spa or retreat if that would help with your anxiety—if it is that."

I didn't reply as he crossed the space between us and took my hands in his. "We'll figure it out," he said. "We always do. I just want my Chloe back."

His Chloe was dying.

His Chloe was slowly fading away into nothingness.

She was sitting at the bottom of the ocean, the pressure breaking her body down bit by bit. Cracking her walls and thinning her boundaries. She had been in this place before, though further down, in the dark where light couldn't reach, but she'd swam out of it and grown thicker skin.

The newest Chloe was banging on the iron threshold, growing gills and learning to breathe.

And fuck, did it feel good to breathe underwater.

I didn't reply as he kissed my cheek.

"Dinner is in a couple of hours," he said. "The chef has some appetizers out if you're hungry now."

"I'll be in soon," I said with a thin smile.

Molly was waiting for Tyler at the pergola, hugging a glass of wine to her chest. She held her hand out as he reached her, and they turned to go inside, but not before Molly gave me a dirty look.

I resisted flipping her off.

My phone buzzed, and as I looked down at the message, my shoulders fell with a sigh.

If you're home, open the door.

I studied Gavin's message, reaching and pulling back from my phone as I debated whether to answer. I itched to talk to him, and after the conversation Tyler and I had just had, I was almost ready to give in.

I'm not there, I said, though I wanted to say so much more.

I didn't wait for him to text me back before I gathered my things and headed back up the hill toward a future I was quickly realizing I didn't want.

Dinner was… awkward, to say the least.

As was the entire night with Tyler.

He, again, tried to be intimate, and this time, instead of giving in and jerking him off, I rose from the bed and wandered outside. I slept with a blanket on the couch under the pergola, and honestly, it was the best sleep I'd gotten in weeks.

John had woken me up with a cup of coffee, and we'd chatted for a while about business. But as everyone else began to wake up, I retreated into the bedroom to pack.

Tyler left me at the front of the airport with a kiss and a quick "See you soon" before the driver took me to my private flight.

I didn't realize how lonely the jet would feel until I was sitting in the cushy seat by myself, and the stewardess came to bring me a drink.

The same captain as before greeted me, though he didn't just ask about getting going this time. He sat in the chair across from me like we were old friends and crossed one leg over the other.

Mirth danced in his blue eyes, so much that I shifted uneasily away from him. I forced a smile, then looked down at my tablet, hoping he would think I didn't want to talk to him. I had pulled up a newly released demon romance and was eager to escape into the fictional world.

"Did you have a good weekend?" the pilot asked.

My lashes hit my eyelids as I lifted only my gaze to him. I didn't like the sarcasm in his tone.

"It was fine," I replied.

His smile widened. "Family can be tough, especially around weddings. *Everyone* has an opinion. It's exhausting." He tilted his head. "But you know this too well."

"It's stressful for all of us," I muttered, ignoring the last sentence.

"At least this time, you have some say-so, right?"

I stopped pretending to be on my tablet. "What are you talking about?"

"I mean, your father isn't dropping you off atop a mountain in—" He paused upon meeting my confused eyes, his smile softening. "Sorry, you look just like a friend I once knew."

It was the same smile Demi had looked at me with.

I tucked my hair behind my ear and avoided his gaze. "Sorry to disappoint, but this is my first marriage."

Atop a mountain?! That poor girl.

An audible sigh left him, and he clapped his hands on the armrests. "Well. Either way. Congratulations. I'm sure it'll all work out," he said as he stood. "Ready to get underway when you are," he added.

"Let's go," I said. "Wait, did Tyler pay you for this flight yet?"

"I always get paid in advance," the pilot assured me.

"Give Tyler back half. I'll pay you for this leg of the trip and a tip."

His eyes moved to one of the stewardesses, who shrugged, and he retrieved his phone to send an invoice. Call me paranoid, but with the possibility of Tyler and I breaking up, I didn't want him to think he had paid for anything of mine.

I knew he loved money more than he loved me.

As I sat back in my chair, the captain's previous questions and talk of that girl ran back through my mind. I wondered who this girl was that people seemed to be mistaking me for.

The plane lifted off the ground, and I decided to let it go as I leaned over to look out the window.

I had too many other things to worry about than figuring out who some stranger was that looked like me.

Chapter Twenty-Five

Chloe

I couldn't sleep for a week after returning from the vineyards.

Tyler had landed in Tokyo that morning. The time difference between Tyler and me was astronomical, so we weren't talking much.

And for the first time, I decided I didn't care.

At *all*.

I had once loved that he was gone so often. It gave me time to do my own thing, have my own life without him, and still feel loved and comfortable even in his absence. It excited me to see him—like every flight home was a special occasion. I'd plan a date, get waxed, meet him at the door in lingerie…

I was beginning to realize it shouldn't have been like that. I shouldn't have felt he needed to be a thousand miles away for me to have my independence. I shouldn't have felt like any relationship was a trap and that the only way I could be myself was if my partner wasn't there.

Shouldn't the person you share your life with bring out the best parts of you, not make you feel you should hide them away?

I sank my head back onto the cushion, taking a break from the design I'd just been working on.

The worst part wasn't that things with Tyler were going downhill or that I couldn't sleep. No, the worst part was not talking to Gavin.

He had texted me a few more times throughout this last week and came by the office once, but I had ignored his messages and asked Jasmine to tell him I was in a meeting.

I remained mad at him, only *not* for what he'd said, but rather for even saying it. I was furious that he had turned my life upside down and made me question *everything*.

Most of all, I was mad about how he made me feel.

Despite all of that, I desperately wanted to talk to him. I had picked up my phone multiple times over the last week to reply to his messages or send him photos of designs for his input, but I hesitated every time. Having him back in my life had made it feel so much more complete—like having a long-lost best friend return.

A best friend who I wanted to touch and kiss and wrap myself up in morning, noon, and night until neither of us could breathe.

I was so fucking needy for flirting and lascivious sex that anything less wasn't worth the energy. I hadn't had sex since May—whenever Tyler tried to initiate it, all I could see was Gavin's stupid face. Intimacy with Tyler felt so *wrong*. Even just touching his hand threw me off. I wasn't even sure I'd told him I loved him since Gavin had returned to my life.

Everything Gavin and Lana had said that day repeatedly played in my mind. I was walking through the last five years, day by day, investigating every feeling and why I'd had it.

Had I genuinely settled for Tyler because it was safe? Did I not think I deserved to feel any happier than I did when I was with him?

I exhaled an audible groan, the shape of the white ceiling fan staring back at me in the light of the television. I watched it spin around and around, hating being so confused and frustrated.

My phone buzzed. I glanced toward it, breaking from my

daze. A text notification bubble was on the bright screen. I assumed it was Tyler and leaned over to read the message.

Can I bring you breakfast tomorrow?

Not Tyler.

Gavin.

Breath shuddered in my throat. I stared at the screen, unable to function or think of a reply.

Chloe, if you're awake, please talk to me. I was a dick.

I bit my bottom lip, hating that the sentence had almost made me smile.

And a jealous asshole.

I finally picked up my phone. **No, you had it right the first time. Asshole is too mild a way of putting it,** I replied.

Three dots strummed the bottom of the screen, disappearing and reappearing with a second between like he was typing and deleting.

Hi, he finally decided to say.

Hi, I said, smiling at the screen.

I didn't mean to wake you.

You didn't, I said. **I haven't been able to sleep for a couple of weeks.**

Neither have I.

Maybe we should have a slumber party. Night owls united.

I like the way that sounds.

My thumbs moved over the keyboard, looking for a word to type. But Gavin beat me to it.

I'm sorry, he wrote.

For what? I asked.

A lot of things. Things that I'd rather say to you in person.

Like over breakfast tomorrow?

I thought you were inviting me over for a sleepover.

Not tonight, I wrote back, smiling at the screen. **Too much work to do. The big dating app company I'm working for has these impossible deadlines, and their CEO is a terrible**

distraction.

It sounds like I should have a word with him.

You should. He's already devised the best marketing scheme to date. It'll be hard to beat it.

What scheme was that?

Naughty candy hearts.

There was a pause, and I knew he was debating where to go with this conversation or how far he could push it.

They were fun, weren't they? he finally typed.

I stared at the phone and bit my lips together, knowing what I wanted to say but hesitant about what it might lead to. Yet, a restless feeling inside me threw caution to the wind, and I decided—

Fuck it.

Have you used them with anyone else? I dared to ask.

I haven't. You?

I once asked Tyler to play. He said they were stupid.

Shame. He missed out on a good time. Only one person I know would get so excited about a heart that said 'good girl.' Your reaction to that candy is worth everything.

Heat beat on my cheeks. My teeth gritted together as I tried to stifle the smirk on my lips. **What can I say? I like the gratification. One of the reasons I enjoy sucking cock. You all make the best little noises.**

Three dots appeared and disappeared again. I bit the inside of my mouth as I awaited his response.

Fucking Styx, Chloe, he said. *Warn someone. I just dropped my phone.*

I laughed. **I'm sure you can afford a new one,** I wrote back.

God, I had missed this so much.

I had missed our flirting, our need, our passion.

I missed being the only object of someone's desire.

Do you know which candy was my favorite? Gavin texted.

Tease me?

Gladly. I'm free now. Are you alone? Would you prefer my tongue or my hands first?

I meant the candy, I replied, though I couldn't stop beaming like a foolish teenager.

Sure you did.

I wanted to slap his perfectly sculpted face.

That one was fun, but no, he said. *My favorite candy was you.*

Heat pooled in my gut and spread between my thighs, making me clench my legs as I crossed one over the other.

Flirt, I replied.

Only with you, baby.

I was chewing my lip so hard that I tasted blood. Visions of his face between my thighs filled my mind. Every stroke of his tongue, every command he'd given me—telling me to watch him feast, to beg for him… I remembered it like it was happening right then. My clit began to throb, prompting me to rub my thighs together.

I knew I would be using one of my toys after this conversation.

A photo came through then. A picture of snow, of a city in the background, and a woman standing in underwear, a sweater, and fuzzy socks, her head leaned back toward the sky, tongue sticking out—

Me.

The woman was *me*. I didn't even know he'd taken a photo that night. Yet, there I was, carefree and smiling like I didn't care if I did or said anything embarrassing, enjoying the freezing cold and not worried about neighbors catching me in my underwear on my balcony. Not caring about what they might say if they witnessed us doing what happened next.

"*I have you,*" he had said when he held me on that tiny railing.

That small moment, the trust I'd felt with his holding me, with how he listened to my small talk of grief and memory…

it had been a turning point in our night. Somehow, in those few minutes, I'd felt more comfortable in his presence than with anyone previously, as if I'd known him a lifetime before.

God, that sounded absurd.

I tapped the photo and let the picture fill my screen.

I looked so fucking happy.

My head sank onto the pillow behind me, and I pulled my blanket tighter. *I didn't know you took that,* I texted him.

I look at it on my good and bad days, he said. *Though most especially on the bad ones.*

Why on your bad days?

To remind me how life is supposed to feel.

My chest warmed and tightened all at once. I stared at the words for a long minute, knowing he was right. I wasn't sure what to say.

Three dots on the screen saved me from thinking of something.

I'm sorry I didn't find you sooner.

My chest constricted at those words, and I swallowed the emotion bubbling on the surface, my thumbs hovering over the screen.

I know I'm too late, he continued.

Time stood still. The sound of my pounding heart pulsed in my ears. Heat spread from my neck and cheeks, and I finally found my voice.

You're not.

I stared at my reply for what felt like forever, ears burning that I'd actually said it. Three dots appeared again, and I replied before he could.

Goodnight, Gavin.

I quickly tossed the phone face down onto the cushion like it was made of lava, and I tried to avert my attention to the tv show I'd left playing.

With every passing nanosecond, I glanced at the phone, expecting it to ding with some sort of reply.

I didn't know what I wanted him to say. Did I want him to ask me to clarify what I meant? Would he ask? Had the last two texts even been sent out? Shit, why had I said that? Was I just feeling lonely? Why—

The phone vibrated, and my heartbeat skipped. I chewed on the inside of my mouth as I stared at it long enough that it buzzed again with the reminder alarm.

I snatched it up and read the message.

Hey, love.

Tyler.

A brief moment of disappointment washed through me, followed by gut-wrenching guilt as I looked at the next message from Tyler.

I hope you have a good night's sleep, C. Maybe I'll catch you tomorrow.

A long sigh left as reality hit me in the face. Gavin—Eros, Cupid, whoever he was—was a fantasy. A long-lost dream that I would likely cling to when I was middle-aged, and my friends and I spoke about past lovers.

Call me later when you can, I texted Tyler before slumping into the chair again.

I will. I love you, Tyler replied.

I didn't text him back.

Chapter Twenty-Six

Gavin

I held tight to the bag of pastries as the elevator ascended upward, loaded with employees of various floors. I hadn't slept. My stomach was so twisted that I was nauseous. Lightheaded.

You're not.

I had lost track of time staring at that text message.

I hadn't stopped thinking about Chloe in the ten days she'd been absent from my life. Persephone had come by my office again to check on me. Upon hearing that I still hadn't spoken to Chloe, Persephone had asked if she needed to make a trip to Chloe's office to talk to her, but I had begged her not to.

The last thing I wanted was for Chloe to be bombarded by a goddess who might slip up and tell her who she was.

I was glad Hermes hadn't been seen in a few years. Had he gotten ahold of this gossip, my mother would have already visited Chloe herself, and I might have lost Chloe due to her intervention.

Whenever I'd texted Chloe and not heard back from her, my mind went to the worst. I was terrified of losing her again. I couldn't. I didn't know what I would do if I did.

She was my weakness and my strength, and I needed her home in my arms.

The elevator dinged on her floor, and I filed out with a few of the employees I'd met previously. My gaze went straight to Chloe's office, finding her standing by the table in the middle, her palms pressed into the surface. She wore a black jumper that day, a rust-colored tank beneath it, and white sneakers.

She was so effortlessly adorable that my cock stirred upon seeing her. I straightened my shirt out, nerves wracking my insides. I wondered if I would ever get over that feeling or if I would be doomed to stammering in her presence every waking day—if she would have me that long.

I knocked on her door twice, and her face lit up when her eyes met mine.

Fuck, it was painful.

She was an enigma that I was determined to figure out. I know we had only been apart ten days, but for me, it had felt like years—longer than the five years we'd previously spent apart. And maybe it was because I knew who she was now or had started getting used to having her in my life.

Either way, I had never felt such agony at seeing someone again.

I yearned for her more than my mind could fathom. It was beyond love, beyond need, beyond desire. It was a craving in the depths of my soul, and it took every fragment of my dilapidated willpower to keep from scooping her into my arms, kissing her, and telling her everything.

"Morning, Gavin," she said as she straightened. She eyed the bag in my hand. "I believe you said you had some apologizing to do," she said, propping her hand on her hip. "Is this it?" she asked, nodding toward the coffee.

Something felt different. Even her smile seemed less tense. How she looked at me—her eyes dilated, relaxed shoulders, and beaming face… I was curious if something had happened over this last week with her and Tyler or if things had changed between them.

I couldn't get my hopes up too quickly.

"Gavin?"

I blinked twice, a sharp inhale rushed through me, and I set the bag of pastries on the table, along with her coffee, as I forced my earlier thoughts into a deep, dark corner of my mind.

"Apology breakfast. Apology coffee. And…" I stuffed my hands in my pockets and stared at her smiling figure, nervous about the question I was about to ask. "I wanted to see if you would join me at an Arrow event tonight."

"What kind of event?" she asked.

"Speed dating," I replied, grinning.

She snorted and clapped her hand over her mouth. It was so fucking cute.

"How does that work when I'm engaged?" she asked.

"Take the ring off. Flirt a little. We'll have fun," I said.

She hesitated, shaking her head and moving toward her desk. "I don't know…."

"It's harmless," I said. "Call it a work event."

"I have so much to do with my *actual* work," she said, and I knew she was making excuses. She grabbed her tablet from the desk and began perusing through a few files. "Where is it at?" she asked.

"My office," I said. "It's for Arrow employees and partners. We like to try out ideas before rolling them out to the public. If tonight is a success, we'll have sponsored events all around the country at the end of August and throughout September."

"What's the angle?" she asked.

"Cuffing season," I answered.

Chloe stopped walking, fighting a smirk. "Please tell me there are handcuffs involved."

I shrugged my shoulders, starting with a shake of my head, then worked it into a nod. "Of course."

"How does that work?"

"I can't tell you unless you come," I replied. "Confidentiality and all. You could leak my great ideas to some other dating app. There will be a non-disclosure agreement."

Chloe laughed. "Top secret dating schemes by Cupid himself," she teased.

My chuckle met hers. I braced my hand on the table at her side and watched her thumb through the designs on her tablet. However, she didn't seem to be looking at any of them.

"Come on," I said, ready to beg. "It'll be fun."

"Just friends?"

"Is there another option?" I asked.

She gave me a raised brow look, and I scoffed.

"Just friends," I agreed, my smile softening.

She sighed, sat the tablet on her desk again, and looked up at me. "Okay," she agreed.

Chapter Twenty-Seven

Chloe

"I can't believe you talked me into this," I said as we walked around the corner to Cupid's Arrow headquarters after work.

"I know how much you love games," he bantered, prompting a playful glare from my face, and he laughed. He hadn't stopped grinning since I'd met him outside my apartment.

I'd left my ring sitting on the kitchen counter.

Gavin reached for the door, ready to let me through first, but the moment he opened that door, a voracious hum of noisy laughter and chatting hit me. We stepped through the threshold, and I gaped at the sea of people on the bottom and second levels.

Chairs and tables were in lines, all mismatched and of different heights. It was clear this was a practice run as it looked like they had simply moved all the furniture they already had to set up the game. On the second level, some people hovered by the glass banister, drinks in their hands and leaning over the ledge to look down. A table sat at the top of the stairs back by the wall, and I could see Avril and a few other workers getting people signed in and handing out handcuffs, keys, and name tags.

"Wow," I managed. "Do all of these people work here?"

"Most of them. Their friends and partners were invited to

give things some added interest." He nudged my side and grinned down at me. "Come on," he said, taking my hand and nodding toward the stairs.

I twisted my lips, still in disbelief that I'd agreed to this, and squeezed his hand.

Gavin was a celebrity at this place.

People stopped mid-conversation to greet him, and he clapped a few colleagues on their shoulders, smiling and talking to each of them, knowing them all by name and asking if they were ready for fun.

I was glad I had worn my black overall shorts and a green long-sleeve top instead of the skirt outfit I'd tried on. The stairs were steep, and I was pretty sure if I'd worn that skirt that my ass would have shown to everyone.

Even going up the stairs, people called out to Gavin.

Avril greeted us at the top, smiling widely between us and with name tags ready.

"I see you've dragged our newest partner into this," Avril said, grinning at me.

"Dragged would be the keyword," I said.

"It was the intrigue of take-home handcuffs that did her in," Gavin said, winking at me over his shoulder.

I rolled my eyes, let his hand go, and gave Avril my full attention. "Do I need to sign anything?" I asked.

Avril held out a hand. "Right this way."

Once we were signed up and given name tags, two keys, and two sets of fuzzy black handcuffs, I turned back to look at the people waiting for the game to start. Arrow's CFO, Zayn, came up to talk to Gavin before taking to the top of the steps and speaking to the crowd.

Gavin turned to me, tuning Zayn out. "If you need saving, you know the word," he said softly.

I almost frowned but then remembered what he meant. "Arrow?" I asked, recalling the safe word he'd once given me.

He smiled. "I'm impressed you remember," he said.

A soft huff of amusement left me, and I looked directly into his eyes as I said, "Gavin, I remember everything."

His tongue darted out over his lips, and his smile faded slightly. "Not everything," he said.

"Rule number one—" Zayn's loud demand pulled me from our conversation. I looked over just as he held up a set of keys and began pacing at the top of the steps to start the game.

"—Do not lose your keys. You have two: one for your cuffs and one for someone else in this room. That someone also has your key. On the key that goes to your cuffs is a number, and that number determines which group you'll be in. Now, I want everyone to take their handcuffs out and lock both around your wrists," Zayn said, holding up a pair of cuffs.

People exchanged glances, and Zayn grinned. "Come on, I know all of you like bondage," he said, and the room laughed. "Both cuffs. You'll have to figure out how to maneuver using both hands for the next hour."

People did as they were told, some having friends clasp the cuffs on their wrists, laughing nervously as they did.

"Each group will have ten minutes total. At the end of those ten minutes, Avril will be dinging the timer chime. There are five groups, ten people in each, so you'll get one minute each to chat and see if your key works in their handcuffs. At the end of that minute, you will switch partners, and at the end of ten minutes, Avril will call out the next group pairing. Now, if you find your match, you can either pull from the game, come upstairs and mingle, or you can continue playing to chat with everyone else and then meet up with that person at the end."

I leaned in closer to Gavin. "What exactly is the goal with the cuffs?" I asked.

"It's an easy, fun icebreaker," he said, arms folded over his chest. "Helps the minute flow more naturally than the interview style like most speed dating events can feel. Also, the person with your key might be someone you wouldn't have considered just swiping profiles."

"I like it," I said, and he turned his head, our gazes meeting.

"Really?"

"Yeah," I said. "It sounds fun and not completely awkward. And I like how open this all is. No labels. "

"We believe in an inclusive concept here," he replied. "Everyone deserves love. You might even find a new best friend if the relationship part doesn't work." He nodded toward the key in my hand. "What's your key number?" he asked.

I looked. "Five. Yours?"

"One," he replied.

"How many godly tricks have you played with the pairings?" I asked.

"Ah, that's for after they're paired up," he said. "Sometimes people need a nudge."

I still wasn't sure if he was joking or not.

He turned into me then and took my cuffs from my hands. Eyes never leaving him, he spread the metal open wide on one wrist, the soft fuzz brushing my skin, and he clicked it closed. That little click made my breath catch. He didn't put the other one on, and I was grateful not to have to walk down the steps with my hands bound in front of me.

I reached for his cuffs and put one around his left wrist, my heart stammering the entire time as I remembered all the ways he'd taken me the last time I was wearing handcuffs and threatened him with them while pleasuring him in the shower. I was sure my cheeks were pink when I locked them securely.

"Are you thinking of a fantasy you'd like to share?" he asked, his voice deep.

"Don't you wish," I said, though the image of him with his hands behind his back while I sucked his cock played at the edge of my mind.

"Are you sure?"

My lips pulled behind my teeth, gaze unable to resist glancing down to his pants before meeting his eyes again. I tugged his cuffs. "Just things I didn't get to do," I said.

His gaze blew with desire. I wondered if his heart was beating as erratically as mine.

Zayn began a chant of 'Cupid's Arrow' back and forth with the crowd, making me lose my focus on Gavin as the room erupted in cheers. Avril clapped her hands twice and stepped up beside Zayn.

"Everyone, to your group tables! Let's go, people!"

Gavin grinned at me. "See you on the other side."

As he walked away, my stomach launched into my throat, and I turned to face the now mingling crowd.

Here goes nothing.

I couldn't stop laughing.

It was apparent the patrons weren't taking this game seriously.

The room was loud.

The decor was tacky.

The pickup lines were cheesy.

It was so much fucking fun.

Trying out keys in everyone's cuffs proved to be the most

challenging, aside from all of us looking silly as we two-handed drink cups every time we needed more alcohol.

Occasionally, I looked for Gavin in the crowd, and I found him watching me nearly every time. Those quiet, shared smiles made my knees weak. He walked around the room when he wasn't gazing at me or playing. Observing the interactions, I knew. Calculating and making a note of every flaw that he saw needed adjusting.

Nudging a few couples together, if he was to be believed.

I still hadn't matched with someone when Avril called Table Five to go to Table One for our last ten minutes. Some on my team had found their matches but were having too much fun to stop playing. Even with the handcuffs off, they continued to treat every speeding minute with jokes and eventually introduced themselves.

Upon seeing that Gavin hadn't worked his handcuffs off yet, my brow raised. His chin lifted smugly, tongue darting out over his lips as he gazed down at me with the most sinful look in his eyes.

My thighs tightened at the mere sight of it.

"Ready to be set free?" he asked.

I almost laughed. "You planned this?" I asked.

He maneuvered his key between his fingers and smirked as he placed it inside the lock. It clicked, and he slowly pulled them off, the metal tip grazing my skin. "Couldn't have anyone else taking these off of you," he said.

"Or on me." I took my key out and put it in his handcuffs, releasing the lock and his wrists. He softly grasped my forearms when he was free, his thumbs massaging my pulse points, and my breaths went jagged at the touch.

"I wanted you to get through the entire game," he admitted. "I knew you would be honest with me about any flaws that might have come up."

"Will no one else?" I asked.

"They will, but most of them know each other. I needed someone completely new to play it. An outsider's opinion."

"I'm happy to oblige," I said.

Pizza was waiting for everyone upstairs when the game was over.

We were asked to put our thoughts onto suggestion papers they'd had printed, then put them in a box for Avril and Gavin to go through the next day. We were encouraged to write anything we loved or might have wanted to change.

I grabbed a couple of slices of pizza and a beer, then sat by the window at one of the tables to look out while Gavin talked with everyone.

He was so charismatic that I couldn't tear my eyes away. The way he moved through the crowd and knew every person's name, their significant others—I even heard him asking about someone's children.

It was an hour before he navigated over to where I sat.

"You look like you're trying to figure it all out," he said.

I pushed him a plate with two slices of pizza I'd grabbed for him before it ran out, then took a sip of beer and inspected him to the point that he smiled almost nervously.

I wasn't used to seeing him nervous, yet now I'd seen it twice in one day.

"How do you know everything about everyone here?" I asked.

"Ah..." he sat back in the chair and looked around the room. "Most of them have been working with me since day one, and after ten years, they're practically family."

"These people have been here since the beginning?" I asked in disbelief. "That's wild for a company nowadays."

Gavin shrugged. "You treat people with as much respect as you wish to receive, and sometimes it works out."

"Most employers only care about the work getting done, no matter how it gets done," I said.

"I'm not most employers," he said. "Can't imagine you would only care about that with your employees."

"No," I said. "No, I've worked for enough assholes over the years. That was one of the reasons I had quit completely and started doing contract work like I was doing when we first met."

"How did you end up with Ezzie?" he asked.

"I actually met her at a convention in Toronto. She was running around on the phone and had three clients signing there. For some reason, she spotted me and asked me if I could help her round up one of her celebrities who had decided to get up and go to the taco truck outside instead of staying in and doing his job. Our no-bullshit attitudes got along great, and when my workload became too much, she was who I instantly called. At first, it was all remote. We had never even met some of our employees until the offices opened. You should have seen how we did interviews when we moved out here. "

I laughed at the memory, and Gavin smiled.

"Is there a special way to conduct them?" he asked.

"We were sat in the middle of the thirteenth floor with only our laptops and a few cushions," I said. "The ones who came in either took one look at us and turned around, or they stayed to hear what we had to say. We heard their stories and concerns about working for a startup, too. We had barely enough in the bank to cover rent, electricity, and payroll, and for the first six months, we all worked on those little food tray tables or the floor in the back corner. Construction was done on the fourteenth floor first, and we all moved in there while the other floor was done."

I sighed, remembering those first few scary months when we didn't know how things would work or if they would.

"It was our dream," I said.

"I wish I'd seen it," he said, and I met his eyes.

I gave him a small smile. "I think things worked out. If I had been with you then, I don't know that I would have met Ezzie, and maybe I would have moved across the country earlier than I was meant to."

"Do you believe in that kind of thing?" he asked. "Fate. What's meant to be and a predestined life and everything."

"Are you asking if I believe in the universe and patterns or if I believe in the three women called the Fates who control our destinies?"

Gavin chuckled under his breath. "There are many things wrong with that statement, but I'm going to let you slide this time," he said.

"Oh, really? Will you give me a thorough education on Greek mythology one day?"

"Maybe I will," he said. The rim of his bottle touched his lips, and he sipped the beer as he said, "Depends on if you're a good girl or not."

My mouth twisted, not out of annoyance, but in an attempt to hold back the flirt that threatened my lips.

And he knew it.

That dimple shone with his crooked smile, and he sat up in his seat. "I'm asking if you believe in either," he said.

I eyed him again, took another drink, and pondered his question. "Lana is always going on about listening to the universe and manifesting your own destiny and everything. I've never really thought much of it. Although I think... I think it's possible. Maybe there are a thousand predetermined destinies, and our choices send us off on one of those paths. And maybe those who actually give the universe a chance to speak are the ones who have some insight into those various paths, so we see that path and all the steps it takes to get there."

"And soulmates?"

A slow smile lifted on my lips. "I think our souls have

many different counterparts for many different reasons, and maybe a different one for each part of our life. They make your life a little more complete. For instance, I think Lana is one of mine. We were definitely meant to find each other."

Gavin stared at me for a long enough moment that I had to shift in my seat. I squinted at the look on his face. "What?" I asked.

"You didn't say your fiancé," he said.

I took a long sip of my beer, never losing his gaze, and I considered it. I'd never really thought of Tyler as a soulmate. He wasn't a craving that I missed when we were apart. My soul—if that's what it was—didn't ache in his absence or reach out for his touch when he was there. Whether it was his touch on my body or my mind, I didn't…

I gulped back the last of my drink and cleared my throat. "I should be getting home," I said, avoiding his gaze.

"What's there to do at home?" Gavin asked.

"Laundry. Work. Ice cream," I answered. I gathered my things and stood. I heard Gavin chuckle, and I finally looked at him again.

The bastard was smiling.

"What?"

"Nothing," he said. "Did you write your suggestions down?" he asked.

"I did. You'll know which it is. I also drew a dick."

Gavin's smile widened. "Hopefully, a very large one—"

"Veins and everything," I said, chuckling softly. "A nest of curls."

He laughed under his breath. "I can't wait to see it." He looked me over in silence then, that soft smile lingering on his lips. "Come on. I'll take you home."

Nerves filled my stomach and rushed through my extremities as Gavin shook hands and said his goodbyes while walking to the exit. A few people I'd talked to during the game hugged me, and the people… the people felt like an extended family. There was a contagious energy in the room, and I couldn't keep the smile off my face.

And Gavin didn't stop smiling at me.

The way he looked at me was the same stare I'd woken up to the night we'd spent together so long ago. Wonderment. Joy. Desire. I didn't understand that look. No one else stared at me that way, which confused me.

I regarded him as we strode down the sidewalk to the parking garage where his car was.

"Why do you look at me like that?" I asked him.

Hands in his pockets, he shrugged and glanced forward. "Why shouldn't I?"

"No, I mean the *way* you look at me," I said. "It's…" I tried to put it into words, but the only ones that entered my mind sounded ridiculous.

"You don't like how I look at you?" he asked.

"No, I do. I—" I paused and shook my head. I loved how he looked at me. Even if I didn't understand it, it didn't stop me from wanting to be seen like that every day. "I do like it. I just don't understand it," I said.

His smile softened, and he chuckled under his breath. "When is your fiancé home?" he asked.

"Ah… He'll be away two more weeks this time," I answered. "He was gone all of last week, too. Probably the longest he's been gone for a year or more."

"Business?"

"Tokyo."

"What's in Tokyo?"

"I'm not sure," I admitted as we reached his car. Gavin opened the door, and I hopped inside. I waited for him to get in and start the engine before continuing. "I rarely ask about his ventures. They all seem complicated."

"How so?"

"In that, I'm not really interested in them," I confessed. "I tried in the beginning. I asked about all the deals and the startups he was investing in—I *still* ask about the startups. Some of them are worth it. But then there are ideas I can't help but laugh at because he and his partner have no clue what they'd have to do to pull them off."

"Like?"

"Like backing what would have been the next Fyre festival."

Buoyant laughter left Gavin's lips. "Seriously?" he asked, and I joined his laugh with another nod.

"Seriously," I said.

"Wow. Shit, I hope you talked him out of that one," Gavin said.

"I did, thankfully. I made an entire chart of everything he hadn't thought about, and he and his partner backed out pretty quickly."

"Thank fuck for that," Gavin said. "You don't ever go on the trips with him?" he asked.

"And what? Sit at the hotel pool while he goes out to fancy dinners, cigar lounges, and meets other rich pricks?" I laughed. "I'd rather sit at home in my sweatpants and watch the home shopping network than think I was getting in his way."

"Why couldn't you go with him to the dinners?"

"Tyler says I'd be a distraction," I said.

Gavin's brows furrowed as he stared at me. "What?"

"He says the trips are for business, not pleasure, and bringing me would distract him from his job." I sighed and pushed my hand through my hair, not liking where the conversation had gone. The subject had been a fight I'd once had with Tyler when he'd traveled to a few places I also wanted to visit—namely, New York City. I had argued that I wouldn't be in his way, that I would take in the city sites myself, and that he would only see me back at the hotel at night. But that wasn't enough.

He'd promised to take me on a real vacation there one day, though we still hadn't booked that trip.

"Can we just… can we not talk about this?" I asked, frustrated that talking about it had nearly ruined my happy mood. "It was such a fun day. Let's not ruin it with things I can't change."

Gavin's grip on the steering wheel was so tight that his knuckles were white. I could feel his energy change, and I knew it was taking everything in him to hold back what he wanted to say. I didn't know whether I wanted to hear it or not. I almost wanted him to scream at me and tell me to wake up again. I needed that push and pull. I wanted to fight with him, slap him, and have him haul me into his chest and shut my mouth with his kiss.

"Go ahead," I muttered.

"With what?" he asked.

"Whatever it is you're thinking," I replied.

Gavin switched hands on the wheel. "I'm thinking about you sitting at home alone in your sweatpants and a messy bun, ice cream in hand, a cooking show on your television, and I'm thinking that that sounds more interesting than any business trip I could ever plan."

A smile dared to show itself on my lips. "Really? That's what you're thinking about?"

"I'm willing to bet there are stains on the shirt you're wearing and mascara smudges under your eyes because you forgot to wash your face," he said, beaming at me.

My mouth dropped. "What—There is—well, not on all of my shirts. And how do you know that I forget to wash my face?"

"Probably take-out strewn on the coffee table," he kept going.

"I clean up after myself," I argued.

"I bet you only clean up the day before he gets home," Gavin said. "Because you get to be yourself when he isn't there."

"So says the god with a maid that cleans up his messes," I said.

"Yeah, she's hot too." Gavin grinned, and I couldn't stop my own.

"Are you trying to make me jealous?"

"Is it working?"

I chuckled, and my heart swelled at the expression on his face. We were pulling into the garage beneath my apartment building then, and I knew Gavin had said all those things just to make me laugh and forget about what we'd just been talking about.

It worked.

He reached over and gently squeezed my knee as he pulled the Jeep into a parking place.

"There's my girl," he said before bringing my hand to his lips.

It was a few seconds before his eyes left mine, and his

thumb caressed my knuckles the entire time, making my whole body squirm with need.

"I'll walk you up," he said softly.

I should have said no. I should have said I could handle getting in the elevator and walking to my door alone.

But I didn't.

Every second in that elevator made my hands clammy. I could feel how tense he was beside me, too, and I wondered if his insides were as restless as mine. I didn't know why. He was a friend—*only* a friend.

My hands stretched with jittery nerves. We glanced at each other once, apprehension in his eyes, as though he was taking me home after our first date, and we were both wondering if there would be a kiss at the door.

I considered asking him to come inside to watch a movie, order late-night food, and stay up talking about whatever came to mind. Only that was too dangerous for my lonely heart, and I knew better than to think my willpower would be significant enough to deny him again after what happened in the storage unit.

Gavin followed me out of the elevator and down the hall to my door, where we both paused as I fumbled for the key. And when I found it, I put it into the lock and looked back at him.

My back pressed into the door, my hand still on the knob, but I couldn't twist it, not with how he stared at me there.

"Thank you for today," I managed. "I don't think I've ever had so much fun speed dating. You probably shouldn't have people walking around restrained, however. Especially with drinks involved."

Gavin huffed amusedly. "Was that your suggestion? To get rid of the handcuffs?"

"I didn't say get rid of them completely. Maybe just put them on one wrist so people still have mobility, and you're not getting sued for someone tripping on their heels and falling into a table."

His smile widened. "This is why I wanted you to play."

"Are you sure that's the only reason?" I asked, leaning into the doorframe.

I loathed myself for the flirtatious tone on my tongue, and the young-in-love smile I knew had spread across my stupid face for most of the day. Fucking hell. I hadn't smiled like that in years. What the hell was wrong with me. How did he make me feel—no, how dare he *make* me feel this way.

Gavin gave my chin a flick, the endearing gesture spiraling my heart almost out of control. His crooked smirk met me, and he didn't say anything else as he turned on his heel and headed toward the elevator.

I forced my legs to move and my hand back on the key in the lock. I needed a cold shower and a large glass of wine. Or a bubble bath in the hottest water I could stand, anything to try and drown out the butterflies now making their way from my stomach to my fingers and toes to between my thighs.

"It's how you look at someone when you can't stop thinking about them."

Fuck.

My heart skipped.

I paused, my hand still on the door as I glanced in Gavin's direction. He had let the elevator doors open and close, now slowly enclosing the gap between us again as he spoke.

"What?" I managed, my voice shaking.

"The way I look at you," he said.

The butterflies in my stomach swarmed into a lump that settled in the pit of my chest. His tongue darted over his lips, and he continued speaking even as I opened my mouth to tell him we should call it a night.

"It's the way you look at someone who makes you feel truly alive, like the rest of your life has been nothing more than a string of dreams tied together with twisted twine that you just can't seem to get right—not without that last piece of thread to braid it all together," he said. "It's when you only see them in the middle of a crowded room. It's how you look at the person you want to hold while you fall asleep, the person you want to feel around you when you wake up, who brings you joy, and who it agonizes you to be apart from."

It's how you look at your soulmate and the person you can't stop yourself from falling for.

The last sentence was a whisper in my ear, a murmur barely audible like it had whispered in on the wind and was meant to be said aloud, but he was too scared to say it.

It wasn't true. It *couldn't* be true.

He reached up to push a stray hair from my eyes, his gaze traveling over my face. "And it's how I'll never stop looking at you," he said softly.

I couldn't breathe.

Gavin leaned in, and every muscle in my body stiffened. His lips hit my cheek and then my jaw, and he squeezed my wrist as he pulled away. Hunger clouded his dilated eyes, making my heart constrict.

"See you soon, Chloe," he whispered.

"Goodnight, Gavin," was all I could manage before forcing my hand to twist the doorknob, knowing that if I didn't, I would stand there and exchange 'goodnights' with him until one of us gave in to the pull between us.

The door clicked behind me, and I finally exhaled the breath that had staggered in my lungs. I stood with my back to the door, relaxing there and gathering my wits. My eyes closed, and all the laughs and smiles from that night replayed in my head.

I was giddy and edgy all at once. My insides were a tangle of nerves and happiness and outright nausea. Heat beat on my cheeks. My heart was an erratic mess. I couldn't stop smiling, couldn't stop shaking from all the emotion moving through me. It burned the back of my eyes and pricked my skin.

I didn't realize I was sliding to the floor until I felt the cold hardwood under my ass.

Shit.

Shit. Shit. Shit.

I lunged for the couch, grabbed a pillow, held it to my face, and screamed into its padding. All I could see was his eyes on me. All I could feel was his lips lingering on my cheek and jaw.

After a few minutes, I forced my body to move, deciding that I needed an icy shower to bring myself back to reality.

My ring remained forgotten on the kitchen bar.

Chapter Twenty-Eight

Gavin

Every day, I grew more and more restless over her.

The feelings were growing, not only that ache for who I knew she was but just for her. I was falling in love with her all over again, and the thought of her not eventually leaving her fiancé was beginning to wear me down.

I had to fight.

I knew she felt what I did. When she thought I wasn't looking, I could see it in her eyes. I could feel it every time I touched her, and it was written in that cute little smile she gave me when she thought I was being ridiculous. Fuck, that look was burned in my memory. All of her was burned on my skin. Whenever I thought of being with her, my heart yearned painfully.

If this was what it felt like to fall in love with her, I didn't know that I wanted to feel the pain I'd forgotten upon losing her—the pain I knew I would feel again if I was an idiot. Just the thought of it sent me to my knees.

Her fiancé was gone for two weeks, and I knew that was how long I had left before she was lost forever.

A text came through as I sat outside on my balcony by my infinity pool, taking in the morning sun and sipping my coffee. The noise of the ocean waves filled my ears, along with the joyous sounds of the surfers catching waves.

Morning entertainment, I liked to call it.

My heart skipped at the name on the screen as I looked at my phone.

I think I need to get an orange safety vest to walk from my car to my office, Chloe texted me.

I smiled, loving that she had texted me something out of the blue, especially after we left things last night. I had been nervous saying those things, even scared she would tell me to vacate her life.

She needed to know that was how she deserved to be looked at, that any first-time phases of butterflies and flirting would never fade with us. She deserved to be loved and truly feel it every day, and I would do that.

Why's that? I asked.

Third time in two weeks that I've nearly been taken out by either a skateboarder or cyclist, she replied.

You do wear a lot of black and green, I said. *Maybe they think you're in camouflage.*

I'm wearing pink today.

Is that your shirt color or lingerie color?

I don't have pink lingerie.

We should change that.

We?

As your friend, you should have a pink set.

So says Eros. Isn't pink your favorite color?

My favorite color is whatever shade of lipstick you're wearing.

Today is a bright reddish coral. Forever Dior.

Dior lipstick?

I splurge on good makeup.

What else will you splurge on?

Books. Lingerie. Staple clothing like jackets or jeans. Practical things.

I didn't know lingerie was considered practical.

Expensive lingerie is essential when your tits are like mine,

she said. *A good bra is hard to come by. And sexy lingerie that actually fits my figure is exhausting to look for.*

Is this why you save money? For books and lingerie?

What else is there to spend good money on?

I scoffed at her joke as I took another sip of coffee. *Will you be in the office after lunch?*

I have a work excursion with Ezzie this afternoon.

What's a work excursion?

It means we take the afternoon off to go shopping and call it 'work.'

Will you send me pictures? I asked.

What exactly do you think I'm buying?

It sounds like you're buying pink lingerie.

I'll see what they have, she said.

I smiled as I sat my phone down and stretched my arms back, groaning with the feel of my muscles begging to move. I kept looking at my phone and waiting for it to light back up with another message from her, though after it remained dark for ten minutes, I finally picked it back up.

Will I see you today? I asked.

It was another five minutes of anxiously waiting for her response before she wrote back, *I don't think so.*

Tomorrow?

Why? Do you miss me?

Like you wouldn't believe, I admitted.

You just saw me yesterday.

I know. It's been an agonizing twelve hours.

They say absence makes the heart grow fonder.

Absence from you makes me weak.

The three dots strummed the bottom of the screen. *Maybe Thursday. I'll have some designs ready for you then.*

Three days.

I groaned inwardly, but I knew I couldn't push it.

I'll take it.

I glanced at the time. It was almost time for the heated yoga class I liked to attend downtown. It was a twenty-minute drive, so I changed clothes, grabbed my water, and made my way out the door, all while fantasizing and wishing I was the one going shopping with her instead.

I drove by Chloe's workplace on the way in.

Not to see her but to check on something that had come to mind while I was in yoga class.

Her mentioning someone on a skateboard irked me. I remembered the one that had nearly run the two of us over in the park that day, and it had me curious as to if it could have been the same person.

It was a little ridiculous. Plenty of people had skateboards around this town, and there may not have been any reason to be suspicious.

Yet, I was.

I drove slowly around the area, scoping out the parking garage and the nearby park where we'd run into him the last time. I was on my third turn, about to take the exit toward my building when I finally spotted him.

The middle-aged man stuck out against the younger crowd. He was gliding along, his hands in the pockets of his black jeans, wearing a backward navy baseball hat, and wavy blonde hair sticking out over his ears. That same uneasiness washed over me, the hair on the back of my neck standing. And when I saw the wings drawn on his Converse sneakers, I almost wrecked my Jeep.

The nosy little shit.

I wondered why he was following Chloe, though—if he knew who she was, if my mother had perhaps put him up to follow me and if he'd seen me with her in the park that day.

Fuck.

I deliberated whether he'd seen our fight, and I really fucking hoped he hadn't. Every god would be onto us if he had, and I wasn't ready for that kind of attention, not to mention it would have alerted the one that had stolen her and warned them that I was poking around things. I intended on finding that out on my own, and I would bring down every bit of wrath I was capable of upon them when I did.

I parked my Jeep in the lot between the grassy park and the beach, keeping an eye on the god I was stalking as I pushed my arms through my jacket and exited. He was back a little way but riding up quickly. I grabbed a frisbee from someone's car and threw it onto the sidewalk as he passed by.

The rider face-planted, his board flipping out from under him. He cursed and grabbed his knee, and I coolly picked up the board.

"Oh, look at that," I said, grabbing him by the arm. "So, *sorry*. That was my fault."

"Fucking Styx," he muttered. "You should watch where you're throwing that. Someone might get—" His eyes widened when his gaze met mine, and I squeezed his shoulder.

"Shit," he grumbled under his breath.

"Hello, Hermes." I picked up the frisbee, angled it toward the car it had come from, and then pushed Hermes forward. "Let's take a walk."

"This isn't exactly how you greet your father—"

"The number of you that think that is *astounding*," I interjected.

"Ask your mother. She'll tell you—"

"My mother likes being admired," I cut him off. "She'll tell anyone what they want to hear just to keep them swaddled around her pretty little finger." I glanced at Hermes, the blonde hair sticking out from under his baseball cap over his ears, and I scoffed. "Is this hat to hide your receding hairline? Or do you think it helps you blend in?"

"What does it—"

"What are you even doing with a skateboard?"

"What's with the drill? Are you—Wait—" He rounded in front of me, holding his hands up. "What are you hassling me for? Aren't you some busy hot-shot technician that can't even make time for your family?"

I smirked and pushed past him, hitting his shoulder when I did. "Well, you have been hanging out with her lately," I said. "And it's app developer, not technician."

"Oh, excuse me, Mr. Fancy-Pan—"

"Why are you following me?" I asked, stepping in front of him again.

Hermes stuffed his hands in his pockets, his mouth twisting as he considered me. "Who says I'm following you?"

"Oh, right. I meant following Chloe," I corrected myself, my nostrils flaring at the look of false innocence in his eyes.

"Chloe… Chloe, Chloe, Chloe… Hm… Nope, doesn't ring a bell—"

If we hadn't been in a public place, I would have grabbed him by the throat and hoisted him in the air, let him spurt and sputter on his own spit as he stammered out the truth.

I jerked forward, causing Hermes to flinch, and the reaction lifted my lips.

"Think harder," I said.

"Oh, the *girl*," he finally said, and I wanted to pummel him for the sarcasm in his tone. "I think you mispronounced her name. It's *Psyche*, isn't it? Or is she not your long-lost wife?"

I gritted my teeth, trying to quell my rage. It was another minute before I moved, letting a huff of amusement leave me as I clapped him on his shoulder and gave him a wry smile. "Tell me, Hermes. What are you doing now? Can't be spending all your free time stalking other gods and pretending to be young."

Hermes judged my facade. My jaw clenched as my fingers dug into his clavicle. "Private jet service," he answered, strain in his tone. "You have the money, and I have the plane."

"No questions asked?"

"Wouldn't want anything to incriminate me, would I?" Hermes said.

"Because you're so wholesome, right?"

He twisted out of my grasp, and I let him free. A grimace stretched over his face as he rolled his shoulder. "Fucking Styx, kid. Glad to know that grip hasn't changed. What's with the aggression?"

"You're following us," I said.

He rubbed his collarbone. "It's not what you think," he said. "Your mother told me about your outburst the other week and wanted to know if I could find out how you suddenly knew Psyche. I volunteered to help."

"Did you know who she was talking about?" I asked.

"No, actually. Another reason I wanted to help. I was curious about who and what could cause her such distress. It was maddening to see her like that."

I chuckled under my breath. "All of you. Wrapped around her finger," I muttered.

"And you have her wrapped around yours," he said, glancing up at me. "Let's face it, kid. You're the one person she would move mountains for—and has. Multiple times over."

I ran a hand through my hair. "This is one mountain she should never have touched."

"I don't disagree," he said. "The first time I followed you was in the park, and the moment I saw the girl, I knew who she was. I remembered everything about her, everything that happened, and it killed me that I had forgotten her."

"I thought Mother said she only tampered with the memory of my closest friends?"

"She didn't exactly have the power to do that on her own, did she?" Hermes cocked a brow, throwing me for a loop. "I'm sure she only gave the order, and once she did, it sounds like it was botched."

"You seem to know a lot about this, Hermes," I drawled.

"Only theories," he answered.

"Doesn't tell me why you're still following us," I said.

Hermes shrugged. "What can I say? I love a good love story."

"The last thing I want is you gossip-hopping between every god and telling them who I've found—"

"I wouldn't do that to you," Hermes said, and seeing the look on his face, I believed him.

"Thank you," I said.

Hermes nodded. "Now, are you done hassling me? Can I get on with my morning ride?"

"Ah… yeah," I gave in. "I have to be heading into the office, anyway."

Hermes propped the board against his leg, moving as though he was about to speed off. "I will tell you this," he said. "She's just as beautiful as I remember. Maybe that's why Aph is scared."

"What does she have to be afraid of?" I asked.

"Seeing you get hurt again."

A rope twisted around my heart as I looked at the beach and let his words sink in.

"See you around, kid," Hermes said.

He rolled away with a few pushes of his foot, and I was left standing on the busy sidewalk, trying to figure out what to do next.

Work was the best distraction I could think of—aside from throwing myself into freezing cold water to numb myself. We were going through some of the comments from the speed dating event. Most were basic—better handcuffs, longer time to talk, whether they should stay in the game after they'd matched. But a few, like Chloe's, were helpful.

Avril had a whiteboard out in the conference room to keep track of the useful ones. It was just her, Zayn, our PR manager, Louisa, our lawyer, Stella, and me. We had to keep Zayn in the room to ensure we weren't overspending, as he liked to remind us that we did. And as for Stella, I had decided to start bringing her into these meetings after Chloe had mentioned the word 'lawsuit' over the handcuffs.

"This one says we need blindfolds," Avril said.

Zayn scoffed. "Blindfolds and handcuffs. I think they just want to fulfill some fantasy of their own."

"Maybe we keep that idea for another holiday," Avril said.

"You can't blindfold people and ask them to walk around," Stella said.

Zayn sat up and gave me a look. "Who invited her?"

"We're trying it out," I said, leaning back in my chair. "Better to have her in the room while we're bouncing ideas than have to scratch them and start over once she gets wind."

"I've been telling you to bring her in for years," Louisa

said. "There's only so much I know."

"So, scratching blindfolds altogether," Avril said, drawing a line through the word.

I cleared my throat and shifted in my seat, making Avril look back at me, and I shook my head discreetly.

Louisa pursed her lips. "You can't blindfold people and have them walk around at a party. Especially with drinks."

"Blind dates," I said simply. "Meet your match and judge them purely on the connection. We can target people who have selected that they want an actual relationship."

Zayn slapped the table and pointed at Avril. "Post it," he said enthusiastically.

"You'd have to have moderators. A time limit—a *drink* limit," Stella said.

"Everyone calm down. We're just brainstorming," Avril said.

My phone buzzed as she picked up the next suggestion paper from the pile. Avril said something about themed cocktails, and Zayn began naming off every idea for drinks that he had, although my attention drew to the message on my screen.

I found it, Chloe said.

I picked up my phone and pulled it into my lap, crossing my ankle over my knee. *Found what?* I asked.

The sexiest pink lingerie that there is.

I stirred slightly in my seat. *You can't claim that unless you share it*, I said. *You have to have multiple opinions to declare something the sexiest ever.*

Are you asking for a picture?

If you're willing to share.

Okay, but I hope you're at home.

Why?

Because I don't think you'll be able to keep it in your pants once you see this.

I'll be the judge of that.

A picture came through then, and I nearly dropped my phone. I had to clamp my lips together to keep from grinning outright. Still, as everyone was arguing about drink names around me, I doubted they noticed my silence.

Chloe was wearing a pink T-rex onesie with a tail, a ridged spine down the back, and a hood with eyes and teeth. I laughed, but gods dammit, she was even sexy in that thing. It hugged her shape, the pink color bringing out the pink of her lips, standing stark against her dark hair while accentuating her skin. She was laughing, and I was curious if Ezzie had said something as she was taking the photo of her.

I know you're joking, but this is sexy as fuck.

You like it?

I fucking love it.

You're so weird

This picture is going on my wall with the other one, I said.

You have a picture of me on your wall?

It wasn't on my wall. But I had printed out the picture of her in the snow and put it on the dresser in my bedroom. I looked at it nearly every day.

Does that creep you out?

Only if you have it in any frame other than a cheesy one with big red and pink hearts.

I smiled. *What else would I have it in?*

Something aesthetically boring, she replied.

Never, I said.

"Earth to Gavin," Avril said, snapping her fingers expectantly.

I finally looked up, noticing the silence, and realized everyone's eyes were on me. Zayn was grinning widely.

"Only one thing can cause that kind of distraction," he teased. "It's that girl, isn't it?"

I placed my phone face down on the table and cleared my

throat. "What were we talking about?"

"You can't get off that easy," Zayn said. "Spill. What did she send you?"

"I don't know what you're talking about," I said.

Louisa snickered. "I talk to Ezzie all the time," she said. "She says you're at their office at least three times a week."

"Isn't that girl engaged?" Stella asked.

But Avril was looking at me with a proud smile on her lips. I pleaded to her with my eyes, and she tapped the whiteboard twice.

"Back to it," she said. "We have a deadline for this. You can harass the god of love on your own time. Right now, you're mine."

"Ooh, that's spicy, Av," Zayn joked. "Are you going to punish us?"

"I very well might," she replied. "The next suggestion—" She paused, a look of surprise on her face. "Now, that is a cock drawing," she said as she shifted around the paper for us to see.

"Oh shit, let me see that," Zayn said as he stood and took it from her hands. "Damn," he drawled. "Veins and balls and everything." He turned it around, and I snorted, prompting everyone to stare at me.

Gods damn, this woman.

Chapter Twenty-Nine

Chloe

I was a glutton for punishment.

I was texting Gavin every day.

Morning. Noon. Night.

I had yet to hear from Tyler, which was odd. I knew it could have been the time difference since he was in Tokyo, or at least that was what I was blaming it on.

It definitely *wasn't* because I was so obsessed with Gavin.

No.

No, that couldn't have been it.

"Five things on your bucket list," Gavin said as he sat beside me at the office table on Thursday.

He had brought burgers and fries for my entire team to munch on while we showed him progress on the designs for his company. I estimated another week to put the final touches on them before we would be done. My team happily took the afternoon off with Gavin's approval on everything.

I chewed slowly on one fry, considering his question but also trying to extend as much time with him as possible.

"Skydive," I answered, counting the list off on my fingers. "Travel. Go on a sailboat—"

"You have to be more specific with travel," he said. "Where do you want to go? Besides Greece?"

"Rome. Or rather Italy, in general," I answered.

A soft smile lifted his lips. "You really like Greek and Roman things."

"I love it—okay, there's one of my travel items. To see all the relics and architecture relating to the Greco-Roman world."

His chewing slowed as he stared at me, and I chuckled under my breath, remembering who he was.

"That probably seems silly to you," I said.

"No, not at all." He grabbed another fry and popped it into his mouth. "I could use a refresher. It's been a long time since I've seen the old world."

"Who says I want you with me?" I asked.

He balked. "Who better to be your tour guide than a god?"

"You'd probably just show me all the statues of yourself and forget about everyone else."

"I mean, statues of me do come first—"

I shoved him, and he laughed, falling off balance slightly as he swallowed his food.

"What else, sweet girl?" he asked once he'd collected himself.

"Ah…" I searched my brain, debating and thinking about everything I'd ever said I wanted to do. "Visit every historical library," I said.

"What do you mean?"

"I mean… not your normal local library, but the huge, architectural beauties that seem to go on and on forever. The ones you walk into and someone has to pinch you because you think you're dreaming."

"I don't think they have smut in these libraries," he said.

I scoffed. "Shut up," I muttered, and he smiled at the table before glancing back at me again.

"Are all your bucket list items about traveling?" he asked.

"I feel like the world is so big and yet so tiny compared to the rest of the universe. Why wouldn't I want to explore as much of it as I can?"

"Maybe that should be a separate list," he said. "What do you want to do that isn't travel-related?"

"What do you mean?"

A solemnness settled in his eyes, and he sighed as he leaned back in his chair. "I mean… things like laughing so hard that you spit drink out of your nose. Watching the sunrise every morning holding the person you can't live without. Feeling pain that you think you'll never recover from."

"Love without fear," I said without thinking, my voice barely audible.

I twisted my straw wrapper and let the sentence rest between us like it was hovering in the air, written in a bubble just waiting to burst. I glanced at the clock on the wall, saw the time, and pushed my chair back.

"I should be getting back to work," I said as I stood.

"Me too," he said, rising to his feet. "What are you doing this weekend?"

"No plans," I said. "Why?"

"Maybe I can take something off your list," he answered. He gave me a smile as he leaned in to kiss my cheek, then flicked my chin in that teasing way that made me blush.

"I'll text you later," he said.

Ezzie appeared at the door then, knocking twice and nearly scaring me out of my skin.

Ezzie's brow lifted as Gavin moved by her and headed toward the elevator. I huffed at the look on her face and shook my head, knowing that she would say something about his being at the office so much when that door closed behind her.

"Don't try to tell me that he's only here to keep an eye on the designs," she said. "The project is nearly done. I think you're hanging onto those final edits just to have an excuse to keep him around."

I started gathering up my papers strewn on the tabletop. "If I am?" I asked.

Ezzie grinned. "And she admits it," she drawled.

I threw trash at her face. "Shut up," I muttered, though I couldn't stop smiling like an idiot.

"Fucking hell, I love seeing you like this," she ragged me.

"Is it really that obvious?" I asked.

"God, yes," she said. "As someone who has known you before and during your relationship with Tyler, I can say that this is the happiest and most yourself I've ever seen you."

"Gavin is just a friend," I said.

"You sound disappointed," she bantered.

I chuckled under my breath as I sat down at my desk. "What did you need?"

"Actually, I came to talk to you about that vineyard you suggested," she said, sitting in one of the chairs. Her eyes narrowed at the seat, hands moving up and down the fabric. "This is nice," she said, staring at it. "Is it new?"

"It is. I used your credit card," I told her.

"As you should," she replied. "Anyway, Raegan and I did a tour and agreed it was the best venue we'd looked at. So, we asked about dates, and..." Her eyes lifted to mine, and I tilted my head.

"Are you enjoying keeping me in suspense?" I asked.

Ezzie's smile widened. "We're getting married September 16th."

"Holy shit," I muttered. "That's so soon. Shit, I need a dress."

"Yeah, so we're thinking formal, but not black tie. Open bar. Live band for the ceremony, cocktail hour, and beginning of the reception, and then a DJ for the last hour or so. Lots of dancing. It'll be a very relaxed ceremony and day. We just want everyone to have fun," Ezzie said.

"Plus one?" I asked, and Ezzie smirked.

"Why? Thinking of someone other than your fiancé?" she asked, batting her lashes.

"No," I said, though the idea of going with Gavin to a wedding surrounded by my friends and laughing and dancing with him made my heart swell.

"When can we go shopping again?" I asked.

"When is Lana coming?"

I wiggled my mouse and looked at the calendar on the computer. "Two, almost three weeks. She's staying the entire week before my wedding."

And the mention of that wedding seemed to poison my giddy mood.

"Does Tyler know that?" Ezzie asked.

"I booked her a hotel on the water," I answered. "Did you find a cake yet?"

"Not yet. Why?"

"I don't know the name of the bakery that Tyler's mom found, but the tasting we had was the only good thing to happen that entire weekend," I said. "I'll find out the name. She will probably text me about roses today."

"She's still on about those roses?" Ezzie asked.

I gave her a look and Ezzie grinned.

"Right, well. You have fun with that," she said as she stood. "Date this weekend with Gavin?"

"Ah… not sure yet," I said. "He mentioned something about checking an item off my bucket list. I—" My face faltered at her smirk, and I huffed in response. "It's not a date."

"Sounds like it is," she said. "Have fun with your boyfriend while the fiancé is out of town."

I glowered terribly at her, and she gave me a teasing wave as she left the room, still laughing to herself upon striding to the elevator.

My phone buzzed, causing my heart to skip, but the name that came up had me sitting back in the seat with disappointment coursing through my veins.

Four more weeks until you're Mrs. Drake, Tyler texted.

Final countdown, I texted back.

Although, I didn't say to what.

Gavin knocked on my door at 9 A.M. on Saturday.

I had just woken up, still in my pajama shorts and a tank, my hair in a messy bun atop my head. When I opened the door, he was leaning against the doorframe, and his brows raised slightly.

"Is this what you look like every morning?" he asked.

I cursed the ache of my heart and the heat creeping up on my cheeks at standing there so disheveled and scantily clothed. However, no coffee was running through my veins, so it was all I could do to yawn and manage, "I usually sleep naked. Why?" in the midst of it.

His eyes ran over me, and I knew he was envisioning me with less clothing on than I had. "Ah… nothing," he said.

"Liar," I said, leaving the door open for him to enter as I strode away. "Do you want coffee?" I asked him, making my way to the machine.

"Don't you want to know why I'm here?" he asked as he closed the door.

"I do, but I need coffee first. So, you'll just have to wait for me to be ready to hear whatever you have to say." I pulled two mugs down from the cabinet before prepping the espresso machine.

He settled onto one of the barstools, pulling his booted foot onto the first rung. I could feel his eyes on me as I made coffee the way I liked—extra strong with oat milk and caramel. The smell wafted through the apartment, filling me with that fresh morning feeling. And when it was done, I brought both cups to the bar.

I leaned an elbow against the counter before him, hugging the coffee in my hands and pressing it to my mouth. His tongue swiped across his lips, and he reached out, fingers toying with the hem of my pink silk shorts.

Too close. Too dangerous. Too early for my willpower to be in place. With how sleepy and needy I was for touch, he had about six inches of space to cross before I would have let him fuck me across this countertop.

When his gaze lifted to mine, I didn't bother trying to hide how terribly I needed to shift the weight on my feet, my pussy pulsing from his touch on my thigh.

"What are you doing today?" he asked, his voice deep.

"Being lazy," I answered. "Someone has been keeping me up late texting, and I thought I would just be laying in bed sending him pictures all day. Maybe eating junk food and having a vodka later."

"What kind of pictures?"

"Well, you'll never know now. You're here," I said, tilting my head.

"Tease," he said, his hand grasping at my flesh.

I nearly smiled, my heart doing a somersault with his fingers on my thigh. "What are you proposing?" I forced myself to ask.

"I was going to propose skydiving and dinner, but now that you've mentioned lying in bed and pictures, I might reconsider."

"I didn't say you could lay in bed with me," I said.

"Killjoy," he muttered.

"Wait—skydiving?" I asked, realizing what he'd said.

His smile broadened. "Thought I would help mark something off your list."

"I don't think I woke up prepared for skydiving this morning," I said, nerves sweeping through me. "That's… you're not fucking with me, are you?"

"No," he replied. "And it's a couple of hours north, so you have plenty of time to talk yourself in and out of it."

"Oh, well, that's key because I think I need to have at least one freak-out about it," I said.

"As should any normal person."

I took a long sip of my coffee, staring at the amused expression on his face. "Do you know what I think?" I asked.

"What?"

"I think you just want to be strapped to me thousands of feet above the earth," I said.

"I do. Nothing counts that far up," he agreed.

"Such as…"

His fingers tightened so much into my thigh that they indented in my flesh. I sucked in a sharp breath.

"You'll have to come with me to find out," he said. "Do you trust me?"

I considered his question, drinking my coffee and letting it warm my insides. Although, it could have been his touch that had me warm to the point that I felt heat in my ears.

"You really shouldn't do that," I managed as his hand cupped just beneath my ass.

"Make me stop," he dared me.

Our eyes locked as I took another long sip of my coffee, unable to escape his addicting caress. His throat bobbed with his stare, and I think I forgot to breathe. God, that touch. The roughness of his fingers, how large his hands were, and how they pressed into my skin…

I had fucking missed this.

And he knew it.

"I need a shower first," I blurted, inhaling sharply and pulling away from him before I ended up straddling his lap or sitting on the counter so he could have me for breakfast. I

rinsed the cup out and sat it on the drying towel, repeating, *'it's only lust'* in my head over and over again.

"Think of me," he called out as I headed toward the bath.

I flipped him off but knew I would.

I half expected him to make his way into the shower with me, and every time I heard a noise, my heart jumped.

I wondered how much longer I would last before complete combustion.

He was waiting for me an hour later, scrolling through his phone in the same spot he'd been before. I had chosen ripped jeans and a basic band tee to keep my style simple since I would be flying through the air. I didn't know if my stomach was in knots from the thought of skydiving or being with him.

"You never answered my question," he said as I appeared again in front of him.

"What question?" I asked.

He hovered over me, gaze seeming to devour me whole. "Do you trust me?"

I paused for a beat, my heart stammering as our eyes locked. "Yes."

Chapter Thirty

Chloe

Life before Gavin walked back into it was beginning to feel like a distant memory.

Skydiving had been so much fun that he'd retaken me on Sunday. All that adrenaline, the screaming, the wind, the jump… I was impressed that I hadn't given in to that desire for him. It had been so intense that I'd made him bring me home immediately after on Sunday so that I didn't do anything impulsive.

Just lust. Nothing more.

Because that was all it could be.

Anything more was too frightening to consider.

It had already been another week. Gavin had brought food twice to my office, and we'd texted throughout the days like best friends that needed to tell each other everything.

Tyler would be coming home on Monday.

I wasn't ready for reality to come crashing down on me.

The last two weeks with Gavin had felt like a month, like Tyler was some distant memory far in the back of my head, and my wedding to him wasn't just three weeks out. Although, the texts I kept getting from Tyler's mother ensured I remembered it. Apparently, rain was forecasted for that week, and there was no telling her that weather forecasts three weeks in advance weren't reliable at all. I wondered if that was why Tyler had left so close to the wedding—so he wouldn't be stressed about the little things coming from his family.

My family didn't seem to be bothered. All my mother kept asking was if her dress was nice enough. She had bought one but continued shopping to look for others in case she found a nicer one.

Despite all that, I still felt like I was in some giddy little bubble. As if that was the nightmare and my days with Gavin were reality.

Every workday, I spent too long staring at the elevator doors, my heart jumping every time its bell chimed in anticipation of Gavin making an appearance, and every night, it was him I was texting right before I fell asleep.

I wanted to be mad at Gavin for making me a silly teenager all over again. It felt like the beginning of a relationship—something I had sworn to myself I would never feel again—where there was so much hope, butterflies, and downright bliss. The kind that kept you up at night because, for once, your reality was better than your dreams.

It was disgusting and terrifying and amazing all at once. The last time I'd felt this way, it had turned into something I barely escaped. *That* thought kept me level and reminded me not to trip over my feet as I strode further and further toward a four-letter word that I refused to utter.

But it was so fucking hard denying it.

"Your toaster is smoking," Lana said over our video chat on Friday morning.

The smell of burning toast broke me out of my daze as I stared at my phone, waiting for Gavin to text me back.

"Shit," I said, scrambling for the toaster. The black toast burned my fingers when I grabbed it, and I nearly threw it onto my plate.

"Fucking hell—"

My phone buzzed, and I forgot about the burnt toast so

quickly that I practically gave myself whiplash.

So early, baby, he replied in response to my saying something about the beauty of the sunrise.

Here I thought gods woke with the sun to work on their chiseled physiques, I texted back.

I usually do that after coffee. Why? Would you like to come over and watch me sweat?

No, I blurted.

I love when you lie.

"So… who are you texting?" Lana asked in a sing-song voice.

I didn't even realize I was grinning at my phone. Had forgotten I was on a video call with her.

"It's nothing," I said, basically throwing my phone across the counter.

I wiped my face with my hands and pushed my hair back behind my ears, forcing myself to ignore my phone when it buzzed again.

Shit.

"Could it be a certain ginger god?" she teased.

I chewed at the inside of my mouth to keep from smiling outright, looking down at the counter to hide the heat on my cheeks. "No," I forced out.

"God, you are the worst liar—"

"If you were here, I'd throw something at you," I said as I turned and removed a carton of eggs from the fridge.

"Skydiving, texting every minute of the day, burning your food, lunch dates… tell me, Clo, how exactly have you managed not to fuck him yet?"

I cracked open an egg into the pan. "Extreme willpower and lots of toys," I muttered.

Lana snorted, and I glared at her over my shoulder.

"So, what's the plan, then?" she asked.

"What do you mean?"

"I mean, your fiancé comes back on Monday. You can't tell me with a straight face that you're going to sweep all of this under the rug as though it meant nothing," she said.

"Lana, can you please let me enjoy this weekend," I sighed. "I'll think about all of that when Tyler gets back. I just…" I braced my hands on the countertop, hanging my head. "I don't want this feeling to end. Everything seems to fall apart when it does."

"It doesn't have to," she said.

I clenched my jaw. I didn't want to think about what had to happen come Monday. Ignoring it was much easier for me. And Gavin hadn't asked…

I knew I couldn't keep stringing him along. I couldn't keep denying myself of him—whether it was love, lust, or something in between.

"What if I forget who I am again?" I asked softly.

Lana hugged her hands around her coffee. "You haven't yet," she said. "If anything, you've been more openly yourself than I've seen you in a few years. You're not putting on a face when he's around. You're still… *you.*"

"What does that mean?" I asked.

"You do that with Tyler," she said. "You sober up around him, you don't laugh as loudly, you don't get as excited. It's like you think you have to be reserved. I'm not saying submissive because you're not, but…."

"I lose a part of myself when he's around," I said, scrambling the eggs in the pan. I plated them and turned back to Lana, barely picking at the food as I let the realization move through me.

"Let's get through the weekend," Lana said. "Does Gavin have any plans? More skydiving—I still can't believe you did that without me," she added, brow elevated.

"We still have our dream New Zealand trip and skydiving adventure there that's reserved only for you," I assured her.

"And no, he hasn't mentioned plans."

My phone buzzed again, and I itched to answer it.

Lana snickered behind her cup. "So fucking cute," she muttered.

"Oh, shut up," I said.

Ezzie was exiting her car at the same time as me when I arrived at work an hour later. She had a massive grin on her face, and I knew she had some secret she was eager to get off her chest. A leather midi pencil skirt, black lace tank, and pink cape adorned her luscious body that morning, and I whistled at her across the parking garage.

"Have I told you how much more you're glowing with that ring on your finger?" I asked as we caught up to one another.

"And have I told you how much more you're glowing since taking yours off?" she asked, and my heart dropped as I realized I'd left my ring on the kitchen counter after washing dishes.

"Ah, fuck," I muttered, cursing myself for the mistake.

Ezzie snorted. "Don't worry. If anyone notices, just tell them you took it to be cleaned."

"Is that something I'm supposed to do?" I asked, genuinely wondering.

An amused sigh left her, and she draped her arm around my shoulder, giving me a comforting squeeze. "You're adorable, and that's one of the reasons I love you," she cooed. "But really, you should have it cleaned before the wedding," she added.

"Noted," I said. We hit the sidewalk then, the sun cascading over us. "What's the good news you're ready to spill?" I asked.

"Dress shopping tomorrow," she said. "Do you want to come with me?"

"You haven't found your dress?" I asked. "They take months to come in sometimes."

Ezzie shrugged. "I called a few places yesterday with some on the rack I could try. What do you say? You need to find a dress, too—that is, if you don't have other plans." Her perfectly manicured brow raised, and I chuckled softly.

"Even if I did, dress shopping with you comes first," I said. "Where are we going?"

Ezzie opened the door to the building. "Well, there's one place an hour or so away I wanted to check out. If I don't find something there, and you're free next weekend, there's another a few hours south. Although that includes staying overnight at a hotel, so we'd make a full weekend out of it."

"Consider me your date," I agreed.

Jasmine had more messages than usual to go through when I arrived on my floor. I hadn't heard from Gavin since that last message while I was on the call with Lana. I knew he was likely exercising or getting ready for work, so his silence shouldn't have made me anxious.

Yet it did.

By the time two hours had passed at work, I realized I hadn't done anything more than open up and reply to a few emails. I glanced at my phone for the thousandth time, hating myself for how distracted I was, then picked it up and threw it across the room. My hands slid into my hair.

Stupid. Stupid. Stupid—

"Whoa."

My heart dropped, and I looked at the door wide-eyed.

Gavin stood there, two coffees in his hands, brows furrowed. He was looking between me and the phone on the ground, waiting expectantly for me to comment.

"Gavin." I stood, but he just smiled, which made my nerves relax. "What are you doing here?"

"I didn't know I needed an excuse to see you," he said.

"Kind of helps with the alibi when you do," I replied.

He grinned crookedly and closed the door behind him. "I dropped my phone in wet cement going into my office, so I wanted to come over and let you know."

"Wait, back up," I said. "How did that happen?"

He handed me my coffee and sat sideways on the opposite side of the desk. "I was texting you, not watching where I was going. Ran right into it."

"You… walked into wet cement—wet cement that was probably sectioned off—because you were too distracted texting me?" I asked.

His hand ran through his hair. "Something like that," he muttered.

I clapped my hand over my mouth to hide my outright grin. "That's the cutest thing I've ever heard."

"It was a sign from the universe that I shouldn't have been sending such a cheesy message," he countered.

"Why? What was it?"

"Doesn't matter," he said.

"Come on. Tell me," I argued. "Please. I love cheesy things."

"Do you like hockey?"

My mouth snapped shut, all thought of whatever text he had been sending now amiss at the mention of—

"I'm sorry, I think I blacked out for a minute," I said, shifting in my seat and blinking. "I thought you asked if I liked hockey."

"Do you?"

"I love hockey," I replied.

Gavin smirked. "I have tickets for the Sharks preseason game tonight. By the glass. In the corner. Right where the action is."

"How did you get those?" I asked.

He shrugged. "I know a guy. Do you want to go?"

I was giddy just thinking about it, and I tried not to grin as I settled back into my seat. "Oh… do you really want to take me there?" I asked. "I don't think you're prepared for hockey-game-Chloe. Even if it is a scrimmage."

"I am fully prepared for hockey-game-Chloe," he said, that smug look on his face.

I regarded him again, debating whether or not he should see that side of me.

"When are you picking me up?"

Chapter Thirty-One

Gavin

I thought I had prepared myself for whatever person Chloe had warned me of that might come out at the hockey game. I thought she could do nothing to make me fall in love with her any more than I already was.

I was wrong.

Chloe was an animal.

From the moment the players had their first face-off, she was cheering, clapping, and yelling. And the longer the game went on, the more comfortable she got making friends with the people around us. She was her most primal self—completely undone of any restraints that might have held her back in other aspects of her life. It was as if she allowed herself freedom there, zero fucks given to anyone who might judge her for her excitement.

I took my phone out to take a photo of her after she'd shouted something at the glass. She caught me and stuck out her tongue, then sat back in her chair, her body leaning into mine, and she took the phone from my hands to take a selfie of us. My heart stammered at the laughter in her eyes and the genuine smiles on our faces. I wanted to grab her and kiss her, take another photo as I claimed her as my own.

However, her attention was again on the game when the players drove the puck to this end, and I had to swallow the lump in my throat. Every time she looked back at me, I lost track of what was happening on the ice. I didn't even know the score.

Looking back through my pictures, I realized the last two weeks had been nothing more than photos of her, of our time together, of her and I living in stolen moments. Living without her seemed like a waste of the centuries I'd simply waded through.

When the first period was over, Chloe sat back in her seat, exhausted from the effort of her enthusiasm. I put my phone in my pocket as she wiped her face and pushed her hair back, leaning over her knee and turning toward me. She chuckled under her breath.

"I told you you wouldn't want to be seen with me at a hockey game," she said.

"Baby, you're the highlight of the fucking game," I said. "I didn't know you liked hockey so much."

Her smile broadened. "Lana used to fuck one of the players on the Cyclones back home," she said. "It was an easy sport to love."

"You and Lana together at a game? That sounds dangerous," I said.

"Oh, it was," she agreed. "When Tyler and I first started dating, we all went to a game together, and I embarrassed him so much. I think he actually walked out and watched it by the concession stands. It was his first taste of Lana, and he still hasn't recovered."

"Whenever you tell me a story like that, I can't for the life of me figure out why you're with him," I said bluntly.

She laughed. "Well... maybe I thought he was safe. That he was the best I would find when I realized I would probably never hear from you again—that you had no way of finding me once I deleted everything and moved."

"And yet, we're here," I said, reaching for her fingers.

She smiled at the ground before glancing back at me. "As Lana would say: look at the universe."

"Look at the fucking universe," I repeated.

Her eyes stayed on me for a beat, long enough for my heart to stumble.

"What are you thinking?" she asked.

"I'm thinking about how I never want to see that smile fade from your face and all the ways I can be sure of that," I answered. "What are you thinking about?"

Her bottom lip drew behind her teeth, eyes darting from my own to my lips, and I stilled when she leaned into me. "I'm thinking how every time I see you looking at me like that, I want to kiss you," she said softly. "I'm thinking that these last couple of weeks, I've been happier than I've been in years, and how I still feel like myself when I'm with you. I'm thinking that for the first time in my life, a relationship doesn't feel like a trap, that you are terrifying and thrilling and addicting all at once. And I'm not sure how much longer I can resist not having you."

I angled closer, my ears ringing. "So, stop resisting," I said. "You already have me, baby."

Her bottom lip quivered as we sat there motionless, so close that we shared visible breath, our foreheads almost touching. My eyes closed as she inclined her head, and our lips brushed faintly. It was a whisper of ecstasy that nearly sent me to the edge of no return.

I almost fell when she jolted out of her seat.

Cold air washed over me, breath finally leaving my lungs. I looked up at her as she crossed her purse over her body. Her face was red, her chest heaving like she, too, was catching a breath.

"I need to use the restroom," she said in haste. "Do you… do you need anything?"

I blinked out of the daze and shifted in my seat. "No, I

think I'm okay."

"I'll… I'll be back in a minute," she said before darting off.

Gods, that was a disaster.

I slumped forward in the seat, took my backward baseball cap off, braced my elbows on my knees, and shoved the heels of my palms in my eyes. Fuck. I hoped I hadn't scared her more. I hoped she wasn't running out of the building and grabbing a cab to her apartment.

The man behind me reached over and clapped me on the shoulders, shaking me slightly as he laughed, and I knew he had seen what had happened and perhaps thought it amusing. I hung my head in my hand, wiping my eyes to eliminate the anxiety of that almost-kiss.

"Killing you tonight, huh?" the man asked gruffly.

I recognized that voice. I sat up, grasping the ends of my armrests as I turned, and when I confirmed who it was, I scoffed.

"Fucking Styx," I said, smiling and shaking my head at Ares's smirking figure. "What are you doing here?"

Ares grinned. "You know I like hockey," he said.

"I'm fully aware," I said. "You own the team. I meant, what are you doing down here with the regular people?"

"I saw you and the girl on the big screen," he said, pointing to the large screens over the ice. "Thought I would come to talk. You two want to sit in the box for the rest of the game?"

"Ah… maybe. I'll ask when she returns, though I think she prefers being down on the ice." I glanced up at the box, expecting to see any of his friends—

Fuck.

"She's here?" I asked him, seeing Aphrodite in the box, too.

Ares sighed. "Yeah, yeah. Why don't you bring your girl up and introduce her?"

"Why? So she can harm her again?" I asked.

"She'll behave," he swore.

I looked back up at the box, seeing my mother standing there with her arms wrapped around her chest, looking almost... *normal* as she wore an oversized jersey, leggings, a jean jacket, and tall boots. It was a side of my mother I rarely saw—a side of her that was usually reserved for Ares.

"I'll think about it," I said.

Chapter Thirty-Two

Gavin

"Do you want another drink?" I asked Chloe toward the end of the second period.

She turned, her eyes dilated and hungry for the game happening before her. A wild look of happiness and adrenaline rushed through her with every slap and hit on the ice.

"I want to grab it before the period ends, and there's a rush at the stand," I told her.

"Yeah, I'll take another beer," she said, handing me the aluminum cup.

Players ran into the wall then, and she turned back to the game, yelling obscenities and insults at the top of her lungs. I reached over and pinched her ass as she lunged out of the seat, then got up to run to the concession stand when the players stalled in the middle of the ice.

The game became a hum as I hit the top of the steps. I glanced at the tv screen by the restrooms, seeing the Sharks score, and I knew Chloe was probably celebrating with the fans around us. I laughed inwardly at the thought as I set our cups down at the stand and ordered two more.

Someone walked up behind me, standing almost too close as I waited for the drinks. My attention turned to the screen again behind the kiosk, and I tried not to let it bother me. I knew the person was more than likely drunk and unaware of their surroundings or personal space.

"Hockey games are all the same," the person behind me said, the tone of their voice a deep, sarcastic drawl that made every hair on my neck stand on end. "Skate, hit, fight, score…." He scoffed, and I saw him lean against the wall in my peripheral. "You'd think they'd take all their sexual frustrations out on something a little sexier than a puck. Wouldn't you agree, Eros?"

My entire body went on alert. Every muscle and feeling down to the tiniest molecule in my blood seemed to still. I knew the voice. I knew the sardonic way in which he spoke.

My left hand clenched around my drink and nearly crushed it as I peered sideways at his smug figure, and the happy mood I'd been in instantly vanished.

"What… are you doing here, Apollo?" I almost hissed.

He hadn't changed—his ear-length blonde hair remained the same messy shag it had always been, looking like he'd had someone tug and pull it to their liking just so that he appeared freshly fucked. Those usually innocent blue eyes were just as dark and hateful as they always were when he looked at me. The *perfect specimen*, as he'd been described over the years with his sculpted body and chiseled face, always shaved, clean, and effortlessly pure.

He leaned his shoulders back against the wall, his leg bent, brown boot pressed flat against the brick. Tiny streaks of what seemed like gold shimmer paint glimmered beneath his eyes in a sunray pattern.

"In town on tour," he replied with a shrug. "Just stopped by the box to see my brother when I spotted him in the regular seats with who other than his little protege. I thought… why shouldn't I, too, see my old friend? Perhaps see what he's been sinking his dick into lately since he's had such a fondness for stalking my own endeavors."

"You're easily riled up," I said. "Makes fucking with your love life all the more exciting. Tell me, have you had any more nymphs turn themselves into trees just to get away from you?"

A twinge of annoyance ticked in Apollo's jaw, nearly making me smile.

"One day, you'll realize what a mistake that was," Apollo said as he pushed off the wall.

I set my drinks down on the counter again, a soft chuckle escaping me as I sized him up, facing him again, our torsos aligning.

"Yeah? What are you going to do about it?" I asked. "Millenia's later, and I still haven't felt this so-called wrath and regret you once promised me."

The left corner of Apollo's mouth flinched as he huffed amusedly and stepped back. "It was nice seeing you, nephew," he said, the smug smile on his lips making the blood in my body stop circulating. "Be sure to tell your adorable little girlfriend I said 'hello.'"

The devious glint in his eyes made my stomach hollow. I stared after him as he left down the hall. A vicious urge reared its ugly head from deep within me. I wanted to follow and make him regret ever mentioning her, ever *looking* at her.

Because if he ever touched her…

The end-of-the-period buzzer went off, and I ambled back toward our seats, but not before pausing at the stairs to text Ares.

You didn't mention your brother was here, I texted him.

He only dropped by to say hello. Has a show to get to, Ares replied. *Why? Did you bump into him?*

Something like that, I replied. **Is he leaving for good? I don't want him anywhere near Chloe if I bring her to the box for the last period.**

He won't be back. His gig is across the complex, a half-mile away. He's onstage in twenty minutes.

People began making their way up the stairs. I stuffed my phone in my pocket and descended to our seats. Chloe was stretching when I reached her, the oversized team jersey rising just enough that I could see where she'd tucked a small section of material into the black high-waisted shorts and stockings she wore beneath them.

"You missed the best goal of the night," she said as I reached her. "Fucking amazing five-hole. Goalie never had a chance."

I smiled at her enthusiasm. "How do you like these seats?" I asked.

"I've never been this close to the ice before," she said. "It's insane. A little overwhelming at times, but amazing. My ears are a little numb. Am I talking too loud?"

"Do you want to go somewhere quieter for the last period?" I asked.

"Like where?"

I gave an upward nod to the box, and she frowned. "How the fuck are we getting in there?"

"I know a guy," I said. "But it's up to you. And if you get up there and prefer to be down here, we can always come back."

"Who's the guy?"

"Ah… possibly my father, though there's been some debate about it," I answered truthfully.

The light in her face waned, along with her smile. "Wait, you mean… like another…." She glanced around us for any onlookers. "*Another god?*" she mouthed.

"Does that scare you?" I asked.

"A little, yeah. That is if you're not full of shit," she answered, arms crossing. "You still haven't proven it."

"I will, baby," I said. "One day, I'll show you." I stared at her another second, then nodded toward the box. "What do you say?"

Chloe's gaze moved upward again, debate twisting on her pursed lips. "Is it Ares?" she asked.

"Yeah," I answered.

"Is he hot?"

I huffed, running my hand through my hair. "I mean…"

She laughed as she pushed past me. "You're cute when you're nervous." Her right foot landed on the bottom stair, and she jerked her chin upward. "Let's go, Eros. Introduce me to *Daddy*."

I nearly fucking lost it at the teasing glint in her eyes. The way she'd said my name, then ruined the entire moment by calling Ares… *that*. "Please never call him that again," I managed, grabbing her by the waist as I caught up with her. "Fucking gods. I'm begging you."

"That's all going to depend on what he looks like," she said.

"I've changed my mind," I said as I tried to drag her back down.

"It's too late," she said, tugging me forward. "Let's go."

Ares met us at the club level, giving his security a clap on the shoulder before ushering us up.

Chloe blushed as Ares kissed her hand, and I shoved him for being his usual self.

Though, when Ares led us toward the entrance to the box, Chloe turned around, delight on her face, and she mouthed "Daddy" to me with a grin wider than I'd ever seen. I grasped her arms and pulled her struggling figure into me, her back against my front. She kept moving forward as a laugh left her, slipping from my arms and instead entwining her hand in mine. The contact and precise fit wrenched my stomach.

My mother was watching the game when Ares opened the door. Chloe slowed slightly as my mother turned around.

Aphrodite's eyes widened just noticeably, her hands clamped on her elbows, but that was all the movement of recognition she gave at the sight of Psyche.

"Someone I forgot to mention," I said to Chloe as we approached Aphrodite. "My mother. Mother, this is Chloe, Chloe… meet Aphrodite."

Chloe's mouth hung open in disbelief, and my mother seemed to revel in that surprise.

Her stern face softened, and jaw clenched like she was holding back emotion. "Hi, Chloe," she said, sounding like she was greeting an old friend. "It's good to see—meet you," she nearly slipped up.

I had to nudge Chloe in the side just to break her out of her stupor.

"Oh… oh, fuck. You're *gorgeous*," Chloe said, and I wasn't sure she'd meant to say it. She covered her head with her hand, shaking her head. I'd never seen her embarrassed like that.

"Sorry, I meant to say it's nice to meet you," she recovered. "Gavin didn't say anything about his mother being here," she added with a glare my way.

"Would that have deterred you from coming up?" Aphrodite asked.

"I definitely would have gone to the restroom to make sure I was presentable first and didn't have chili on my face from the hot dog I ate earlier," she said with a nervous laugh.

Aphrodite beamed. It was a slight smile that wasn't sarcastic or full of malice. But rather, one that told me she was genuinely trying, or perhaps seeing Psyche in the flesh again after all these years, had her wanting to be civil.

Of course, it could have been my threat to never speak to her again.

Either way, it was a pleasant change.

"Hello, son," she said before hesitantly hugging me. But

once I was in her arms, she seemed to relax.

"I'm sorry," she said in my hair.

I appreciated those two words more than I did anything else.

My mother's attempt to be friendly and give Chloe a chance impressed me. She offered her a drink and asked about her work and life. She even made a joke about her spending time with me. And by the time Chloe made her way over to me, standing by the edge of the box, my mother seemed more at ease than I'd seen her in centuries.

"Everything okay?" I asked.

"You know, I thought your mother would be a pretentious bitch, but she was actually very nice," Chloe said.

I smiled as I sat in the seat behind us. "That's surprising," I said. "Although it makes me happy."

Chloe was staring at me when she sat down beside me. I gave her chin a quick flick, making her grin widen, and asked, "What?"

"Thank you," she said.

"For what?"

"For not lying to me," she said. "For introducing me to them as they are to you, not giving me false names or some lie. Although, now I am wondering how many other gods I've met that are parading around as normal people."

I chuckled softly. "I'll introduce you to all of them," I said. "Except Apollo."

"What's wrong with Apollo?"

"He's an asshat who doesn't deserve your presence," I replied.

"Wait, didn't you two get in some fight about a girl?" she asked, apparently pulling some memory of a myth she'd read in the past.

I sighed. "Long story short, he insulted me, and I got revenge by striking him with a love arrow and striking the nymph he fell in love with with a blunt arrow. She ended up hating him so much that she turned herself into a tree." I almost laughed as I remembered.

"That's a little mean," Chloe said.

"It was very entertaining at the time," I said.

"I'm sure he didn't think so," she said. "How would you feel if someone took away the love of your life?"

Someone did. Someone stole you from me, and my mother erased you from history to shield me from the pain of it—was what I wanted to say.

"He's had plenty of lovers before and after," I said instead. "Believe me. Right now, he's touring as a musician. He has all the groupies he wants."

Chloe stiffened slightly. "I once dated a musician," she said in a small voice.

"What happened?" I asked.

"Ah…" she looked down at her hands, her hair falling over her eyes. "I had to delete all social media and move apartments."

Her gaze lifted to mine as my heart plummeted. I thought she might say more, but she leaned back in the seat and slid sideways, her body molding perfectly into mine, and I draped my arm across the back of her chair.

"Soon," she said.

I kissed the top of her head and squeezed her shoulder, but I didn't reply. I was eager to know who had hurt her so badly that she'd tried to erase herself—if she would even tell me his name. I wanted to know who had made her so scared of love, so afraid to be with someone she might fall in love with, that she had thought it safer to settle for someone she barely liked.

I wanted to know who had thought they could bruise her soul as they had and whose name I would be writing on an arrow not designed for love or spite but for an eternal prison within their mind—driven into madness by solitude in complete darkness.

I hugged her a little tighter at the thought.

Her adrenaline was fading without the boost of the crowd and the fighting players in her face as we sat there. But I savored that closeness as the game went on.

"I think I want to go back downstairs," she said a few minutes later.

"Why?"

"Because the longer I'm this close to you without the noise of the crowd and the distraction of the players in front of me, the less willpower I'm capable of maintaining, especially with how sexy you look in this backward baseball cap." She glanced back over my shoulder. "And—"

"You think I'm sexy?" I interjected.

She stifled a coy smile and pushed her hair over to one side, revealing the shoulder that her oversized jersey kept falling off. Greed lifted her dark eyes, so much that I nearly pulled her into my lap, shoved the rest of the people out of the box, and then spanked her over my knees for testing me like this.

"I'm ignoring that question because you know damn well how sexy you look tonight," she said, prompting me to grin wider.

I jerked my chin upward. "What's the other reason you want to go back downstairs?" I asked, my voice deeper.

Her thighs brushed together like she was desperate for friction, which didn't help my need for her. Gods, this fucking night. I didn't know how I was supposed to just let her go at the door later.

"And..." She shifted in her seat, wholly facing me. "I honestly don't think I should lose that kind of control in front of your *very* overprotective mother."

I chuckled under my breath. "What gave that bit away?"

"Oh, I don't know. Maybe the way she drilled me," she said, though she didn't seem put off by it.

"She said she would behave," I said.

Chloe laughed. "She was very nice about it. I imagine she treats all of your girlfriends like that," she said.

Both of us had spent half of the night forgetting about the ring on her finger, yet with those few words, the memory of what we were crashed upon us like cold water.

She swallowed, clearing her throat, and her eyes downcast briefly to the floor. "Downstairs," she said quickly.

We said our goodbyes to Ares and Aphrodite, and my mother looked like she was on the verge of tears as I pulled back from hugging her.

"Eros, I need to talk to you," she said softly.

"Not tonight, Mother," I said, almost pleading for her to let me go.

"Come home then," she said. "Please. Before Zeus's party. I need to talk to you."

I glanced at Ares, who shrugged, then back to her. "Is everything okay?"

"No. No, I…"

Ares slid his arm around her. "Just come home before then."

I wasn't sure what she was being so weird about, though I didn't have time to get into it then. Chloe was standing at the door waiting on me, and I let Aphrodite go to follow Chloe back downstairs.

"Everything okay?" Chloe asked.

"I'm not sure," I replied. "She gets weird sometimes."

"So, about what I said a few minutes ago—"

"It's fine," I said, assuring her I knew it was a slip-up. "I know what you meant."

We didn't speak again as we made our way to our original seats, and when we arrived, we were greeted with high-fives and shouts of happiness—or, rather, Chloe was. She continued cheering for what was left of the game, though I sat in contemplation and only watched her.

At one point, she took my hat from my head and put it on her own, causing my entire body to erupt in restless desire.

Fuck.

She would have to take it off before I got in any vehicle or elevator with her.

I would lose my fucking mind if she didn't.

When the final buzzer blew, she and the other fans around us celebrated, and she even bent down to hug me.

After a few minutes of chatting with the others and coming down from the high of the game, Chloe sighed and paused before me. A hum surrounded us with the murmurs of fans leaving. I spread my legs, and she settled herself there, her legs hitting the edge of the seat I was sitting in.

"Tired?" I asked her.

"Exhausted," she said.

I smiled crookedly as I peered around us, people piling out of the stadium in a push, and when I glanced at her again, I couldn't help reaching out for the hem of her shirt and toying with it between my fingers. She was irresistible. I wanted to touch her every chance I could, even if it were just the hem of her clothes or a whisper of her delectable thighs.

Gods dammit, these fucking thighs.

I needed her to wrap them around my face.

"Do you want to chill out here, or are you in a rush to get home?"

"Which one involves more time with you?" she asked.

I sat up, my breaths short as I stared at her standing between my legs, her shorts digging somewhat into the tops of her thighs. I let my fingers tickle over those stockings and run under the distressed hem.

"Here," I said.

Her bottom lip sagged when I touched her. "I like when you do that," she said, her eyes still on me. "When you touch my thighs like you can't resist them."

"I can't," I said as I sat up more, my left hand following the same movement as my right; thumbs brushing under the hem, as my other fingers clasped the backs just below her ass. I massaged her flesh as we stood there, staring at one another in a moment we couldn't control. She pushed her hand through my hair, making goosebumps rise, and I groaned under my breath.

"I like when you do that," I managed, leaning in to kiss her stomach below her breasts. "When you push your hand through my hair like you're using it as a handle."

A smile flickered on her lips. "It's a good handle," she said with a tug.

I huffed under my breath and leaned forward, mouth catching on the button of her shorts. "Are you ready to get out of here?" I asked.

"I don't know," she said. "I'm quite enjoying this thigh massage."

I pinched her ass cheeks, making her jump, and she pulled at my hair, tilting my head back.

"The massage can continue in other places at your apartment," I said. "Or in the car. We have a driver, you know."

"I'm not getting naked in the car," she said.

"I didn't say you had to, however now that I know you *want* to…." I started to bury my face between her breasts, but she hauled me away with a laugh. I sat my chin there instead and peered up at her.

"You're so fucking beautiful," I whispered.

Another chuckle left her, and she pushed me away, stepping out of my grasp. "You're an absolute flirt," she laughed.

"I need my hat back," I said.

"Oh? Why? You don't like it on me?"

"That's the problem. I like it too much on you," I answered. "All I can think is how sexy you'll look wearing it with tiny shorts and tall socks, your hair laying over your breasts—"

"That's very specific," she said, her grin wide. "Should I leave you to your fantasy? Get my own car home?"

"Don't you fucking dare," I hissed as I stood and reached for her arm, pulling her back into me and making her gasp.

She gripped my shirt, and I slipped my arms around her waist to secure her body against mine, not caring that the security guards were beginning to usher people out.

She was in my arms, and if I didn't quell my thirst for her, I wasn't sure how I was going to go on living.

My heart beat in my ears, all awareness of the room evacuating from my mind. Her gaze began to dart back and forth from my eyes to my mouth, lingering on the latter for longer than she should have. I wanted—*needed*—to kiss her. This was excruciating, the craving making my muscles stretch, wind, and twist in agony.

"How am I supposed to breathe when I'm this close to you?" she whispered against my lips.

I moved my hand up to her neck, the space between my thumb and forefinger resting on the front of her throat, and I tightened my hand. "You breathe when I tell you to," I whispered. "Tell me, baby, is your pussy aching as much for me right now as I am for it?"

I knew I was walking on thin ice, knowingly causing myself distress by touching her as I was. After tonight, after being so near her, laughing with her, all the stolen glances, the small touches…

Fuck everything that was keeping us apart.

"It's not," she breathed, her bright eyes meeting mine. I felt her shift, her thighs rubbing together, prompting the right corner of my mouth to rise.

"You're squirming with the fantasy of me reaching between your thighs during the ride home, aren't you?"

"No," she lied.

My gaze roamed over her face, and I increased the pressure from my thumb. "My little liar," I whispered. Our open mouths brushed, my heart staggering in response. Her grip tightened on my shirt, the gap between us enclosing. All that held me back was that final acute distance and her hesitation.

"Tell me your heart is racing as fast as mine," she breathed.

"Sprinting out of my chest," I managed. I squeezed her waist, swallowing the dryness in my mouth. "Chloe—"

The bright ray of a flashlight washed over us, breaking us from our trance. "Let's get moving," a guard said. "Move it along."

I licked my lips as I dared Chloe to do something drastic, to tell either the guard or me to fuck off.

But she grabbed my hand and pulled me toward the exit.

One of my cars was waiting for us out front.

The driver tried to talk to us, and Chloe politely conversed with him. Though, I wondered if it was just to keep her mind occupied after the entire night or to keep from noticing my hand on her thigh.

I yearned to touch her in more places than just her legs. My ears rang, body numb with desire. I wasn't sure I could walk away from this as I'd done in the past. This night felt final, like my last chance to win her back. My last chance was to tell her I belonged to her in every way, that she had my heart, soul, and everything in between.

As we pulled up to her building, I took her hand and led her inside without asking whether she wanted me there. We were the only ones entering the elevator on the first floor, and before she even made it inside, I hit the 'door closed' button to keep it that way.

She nearly tripped when I yanked her into me, the doors shutting behind her. Her chest lined up with mine. I wrapped my hand around her waist upon hearing her breath catch in her throat, a gasp leaving her as her hands moved to my cheeks.

Time stilled with the magnetism between us. Our mouths were so close, opening and closing like we could taste each other. I sensed her begin to tremble at holding back.

"It's torture being around you like this," I whispered.

"So why do you keep coming back?" she asked.

"Because staying away would be worse."

My forehead came to a rest against hers as we staggered there. And with each bell of the next floor, we drowned together. Our eyes closed, holding each other and breathing in the ease of this, the comfort and home of being in the other's arms.

"Chloe…"

"Shh…" she whispered. "Don't say anything. I want to savor this."

If there had been music, I would have danced with her. I would have spun her around and made her laugh. But it was all I could do not to close the inch between our lips.

Even when we reached her floor, we didn't move. She grappled behind her and hit the lobby button again as if that elevator ride was the last thing we would ever do together.

Fate had different plans.

The chime sounded on a different floor for the elevator to stop. We broke out of our daze and moved into the far back corner. I held onto her waist and turned her around so her back would lean into my front. An older couple and a group of friends entered the elevator with us, squishing us into that corner.

My eyes closed again as I inhaled the scent of her hair, my fingers tightening just enough on her waist to feel her recline against me. Her back on my chest, her ass against the tops of my thighs, arousing my cock. I wanted to curl my arm fully around her, dip my fingers between her legs and hear that moan in my ear as I bit her neck and teased that sweet cunt.

"Gavin..."

I couldn't tell if it was a plea to stop or go on. I glanced down at her, noting her extended neck, closed eyes, and short breaths. Her ass shifted into me, and my body practically surrendered to the feeling.

I wrapped my arm around her waist, her hand laying atop mine, and my forehead rested on the back of her head.

Fucking Styx.

Forget the rest of the people on the elevator.

Forget the rest of the world waiting outside.

Forget the reality of our situation.

Her fingers entwined with mine so perfectly, and I pulled her closer. Somehow. I wondered if this close, if this quiet and intimate, if our souls would realize who we were.

With every floor change and group of people moving on and off the elevator, my lips brushed her neck, and each time I kissed her, she seemed to sink a little further into me.

"What if we stayed here?" I whispered in her hair. "What if we created our own reality right here in this elevator and never left."

Her head lay entirely on my shoulder, and she looked

sideways at me. "What if we ran away?" she whispered. "What if we jumped in your Jeep and never looked back?"

"Baby, you say the word, and I'll follow you to the end of the earth."

The elevator dinged again. People began to move. They shuffled about, and I realized that we might have the elevator to ourselves again for a minute or two. Both of us stood breathless as the onlookers exited, and the moment the doors closed, a switch turned off in our heads.

She turned into me, grabbed a fist full of my shirt, and hauled me against her. I reached around her and slammed the emergency stop, jerking us both and making us hold each other tighter.

"I hate what you do to me," she hissed, staring at my lips.

"I hate what you do to me too."

Chapter Thirty-Three

Chloe

I couldn't stop shaking.

Fuck, after this entire night… after forgetting about the world with him for a few hours, I wasn't ready to go back to anything less. I had thought he would finger-fuck me right there in the elevator or sometime earlier in the night and had been prepared to stifle my moans and keep a straight face if need be.

Only this was almost worse.

"I want to kiss you." His breath tickled my ear, a chill running down my spine. "I want to touch you, hold you, and call you mine." The hand on my ass moved to my neck, pushing my hair back as he wrapped his hand beneath my jaw. Every muscle in my body weakened at the simplicity of that touch, of the ownership and confidence in his knowing what that would do to me.

I couldn't speak. I wanted him to touch and kiss me too. I wanted him to push me against the elevator wall and hold my throat while he plunged his fingers inside me with reckless abandonment. Each second I remained in his arms was a second closer to combustion.

And yet, I couldn't pull away.

I opened my eyes, only to be met with his. Desperation filled his gaze as the hand on my neck moved to cup my face, his thumb running across my bottom lip.

"Tell me I can never have you, and I'll walk away," he whispered. "I know what you said, but I need to know that it wasn't just you feeling lonely. Tell me I'm too late."

My heart hurt. Breath escaped me. It felt like so long since I'd sent that text, even though it had been less than two weeks. I was trembling. Broken. And the words that came from my lips were an admission that I hadn't allowed myself to admit aloud.

Not until now.

"Say it," I whispered.

"Say what?"

"Say that I'm making a mistake," I said as my gaze lifted to his. "Say that what we had was more than just a one-night stand. Say that you looked for me, and tell me that I'm not completely crazy for feeling like something is missing every time I look into Tyler's eyes."

I grasped his shirt, and his fingers creased on my waist. Pain and hunger and sorrow filled his face. He looked hurt, not for himself, but for me.

"Tell me everything my heart has begged to hear from you since I said yes to him on one knee. Tell me why when he proposed that I only thought of your face and why every time it snows, my heart feels like the pieces are still on that fucking balcony."

"Chloe…"

"Say that you're here," I continued before he could say more. "Say that you found me, and you're not leaving here without me. Say that this time, it's real."

"It was real the last time," he whispered. "I was just stupid enough to walk away from you."

"Don't."

"Don't what?"

"Don't walk away this time."

The elevator rattled and jerked, and once more, it was moving.

I released him and cleared my throat. My face was beet red and burning. I inhaled a sharp breath, intent on ignoring what I'd just said and readjusting myself to be presentable for the elevator door to open, but—

Gavin grabbed my arm and whirled me into him, his body engulfing mine, and before I knew what was happening, he kissed me.

Oh, *fuck* yes.

God, his lips. This unhinged kiss. His squeezing hands. His absolute *need* for me…

I opened up to him without hesitation, trying to claw my way into his body as he raked his way into mine. I craved it. I craved *him*. He was an addiction and obsession that I didn't want to recover from. With every hungry stroke of his tongue against mine, he claimed my body, heart, and soul.

We were a mess of chaos and desire, and we had fought this far too long to stop.

He couldn't decide where to grip me first: my jaw, my neck, my waist, my ass. Those hands moved all over me as though he could consume me all at once. His hat fell to the ground as my fingers writhed into his hair and tugged at the thickness of those ginger strands.

This was… fucking hell, this was *everything*.

I knew the kiss was wrong, and I didn't give a fuck. Not right then. Not at that moment. I'd driven myself crazy trying to deny what I felt. But dammit, he was here, and the way he was kissing me…

I was so fucking in love with him.

And for a few brief moments, I was okay with that.

The elevator door opened, and we staggered out of it, still in that embrace, too afraid to pull apart for fear that it might be a dream. Thank fuck, no one else was there. He hurriedly guided us, my back slamming into the opposite wall. His hands were all over me—my face, my waist, squeezing my ass and pulling my thigh around his hip. It was as if five years of desperation flooded us both in that kiss. Like we could devour the other's soul if we tried hard enough. I scraped and stammered and begged with my body for him to never stop. I didn't know what to do with reality if he did.

I could feel his erection against my abdomen, and dammit, I wanted him.

I wanted him *so fucking desperately.*

But Gavin staggered back, and I almost sank forward as we separated. Both of us heaved with those stolen breaths. I grabbed to the wall, my thighs squeezing at the throbbing between them.

He pressed his hands to his hips. "Tell me not to follow you to your apartment," he managed.

"Why?" I breathed.

"Because once I'm there, I won't stop," he admitted. "Chloe, I don't even think I would concede to your safe word. This is as far as my willpower goes when it comes to holding back from you, and I'm not entirely sure how I'm doing this." His tongue darted out over his lips as he gazed over my body —from my disheveled hair to my hiked-up shorts that bared my thick thighs to the V-neck hockey jersey half tucked in and falling over the lacy bra I'd worn.

He bit his knuckle, almost growling under his breath. "Fuck, and you're wearing that, too?" he said as he noticed the lace. "Tell me to get in the elevator and go home," he almost begged.

"What if I don't want you to go home?" I blurted.

His hands ran over his face, and he dropped into a squat. An agonized noise left him. And when he stood again, he braced his hands on his hips again like they were the only thing holding him back from touching me.

"I'm not fucking you out of pure lust anymore. You're going to be *mine* when I take you again," he said darkly. "You won't remember that another man ever touched you because the only thing you'll ever feel on your skin, on your soul, or inside your body for the remainder of your days is *me*. My lips, my hands, my dick. You will be wholly and unequivocally mine, Chloe. And I don't think you're ready for that."

I didn't know what to say, and he knew it.

He sighed and stepped up to me again. Hesitantly, his lips pressed to my forehead, temple, and cheek. "I'm heading to Atlanta in the morning for the weekend," he said. "There's a conference I like to attend with Zayn every year." His hands wrapped into mine, and he stared into my eyes.

"Gavin..."

"Don't make me any promises," he whispered. "Take this weekend and figure it out."

The only thing I could do was nod.

He was gone with the next chime of the elevator, and I was left in that hallway to the torture of my own throbbing heart.

Chapter Thirty-Four

Chloe

My texts with Gavin on Saturday were few. He was getting on a plane with his friend, and I was in the car with Ezzie for dress shopping starting at 9 A.M. that morning. Yet on Sunday, I woke to breakfast, a book, and a single sunflower delivered outside my door.

I hope it's not too much, the note on the breakfast bag said.

I smiled at the sunflower before looking at the small book he'd left. And when I saw the art on the front, I snorted so unexpectedly that I dropped my breakfast, trying to clap my hand over my mouth. Another note fell out of it, and I reached down to grab it.

You should have seen the cashier's face when I took this to the counter, it said. *If you already have it, let me know. I'll buy the entire library to get one you don't have if I have to.*

I had the book on my tablet, but a physical copy had yet to make it onto my shelf.

I set all of it on the counter when I went inside and grabbed my phone to text him.

Thank you, I said.

He texted me a few minutes later while I was settling in front of the tv. *I know you don't like gifts, so I tried to get you something you had use for*, he said.

Food and books are always the correct answer, I replied.

I'm heading into the conference room now. Can I video you later?

Video? Seems like a big step, I bantered.

I miss your face.

Goddamn, these butterflies.

Okay, I said. **When do you get out of the conference?**

It'll be after nine here once we get back to the hotel. Is that okay?

Yeah. I'll take a nap.

I love the way you look when you wake up.

I chewed my lip so hard that it hurt, unsure what to say next.

Gavin replied before I could.

I'll text you later.

I spent most of my day hugging my blanket around me and staring at the television. I tried reading, but my mind kept wandering to him, to that kiss. Fuck, that kiss. It had been everything. I could still feel that need in my bones, see the desperation and greed in his eyes when he'd held himself back from going to my apartment.

I had to catch myself a few times when I thought of a future with Gavin.

The need for him to be in my life was overwhelming and terrifying. Such a need that I was envisioning how to tell Tyler to go fuck himself when he arrived home the next day.

I needed to.

I needed to say to him it was over, that I had found something greater, something more than I'd felt in a long time.

However, when that thought entered my mind, I had to make myself a drink.

Giving in to Gavin meant facing the irrational fear that had lurked in my mind since meeting him that fateful night—losing myself in a relationship again, ignoring family and friends and commitments just to please him. With Tyler, he was gone so much that it didn't matter. I could continue being myself when he was gone, but with Gavin…

I knew I was possibly being paranoid after what had happened with Aidan. I didn't want to go back to that person —I *couldn't* go back to that person.

But maybe Lana was right. Perhaps I wasn't forgetting myself with Gavin. I had been myself the other night at the hockey game. I had been myself during every lunch, text, walk, and car ride. He had made me feel more complete than I ever had. More *free* to be me than I ever had, even encouraged it.

The realization made my heart swell, and I fell asleep waiting on Gavin's call.

An impatient and heavy knock sounded on my door.

My eyes opened to the haze of the living room, the television loud with the home shopping network on. I groaned at the lateness, my body aching from awkwardly falling asleep. Another knock, this one more insistent than the last. I debated whether to answer it but finally rose off the couch at the third persistent rap.

"I'm coming," I called out. "Fuck, calm down."

I was still in a daze when I reached for the knob and opened it. A man leaned against the door frame, messy blonde hair sticking out from beneath a black beanie, and a slim shirt fitted on his long, trim torso. And when his lashes lifted, revealing his dark blue eyes, all sleepiness evacuated with the plummet of my heart, and horror rushed through my veins.

His mouth quirked upward. "Hello, sweetheart."

Aidan.

I threw the door shut, except he caught it with a slam of his hand upon the wood. It propelled inward and almost hit me as I tried to bolt from his reach—

He caught me around my throat before I could sprint away. A piercing scream left me. I wailed at the top of my lungs, desperate for anyone, *anyone* to hear.

Aidan. Fucking *Aidan.*

His hand clapped tightly over my mouth, muffling my screams and making me choke.

"Shh…" he hissed, kicking the door shut behind him.

Tears sprung from my eyes. I squirmed, writhing against him. I couldn't breathe. His other hand was so secure on my throat that my windpipe felt like it was being crushed.

How had he found me?!

Fuck. Fuck. *Fuck.*

I wanted to vomit. Wanted to burst into tears and break down into a ball.

He tilted his head as he backed us closer to the kitchen. Every step felt like an eternity, one step closer to the final moment when he might decide if I wasn't his, I wasn't anyone's—just as he'd threatened before.

"Did you honestly think you could outrun me?" His voice was as terrifying as I remembered. Deep and rich and horribly sinful. "You were always so stupid." Raging eyes boring into mine, he lifted one finger off my cheek. "Promise not to scream."

I was shaking so much that I didn't know how I was still standing upright.

How had he found me?!

The sentence kept repeating in my head. A hushed, panicked earworm destined to drive me into madness. I inclined my head slowly in agreement with his question, and released my face one finger at a time. Sobs choked in my throat as my back hit the counter.

"Three years you've evaded me," he hissed. "Three years and you slip up in some rich boy's family photo, his sister bragging about her brother's wedding of the year and the pretty girl he's marrying."

My stomach dropped. God, I was going to vomit all over him. Not that he would care.

"Did you forget that you belong to me?" he asked, his face an inch from mine.

"I'm not—"

He struck me across the face, and I fell into the barstool, barely grabbing in time to stay on my feet. The sting reverberated in my skin down to my teeth.

"I told you once, Chloe," he said, standing over me. "You belong to me."

I peered through my disheveled hair, gripping that barstool so much that my knuckles were white.

The wine bottle I'd been drinking from was on the counter.

"And if you're not mine, no one can have you."

Aidan's hand threaded in my hair. He jerked me upward—

I lunged for the wine bottle and threw it over his head as he whipped me around. It crashed into his scalp, shattering over us, and I bolted. Screamed at the top of my lungs. I jumped over the couch, trying to grab my phone before running into the bedroom—

He grabbed my hair in mid-air and yanked me backward. I landed on my spine, my head slamming into the hard floor, and for a moment, I could only groan at the pain and stars behind my eyes.

"Fucking bitch."

My phone was buzzing. Gavin's name appeared on the screen. I scrambled for it, swiping the answer button in a rush. "Gavin!" I nearly screamed his name into the phone. "Gavin—"

But his slow chuckle caught me off-guard. Blood evacuated from every cranny of my body. I stopped squirming, stopped breathing.

"Did you like my surprise, baby?" he asked, his voice sinister and profound.

No.

No. No. *No.*

"Gavin?" I managed, heartbeat thudding in my ears.

Hands grabbed my ankles and snatched me in reverse. My nails dug into the rug and the floor, grabbing for the chair, even as my writhing did nothing. The couch became a blur. The rug was a distant thing that my nails couldn't catch. The living room grew darker, smaller. I screamed, screamed, *screamed*—

I bolted upright off the couch so fast that I fell to the floor.

Sweat beaded on my forehead. The television was on the same reality tv show it was on before. My heart continued to throb in my ears. I threw the blanket off me and scrambled away from the couch, the rug, the tv—everything that had just been in my dream.

Dream.

It had been a dream.

Just a dream.

Cold relief washed over me. I buried my head in my hands, tears streaming down my cheeks. My heart didn't want to slow down, even with my deep breaths.

Shit. I hadn't had a dream like that in months. The last time had been over Christmas when I thought I'd seen Aidan on the streets, but I had looked up his band and found out he was across the country. Thank fuck, Lana had been in town to keep me sane.

I rubbed my hands over my face and hugged my knees,

reminding myself to breathe.

He isn't here. There are no pictures of you out there. You're safe. You're okay.

My phone vibrated on the glass coffee table, making me jump. I was positive my heart completely stopped at the surprise. But as I slowly rose to my feet and saw the name on my screen, I sighed.

Are you awake? Gavin asked.

I didn't reply until I had gone to the restroom to put a cold towel on my neck and then pour myself a vodka soda. Gavin had texted again by the time I sat back on the couch, and finally calmed down from the scare. Though, I still made sure to tilt a barstool beneath the doorknob.

Or am I too late?

For you, I'll always wait, I replied.

You'll never have to again, he said. *Can I call you?*

I sat up and pulled the blanket around my shoulders as I opened my computer on the coffee table. **Sure**, I texted him.

The call came through, and I gave myself one more look before answering it. His face popped up on the screen, only illuminated by the light from his computer, and the shadows lit his godly features in the best way. His lips quirked on the right side, that crooked smile making my muscles weak.

My home was on the screen, and my mind eased as the remainder of that fear was pushed to the very back of my mind.

"Hey, baby," he said softly.

"Hi," I replied, enjoying the warmth and comfort in my soul as we settled into a soft lull to admire one another.

"How was the conference?" I asked.

"Fun, actually. Though, most adventures with Zayn are," he answered.

"I think we should hook him up with Lana the next time she's here," I said, solely based on the few minutes I'd spent with Zayn at the speed dating event.

"Something tells me that would be dangerous," he replied.

"Definitely," I said. "They might burn the city down, but at least it would be entertaining."

Our soft chuckles resonated in the space, and I couldn't help resting my head on the back of the couch. I could tell he was itching to say something by the intense way he watched me, like a question was just on the tip of his tongue, and he was only waiting for the opportunity to say it.

"How was your day?" he asked, though I knew that was far from his actual question.

"A little boring, honestly. I watched tv, did a little reading —"

"Did you have the book I got you already?"

"I have it in an eBook, but not a physical copy."

"Dammit," he said under his breath. "I guess I have to find more."

"You know I can't keep these books here," I said, batting my lashes. "They wouldn't fit Tyler's aesthetic."

Gavin's smile widened. "I have somewhere you can keep them."

I tried not to grin or blush, but he knew me too well, and I could hear his scoff as I pushed my hair back off my face.

"Did I wake you?" he asked.

"Not really," I said. "I woke up about five minutes before you called."

My smile must have faltered, or a solemnness threaded my voice because Gavin leaned up toward the screen, his eyes narrowing.

"What's wrong?" he asked.

"Ah… it's nothing. Just a bad dream while I fell asleep on the couch," I replied, squirming slightly. "Actually, it was more like a nightmare," I muttered.

"Was it about him?" he asked. "Your ex, I mean."

I considered telling him. He deserved to know what had happened, deserved more of an explanation than this back-and-forth I had been giving him. And if I wanted to indeed be with him…

"Yeah," I answered. "I dreamed that he found out where I was."

Hurt and frustration clouded his eyes. "That's why you deleted everything," he realized, saying the sentence to himself more than to me. "Chloe, did he hurt you?"

There was expectancy in his tone, and I avoided his gaze.

"It's not exactly something I want to discuss over video," I said. "But when you get back, once all of this is over, I will."

Gavin surveyed me quietly. "Do you know what I kept thinking about all weekend?" he asked, and I fucking hoped he was changing the subject.

"What?"

"That kiss."

I wanted to kiss him again for the shift in conversation. My heart swelled, not just with the mention of his lips on mine, but with how he seemed to ease my mind of things that haunted me.

"I don't think I've stopped thinking about it either," I admitted. "I don't think I've stopped thinking about the last two weeks with you."

"You say that like it has to end," he said.

I hugged my blanket tighter and asked, "When do you get back tomorrow?"

"Flight is early in the morning. I should be back around lunch."

"So, you're out of the office?"

He nodded. "Why?"

"I have the final design proofs for you," I said. "Ezzie told me that I needed to get you to sign off, that I had put off getting your final approval for too long now."

"How long have you had them ready?"

"Almost two weeks," I admitted.

A smile tugged at the corner of his lips. "Did you think I wouldn't want to see you if I didn't have a work-related reason to?"

"I think I was covering my ass in case anyone asked," I said.

"So, once I sign off... I'm no longer allowed to bring you coffee or lunch?"

"Nope."

"No longer allowed to text you?"

"Nope."

"What about taking you out on the weekends?"

"Not at all," I said, hiding my amusement.

"Well, we're just going to have to come up with another excuse," he said.

"Really? Like what?"

"That's up to you," he said, and butterflies swarmed my stomach.

I sighed as I stared at him, unable to keep the small smile off my face.

"What are you thinking about?" he asked.

"You," I answered. "And how I wish you were sitting on this couch with me so I could tell you everything."

"Is that the only reason you want me there? To talk?"

I scoffed. "Are you asking if I'm thinking of every way I want you?"

"Are you?"

"It's certainly possible that I was planning to dig into my toy collection tonight with the thought of you on my mind," I admitted.

"You have a toy collection?"

"Well, my fiancé is out of town a lot. So, what do you think?" I asked as my heart began to speed up.

"Like a sex toy collection?" he asked.

"Yes."

"When you say collection…."

"I don't mean just a couple," I said. "I mean, quite a few. I like exploring." I chewed on my bottom lip as a thought came to mind, restlessness suddenly in my veins. "Do you want to see them?"

Gavin's tongue swiped across his lips as he shifted in his seat. "You're going to show me your toys?"

"Does it make you feel inadequate when your partner has them?"

"No," he said. "Toys are fun. What does your fiancé think about them?"

"He only knows about one," I said. "He's a bit intimidated."

"Really," Gavin said, and I glared at the smug smile on his lips. "So, he hasn't used them on you?"

"Unfortunately not. Which is a shame. I think partner play is fun."

I could see the fantasy in his eyes—using a toy on me while he tortured me in his own way. I sucked my bottom lip behind my teeth, waiting on his response.

"Show me," he finally said.

I picked up the computer too eagerly and trotted to the bedroom in too much of a rush, though Gavin only responded to my eagerness with a broader smirk.

I set the computer on the bed and pointed it toward me as I opened my dresser drawer.

"Fuck, what kind of shorts are you wearing?" he asked.

I looked down, realizing I was wearing the shortest pajama shorts I owned, and the curve of my ass was probably hanging out of the back.

"Ah… I don't remember the brand. Why?"

"I was going to invest my entire life's savings in them," he said, still looking at my legs. "Fucking Styx, Chloe. You know what your thighs do to me."

I snorted but slapped one of my thighs and then grabbed it, teasingly indenting my fingers in my skin. "Would you like me to put on something less distracting for you?"

"Gods no," he said. "But if you turn around and find me with my dick out—"

"Gavin, I'm about to show you my sex toy collection," I said, tilting my head. "What do you think we're doing here?"

His smile slipped, quickly replaced with an eagerness I craved, and he sipped his beer. "You tell me."

My mouth flinched like it might curve upward, but I turned back to the drawer, hiding my blushing face with my hair, and laid each of my toys on the bed.

I had a few different kinds—vibrators, dildos, one grinder, and a few eclectic ones that I'd bought purely out of curiosity.

"Is that a tentacle?" Gavin asked.

I resisted laughing. "Three A.M. plus vodka, and one smutty read later…." I reached for the thing and held it up. "It's very… interesting," I said.

"Inspired by one of your books?" he asked.

"Well, the appeal there is all the suction, which, unfortunately, this one doesn't have. Maybe you should invent it," I said.

"You've inspired me," he said, and I almost laughed, but he nodded toward a couple of the smaller ones. "Vibrators?" he asked.

"Always reliable," I said.

"And the big blue cock?" he asked, and I knew he had been eyeing the dildo.

I picked it up and sat down on the bed. It was the one I used most when I thought of him, when I needed to feel that deep penetration and stretch that made me cry out. It wasn't the same by any means, but I liked to pretend it was him I was riding, whose cock pulsed inside me. My pussy began to throb as I thought about it, and I didn't realize I was stroking the dildo until I began to speak.

"Girthy, just like I like. Have to have the realistic one, of course. Suction on the bottom. And this one comes with a fun little remote," I said as I held up the black controller. "Great for those extra lonely nights."

My mouth dried when I looked back at the computer and saw Gavin's hand on his pelvis, his slight erection visible through his dark grey sweats. He took another sip of his drink, lifted his hips, and pulled at his pants.

My lip drew behind my teeth again, eyes lingering on that erection for long enough that I knew he had caught me. Gaze lifting to his, I asked, "Tell me what you're thinking," though I barely heard my own voice.

"I'm thinking how much I'd love to see you riding that cock as you rode mine," he said, and the rasping way he said it made my thighs clench.

I swallowed, heat rising on my cheeks, and I reached into the back of the drawer, my heartbeat thudding as I grasped my last toy. Gavin was smirking at me when I turned back to him.

"What?" I asked, sitting on the bed.

"I didn't realize you were actually a collector," he teased.

"I enjoy myself, okay?" I said, chuckling with him. "Is that a problem?"

"No, I love it," he said. He jerked his chin toward the pink C-shaped one in my hand. "What's this one?"

"This is my last one," I said.

"Bummer," he replied.

"No, I think you'll like this one the most," I said, making him more attentive.

"Why's that?"

"I bought it because Tyler was away so much, and I

thought it would be a fun way to be intimate while apart."

"Why? What does it do?"

"Three things: suction, licking, and G-spot simulation. And the best part? It's controlled through an app."

I watched the playful delight that had just been in Gavin's eyes fade into utter desire. *Hunger.* He shifted in his seat, tongue running across his lips once more, and he stared at the pink vibrator.

"Explain," he said.

"I actually spent a lot of money on this and have only used it once," I admitted. "It's the LoveDistance app. It connects through the QR code specific to this one." I bent over again, pulling the box out from the back.

"What happens if it connects to someone else's?" he asked.

"Then someone else is in for a wild ride," I answered.

My lashes hit my eyelids when I lifted my gaze to him again, the paper with the code on it in my hand. He had his phone out, and I knew he was searching for the app.

"Did you ever try it?" he asked.

"Not with Tyler. I've used it on myself. The app has some fun 'playlists' as they call them."

Gavin shifted in his seat again, a seriousness on his face as he scrolled through, deciphering and reading all the pop-ups that came when you first downloaded it. I was still staring at the instruction manual when I saw him reach over to the nightstand and—

"You wear glasses?" I asked, seeing the black frames he was putting on.

A smile flinched on his lips. "I'm millennia's old. Something is bound to go bad after a while. They're only for reading or if I'm staring at a computer for too long, though," he said.

God, he was hot in those fucking glasses.

"What are your other weaknesses?" I asked.

"Weak knee. Occasional ringing ear. Bad shoulder. You." He shrugged. "I could be taken out any minute now."

"Poor thing," I taunted. "So, do you want the code?" I asked him after another minute.

He looked at me over the frames. "Ah… for research only," he said, and I felt my mouth twist to stop from smiling.

"Of course." I held the code up to the screen, and he scanned it, then leaned back against the pillows again.

The bulge in his sweats was more noticeable. He kept glancing at me as he thumbed through the directions and options. Noise emitted from the toy with his first choice, and I held the suction end to my palm. My skin sucked into it as he had it on a slow setting. My gaze moved to his, and he changed it to a pulse.

"What does that feel like?" he asked, his voice husky.

"It feels like… it's too steady, I think. Should be more organic like it would be in real life," I said. "Try the licking one."

My thighs squeezed at the concentration on his face, his determination to figure this out. I loved how curious he was about it.

"You know, as the God of Lust with his own dating app, I thought you would have known about this by now," I said.

"I've heard of it, but I haven't used it on anyone," he replied. "You're the only person to have ever held my attention enough to warrant a video chat."

He changed the setting then, and a pulse moved between my thighs as I saw that he was in total control, with no playlist or specific setting. He was pressing those buttons and responding only to my face. I met his gaze, and a slow smirk spread on his lips.

"Better?" he asked.

I squirmed slightly, rubbing my thighs together, and his gaze fell on my hips, his own hand moving to his lap, where he gave his rousing cock a few slow strokes. I almost whimpered at that—just seeing how much he was turned on from merely thinking about controlling my orgasm. And when I could see his entire cock outlined beneath those pants, I sat on the bed, my mouth watering at the possibility of just looking at his dick again. *Fuck.*

He changed his rhythm on the toy, all hesitation thrown to the wind.

"Take your dick out," I said eagerly.

"Take your shirt off," he countered.

I snickered under my breath. "How about a game then?"

"I'm listening," he said.

"Maybe truth or dare?" I suggested. "That doesn't count, right? It's just a game, after all. And we're only following the rules."

His gaze stayed locked on mine for a long moment, and I wondered what was going through his mind.

"Truth or dare, sweet girl," he finally said.

My heart thumped so erratically that it plummeted to my cunt. I inhaled a sharp breath. "Truth," I answered.

"Is it true that you always think of me when you use these?" he asked.

"Yes," I breathed. "Truth or dare."

"Dare," he said.

I wet my lips as I considered him. "I dare you to take off your shirt."

Gavin smirked. "Too easy, baby." He stood and pulled his shirt off over his head, his lean muscles rippling when he moved. Fuck, I'd nearly forgotten about the tattoos all over his arms. I hadn't seen his torso since he'd been back in my life. He had a few new tattoos across his pale chest, though the one that caught my eye was the one at the right vee of his pelvis.

"Is that… is that a skeletal unicorn?" I asked.

A quiet laugh left him, and he pulled his pants down just enough that I could see the macabre drawing—and it was, in fact, a skeletal unicorn. It looked like hair was melting off the bones, the decay of that majestic creature, unlike any fantasy drawing I'd ever seen.

"That's horrifyingly beautiful," I said. "Why that one?"

"Ares and I get tattoos together sometimes," he admitted. "Sort of his way of bonding with me."

"You get tattoos with Daddy?" I mocked him.

His head sank onto the pillow. "Don't ruin this, baby," he said as he pulled his pants back to his waist, only not before giving me a glimpse of his dick and the indentions of his pelvic muscles.

I sank sideways onto one of my pillows, nearly mesmerized by the quick peek.

"Truth or dare?" he said.

"Dare," I said.

"I dare you to take off your shirt," he said.

I sat up again and pulled my shirt over my head, making sure to go slow as I did. I fluffed my hair to one side as I tossed the fabric to the ground. It was so late, I wasn't wearing a bra, and the bob I saw his throat take made me smirk.

The cold air and the look he was giving me had my nipples peaked. I grabbed my breast, squeezing and massaging it as he had done.

"Truth or dare," I asked.

"Dare."

"I dare you to tell me which toy to use first."

He groaned as I touched myself. "The one we're playing with. You don't know how hard the thought of controlling your orgasm thousands of miles away makes me."

"Slow down," I said, sinking back into the pillows and spreading my legs wide. I moved my hand between my thighs over the fabric of my shorts, feeling how wet I already was from just our talking.

"Fuck, baby," he hissed. "Truth or dare?" he asked.

"Truth," I managed.

"Is it true you want to take your shorts off and show me how wet you are?"

Fucking hell, I did. I slipped my thumbs beneath the waistband and shimmied them off, flicking them off the bed after. Gavin grabbed his computer and held it closer, his eyes so dark that I barely saw any green surrounding them.

"Gods dammit, you're sexy." He sat the computer down and wiped his face harshly. "Fucking Styx, baby. I want to devour every part of you."

I leaned back on the pillows again and spread my legs, one hand going to my pussy, the other squeezing my breast. "You want this?" I asked, a finger on either side of my clit, imagining it was his hand there and not my own.

"I want to savor you," he said. "I would crawl on my knees just to taste what's forbidden to me."

"Truth or dare?" I asked.

"Dare."

"I dare you to show me how much you want this," I said, toying with my clit.

He sat his computer on something, and I watched as he shuffled his pants off. I was parched at the sight of his cock again, yet the only drink that might satisfy me was the taste of his dick in my mouth.

I had almost forgotten how nice of a cock it was. *Fuck*, I wanted that inside me.

I reached for the dildo on the bed and saw Gavin swallow, his fist tightening on the head of his dick. Precum spilled over, and I almost whimpered at how much I wanted him in the bed with me.

Spit dribbled from my lips onto the dildo. I pretended it

was his dick I was about to put in my mouth, making me salivate more.

"I wish you were here," I admitted.

"So do I," he said. "Shit, Chloe," he managed when I stuck my tongue out to run down the shaft.

My lips puckered as I took it into my mouth, slowly making it disappear and hitting the back of my throat. I hummed around it, and Gavin cursed again.

"You're going to make me come," he rasped. "You don't know what the sight of you doing that does to me."

I removed the dick from my mouth and moved it between my breasts, across my stomach, and then between my thighs. "What does this do to you?" I asked as I positioned it at my entrance.

His chest caved.

I *loved* this.

I loved watching what I did to him without even being in the same room. He swallowed and began to stroke himself quicker. Harder.

A sharp gasp left me when I pushed that cock inside me, watching it slowly move in and out of my pussy as I worked it. I had to adjust myself on the mattress and move the computer slightly so he could see better.

"That's it, baby," he hissed. "You can take it. Put me inside you."

The words sent me further down the rabbit hole.

"Fuck, Gavin," I said, twisting that dildo, my hips moving as I got used to the fill. I grabbed the sheets with my other hand, my head throwing back onto the mattress.

"You're so fucking beautiful," he said. "Taking that cock like the good little whore you are."

My delighted eyes flew open to the computer, surprised he had called me that. A lump of yearning formed in my stomach, my teeth chewing the inside of my mouth to keep from smiling, and I swore my pussy throbbed around that dildo.

He smirked at me like he knew the answer to his question before asking it, yet he wanted to hear me say it nonetheless. "Is that too much for you?" he asked in that throaty rasp that I loved.

"Fuck no," I said breathlessly. "Keep going. Tell me I'm your dirty whore."

He snickered under his breath. "Tonight, you are, baby," he said. "Look at you. Salivating for another man while your fiancé is across the world." He tutted his tongue. "So greedy."

I had the toy nearly all the way inside me, and my back arched off the bed to take it in further.

"How many times have you imagined me when you use that, baby?"

"Every time," I said, my mouth open to the ceiling as I squirmed at the fill. Behind my closed eyes, I saw him above me, thrusting his cock torturously inside. I imagined him holding my wrists flat into the mattress, securing me in place.

"One day, you're going to take me and that toy," he said. "Do you think you'd like that?"

"Fuck, yes," I managed.

"Tell me how it feels inside you," he said.

"Full," I managed. "Full and—*god*, I don't know if I can take much more," I added as I arched my hips to match the movement of my hand. "Shit, Gavin. You feel so good inside me. I don't want to stop."

"Don't stop, baby," and I could tell by his stiff voice that he was reaching his own end. "Fuck, Chloe."

I looked at the computer. His head was thrown back, that strained expression on his beautiful face. My pussy pulsed, and I took advantage of his lapse in paying attention to me.

"Right there," I said, slipping the cock from inside me and eagerly sitting up so I could watch him. I groaned with the release of it in my swollen pussy, my insides aching for that finish. Nonetheless, I was too fascinated by him.

"Fuck, Gavin." I gasped in a high pitch, letting every sound I'd ever made to fake an orgasm roll off my tongue. "Shit, I'm coming. I'm—Come with me—"

Every vein in his neck appeared with the tension of holding himself back. He cursed under his breath, his hand moving up and down with a squeeze and accelerated rate, and as I moaned out a scream, he spilled over his hand.

The expression on his face was absolute ecstasy. Fucking hell, it had felt good to watch him come like that.

It didn't feel like that with anyone else. I was even breathless, and I wondered if this was how he felt when he watched me.

His eyes were dazed when he finally lifted his head. When he saw me sitting up and smirking, the dildo tossed to the side, he looked like he might laugh.

"I didn't know I could make you come with just my voice," I said.

"I thought you were coming with me," he said, tongue running over his dry lips.

"God, I wish I could kiss you," I said, laughing at how cute he was.

"You're going to pay for that," he said, and my lips puckered playfully as I glanced at the one he wanted to play with.

"I fucking hope so," I said as I picked up the vibrator.

Our eyes were locked onto one another as the toy slipped effortlessly in my entrance, the C-shape curling within me, and, with a bit of adjustment, the outside suction settled comfortably on my clit. I sat back on my calves, my knees spread wide in front of the camera, and I scratched my nails down my thighs.

"All yours," I said. "Make me come, Eros."

A smirk lifted the right corner of his lips as he held that phone. "You might regret this in the morning," he said.

"Why?"

"Because I'm not going to stop."

Every inch of my body was already on edge in anticipation.

I didn't know what it was about that moment, about the waiting and not knowing what he might do, but god, I was starved for him.

And when the first stroke of the tongue moved across my clit, I let out an audible exhale.

"Fuck," I muttered, wanting to sink back into the mattress as he started his slow torture. My eyes rolled, my body becoming limp with every stroke.

"Shit, Gavin—"

"You like that?" he asked. "Look at me."

I did, and I nearly fell apart at his appearing so calm and collected there. Watching me. Controlling me. Fucking hell, it was hot. He wasn't just pressing buttons. He was responding and memorizing my every move, calculating what each setting did to me, the combination of the outside actions and the G-spot gyrations inside me.

My hips undulated against the tease as he alternated the sucking and tongue movements, the pulsing and thrusting inside me. My fingers gripped the bed sheets so firmly that the fabric began to come off.

I was an erratic mess of moans and nerves. I couldn't stop crying out his name. Cursing the air. Pulling my own hair.

I whimpered as the first orgasm poured through me. It waved over my body from my head to the tips of my toes. I could feel it in the strands of my hair.

"That's it," he encouraged me. "Moan for me, baby. Cry out my name when you come."

His name was the only name I ever wanted to moan again.

It tasted too good on my tongue, and it felt like ecstasy in my pussy. I grabbed my breast, squeezing and bruising my skin.

"Fuck, Gavin," I sang with the pulse. "God, I wish it was you inside me. I need you," I pleaded.

I heard him curse under his breath. "I love it when you talk like that." He switched settings, and I whimpered with the drive of another orgasm threading through me. "How do you like that?"

"Shit, that feels good," I cried, tears pricking my eyes. High-pitched wails left me as I wriggled on that bed, thrusting my hips at a pace I couldn't steady. I started to cry out for God, for any higher being, to let me have that next orgasm.

"Eros," My chest caved when I said it, and I heard Gavin's deep chuckle at my side.

"That's it," he said. "My little slut, calling out her god's name when she thinks she can't take anymore. Tell me, baby. Did you once call it out when your fiancé tried to please you?"

"No," I breathed, grabbing the headboard. "He never— *fucking hell*—he never warranted that kind of—shit, *Gavin*— praise," I finally managed. My trembling body sank into the mattress, and I pushed a pillow over my face, almost screaming at that edge.

"I don't think I can—"

"Yes, you can," he said, and the vibrations began to increase. "You're going to give me this next orgasm, baby, and when you do, you're going to scream my name so loud that he hears you in Tokyo."

I couldn't breathe. Every vibration was too much. I didn't know how my body was going to give in again. One after the other like this… god, it wore on me. I wanted to burst into tears and pull my hair out. The toy was constant, steadily rising. I glanced sideways, prepared to plead for him to end me.

"Gavin—"

"Come for me, baby," he said, his voice breathless. "Fuck, you're stunning like this."

"I can't—"

"You can, Chloe," he said. He pressed another button, and I think I screamed. I threw the pillow over my face again, shouting and whimpering into its softness. I couldn't take it. I couldn't catch my breath—

My eyes opened to the dark ceiling, the ceiling fan spinning around and around. I couldn't feel my body. I was spread eagle in the same position I had been in, still twitching, and I heard Gavin's laugh come through the video to my left.

"There she is," he drawled, grinning smugly at my exhausted figure.

Stars danced behind my eyes. I swallowed, realizing how dry my mouth was and how much I needed water and oxygen. My thighs... god, my *thighs*. They felt like jello. My pussy ached with the toy still inside me, and I was thankful that it wasn't continuing to vibrate.

"Did I just black out?" I asked.

"Yeah," he said. "It was glorious. I think I like this toy."

My head rolled sideways so I could peer at him. He still had on his glasses, his phone out, the light illuminating his smirking face. I flipped him off, and he chuckled softly.

"How do you feel?" he asked.

"I can't really feel anything," I admitted.

"No, I mean... are you satisfied?" he asked.

"For a toy," I answered. "I'm just not sure what I'm going to do if it isn't your tongue on me next time I feel like reaching for this toy," I said without thinking.

His smirk faded slightly, replaced with a longing that told me he was thinking of the next day.

"I don't know what I'll do either," he breathed.

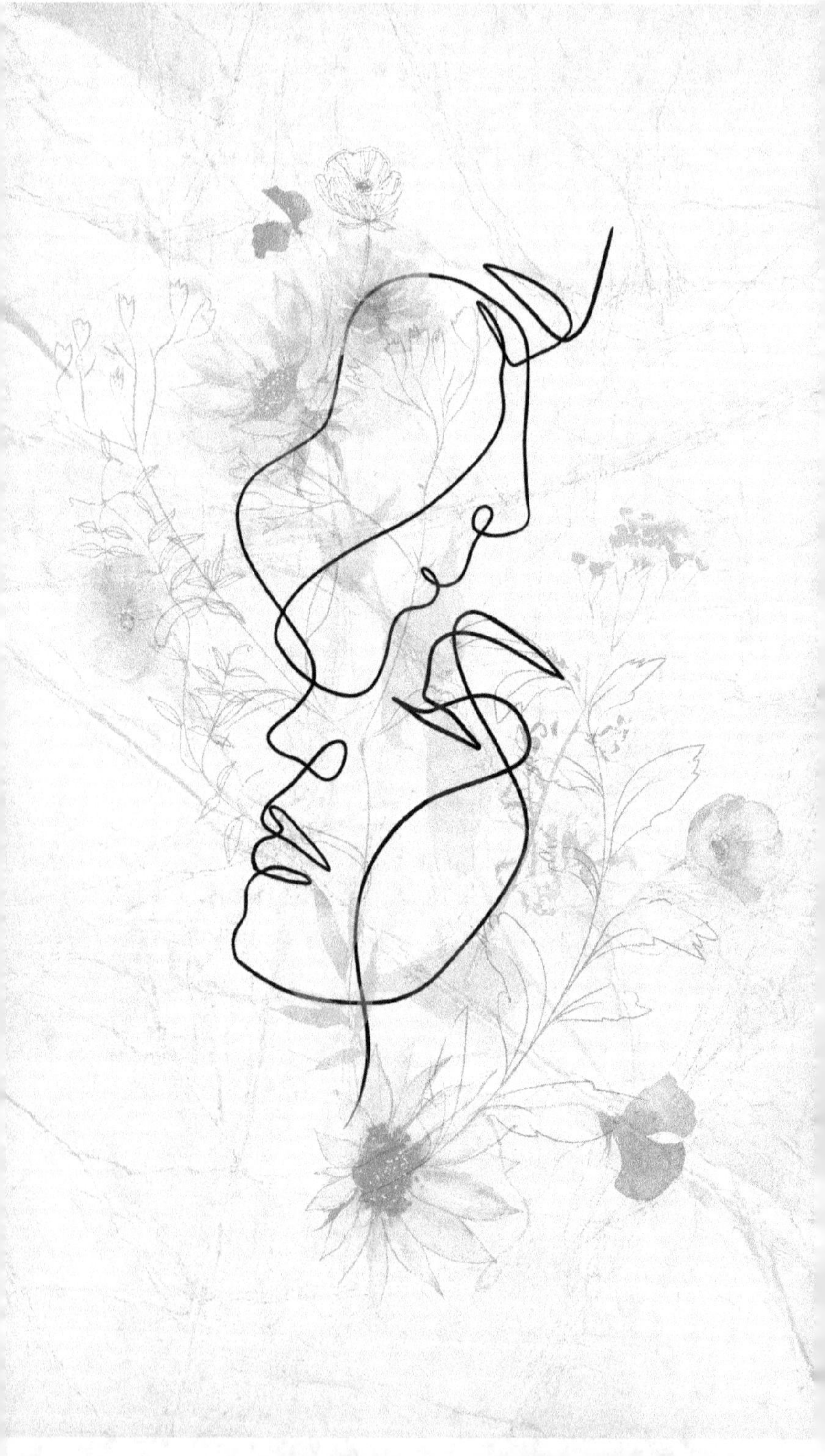

Chapter Thirty-Five

Chloe

Tyler crawled into bed with me a few hours after I finally fell asleep.

I didn't even remember he would be home that night. I'd been so caught up with Gavin that I'd barely noticed three weeks had passed. And when Tyler wrapped his arms around me, I got out of bed.

I could hardly stand to be near him. My body and mind rejected his touch. My ears rejected his voice. I wondered if he even noticed how I was pulling away from him day after day. We had hardly spoken while he'd been away. Part of it was due to the time difference, though it was also that I didn't know what to say to him.

My pussy ached as though Gavin had been with me that night. I spent a little longer in the shower to relish the hot water over my skin, letting it massage me into that haze I'd been in while videoing him. It had been like a fevered dream, so much so that I thought I might have imagined it.

A text came through as I brushed my teeth.

Hey, beautiful.

My stomach knotted as the memory of the night before flooded between my thighs.

Hey, sexy.

Did you want me to come by your office to finalize the designs?

I'm working from home today. Can you come by here after you get settled this afternoon?

Sure. Do you want me to bring food? Wine? Chocolate? Batteries? Candles? Overnight bag?

Something tells me your candles aren't the kind you light to create an atmosphere.

Absolutely not, he answered.

I smiled. **Keep it in your pants, Cupid. Tyler is home.**

Killjoy.

A quiet laugh left me, and my heart began to race as I said, **All I can feel is the ache of that toy between my legs, and all I can think about is how much I wish it had been you.**

All I can think about is how much I wish it had been me, too, he said. *I'll see you this afternoon. Think of me in the shower this morning.*

I already did, I said. **Text me when you're on your way over.**

Kicking him out?

He'll probably be gone somewhere for a meeting anyway.

So, you're saying I should bring the candles.

Gavin.

Don't worry, baby. The first time you let me touch you again, I won't be able to stop, not even if he walked in the door. I'd make him watch all the ways you were meant to be satisfied and make him feel like an idiot for ever denying you any of it.

My knight.

Your dragon.

I smiled at the screen and set it face-down before I could get so distracted by him that I didn't finish getting ready.

For twenty minutes, I enjoyed my morning coffee on my own. Lana couldn't chat that morning as she had an early client, so I took a little time to browse for my next read on my tablet.

"Morning," Tyler said upon coming into the kitchen. He

strode straight for me, his lips landing on mine as though he had genuinely missed me.

It made me nauseous.

My skin squirmed when he held my face in his hands, and I had to force a smile on my lips when he finally pulled away.

"I missed you," he said. "God, you're pretty."

My eyes narrowed. He hadn't called me pretty in… Frankly, I couldn't remember the last time he'd called me pretty.

"How was the trip?" I asked once he had released me.

"Great. The flight was tolerable. I can't imagine not having taken first-class there. Fifteen hours there, twelve back. I need a massage ASAP," he said as he approached the coffee machine.

He stretched his arms over his head, cracking his neck back and forth. I watched him, trying to figure out the best way to do this or if I was doing it that day.

Maybe I would wait another day. I wanted to have my things packed, or at least some of them. I didn't like not having a plan for what came after this. I knew it had to be done, but…

"Clo?"

"Hm? What?" I said, blinking out of my thoughts.

He smiled. "I asked if you felt better about everything," he said, coming around to sit on the stool beside me. "My mother says she's talked to you about some details."

"Yeah, we straightened a few things out," I said. "I'm never going to not be nervous, Tyler. It's three weeks."

Or one day.

I stood then, finished with my coffee, and honestly trying to find any excuse not to be near him. "Gavin is coming over to help me tie up a few loose ends on the project this afternoon," I told Tyler as I rinsed out my mug.

He sipped his coffee, elbows resting on the countertop. "Gavin, as in Arrow's CEO?" he asked.

"Yes."

"He's coming here?"

"Yeah. I'm working from home today and tomorrow," I replied. "The office is a distraction. Too many other things are going on there, and I need to focus on finishing this." I turned and leaned my hips against the counter, wiping the water out of my mug.

Tyler observed me, wariness in his eyes. "You usually don't bring clients here," he said. "Why is this different?"

"Gavin is a friend," I said with a shrug. "He's been very involved in this whole process. Why?"

"It's a little weird," Tyler said.

"Why?"

"Because he's the CEO of a major company—your biggest client—and you're bringing him into my home," Tyler said, a twinge of jealousy in his tone.

"How do you know I don't do this regularly?" I asked. "You're never here," I practically snapped.

Tyler noticed it. He was quiet for a few seconds, taking a long drink of his coffee as we stared at each other.

"You know that'll change in a few months," he said softly.

A boulder sat in the pit of my stomach. My hands clenched and unclenched on the edge of the countertop as an agitated itch worked its way through my bones.

"I've already found us a house," he said. "It's an hour from my parents on the coast."

"I don't know if I want that," I finally said.

Silence dwelled between us again.

"What are you talking about?" he asked after a beat.

My jaw tightened, and I hung my head. "I mean, I'm not ready for all of that. I'm not saying I never want it. I just… I don't know what I want anymore."

"What do you mean you don't know?"

"I mean, I don't fucking know, Tyler! Goddammit—" I pushed off the counter and tugged at the roots of my hair, walking around in a circle. "Shit, this is a nightmare," I muttered.

Tyler stood and rounded the island to come to my side. He took my arm in his hand, trying to pull me into him, but I wrenched away, and he looked at me with a tight-lipped expression.

"I thought you would work all this out while I was away. I thought you would be ready when I got back," he said. "We've been planning this move since—"

"No, *you've* been planning this," I argued. "I didn't know anything about this until a few weeks ago."

"We've always talked about living near my parents," he said.

"Yes, but I thought we were talking in like ten years. Tyler, why would I have started my own company and leased a fucking office space on the other side of the country if I was going to be out of it in less than two years?"

He stared at me for another moment. "I thought you were just… having fun."

A sardonic laugh left me, one that blurted from my lips like I was choking. "What, like a side project? A hobby?" I rested my hands on my hips and shook my head. "Not all of us have so much money that we just open up businesses for shits and giggles—"

"I told you I would help you—"

"I don't need your money," I sneered. "This was my *dream*. My own company, my own rules, my own time. I saved up for that for years. You can't just tell me I have to give all that up in six months."

"So what are you saying?" he asked.

"I'm saying I'm not ready," I finally said.

Tyler rubbed the back of his neck as he audibly sighed and stepped over to the door, where I realized a black box with a ribbon wrapped around it was sitting in the corner. I hadn't noticed it until right then.

I wanted to puke.

"Maybe this will help change your mind," he said as he sat it on one of the barstools.

"Oh, god, no. Tyler. I told you no more expensive gifts," I said, staring at the large black box.

"Open it."

I felt like my teeth might crumble beneath the pressure of how tight I was clenching my jaw. I undid the ribbon in a huff and lifted the lid—

It was a Birkin purse.

A fucking *Birkin*.

I couldn't even touch it.

Bile sat in my throat.

"What… is *wrong* with you?" I hissed, my voice shaking. "What?"

The confusion was evident. He had no idea.

"What's the matter? You don't like it?" he asked.

"The fact that you don't know what's wrong is what's wrong!" I said, nearly losing it. "Why—why, *why* would you buy this for me?" I couldn't breathe. Couldn't think. "Tyler, I lose every bag I own, or… or I spill drinks on them, leave fucking hard candy inside them and they get sticky and gross, and I have to throw them out. I am a disaster when it comes to nice things. Why would you think I need a *hundred-thousand-dollar* bag? That's half of a fucking condo!"

"Not in this housing market," he muttered.

"That's not the point!"

He stepped up to me, amusement dancing in his eyes as he tried to take my hands. I pulled back, but he grabbed my fingers so tight I winced.

"The weekend at the vineyard, my mother kept asking about your bag, your lack of jewelry, and why I hadn't found some more suitable things. You didn't even wear the earrings I got for you while you were there." He shifted on his feet, giving me a small smile as if whatever he was about to say would fix everything.

"Once we move, it will be different. You usually do those things to your bags when you're drunk, something you won't be able to do as much since your friends won't be there, and with kids running around in a few years, you won't have time for it anyway. You'll have so many new friends from mom-dates and daycare, and you'll be around my family more and all of their friends. They spend money like this on bags weekly. Jewelry. Clothes. Shoes. Don't you want a huge closet full of expensive items like this one that you can show off? Don't you want your kids to have that, too?"

I went numb.

Totally numb.

Say it's over.

Just say it, Chloe.

GODDAMMIT, SAY IT.

But my mouth wouldn't form the words. My eyes wouldn't move away from the bag.

I didn't know I was shaking until Tyler's lips landed on my cheek.

"I'm staying at Matthew's tonight," he said, moving away and grabbing his keys. "I'll be back in the morning, and I can finally tell you about this deal. I'm so excited about it, love. We can look at the houses I've picked out and figure out what you're taking and selling from that storage unit you have." He pushed his bag on his shoulder and grinned widely as he reached for the doorknob. "I can't wait. It's going to be amazing. I'll see you in the morning. I love you."

I still hadn't moved when the door closed behind him.

And it was all I could do to not collapse on the ground when I realized what I was.

A basic, pretty girl who he could turn into one of the diamonds he'd put on my finger.

I continued to tremble as I reached for my phone.

Meet me at the park instead? I texted Gavin. *This afternoon. At two?*

He texted back almost immediately. *I'll see you there. Everything okay?*

No.

Chapter Thirty-Six

Gavin

"Fuck, Seph, I don't know what I'll do if she doesn't leave him," I told Persephone as I waited in the park for Chloe later that day. She hadn't said any more than that last text, even though I had texted her multiple times, not only to let her know I was by the dog park but also to ask if she needed me to come to her as soon as I got off the plane. I was worried that something had happened, something with Tyler or even her ex—whatever that story was.

"Is it still the same as before?" Persephone asked, twirling a dandelion between her fingers. "What you remember, I mean."

"It still blanks at Delphi," I said.

Persephone's mouth twisted in thought, and she glanced back behind her at Hades, who was leaning against the tree trunk, his legs extended in front of him, one ankle crossed over the other as he'd placed Persephone's wide-brim hat over his face like he was trying to take a nap. He was dressed more casually than I was used to seeing him— a long-sleeve black Henley shirt and army green joggers. He had his firm forearms wrapped over his chest, a gold watch glimmering with the sunlight. It was a far cry from his usual business suits in the Underworld.

In the years I'd known him, I'd watched his tightly curled

black hair slowly become more salt-and-peppered. He kept it cut in a short fade, and his beard trimmed around his full lips.

Persephone reached over and nudged his leg. "I know you're listening," she said, and Hades grunted behind the hat.

"It's my day off," he said. His deep, accented voice could send a chill down anyone's spine.

"You love the gossip," she said. "Can you fill anything in?"

"I come to the park to let Cerberus be a normal dog," he drawled. "Not participate in a mystery game."

Persephone leaned back and snatched the hat off his face, making Hades glare as the sun hit his dark brown skin. He sat up and wiped his face. "Will this help us get out of here faster?"

"Cerberus is still flirting with that collie over there," Persephone said. "It'll be at least a half-hour before he decides to finally roll in the mud, thus prompting you to decide it's time to go."

"He can roll in the mud back home," Hades said.

I glanced toward the dog park where Cerberus was glamoured to look like a massive blue merle Great Dane instead of the three-headed bulldog beast he usually was. "Why a Great Dane?" I asked.

"The last time I made him look like a poodle, *someone* got angry," Persephone said.

"Watchdog of the Underworld, and you turned him into a show poodle," Hades said.

"Why can't you let him look like a single-headed bulldog or Doberman?" I asked.

"One day, we'll get over the trauma of what happened the last time he was disguised as a Doberman," Persephone muttered, her brow raising poignantly at Hades.

His square jaw tightened. "That girl shouldn't have

touched my dog," he said.

"What happened?" I asked.

"I thought we were talking about your love-life drama," Hades said, finally looking up at my pacing figure.

I stopped walking, my eyes meeting his. "What do you know?"

Hades rubbed his head. "All I know is, you, being you, should never have taken her to Delphi of all places. What were you thinking?"

I wracked my brain for the memory of that day. "I'm not really sure," I admitted. "Fuck, I can't remember. Why? Do you think Apollo had something to do with it?"

"I think the two of you have a shit past," he said. "I'm not saying he's smart enough to pull something like that off or if he has enough courage to cross you. Nonetheless, he might be worth the ask."

I scoffed. "I'm not sure I want to entertain him with the idea that he might have had the gall to do something so stupid. And I certainly don't want to seek him out."

"Are you going to Zeus's little retreat?" Persephone asked, and Hades rolled his eyes. "I'm sure he'll be invited."

"I have no idea," I confessed. "I have no idea about tomorrow, much less two months. Every day has revolved around Chloe and hoping I've done enough that she leaves her fiancé."

Cerberus ran over to the couple, nearly falling into Hades's lap as the mutt rolled over to reveal his belly. Persephone moved so she could pet him, and the beast began licking her.

"Did you hear from Chloe?" Persephone asked as she scratched Cerberus's head.

"Nothing yet," I said.

"But she was leaving him? Today?"

"Gods, I hope so," I answered. "I—"

All thought left me as I spotted Chloe coming down the

sidewalk.

She wore basic ripped jeans and a t-shirt, her straight black hair billowing behind her as she walked.

"Oh my gods," I heard Persephone say. "Oh my—*oh my gods*—"

"Fucking me," Hades muttered.

Stunned silence radiated between them. Only I was already on the move. I stepped out toward the cement, not wanting to shout her name unless I had to. Her eyes appeared swollen and pink like they'd been on the video chat the night before, and I wondered what had happened that morning to cause her such distress all over again. My fists tightened at the thought of her being hurt.

Bewilderment shone in her eyes. She was searching frantically for any sight of me. The moment I opened my mouth to whistle, she looked ahead, and she stopped in her tracks when our eyes met.

Relief spread over her face, her shoulders drooping.

I moved into a trot to meet her halfway, and when we were close, she threw herself in my arms.

I hugged her close and pulled her off the ground. Her face was red, eyes swollen and glistening. And the way she was hugging me... it made my chest hurt. She'd been so playful and more herself last night and this morning. I had to know what had changed—

Or if she'd broken up with him.

"Are you okay?" I whispered into her hair.

Her feet landed on the ground. She pulled back, and I kissed her forehead softly, her hands landing on my forearms and squeezing.

"Yeah," she said with a sigh. "Just realizing some things that I hadn't seen before. And now, seeing you... It just makes it all so much more real."

I held her cheek, my thumb brushing beneath her eye. I

wanted to kiss her. I wanted to kiss her and ask if she'd done it, except I didn't want that pressure to stagger between us.

A dog barked behind us. Chloe's eyes widened, and I realized too late that Cerberus was bounding toward us. He reared up on his hind legs, his large paws flopping on her arms. Chloe released me and grabbed his feet. The beast was as tall as her standing upright.

"Whoa—"

"Oh fuck, I'm so sorry," Persephone said as she ran to us. She grabbed Cerberus by the collar and pulled him down. "Sorry, Eros. I didn't know he would be so excited."

"It's fine," Chloe said, almost laughing. "It's fine. He's…" Her voice waned as she realized what Persephone had called me. Her brows narrowed, and she looked between us. "Who is this?"

My mouth pressed into a thin line at Persephone, knowing she'd let Cerberus free to give her a reason to intervene. But she just smiled, and I noted how bright her eyes gleamed.

"Persephone," she said, her voice a little weaker than it had been moments before.

"Ah… Chloe," Chloe hesitantly replied. "Hang on—"

"The grump back behind me is my husband," Persephone said, and Chloe looked around Persephone's figure to see Hades rising to his feet. Her face went pale, eyes wide, and she looked up at me.

"What—"

"Can I hug you?" Persephone asked.

"Um, I guess…"

Persephone swept her arms around Chloe before she could finish her sentence. Hades grabbed Cerberus by the collar and locked his leash on him, then gave a look that read an apology for how his wife was crowding Chloe.

Chloe's eyes narrowed at me as she stood there and let Persephone embrace her.

"Hang on," Chloe said, still confused when Persephone finally released her. "You're like... like *the* Hades and Persephone?" she asked.

"I don't know about '*the*,'" Persephone said.

"Oh, no, there's absolutely a 'the' in front of your names," Chloe countered. "Am I supposed to bow?"

"You meet Aphrodite and Ares, but these are the two who make you nervous?" I asked her.

"She's the Queen of the Underworld—"

"You introduced her to your mother?" Persephone asked me. "You left that part out when we spoke last."

"It was just on Friday," I said.

"She's pretty intimidating," Chloe said.

"Don't let her fool you," Persephone said. "She's that way because she wants you to think you're inferior. She's surely jealous of your beauty. It's why last time—"

"I think we've overwhelmed her enough, my love," Hades said, his hand on Persephone's elbow. "Cerberus needs a bath." He tugged her slightly, and I gave him a tight-lipped smile in response.

But Persephone couldn't stop beaming at Chloe.

"You'll see her again," Hades reminded her.

"Oh. Right. At Zeus's retreat, maybe," she said as she looked at me.

I held a hand up. "Slow down," I told her.

"Zeus hosts a retreat?" Chloe asked.

"Every few years," Persephone said. "It's—"

"Hey, Seph?" I said, trying to rein her in. "Can I give you Chloe's number later?" I asked as I tucked my hand around Chloe's waist.

A heavy, albeit nervous, sigh left Persephone as she continued to grin brightly at Chloe. "Fine," she agreed.

As Hades wrangled Persephone and Cerberus, and the three ultimately started down the sidewalk, I turned to Chloe, who was still captivated by our guests.

"You know, one day, I need you to tell me where you found all these great actors and actresses to play the parts of gods just to keep up the charade," she said, her hands resting on my chest.

Her hips pulled flush to mine, and I smiled down at her. "One day, I'll show you it isn't one."

She smiled wider, her eyes darting from my own to my lips, fingers moving up my chest to my cheeks. My heart began to stumble as I gazed at her.

"You are a beautiful torture," I whispered. "Sinful damnation from the gods."

Chapter Thirty-Seven

Chloe

I didn't see Hades or Persephone leave or have time to comprehend that they were indeed royalty or that they had glamoured Cerberus to look like a Great Dane.

All I saw was Gavin.

All I *wanted* was Gavin.

He was holding me, and I was closer to having him than I'd ever been.

There was a pull between us that left me oblivious to the rest of the world—the draw of being so magnetically attracted to someone's soul. That's what it was between us. It wasn't merely lust or something as simple as love.

My soul recognized his as its eternal partner, and I was beginning to accept that.

He pushed my hair from my face, and I covered his hand with mine, allowing his palm to rest on my cheek.

"As are you," I managed.

"I don't know if I can keep denying myself of you," he said.

"So, don't," I almost begged, staring at his lips.

He swallowed, his brows narrowed. "When are you going to tell him?"

A bucket of water practically splashed over my head. I released him and took a step back, unable to breathe at the look on his face. There was desperation in his tone, so much that I could feel how on edge he was, how he was one sentence away from losing it over this.

"Soon," I managed shakily. "Tomorrow. It isn't as easy as just packing up my things," I said. "The wedding is in three weeks. There are many things that I'll have to cancel and people I need to call and…." I hung my head. "It's so much."

"Do all that while you're with me," he said, reaching for my hand. "Just tell him. You're positively miserable. Why can't you do it tonight?"

"He won't be there tonight," I said, frustration rising. "Gavin, what do you want me to do? Just rush in in the morning and tell him it's over?"

"Yes," he said flatly.

"There are numerous things to figure out," I argued. "Where to go, what to tell people, the wedding—"

"Let them figure out what they want to do," he said. "Fuck, tell them to still have the party. Tell them to go stay at the resort. They'll have a great time regardless of if there is a wedding."

A void filled the pit of my gut. I couldn't speak as I watched him thread his hands through his hair, fists grabbing onto the roots as he twisted in a circle. His jaw was tight, pain and frustration written on his face. Seeing him like this made me want to drop everything in sight and give him the world just to see that light in his eyes again.

"Gavin—"

"Dammit, Chloe. I *love* you," he said, his head lifting to mine.

I froze. Tears pricked my eyes. I clenched my jaw. "Gavin…"

"I can't stop thinking about you," he continued. "You are on my mind when I wake up, when I make coffee, when I shower. I think about you while sitting in traffic, when I'm listening to the radio. I think about you walking down the sidewalk, and I see a butterfly. You're on my mind every minute of every day."

I smiled despite myself at that, blinking back my emotion.

"You are the person I want to sit down with at the end of the day and watch shit television with until we both fall asleep together on the couch. You're the person I want to wake up beside every morning and burn breakfast with because I can't keep my hands off you. You're the person I want to love and hold on my darkest days, the one I want to escape this world with on all the others."

His hand moved from my face to my jaw, my throat, where his thumb began torturous circles on my pulse point. My knees weakened, chills erupting on every inch of my skin, and I resisted letting my eyes flutter at the soft touch.

"I want to kiss you whenever I want and make you scream my name in the darkest hours of the night," he continued, his voice quieter. "I need to feel you, taste you, and punish you for making me feel this way."

I grabbed two fistfuls of his shirt and jolted him forward. Our lips were inches apart, and he stared down at me as I said, "How will you punish me?"

"As slowly as you've tortured me," he whispered.

I was shaking, my jaw dropping slightly, lips parting. My forearms were on his chest, our hips lined up, his other hand grasping at the small of my back.

"Tied up?" I asked.

"Hands and feet," he said as his gaze traveled over my face. "Blindfolded. Laid across my lap, then on your knees over my face. I'll watch your ass turn the most beautiful shade of red, and you'll come on my tongue as I taste just how wet my hand striking across your ass made you—"

I was glad of his grip on my waist because my knees weakened at the vision of being tied up and straddling his face. The memory of his tongue between my thighs and savoring my pussy pulsed through me. My heart was racing, and I was sure he could feel it pounding beneath his thumb on my throat.

"—All until you remember how to be my good girl again," he finished, eyes meeting mine again. "Would you like that?"

"Yes," I whispered.

The corner of his lips quirked upward, and he nudged my nose with his. "That's my girl," he breathed.

I drew a jagged breath, our parted lips so close that I could practically taste him. His forehead met mine, eyes closing as he inhaled the air around us. I began to shake again, that fear rising up within me. Talking about leaving, his telling me he loved me, all of it combined into something that I couldn't resist.

I had to tell him.

"Do you know why it terrifies me so much to love you?" I whispered.

"Why?"

"Because you remind me of him," I admitted.

"Of who?"

"Aidan," I answered. "My ex."

Gavin released me, his eyes blown and bewildered. "What… What do you mean? Chloe, I'm not like that. I'm not —"

"I don't mean what he did to me," I managed. "I mean, how consuming you are. How, when you're in my life, I count the minutes until I'll see you again. The way you make me feel… I told you once that I thought I would lose myself again just to have you," I said, swallowing as I peered up at him. "I don't want to do that. I *can't* do that."

"You don't have to," he swore. "You never have to be anyone other than yourself. You and all your perfections and all your flaws. I don't want you to ever lose sight of who you are. You never have to hide any part of yourself from me. I want you—*all* of you. Everything that you'll give me."

"I lost myself with him," I said, ignoring what he'd sworn. "I withdrew from family, friends, and work. I gave him everything. I changed myself so much, I… God, this sounds so stupid," I said, burying my face in my hands. "*I sound so stupid.*"

Gavin took my hands off my face and held my wrists. "You don't," he said softly. "You're not stupid. And you don't have to tell me if you're not ready."

"No, I want to," I said as I tried to push the pain of that shame away. "I want to because I want you to know why what's happening between us makes me want to keep pretending that it's nothing more than one night. I *need* you to know."

He swallowed, agony in his eyes as he examined me. "Okay," he whispered. "What can I do?"

"Hear me," I breathed.

"I do," he promised.

I believed him.

I tucked my hair behind my ear, bile rising in my throat. I was mortified at what I was about to do, but he deserved to hear it. He deserved the truth.

You can do this, Chloe. You can trust him, was the mantra I kept repeating in my head. I knew I could. I knew I could tell him, and he wouldn't judge or call me ignorant for how I'd felt or how I'd stayed.

I was trembling when the words began to spill from my lips, but Gavin held me, and I repeated that mantra again.

"When I was with him… at first, things were amazing. I thought, 'this is it.' This is what love should be. I felt safe, protected, and desired. He made me smile. I didn't even realize how much I was already pulling away from my family and friends, desperate to fill every moment with him. I think I feared he would lose interest if I didn't. However, after a few months, when things became more serious, he changed. He started trying to keep me home. He never wanted me to leave the house, and when I did, he accused me of cheating on him. He began checking my phone at night while I slept. He came to my work almost daily to ensure I wasn't having lunch with anyone else. He told me my family hadn't reached out because they didn't love me when it was because I had become someone unrecognizable."

"I feel like all I ever did was defend him in those early days. I said his job was hard, and that was why he was so frustrated all the time and why I needed to stay home—to make sure he was happy and taken care of, that all his needs were met no matter the cost to myself. I said he was protecting me when they asked me to join them for family dinners or even to see them. I told them he was suspicious because he'd had so many unfortunate previous relationships. I thought… I thought I could heal him. If I did what he asked, if I was the woman he needed me to be, he would learn how to love."

I paused momentarily to breathe, and Gavin wiped away one of the tears from my cheek.

"Do you want to sit down?" Gavin asked.

"No," I said. "No, I can do this."

"You can also do it while sitting if you like," he said.

I knew he was just trying to lighten my troubled heart, and I wanted to kiss him for it. But instead, he entwined our fingers together, and I squeezed them back.

"Take your time," he whispered.

I inhaled a deep breath, ready to get it out. "It took me four years to realize what he was doing wasn't protection and that when my friends had told me I had changed, they didn't mean it as an insult. They were worried about me. Only I didn't know any better. I thought that was how love was supposed to feel, that everyone eventually lost their dreams when they met the person they thought they would spend the rest of their lives with."

"What made you finally see it differently?" he asked.

"I, uh… I didn't make the coffee," I answered.

"What?"

"God, that sounds even more stupid," I said, but Gavin wouldn't let my hands go. "Fuck… Ah, one day, I woke up, and I couldn't catch my breath. All because he was already in the shower, and I hadn't started the coffee. And the panic I felt… the absolute terror and anxiety of him getting out of that shower, and I wouldn't be standing there with his coffee and bagel ready… I had a panic attack and was crying over fucking coffee."

I started trembling as I remembered it, tears clouding my vision as pure panic swam in my veins.

"And when it wasn't finished for him by the time he was ready to go, there was no 'don't worry about it, I can stop by the shop next door to the studio on the way in.' There was no reassurance that such a small mistake wasn't a big deal. No. He screamed at me. He called me worthless and stupid and threw the coffee machine against the wall. He told me I didn't love him because if I did, I would have made sure he had what he needed to get through the day. He accused me of being in love with someone else. And then, he broke up with me."

I wiped my face harshly, my heart stammering in my chest. I had to take a moment to collect myself. The memories were almost too much for me to experience again. But I would get through it for Gavin.

"It wasn't unusual for Aidan to leave a few days after an argument and return with material gifts to make up for it. Promises that he never intended to keep. And I fell for them every time, thinking I was the problem. The only difference that night was that I met Lana. I think I pushed her away so many times. I pushed and pushed, and I returned to him one more time. However, there was something about how she made me look at things, and it was like I woke up from a fever dream where I'd been a prisoner. Packing still terrifies me. Walking out of that door for a final time and never looking back… I can still remember how scary it was. We had been broken up for three years when I met you. And I think on that Valentine's night with you, I felt something I had once felt for Aidan. The desire and need for another, except it was even stronger with you. And it frightened me."

"I have worked myself to the bone at becoming *me* again," I kept going. "Some days, it still feels like it isn't enough. And I think, when I started dating Tyler, I thought, okay this is the one. This is safe. Here's someone nice, who likes me, who isn't dangerous by any means—someone I knew I wouldn't fall for so quickly I'd forget everything I'd worked my ass off for. I even still hide a part of myself when I'm with Tyler."

"Do you hide anything when you're with me?" Gavin asked.

I thought about it for a beat, letting the tear roll down my cheek. "No," I realized. "No, with you I feel like my whole self."

Gavin's forehead came to a rest against mine. He held my hands between our bodies, and for a moment, neither of us spoke. My entire soul had been laid out before him. Everything that had molded the person I was, he now knew.

"He doesn't deserve you," Gavin whispered. "Neither of them did, and fuck, I'm not even sure I do. You deserve to feel what love is. You deserve to be your complete self. You deserve to be happy and loved and desired, and I will do that. I swear to you, Chloe. Every day, for the rest of eternity, I will be everything you need me to be. You'll never have to worry about whether you've lost a part of yourself. Because I love you, and I love you for who you've allowed me to see. The *real* you. I love you for every freckle on your shoulders, every person you flip off at a hockey game, for your smutty books, and how you don't know what your face is doing when you think someone is crazy—"

A blurt of a laugh left me, and he smiled slightly in return.

"Believe me, Chloe," he begged. "For every moment of every day, for the rest of our lives. Let me love you."

"I don't want to be scared anymore," I managed.

"You don't have to be," he promised.

My eyes closed as we settled there, my hands on his cheeks, the noise of the beach so close and yet so far. A weight had been lifted off my shoulders, and I felt so much more at ease. I just had one thing left to do, and I had to do it, no matter how much it scared me or how much I dreaded doing it.

I had to do it.

For my soulmate.

"Leave him," Gavin breathed then, his voice shaking. "Leave him so I can give you everything."

My heart dropped. It shattered onto the floor, leaving a void in its wake. Gavin hugged me closer. I wanted to tell him I would. I wanted to tell him I was his, that I would pack my things and run away with him anywhere he wanted.

Because he was my person. My forever.

My soul was his, and his was mine.

But fucking hell, I didn't know where to start.

"I will stand by your side as you do," he said. "I'll bring you boxes and pack up your clothes, toothbrush, and every book you own. You don't have to do it alone. You don't have to fear walking out. Just... leave him, " he pleaded. "I've lost you twice. I can't lose you again."

I started to pull back, to tell him he would never have to lose me again, that I just needed a few days to pack my things and talk to Tyler, but slowly, I felt him sinking in front of me. Dropping down to one knee, hands still clenching me like he couldn't dare let me go.

"Love me. *Marry* me," he said, and a sob choked in my throat. He reached for my hand and brought it to his lips, my heart nearly exploding in response seeing him this way. "Marry me in the mountains of Greece, in your black dress with a bouquet of sunflowers," he whispered. "Just us."

Tears escaped my eyes and fell down onto our hands. I couldn't breathe. Fuck, this *pain*. This absolute agony. I didn't think it was possible to love someone this much.

But god, I did.

I fucking did.

I sank to my knees as he bowed again, and I took hold of his face. I didn't know what to say. I held him, my forehead sinking to his, and he wrapped his arms around me.

"If you need me to beg, I will," he whispered before pulling back to look at me. "I will plead, steal, and do anything else you need me to do. Just say you'll return to me when you leave here today. Say you won't run. Say you love me and are as much mine as I am yours."

I wiped away the tear falling down his face. "You don't have to beg," I breathed. "I'm already yours."

Trembling, we held each other, both too afraid to let go of the other. I wanted to kiss him so badly. My mouth opened and closed a breath from his, quaking in the magnetism of his presence, our bodies and souls yearning for that closure.

I wasn't sure he believed me, and I didn't blame him. Although it was the truth, I was his and had never known how to be anything else. No other relationship could compare to what we had.

"I have to go," I whispered as I released him.

Gavin launched to his feet with me, reaching for my wrist again to pull me back. "Chloe, wait—"

"Gavin, I have to go," I nearly pleaded.

I wasn't running from him. I just needed time to think of how to do this and get what I wanted without severe repercussions.

"Chloe—"

"I need time," I blurted as I met his eyes. "I'm not running. Let me figure this out," I added a little more softly.

He swallowed, his chest falling, and he took a step back. "Okay."

My throat was dry. I wanted to hug and kiss him. But I couldn't. Not yet. He deserved more than a tarnished kiss and touch with this godforsaken ring on my finger.

I stepped up to him one last time, my forehead to his, my hand to his cheek, and he hugged me close. "I'm not running. I swear," I whispered. "I'll come back to you."

I didn't say anything else before bolting off down the path.

Chapter Thirty-Eight

Chloe

I nearly wrecked driving to the apartment.

Tears clouded my vision. My heart, or whatever was left of it, felt like someone had taken a sledgehammer to it. My back ached with the weight of my own anxiety.

When I got to the apartment, I sank against the back of the door and cried. I sobbed for every time I'd put off what I'd known I should do three weeks ago. I wept for the pain I'd put Gavin and myself through. I cried for every day that we'd found ourselves torn apart by my own fears.

That stupid Birkin bag was waiting for me on the counter.

I finally answered Lana's call after I'd cried myself into the shower floor and then laid in the cold bed staring at the ceiling for a while. I imagined how Tyler and our families would react to my calling off the wedding. God, it would be a disaster. However, I had to.

I couldn't go through with it.

I was in love with Gavin, and he was who I wanted to spend my life with.

Happily.

I poured a glass of red wine as Lana told me about her day.

I hardly heard what she was saying. All I could think about was how just one look between Gavin and I could

"|

spiral us into madness. But that's what we were—one breath away from losing all control just to have the other.

I barely noticed that I had stopped drinking my wine and was instead wiping the counter and drying dishes, or even that Lana had stopped talking and was staring at me.

"Babe—earth to Chloe—" I finally heard her say, snapping her fingers at the screen.

"What—Oh, sorry," I managed, breath leaving me.

"What's wrong?" she asked.

"Sorry, I just have a lot on my mind," I said.

Lana took another long swig of her water. "Like?"

The bag snagged my attention in the corner of my eye. I almost turned my wine glass over the top of it, but I couldn't bring myself to do it.

I picked it up and held it in front of the screen, and Lana choked on her drink.

"Is that—"

"Yep."

Lana picked her phone up and held it closer to her face, clearly in disbelief at what I had on my kitchen counter. "Shouldn't you have on gloves when touching that thing?"

"Probably," I said, turning it around. "I'm thinking of pouring this bottle of wine in it and setting it on fire, though."

Lana gasped. "Bitch, no. That's... Fucking hell. Well, on that note, I need you to tell me if I should change my flight."

I sat the bag back in a safe spot far away from the wine. "What do you mean?"

Lana raised a knowing brow. "You're getting married in less than three weeks, and while I would love to wear my sexy dress, enjoy some expensive, delicious food, and hopefully get railed over backward in the coat closet, I would also love to see you genuinely happy. So, I need to know if I should change my flight."

My cheeks heated, and I began absentmindedly wiping my

counter again, staring at the ring on my hand. Emotion pricked my eyes and burned my nose. I clenched my jaw to pull it back, but I could barely hide it with Lana.

"What do you want me to say?" I asked, my voice shaking. "What… Lana, how am I supposed to do this?"

Our eyes met, and she gave me a tight-lipped expression of sorrow.

"There are nearly three hundred guests," I said, unable to hold it in. "Everything is paid for. Food, tables, photography, my dress, the band, the fucking coordinator. Not to mention the guests coming in from all over the world. Tyler's uncle is coming in from Saudi Arabia, for fuck's sake. I just…" I slumped into the chair, setting the phone against the bowl in the middle, and sank my head into my hands.

Lana chewed on the licorice rope she was snacking on, and I could feel her scrutinizing gaze.

"Do you remember when we first met?" Lana asked.

"You picked me up at a bar," I replied, recalling how she'd happily sat beside me and started chatting like we'd been friends for years.

"Hell yeah, I did," Lana said proudly. "Not the point, but after a few drinks, you said something that has stayed with me ever since. Do you know what it was?"

I remembered, and it knotted my chest. "I said, 'I wonder if true love only finds you when you find yourself.'"

"You figured out who you were after that horrible relationship," Lana said. "It was damn hard, but you did it. And then, when you least expected it, Gavin walked into your life. I know you think you weren't ready for him then, but I think you were. You started to believe he was a just one-time find, and so then when you met Tyler, you settled because you had given up on ever seeing Gavin again. But Gavin is here. And you're not happy. Why not give yourself a chance to actually be happy?"

I stared at her without a response, then picked up my wine and downed the entire glass. Lana was finishing her own when I grabbed my bottle to refill.

"Babe, if you had been happy the last few years, I'd be telling you to tell the supposed God of Lust to take a fucking hike and leave you the hell alone," Lana continued. "Truthfully, I'd be calling and telling him to fuck off myself."

"So *how* do I do this? I don't even know where to start."

"Where is Tyler?" Lana asked as she opened up her laptop.

"He's staying with Matthew tonight. They're trying to figure this whole deal thing out. He'll be back tomorrow night. I don't know if he even realized how livid I was this morning."

Lana didn't speak immediately and instead typed away on her keyboard. "Okay. So you have almost a full day to pack."

"And nowhere to go," I muttered.

"Don't worry," she said. "I got you." She hit a few more keys and toyed with the tracker pad for a few more seconds before smiling triumphantly at the screen. "Booked you at that boutique hotel on the surf you wanted to take me to."

My heart was sinking further and further, my stomach weaving into a churning braid of fear and nausea.

"I'm genuinely doing this," I whispered. "I *can* do this."

Lana sighed as she closed her laptop. "Yeah," she said softly. "Yeah, you can. Because you deserve to be over-the-moon, truly happy, not mediocre happy, and turned into someone you're not."

I took a long look around the condo. "I wish you were here," I admitted.

Lana picked up the phone and held it closer. "So do I," she said.

"Change your flight," I almost begged. "Come for moral support, not to see me in a ridiculous dress."

"Oh, I'll see you in that dress," Lana said. "You're going to wear it while we jump off a cliff, and then we can burn it on the beach."

"Twelve thousand dollar dress and we're going to burn it?"

"It'll be the most liberating thing you've ever done," she said. "I'll be sure your god is waiting for you back at the hotel."

My heart fluttered at the thought of Gavin. "He told me he loved me today," I said. "Even got on one fucking knee and asked me to marry him in Greece."

Lana choked, nearly spitting up her entire drink. "He—whoa. What did you say?"

"I told him I needed time. This was after I told him about Aidan," I added.

"You told him everything?"

"Most of it," I said. "I wasn't entirely prepared to tell him what happened when Aidan found me that summer. If Gavin is a god, I hate to know what kind of wrath he might bring down on someone for that."

"Aidan deserves it," Lana muttered. "How long did you tell him you needed?"

"I don't know. A day?"

Lana slumped back in her chair with an exhausted groan. "Fuck all, Clo," she grunted. "You've been blue-balled for weeks now. When did you even have sex last?"

"Like actual sex or…."

Lana's brows raised. "I'm sorry. Have you been holding out secrets on me?"

My lips sucked behind my teeth, and I looked down, avoiding her gaze.

"You fucking bitch," Lana declared. "What!"

"It was just an orgasm," I said, thinking about the storage room. "He didn't even touch me. And then the other night on video chat—"

"You had video sex with him and didn't tell me?!"

"I'm still trying to figure out if it was a dream," I said.

"What about with Tyler?" she asked. "When was the last time you had sex with him?"

"May," I answered. It had been hard for me to get in the mood with Tyler when I could only think about Gavin.

Lana threw her hands in the air. "So, since Gavin came back?"

"Like two weeks after, yeah," I said. "It just… it hasn't felt right. Any intimacy with Tyler has felt more like I was cheating on Gavin than the other way around. There's something… it feels different with Gavin. And I don't just mean love. I mean… it's something more profound. It's like my soul craves his, and I know that sounds crazy coming from me—"

"You have no idea how proud that makes me," Lana beamed.

Heat filled my cheeks, and I didn't know if it was from thinking of him or the red wine. I sighed and looked around at the state of my apartment, and the realization of why it had never felt like a home seemed to hit me.

"Where do I start?" I said softly.

"You grab one suitcase, just like you did the last time, and you put everything you can't live without first," Lana said. "Because in the off-chance you don't get to come back, at least you have that."

I swallowed the lump in my throat. "And after?"

Lana smiled. "I think you know."

Chapter Thirty-Nine

Gavin

I paced back and forth in front of the windows overlooking the beach in my apartment, my hands wringing behind my neck with anxiety. My stomach hadn't stopped twisting. My heart hadn't stopped pounding. I had tried to go for a swim, watch a movie, and even work, but nothing could sway my mind from the turmoil tearing me down.

I'm not running.

The words kept repeating over and over in my head, along with the look on her face when she'd said it, the tears in her eyes. I think I'd blacked out when I'd fallen to my knees.

Gods, I was fucking desperate.

I kept looking at my phone, thinking she might text and ask me to help her pack or pick her up, but the minutes had turned into hours, and I had nearly chucked my phone into the ocean out of frustration.

Sunset had long passed by the time I collected myself enough to order food. Hunger had eluded me, yet I knew I needed to eat or at least have food in case…

In case she showed up.

I sat on my balcony and stared at the stars, the noise of the ocean the only sound in the dark.

It was the only thing I knew how to do at that moment.

My doorbell rang. I looked at my phone one more time—

still nothing.

I left it on the balcony as I went to the door and opened it. As I'd asked, the delivery guy had left the bags on the ground, and I scooped them up to bring them inside. I'd gotten no further than taking two containers out of the bags when my doorbell rang again. I wondered if they'd forgotten to bring something in my order or if Persephone was checking in. She had texted since we'd parted, asking for Chloe's number, though I hadn't texted her back.

The doorbell rang again, and I called out a "Coming!" to whoever was on the other side as I crumpled up the bags and stashed them away. I still had sticky sauce on one of my fingers from a leak in the sweet and sour container and was licking it off my finger when I opened the door.

My heart dropped at the sight of Chloe standing there, tears in her eyes...

And a suitcase.

"Chloe." I started to reach for her, but she backed out of my grasp. My insides writhed with the weight of whatever she was about to say. The lump in my throat reeked of bile, and I had to grab the door to stay upright.

"I'm done," she said, her jaw quivering. "I can't pretend any longer."

"Pretend what?" I managed.

"That what we have isn't real," she breathed, and my knees went weak.

"I'm finished being complacent and comfortable and settling for less than I deserve," she continued, impatience in her tone. "I'm done denying myself true happiness. I'm done being quiet about what I want. I'm so fucking *tired* of being scared. I'm just... I'm just fucking *done*," she said in an exasperated weep.

Her face scrunched up then, her breaths short, bright eyes denying the tears that threatened to fall down her red cheeks.

"But most of all…."

Anxiety squirmed through my bones, emotion burning behind my face. Her gaze lifted to mine, and I forgot to breathe. A tear spilled over as she inhaled a jagged breath.

"Most of all, I'm tired of pretending I'm not completely in love with you."

Her voice was high-pitch, hoarse, and quivering. I staggered slightly, unable to form words or thoughts.

"I love you, Gavin," she wept.

My nostrils flared as I tried to hold myself together. "Did you leave him?" I asked, though I barely heard my own voice.

"Tomorrow," she said. "I know that's not what you wanted to hear, but I couldn't do it over the phone. I packed as much tonight as I could fit." She rolled the suitcase forward and shrugged slightly. "I just couldn't imagine another second without you."

Trembling, I leaned forward, pulled the suitcase from her grasp, and then shoved it behind me, its wheels rolling, rolling, rolling on the wood floor. I didn't bother looking to see how far it went.

Because all I could hear was her saying she loved me, and I couldn't handle another moment without her lips on mine.

So, I kissed her.

Unrestrained. Unadulterated. Unapologetic and unequivocal to anything else. I kissed her like I had wanted to since first seeing her back at that social. I kissed her with my entire soul, with every part of me that belonged to her. Without hesitation and without fear. As though we were gravity itself and the universe depended on our love for survival.

The way I would *never* stop kissing her.

Her arms linked around my neck as she kissed me back. I

could feel it in her kiss, too. That she had let go of everything holding her back and was truly mine this time, and that nothing or no one would come between what we had.

I picked her up beneath her ass, lifted her onto my waist, and slammed the door behind us. Greed threaded through my bones. Fuck, I'd forgotten how she molded to my body, and I needed to taste and touch and fuck every part of her.

I stumbled, intent on moving us to the bedroom, but only reaching the kitchen counter before she grabbed the hem of my shirt. I sat her ass on the top, a pint glass shattering on the floor behind us. Though, I barely noticed.

We broke apart just long enough to pull my shirt over my head. She reached for hers as my lips landed on her neck, my hands squeezing her bare sides as her shirt fell to the floor. She moaned against me, her fingers holding my head against her neck, and I sucked the skin over her collarbone, meaning to blister and bruise her until her body read how insatiable I was for her.

Until her body read that she was mine.

"Fuck, Gavin," she said, her voice pleading. She tugged on my hair and jerked my head back so I could look at her, and when I did, I almost fell to my knees.

Her brown eyes were deep with desire, glistening so perfectly, her pink lips dropped open slightly.

"I need you inside me," she whispered.

My eyes closed, forehead coming to a rest against hers. "Gods, I need you to say that again," I managed.

Her lips crashed into mine, our tongues sweeping desperately against one another, and when she slipped away this time, her teeth dragged across my bottom lip.

"I said I need you inside me," she whispered. "We have every day, for the rest of our lives to live in every fantasy we've ever had. But tonight, I just want to feel you. I want you to fill me until I can't move or breathe from trying to deny my release. I want you to bury inside me until the only air that exists between us is that of our own breaths."

"We'll suffocate together?" I asked, making her smile.

"If it means I'll be with you, yes." Her hands landed softly on my cheeks, beautiful eyes searching my face. "Love me," she practically begged, her words no more than a whisper.

I gulped, my heart an erratic mess as I kissed her hand. "Baby, I'm going to worship you."

She inhaled sharply when my mouth fell upon her throat again, and I sucked a line down her neck, her skin prickling seamlessly with those tiny red dots. Fuck, if I could mark her entire body like this, if I could write my name and brand the pattern of my hands and lips into her flesh, it still might not be enough.

I scooped her onto my waist again, holding her secured legs as I entered the bedroom, massaging her ass through those tight leggings. Gods, I would rip them off her if it meant having her sooner. Her bare skin against mine intoxicated my soul. Everywhere wasn't enough. I wanted to embed myself in her until we were a single entity, and I wasn't even sure that would suffice this thirst for her.

Her nails were on my scalp, tearing at my skin as she let herself succumb to everything we were. Chills erupted all over my body. I spanked her ass, my dick straining already from her feel and the beautiful little noises she made.

Her back hit the mattress, though neither of us could stop kissing the other. Not even when she backed up to the headboard and her legs bent around me. Not even when I took a second to slow down and clench her waist, bruising her skin. I settled between her delectable thighs, her covered breasts heaving against my chest, the lace scratching my skin as my hips ground into hers.

She moaned my name in that desperate whimper when I reached behind her to unhook her bra, and when I pulled back enough to admire her now-naked body, I had to curse myself.

"Fucking Styx, Chloe," I said, staring at her bare tits, her soft stomach. She had a new sunflower tattoo wrapped beneath the underside of her left breast and around her ribcage. Gods, she was sexier than I remembered—utter perfection.

And wholly mine.

A slight smirk lifted her lips, and I couldn't help my fingers grasping around her breast. I was drawn to them and every part of her mind, body, and soul.

"Did you both miss me?" I said aloud, still staring at her breasts.

Chloe snorted. "Are you talking to my tits?"

"Absolutely, baby." I bent lower, taking her perked nipple into my mouth and sucking. Her back arched off the bed, hands hugging my head to her chest. I licked every stretch mark and kissed every inch of them. "Don't worry," I whispered against her nipple. "I'm home, and you'll never be neglected again."

"Gavin!" Her laughter was like beautiful music. She pulled me by my hair to kiss her smiling lips. That fucking laugh. Her fucking smile.

How was I so gods damned lucky to have her in my arms again?

We rolled over, and she landed straddle over my lap. I grasped her hips, sinking my hands beneath the waistband of her stretchy pants, and as she kissed me, I squeezed her flesh. Fuck, I had missed her filling up my hands.

I was obsessed with every inch of her.

She groaned into my mouth, her breasts brushing my chest. With every insatiable move of her hips against my dick, I lost a little more of my mind. Her teeth dragged over my bottom lip, and I sucked in sharply. I was straining against my pants, unsure if I would last very long with the feel of her body on mine again.

I rolled us over again and grabbed her wrists, pinning them above her head as I bent to bite her throat and dip my hand beneath her pants. She whimpered and angled her hips up when I reached her pussy, and as I felt her wetness, I cursed in her neck.

"Shit, baby," I hissed. "You're fucking drenching."

"I missed you," she said, her mouth sagging as I rolled her clit.

My fucking gods, I had missed her too.

I released her wrists to sit back on my knees, then grabbed her pants and worked them off. She lifted her hips to help, and when she was completely bare, I swallowed as I admired my once wife.

Wife.

Shit, that word had me ready to sink inside her.

My lips slammed onto hers, hips moving against her leg as I dipped my finger in her cunt. *Shit.* My dick ached from not being inside her yet. I sucked her jaw again, every slide of my finger atop her hardened clit making her arch into me. She grabbed my pants' waistband and pushed, and I obliged her eagerness by helping her pull them off.

Before I could make her lay down further so I could sink my tongue inside her, she pushed on my chest, forcing me to my back as she bent down, her knees and ass by my chest, her breasts brushing against my left hip. And when her lips wrapped around the tip of my already straining cock, I shuddered into the mattress.

"Fucking gods," I muttered at her tongue swirling around me. "Shit, Chloe." I reached out and gave her ass a loud smack, then gripped it firmly, and she groaned around me. Gods, she was going to have me undone. One look down, and I had to shut my eyes. My dick disappearing into her mouth was enough to send me spiraling.

"Greedy girl," I said, straining to not come down her throat. "You just couldn't wait to have my dick in your mouth, could you?" I asked as I sank a finger inside her.

She hummed around me in response, and I sucked in a sharp breath. "Shit," I groaned. I lifted my hips, prompting her to choke slightly before threading my hand in her hair. Her lashes lifted to look at me, and every time she swallowed my cock, I plunged that digit inside her aching pussy.

One finger, then two, relishing at the noise her pussy was making for me. Gods, I had missed that noise. It was one that only she made, and it was a calling card to my soul. She was so fucking wet, and I knew the only thing that could satisfy that ache was my dick swelling up inside her.

I smacked her ass again, watching it turn the most stunning shade of pink with the sting, then sat up and grabbed her ass, moving her slightly so I could taste her. I spread her cheeks with my hands, admiring her swollen, glistening cunt waiting for me.

Fucking Styx.

I had to taste her. Just for a moment before I fucked her so deeply that her pussy memorized my cock.

She withdrew her lips from my dick as my tongue plunged inside her. She was so fucking addicting. The way she wiggled her ass without even realizing it and moaned my name. I pulled her hips toward me, holding her in place as I devoured that sweet pussy. Her body drooped onto the mattress, submitting to the pleasure pulsing through her.

"Fuck, you taste better than I remember," I murmured against her clit.

"Gavin," she whimpered, her fingers fisting the sheets. "I need you inside me. *Please.*"

I chuckled, my lips touching her clit. I sucked those nerves into my mouth, prompting her legs to spread wider and her chest to sink further into the bed.

"Lie. Beg. Barter… Baby, you sound so beautiful when you're in need," I teased her.

"I need you," she pleaded, her ass pushing into my face.

Holding her body in place, I rose from my back to my knees. She was spread, ready, and waiting. I stroked my dick, precum spilling over the tip, and tapped it on the pink mark my hand had left behind. One sink inside her, and I might be done for. I swallowed to try and contain myself.

Grabbing her hips, I whipped her around. She landed on her back with a bounce, and I descended over her, my lips crashing into hers. She raked her hands through my hair and down my back, drawing blood to the surface of my skin as she lifted her hips.

My dick grazed her drenched pussy, making me groan in her mouth. I released her lips as I reached down and hauled her thigh to my waist, spreading her wide and positioning myself at her entrance.

I don't know why I hesitated, but I did. I took that brief second to lock eyes with her, to truly look at her at that moment. To memorize the haze in her dilated eyes and savor her beauty and desire, my heart began to ache.

I had her in my arms. We had found each other, and once again, we had fought for this. For this moment, for this feeling, we shared.

She was mine. My Goddess. My wife. My Psyche— my *Chloe*.

She blinked as her bright eyes glistened, and she wrapped her hands around my cheeks.

"I love you," she whispered.

I turned my head to the side, kissing her palm, and as I slowly began to sink inside her, I whispered back, "I love you."

A groan left me at the same time that she inhaled a harsh

breath. Her head sank back onto the pillow as mine fell against her chest, and I worked myself inside her, stretching her with every leisurely stroke. Her hips angled off the bed, eagerness driving her body as she tried to take me in. Her hair spread over the pillow, her mouth sagging as she cursed and groaned. And once I was entirely inside her, I had to take another breath.

I never wanted to move from this place. Our bodies connected like this, so molded and fit and perfect. I held her leg higher with my next thrust as if I could somehow force myself deeper. I leaned down to bite the pillow of her breast, every sink of my dick inside that wet pussy sending us both over the edge. Her body rolled against mine, meeting me stroke for stroke.

We were one, our souls entwined.

"I need you to consume me," she said as our eyes met. "I need you deeper, like—*Fuck*—right there. *Right there*—" Her head fell back when I angled myself differently, hitting that spot that would drive her wild.

"What were you saying?" I mocked, admiring the elation on her face.

"Never mind, you found it—*shit*—" She began to squirm, her pussy throbbing around me. "Don't stop," she pleaded as her knuckles whitened on the sheets.

I shifted nearly all the way out of her with every plunge, making sure she kept that look of ecstasy on her face. Her moans grew louder and less controlled, and I felt myself beginning to tremble as I held back my release.

"Fuck, baby," I hissed.

"Gavin, I'm going to—"

"Not yet, baby," I pleaded as my pace picked up. "Fuck, not yet. I don't want to move from inside you." I buried my face in her neck as I held her bent knees by my sides, sinking myself as deep as I could possibly go.

She squealed and whimpered and begged, tears lining those beautiful eyes. I looked between us, cursing when I watched her pussy swallow my cock, and I thrusted a little faster.

"Shit, that's beautiful," I whispered against her breast. "Do you see us, baby?" I asked, making her look at me. "Look at how well you take me, how your body molds to mine." Our eyes met, and I kissed her softly. "You were made for me."

Her mouth sagged, trembling hands back on my face. A tear fell down her cheek, and my pace quickened. Still buried inside her deep. My fingers were bruised on her thigh.

"Gavin, I can't—" she pleaded as her nails dug into my cheek. "I'm going to come. I need to—"

She was so tight around me, her body on its final leg. She sucked in a shaky breath and hid her head in the crook of my neck, teeth bared on my skin and hanging on for dear life as she resisted spilling over the edge.

"Almost," I pleaded, wanting to take us both to the moment of shattering the world around us.

I was nearly numb. Unable to breathe. My body felt like it might combust. Every thrust was one more stolen moment that I wasn't sure was real. Her thighs squeezed my ribs as she began to cry into my neck, and I slapped her ass harshly, making her jump.

I pulled her head back and gazed into her desperate face, my thumb swiping away a tear on her cheek. "Let go, baby. We're there. Let go."

Her mouth slammed into mine, and with that kiss, she surrendered. Her body caved in beneath me. She screamed into my mouth, and I couldn't hold back. I let myself go inside her, my mind drawing a blank, stars forming behind my eyes. I matched her scream with my own audible groan, leaving crescent-shaped scars on her skin and drawing blood beneath my nails.

I couldn't let her go.

We held one another, trembling and broken, our foreheads touching as our bodies struggled to function again.

It was another few minutes before I found the strength to move. As I pulled out of her slowly, my cock glistening with our finishes, Chloe sat up. Her bottom lip sucked behind her teeth at the sight of us, and when I was out of her, cum leaking from her pussy, she groaned.

"Do you like that?" I whispered.

"I love it," she replied.

Our eyes met, and I kissed her again. Long and hard. Pulling her onto my lap as I sat on the mattress. I reached around her waist and squeezed her ass, prompting a perfect little moan to erupt from her throat. My lips moved to her jaw, throat, collarbone, and breast as she hugged my head against her, her delicate fingers threading and tugging in my hair, prompting goosebumps to trickle over my flesh. I sucked her nipple into my mouth, unable to stop kissing her. Fuck, there was no limit to the ways I wanted to have her, and I didn't know how to stop myself.

A quiet chuckle left her as she yanked on my hair, urging me up to her face again. She laughed out my name, and the smile on her lips was so adorable that I had to capture it.

And even still, my heart fluttered with restless need and disbelief that she was once more in my arms.

For real, this time.

"I have so many things I want to do to you," I said upon our parting, my forehead relaxing against hers. "I'm trying hard to pace myself, but you're impossible to resist."

She sat back, her smile soft as she looked at me, as her hands traveled over my face. Her touch was delicate like she was memorizing every line, freckle, and curve. My grin faded as I watched her, and when her palm rested on my cheek, I kissed the inside of it and held her a little tighter.

"Promise me you won't be gone when I wake up," she whispered.

"I promise," I said. "I'm never letting you go."

Chapter Forty

Chloe

I woke up surrounded by the steady arms of the man I loved.

Fuck, everything smelled like him. That sweet, peppered scent. I nuzzled my face into the soft pillow and inhaled deeply, a moan eliciting from within.

"That sound is reserved for me," Gavin muttered into my neck.

I shifted, smiling slightly at the ache between my thighs from our night. "Your pillow smells like you," I said, hugging it closer.

He leaned up and kissed my shoulder, my arm, and my elbow. "I'll make you smell like it every morning from now on," he swore.

I turned over so that I could see him, and I beamed at the sight of his disheveled hair, the sleepiness in his eyes, and his freckles in the light of the morning sun. He gazed at me with that dilated look as he reached out and pushed my hair back.

"How do you feel?" he asked softly.

"Like if I get out of bed, I'll have to face the day," I said. "And I'm not quite ready to do that."

"Okay," he said, almost a promise that I didn't have to move if I didn't want to. His eyes searched my face as we stilled there, and an almost pain stretched behind them.

"Why didn't I stay that morning?" he whispered.

"Because you'd have never made another flight," I said. "I think another day, and we would have fallen harder for each other than we did this time."

"You don't know how happy it makes me when you say that," he said.

"Say what?"

"That you love me."

I leaned in and kissed him slowly, prompting him to groan into my mouth and push up onto his hands on either side of me. I bent my leg, bringing it around his waist as he settled atop me.

"Baby," he said, moving his lips to my neck. "Unless you mean for this to be a little morning delight, I suggest not kissing me like that when we wake up," he said before biting my throat.

I snickered under my breath, relishing the way he devoured me. "Note taken. Gavin cannot keep it in his pants in the mornings," I said as if I were making a list.

"Not with you," he said. He sat up then and reached on the ground for his shirt. I took a moment to admire his back muscles and the way they moved when he did. Those tiny freckles on his shoulders and back made me want to touch him again.

"Coffee should be brewing on the counter," he said when he stood. "Do you want to shower?"

God, he was sexy in the slim-fit tee and navy boxer briefs that fit so snugly that they showed off his leg muscles and the outline of his slightly stiff cock.

I had never salivated over a dick before, but his... his could bring me to my knees at any given moment.

"Chloe?"

"Hm?" I blinked, realizing how hard I had been staring and chewing my lip just thinking about sucking his cock again.

A huff of amusement left him. "I asked if you wanted to

shower," he said. "Or maybe you'd like to reintroduce your mouth to my dick."

Heat spread on my cheeks, and I seriously considered it. "Maybe after coffee," I said, forcing my eyes to his smirking face. "I think I need a few minutes to collect myself."

He nodded. "Balcony sliding door is open. There's always entertainment with the surfers down below."

I slipped on a tank, my boy-short underwear, and a long-sleeved shirt that he threw me out of his closet. I told him my tits would stretch out his shirt, but he didn't care.

A purple sky greeted me when I entered his living room.

Glass walls lined the exterior. Outside the living room was a balcony with a small, curved infinity pool, a lounger, and a small table with two chairs. A few plants, including what looked like a young olive tree, sat in the corners, one vine plant trailing down over the side of the wall, and a tower of vegetable plants sat in the sun.

"There are fresh cherry tomatoes out there if you want any," Gavin said as he took two cups from the cupboard. "I have toast, avocados, and eggs."

I smiled at him over my shoulder, hugging my arms around my chest. "Is that one of those hydroponic growers?" I asked about the plant tower.

"My biggest splurge last year," he said.

I turned around in the room, taking in the feel of his apartment: both modern and rustic—the grey walls painted in a way that looked almost like streaked cement, the dark wood floor, black iron accents. Plants crawled from pots on a few of the thick wooden shelves, bookcases, and other places around the room. Decorative pillows sat on the dark couch, a white blanket lay across the back, and pictures dotted the wall between the halls. I smiled at every little detail.

"Your place is so homey," I said.

Gavin shrugged as he took the bread out of the bag. "It's

my home," he said simply.

"So modest," I taunted him. "I don't think I realized how much you liked plants."

"Persephone is responsible for a few," he said.

"And the olive tree?" I asked.

"Gift from my mother a few years back," he answered. "I think she hoped it would make me want to come home."

I stepped up to the sliding glass door and opened it, and as I did, the noise of the beach down below filled my ears. The wind blew my hair back, and the salty scent of the ocean made me close my eyes.

Peace spread through my bones, my muscles, and over my skin. Peace that I had never truly felt before.

Gavin came through the door and handed me a coffee mug, a large one that said 'Carpe fucking diem (after coffee)' on it, and I laughed softly.

"What?" he asked.

"I haven't drank out of a mug that wasn't purely for aesthetics in a year," I said. "It's nice to see fun ones again."

"I have a matching set of aesthetic ones if that's what you prefer," he said.

"No, I love this," I countered.

As we sat down at the small table and I tasted that first sip of coffee, I let reality slowly come into focus. The warm drink spread through my insides, the hot ceramic heating my hands. I closed my eyes and let the scent waft into my nostrils.

"I have so much to do today," I said upon opening my eyes.

"What time is he home?" Gavin asked.

"I think he said after dinner," I answered. "I don't know. I need to go back through my messages. I had hoped to pack most of my things, so I didn't have to do so much while he was there. I did a lot before I came here, but I hate packing."

A smile slipped on his lips then, one that made my eyes narrow. He settled back in the chair, smug energy radiating off of him.

"What?" I asked.

He glanced at his watch—

The doorbell rang.

I frowned across the table. "Are you expecting someone?"

"I think it's for you," he said.

"Why… why would it be for me?" I asked.

His smile widened, and he shrugged as he brought his cup to his lips. "Just a feeling," he said.

The doorbell rang again. I continued staring at him until he chuckled softly.

"Would you rather I answer it?"

"I don't think I can handle more surprises," I said.

"You'll like this one," he said, and the doorbell rang three times, back to back. "I think they're getting impatient."

I huffed and rose to my feet. "I swear, Gavin, if you've done something crazy—"

"Like what?" he asked, following me inside.

"Like… I don't know… hired a minotaur?" I couldn't think of anything as I reached for the doorknob. "I don't know your gift-giving limits yet."

He was still grinning when I looked at him one last time, and then I swung open the door.

The smirking face of my best friend met me.

"Hey, babe," Lana said.

Tears burned in my eyes. I flung my arms around her, hugging her as tightly as I could.

My best friend was there. She was in front of me. In the home of the man I had practically run away with.

Seeing her there made it all real.

"I didn't know you were coming," I said into her hair.

Lana pulled back. "Of course I did," she said. "Couldn't let my best friend break up with her fiancé and pack everything herself, could I? Plus, you know, I really wanted to stay at that hotel."

I laughed, wiping my cheeks of the tears that had trickled down them. "What… But what are you doing here?"

"Can I come inside?" she asked.

"Oh shit. Yeah—" I opened the door wider, letting Lana in, and I couldn't help but hug her again when the door was closed, and we were in the living room.

"I'm so glad you're here," I said.

"Stop crying," she said, wiping her own face. "You're making me cry."

I chuckled under my breath. "How did you know I was here?" I asked.

Lana smiled back at Gavin as he slipped an arm around my waist. "Ask your… I'm not sure what to call you yet," she said, her head tilting.

"We haven't really gotten that far," I admitted, wondering myself what to call him.

"I messaged her this morning on the Arrow app," Gavin said, and I turned into him, my heart aching at the smile on his face. "I was asking if she knew what was going on. Told her you were here. I was going to pay for her to get on a plane and anything else she needed, but she said she was already on a flight over."

"So, I checked into your room at the hotel," Lana added. "And Gavin sent a car over to bring me here."

"I would have picked you up myself, but she woke up earlier than I thought she would," Gavin told Lana. His gaze moved to me. "I figured you could use the help and support. I didn't think you wanted me to go over and chance Tyler being there."

This man… he continued to surprise me. Making sure my best friend was there while I made such a huge life decision was something I would never have expected from him—from anyone.

I sighed as I looked up at the clock Gavin had on his wall. "We should probably head over there soon," I said.

Lana met Gavin's gaze over my head, and he squeezed my waist. "Putting it off a few more minutes won't hurt," he said. "How about breakfast first?"

Chapter Forty-One

Chloe

Lana helped me pack up my things as I was a wad of nerves.

I honestly didn't have much. I was leaving behind every piece of jewelry Tyler had ever bought me, along with any clothes I knew I would never wear. I left the oversized watch I wore on his dresser and the engagement ring on my finger… I laid it on the kitchen counter, back in its box.

With every trip to the storage unit, leaving him became more and more real. I grew more nauseous the further into the afternoon it got. Every little noise startled me, thinking it was Tyler coming home. I didn't know why I was so panicked. This was Tyler, not Aidan. Lana was there, and Gavin was a phone call away.

Lana and I were closing my last suitcase when we heard the front door open and close. Our eyes met, and I swear my heart stopped beating.

There was an instant of silence in which I stilled, unsure if he would even notice the ring on the counter.

"What the—Chloe? Chloe!"

There was panic in his tone as his footsteps hurried along the floor as down the hall. He called my name again. And again. And then again when he launched himself into the closet and saw Lana zipping up my suitcase, with me standing there in silence next to her as the color drained from his face.

"Chloe," he repeated, his throat bobbing as he shifted from foot to foot. "What are you… What's this?" He held up the ring box. "Why are you—*are you packing?*"

"Let's go to the living room," I said, finally finding my voice.

"No," he argued. "No, what is she doing here?" His eyes landed on Lana. "What have you filled her head with? Are you—"

"Whoa," Lana and I both said. Lana jumped to her feet in defense, but I moved in front of her.

"She's here to help me pack," I said, deciding that if he was going to be a dick, so could I.

"Where are you going?" he asked.

"I'm leaving you," I said, and he took two steps back.

"Leaving—what—why?"

"Let's go to the living room and talk," I said, trying to get him away from Lana.

"Why?"

"Because I don't want you to stand here and think everything coming out of my mouth results from any *ideas* you think Lana might have put in my head. And I also don't want her to punch you in the face, so go."

Tyler glared in Lana's direction but turned on his heel and stomped toward the living room. I grunted under my breath before following.

"If he says anything—"

"If he says anything about you again, I'll hit him my damn self," I said, seeing the wild expression on Lana's face. "We're almost done, aren't we?"

"I will be by the time you tell him to go fuck himself," she swore.

I grabbed one of the laundry baskets and headed down the hall.

He was pacing behind the couch when I reached him, his hand rubbing behind his neck.

"The fuck is she doing here so early?" he asked. "And what do you mean you're leaving? You can't leave. We're getting married—"

"No, we're not," I interrupted him. "It's over. I can't marry you."

Tyler stopped walking. "You're breaking up with me? Where is this coming from? I thought you were just nervous."

I almost laughed. "How did you not know this was coming?" I asked, exhausted with emotion. "After everything the last two months. Are you so oblivious that you had no idea I was unhappy?"

"Everyone kept telling me it was normal wedding jitters!" he argued. "How—why— After everything I've done for you? You're leaving me?"

"Everything you've done?" I balked. "Tyler, tell me what you've done for me? Other than buying me things I don't care for and trying to tell me the kind of future I want. I just told you two days ago that I wasn't ready to give up my life—"

"What the fuck is so special about your life now that you feel the need to hang onto it?" he shouted. "Your trashy friends? Your joke of a job? Chloe, you're better than these things you cling to. You could be *so* much more if you would just realize you don't need them."

My fist curled in on itself, rage rearing its head from deep within me.

"My *trashy* friends have been there for me through things you would have told me I was being stupid over," I snapped. "My *trashy* friends love me for me. And my joke of a job is my fucking dream—something you wouldn't know anything about. God, Tyler. How… How the hell did I ever fall in love with you? Were you just waiting until we were married to cut me off from everyone?"

"This is ridiculous," he said, shaking his head at the ceiling. "You can't be this dumb, Chloe. You're giving up everything I could provide for you."

"I don't need anyone to provide for me," I sneered. "This is half of the fucking problem. You think I need you."

"What's the other half of the problem?"

"It would take me hours to name off the rest of the fucking issues we have," I said. The weight of everything dragged me down, and I didn't have the energy for this quarrel.

I just wanted it to be over.

"We're done." Emotion burned behind my nose. "Nothing either of us says will change that, so why bother with this fucking argument. Do you even truly care? Did you ever love me?"

"Of course I love you." He stepped in my direction, but I quickly escaped his grasp.

Lana appeared from the shadows of the hall then, and Tyler's jaw set as he glanced between us, seeming to realize that I wasn't bluffing.

"What am I supposed to tell everyone?" he asked. "The wedding. The guests. The vendors. Our honeymoon—"

"Our honeymoon in the Maldives had a calendar of meetings attached to it," I said. "Go on the fucking honeymoon. Have the reception. Celebrate all of your family and friends coming in from all over the world by spoiling them with champagne and caviar. I don't care. Just tell them there isn't a wedding."

I grabbed up the laundry basket, giving him one last look. "Goodbye, Tyler."

"No, Chloe, wait—"

He launched for my elbow as Lana twisted the doorknob.

"Wait—" he pleaded, and I met his crestfallen eyes.

"Tell me what I did wrong," he asked, his voice calm.

I thought about it as I hugged that basket to my chest.

"You didn't hear me," I said. "And I never felt like I could be myself. Not with you, not with your friends, and especially not with your family. And I couldn't… I couldn't live that lie for the rest of my life."

"I can change," he pleaded. "We don't have to leave right now. We can wait a few years. That deal—"

I was done with second and third chances.

I was done believing when someone said they would change.

"Tyler, it's over."

I barely spoke as we loaded my last boxes into my SUV. I didn't have it in me to drive anymore, so I gave Lana the keys and plugged in the address for the hotel.

I knew breaking up with Tyler was the right thing to do. I knew I was leaving something that never supported me.

But it still hurt.

When we arrived at the hotel, my knees were wobbly. My body nearing collapse. I wasn't even sure why I was so upset. It was like something in me that had been so perfectly placed together was snapped overnight. I couldn't move my mouth. Didn't feel my heart.

The moment we stepped inside the room, I collapsed onto the floor, and every emotion I'd held back for what felt like years came to the surface.

Lana ordered pizza as I sat in the bottom of the shower, letting hot water cascade on my aching body and mind. God, I was fucking exhausted. All I wanted was to lay there in silence for a week.

But the thought of Gavin filled me with butterflies and warmth, and after a couple of hours, I finally turned the water off.

"About time," Lana said as I emerged, wrapped in one of the hotel robes. "I was going to come to make sure you hadn't drowned."

I huffed amusedly. "Just thinking," I said as I settled onto the bed.

"Yeah, I figured." She slid my phone across the mattress toward me. "Gavin called," she said. "I answered and told him you'd call when you were out, but he said he would text you. He didn't want to crowd you."

I grabbed my phone and scrolled through his message notifications.

I won't bother you. I only wanted to see if you had made it out okay.

I'm here if you need anything.

I love you.

I sighed as I set the phone down. "Three years," I said, sinking onto the pillows. "Three years wasted—*five* years wasted." I shook my head. "I shouldn't have been so afraid that night."

"I don't think it was a waste," Lana said. "I think we're meant to find people for certain stages of our lives. Like stepping stones. Some last. Some don't." She pushed the pizza toward me and then rose to make our drinks. "Vodka?"

"Please," I said as I reached for a slice.

Lana made two vodka tonics and sat back on the bed, raising her glass to cheers against mine. Our glasses clanked, and I drank half of it in the first sip. The alcohol stung my insides, making me bite back a grimace.

"Do you know what we're doing tomorrow?" Lana asked.

"Sleeping?" I replied.

She scoffed. "No. We're going to Disneyland, and we're going to ride every ride and eat all the food until they have to roll us out of there."

A smile graced my lips. "I don't know if I'm in the mood for Disney."

"That's why we're going," she said. "One day. No phone calls. No texts. No drama. We can tell Gavin and Ezzie that your phone will be in my purse. But you need at least one day before all the phone calls start coming in."

The moment the sentence had left her lips, my phone buzzed.

Abigail.

I locked eyes with Lana, who grabbed my phone up before I could think about answering.

"Hello?" she answered. "Yes—no. No, you can't talk to her," Lana said to Tyler's mother. "No, there's nothing you can do. I'm sure she'll call you another day, but she won't be on her phone any time soon. No—goodbye, Abigail."

A loud huff left her when she hung up, though I could hear Abigail continuing to speak. Lana extended me the phone.

"Five minutes," she said. "Then it's going in my bag. You're going to get some actual sleep."

I was eternally grateful for her being there.

I already had texts from Tyler, Tyler's mother, and a few from Ezzie—work-related, as I hadn't told her anything. I texted her first to let her know I wouldn't be in the office the next day either, but I would be in on Wednesday and let her know what was going on then. Her returning message was that she hoped I was okay and would see me when I was ready.

I'm staying at the hotel with Lana tonight, I texted Gavin. He replied back almost immediately.

Okay, he replied. *I'm here if you need me. Are you okay?*

Not really, I said. **Lana wants me to take tomorrow off, just her and me, to try to get my mind off things.**

I think that's a great idea. I won't bother you then.

I'll probably stay here tomorrow night, too.

Okay, he said. *Whatever you need.*

I don't want you to think I'm running.

Chloe, I love you, he said. *And while I would love for you to be in my arms every moment, I know you need time. So, I'll be here waiting when you're ready.*

Thank you. For everything, I mean. Not just for this. But for understanding. For pushing me to go after what I deserve. I could list a million things.

Maybe you can tell me one per day, he said. *Get some rest. I'll see you soon.*

Chapter Forty-Two

Chloe

Lana and I's day trip to Disneyland was precisely what I needed.

We spent the day ignoring reality, and it was only when we got back to the hotel and ordered sushi that I finally looked at my phone again. I had several missed calls, too many text messages, and a cascade of emails. It seemed that when people hadn't been able to reach me through text or calls, they'd decided email was the next solution.

Lana deleted all of them.

The only people I really owed an explanation to were my family.

My sisters took the news graciously, and I was surprised at how neutral they reacted. I thought they would have been upset about the amount of money spent on dresses and the plane tickets, but both said they were fine returning their dresses and taking the vacations anyway. I told them to make sure to call when they were in town so I could at least see them.

My mother, however, had had the worst reaction.

"Chloe, how could you?!" my mother had practically screamed over the phone. "The guests, the food, the dress—how could you call this off? Look at the wedding he had planned. Look at what he can provide you—"

"I don't need anyone to provide for me," I snapped, in disbelief that she was reacting this way. "I'm capable of doing that myself."

"This is ridiculous. Go back over there and tell him you made a mistake—"

"Mother—"

"—Tell him you had a momentary lapse, that you were just lonely when he was gone," she continued, desperation in her tone. "Tell him anything, Chloe. You need this. You need—"

"What do I need?" I asked. "To sit at home alone and feel indifferent when he is there? I shouldn't feel *nothing* for the person I'm meant to spend my life with."

"And what will you do now, Chloe?" she asked. "Idiot girl. You were the only one of your sisters to marry up."

"Is that all you care about? Status? The fact that Tyler had well-known parents? Not the fact that your daughter wasn't happy?"

"The situation the two of you had was what many of us wished for when we married. Our own lives while being provided for, not having someone come home after work and wonder why the laundry wasn't done."

"Don't you dare make this about Dad—"

"You are silly if you think marriage is only about love," she spoke over me. "It's about finding someone to take care of you—"

"That's *not* what I want," I said, my voice shaking as I was on the verge of tears. "Just because you spent your life in resentment and unhappiness because you thought he didn't do enough doesn't mean I have to spend my life like that. I want someone I get excited for, a best friend to share my life with, someone who fights for me and looks at me as though I'm the moon and stars and endless night—"

"That's a fairytale, dear," she grunted.

"Then call me fucking Cinderella," I snapped as the tears

fell down my face. "Because I've already found it."

I avoided telling her who it was, and I would avoid it for as long as I could because I knew the moment I told her who he was, her entire argument about being provided for would have turned around, and I hated that that was all she would see him as.

I had made it to work at least on Wednesday morning. A few co-workers noticed how distracted I was, but I wasn't ready to discuss it. I had only told Ezzie that morning before making my way to my office, and she hugged me and told me she would be there if I needed anything.

I couldn't concentrate. My mind was blank. Absent of actual thought.

I was just so fucking tired.

My phone buzzed back on my desk, and I stopped chewing the end of my pen and staring out the window to see the message.

A small smile worked its way onto my lips at the name on the screen.

How are you today? Gavin asked.

I sat down at my desk and pulled up my email before answering.

I'm okay, I answered. ***I haven't told anyone here yet. Just Ezzie. I don't think I'm ready for all the questions.***

Take your time, he said. *You were engaged for two years.*

It feels like I've wasted so much time and energy trying to deny something that only worked in the beginning.

There was no way to know that.

I should have waited for you.

Three dots strummed the bottom of the screen for a moment. *Are you at work?*

I am. Are you coming by to approve this final?

I don't want to crowd you.

You won't. I want to see you. And I need to close this file.

With everything going on, I forgot.

I'll be there closer to four, he said. *Do you want food, or do you want to order takeout later?*

Takeout. Are you sure you're okay with us staying with you?

He had offered the night before when Lana was texting him. I didn't want him suggesting it out of pity. We could have stayed at the hotel. Although the truth was, I missed him. And even as tired as I was, I knew I didn't have to be 'on' with him any more than I needed to be with Lana.

Of course. I like having Lana around.

Is Lana with you?

She's gone to take some things to your storage unit and checking out of the hotel.

What did she drive?

I let her take my Jeep.

I almost laughed. **I hope you didn't want that back in one piece.**

It's time for an upgrade, anyway.

There was a pause in which I stared at the screen, unsure what to say. So much had happened just over the last 48 hours… I wasn't sure I had taken it all in.

Are you sure you're okay? Gavin asked.

No, I answered. **But I know I will be.**

I set the phone down and tried to finish some work, but the damn thing kept ringing. I was ready to throw it across the room, get a burner phone and only give my closest friends the number.

I looked at it one more time, intending to message Gavin, Lana, and Ezzie and let them know to call Jasmine and have her put them through to my work phone if they needed me, but the name on the screen caught my eye.

Hey, Chloe.

It was John, Tyler's father.

I leaned back in my chair and sighed as I opened up the text thread.

I heard, and I'm sorry, he said. *But I'm mostly sad that you won't be at family gatherings in the future to keep me company. You were a breath of fresh air these last few years. If you ever need anything, anything at all, call me. I don't care if you're with my son or someone else. You deserve real happiness, and I hope you find it.*

I had to clench my teeth as emotion swelled behind my eyes. **Thank you**, was all I could manage back.

Anything, Chloe, he said. *I mean it.*

I know you do, I said. **Thank you again for everything.**

Anytime.

Three texts later, and I had Jasmine lock my phone away in her desk. I put in headphones, pulled up a playlist on my computer, and closed my door. I was determined to bury myself so far into work that I lost track of time.

Thank fuck, it worked.

My eyes were nearly crossing by the afternoon. Jasmine only disrupted me twice to bring coffee, even though I hadn't asked. I didn't even realize it was quitting time until she knocked on my door to let me know she was leaving for the day.

I had so many missed calls and texts. I barely knew where to start.

Three soft knocks sounded on my door, and I looked up to find Gavin standing there.

My heart knotted as I swiveled in my chair. His lips lifted on the right side, eyes brightening just enough to notice, and he quietly closed the door behind him.

"I'm late," he said, his hands in his pockets. "Looks like everyone else has gone home."

I sighed and let the look on his face wash over me, feeling it in my bones. "You're perfect," I said, then glanced over to the rest of the office, noticing that the entire floor was dark.

Everyone else had gone home, and I realized it was later than I thought.

"Shit, what time is it?" I asked as I sat up.

"After seven," he answered. "I ran late at the office with some things, but I hadn't heard from you, so I figured you were still here. Lana is downstairs with Ezzie."

"Are they waiting on us?" I asked, standing.

"I told them to go have a few drinks at the bar across the street," he answered. "I didn't know how much longer you needed."

"Actually, before I forget—" I pulled up the final proofs for Cupid's Arrow on my tablet and strode over to him for him to sign. "Please sign off on this before Ezzie has a fit."

A smile spread over his lips. He started to wrap his arms around me, but I pulled back. "Sign first," I said, resisting a chuckle. "Then you can touch me. This is why it's weeks late getting done."

"Because I've distracted you?" he asked.

"Yes," I said flatly.

He scoffed, took the tablet pen from my hands, and gave the screen a quick signature without looking over what he was signing.

"Thank you for signing away your entire company, Mr. Erosin," I said, clicking on the next screen. "Now, if you just sign over all your accounts to me, we'll be done here."

He snickered softly but signed the next page.

"Do I get to touch you now?" he asked when I sat the tablet on the table.

My chest swelled and ached at how he stared at me with such love and desire. I debated teasing him, making him work for it, but I had missed him the last two days, the last five years... and I intended to make up for it.

"I'm not ready for everyone in this office to know about us just yet, but since it seems everyone has gone home...." I bit my lip, trying to stifle my smile, and Gavin chuckled.

"Don't worry, baby," he said. "Even if someone is hiding in the back, they won't hear you."

His hand landed on my cheek, the other on my hip, and he pulled me into him for a lingering kiss that made my knees wobble. God, I loved the way he kissed me. I loved the way he loved me. It caused goosebumps on my skin and had me restless for more of his everything.

I groaned into his mouth as he pulled away, and he grunted under his breath, still hanging onto my cheek.

"Fuck, I'm glad I can do that whenever I want now," he muttered.

My gaze darted from his dilated eyes to his lips, and I leaned forward, catching his bottom lip between my teeth and dragging him back into me. "As am I," I replied after another kiss.

Gavin settled his hip on the desk, catching me between his legs, his fingers entwining with mine. "Are you feeling any better?" he asked.

"A little, yeah," I said with a sigh. "I might have to change my phone number."

"That bad?"

"That bad," I nodded. "I hope it'll die down in a week or so. Until then… I don't know. Hide?"

He laughed softly, squeezing my hands. "Anything I can do to help?"

"Keep me distracted," I said. "Continue loving me as you do."

His smile faded, his throat bobbing. "Always," he whispered.

Gravity pulled me toward him, our lips meeting hesitantly, deepening with every second. I could feel my need for him swelling as my fingers scratched the scruff on his face, his hands squeezing the curvature of my ass, and I soon forgot where we were.

His mouth landed on my neck when he stood, greed in every swipe and suck of his tongue on my skin.

"Isn't Lana and Ezzie waiting on us?" I asked, my thighs pressing at the way he grabbed me.

"Do you care?" he asked as he straightened over me.

My stomach twisted with the look in his eyes. "Fuck them." I kissed him eagerly, and caution vacated between us.

I pushed his jacket off and reached for the hem of his shirt —unable to get his bare body against mine quick enough. He grabbed my blouse, which nearly ripped with the swiftness of its removal. I could already feel him growing against me, and fuck, I wanted to taste him again. I fumbled with the buckle on his jeans. The zipper and soft fabric of his boxers were obstacles that I desperately needed out of my way.

But he grabbed my hands as I started to pull his cock free, and he stilled over me, his green eyes boring into mine.

"I want you to feel how I feel when I'm with you," he said, breathless.

"How are you going to do that?" I asked.

His gaze darted around us until finally landing on the coat closet, and he broke away from me momentarily to look inside. A soft scarf was in his hands when he returned, and I swallowed at the sight of it. With every wrap of that scarf around his hands, his arms flexed.

"Sit," he said, jerking his chin to the desk.

I peered behind me at everything on my desk and started moving a few of them out of the way, including my laptop, before perching my ass onto the edge. Breath hitched in my throat as he circled that scarf around my head, and when the room became nothing more than a shadowed blur around me, I blindly reached out for his arm.

"Don't fight it," he rasped as he touched my fingers. I felt him lean closer, felt his body's energy just inches from mine, and my chest caved without the aid of my vision. "Give everything over to me," he said, his breath tickling my cheek. "All your boundaries. All your hesitations. Every uncertainty you've ever felt. Let them fall. Free yourself. Put all your trust in me and surrender. I've got you, sweet girl."

His mouth enclosed on mine—a slow, lingering kiss that explored every crevice of my needy soul. And when he pulled away, he placed a gag made from the same scarf in my mouth, and I instantly held my breath.

"Breathe, baby," he said.

Chills ran down my spine, his delicate touch trailing from my neck to my chest and over my breast. I exhaled, my shoulders going limp as I tried to relax for him.

"That's it," he said. "You're doing so well. Now, lift those hips for me."

Every little part of me was on fire. I moved my hands until I felt the edge of the desk, and I lifted my hips, letting him slowly pull my pants down over my hips. I started to sit back down, but he grabbed me around the waist and lifted me again, setting down his jacket beneath my bare ass.

Cold air swept over my legs as he torturously relieved me of my leggings. I had no idea where he was going next, no idea of the way he looked at me or anything. A brief second of fear brushed through me, but Gavin's hand was back on my face as though he had sensed it.

He moved the gag down, his lips landing on mine again. The kiss was a comfort and a promise that he had me. That I could trust him. His tongue explored my mouth, the desire distracting me from where his hands were. I could feel his body between my thighs, feel the magnetism of his palm as it hovered over my thigh.

I flinched when he touched my side, the short stroke tickling my cold skin. He smiled against my mouth.

"Are you going to relax for me?" he asked.

I swallowed, heartbeat thudding in my ears. "Yes."

"Will you remember to breathe?"

"Yes."

He placed the fabric back between my teeth, and I forced an inhale. A scoff of approval sounded from Gavin before he kissed my cheek.

"Such a good girl," he whispered. "Do you know what good girls get, baby?"

I shook my head, my body on the verge of trembling already.

He pushed on my knees, widening my thighs and opening me up to him. And as his fingers trailed up my thigh to my sex, I forced another breath into my lungs.

"Good girls get orgasms," he breathed against my cheek.

I whimpered, not just at the feel of his words on my skin but at the brush of the pad of his finger on my clit. My hands gripped the edge of the desk, hips angling upward as he began slow gyrations over those nerves and dipping into my wetness.

"Fuck, baby," he hissed on my collarbone. "I love the way you respond to my touch."

His mouth pressed to my jaw, licking and sucking over the soft part beneath it. I was a puddle as I anticipated where he might kiss or touch next. His free hand squeezed and massaged my breast, thumb swirling over my nipple.

As he began moving down my body, his mouth making sure to kiss and suck and bite nearly every inch, I drew further into a trance. I had no idea where he was going next.

But I felt him.

I felt him all over me.

I felt him on my skin and inside my body. His name was a brand along my flesh, covering and claiming me whole.

And when I heard him on his knees and felt his nose brush my clit, I wasn't sure how much longer I could stay upright.

His breath was jagged as he blew it out over my clit, and I whimpered in response, saliva nearly choking me from the gag.

"Hello, beautiful," he whispered before kissing those nerves. His right arm wrapped around the top of my thigh as it rested on his shoulder, and he flicked my clit with his left.

"Mm… I'm home."

I almost fell backward onto the desk as his mouth wrapped around my clit, and he kissed it as though he were kissing my mouth.

He devoured me, his tongue teasing, his lips sucking and pulling that hardened bundle into his mouth. Over and over while I could do nothing more than grab the edge of the desk and moan behind the fabric between my teeth.

I had no choice but to concede to his pleasure, and fuck… it felt so good to let go.

Letting go of all worry and stress, the tenseness in my body, and the weight on my shoulders. The only things in existence were the pair of us, and I was wholly his.

The noises he made while eating me, the noises my body made in response to him… I was weak for it. He drew out my pleasure and caused my hips to undulate against his face. Shit, it was so fucking good.

Stars rose in the darkness behind my closed eyes. He reached up and squeezed my tit, thumb rolling my nipple. I didn't know what to do with my hands as his tongue swiped up and down my pussy, then licked inside my entrance.

Each moan that left me was more desperate than the last. I tried to deny myself the cresting orgasm. Fuck, he felt too good, and I didn't want this pleasure to subside. I wanted to ride his face until his jaw locked, and he had no choice but to fuck me backward to quell the need for us both.

Darkness swallowed every hesitation and embarrassment I'd ever experienced. I could hear him cursing against me like he was consumed by my taste. My body began to tremble, to quake in anticipation of that release at the very tip of my tongue. I squirmed against him, but he kept going. Determined to make me spill and spill until I couldn't anymore. Resisting only heightened it. My teeth chattered against that gag. I writhed against his tease, his fingers bruising the tops of my thighs, and I finally collapsed.

The gag swallowed my scream. My hips lifted off the desk.

God, I would never look at my office the same way again.

My muscles continued to jerk as he lapped up my juices, his tongue swirling inside me, to tease me to the edge of another release. But I grabbed his hair and felt him smile crookedly against my nerves.

"Do you think one is enough?" he asked, and I could only give a desperate whine in response. "I don't think one is enough," he said as he kissed my clit again. "I think..." another kiss "...my love has been so neglected..." his tongue sank inside me and swirled, teeth grazing those nerves "... that she deserves more...."

I mumbled behind the gag, tugging on his hair.

"What was that?" he mocked me. I felt him move, lean over my body, and pull the gag out of my mouth.

"I said—" I had to wipe the saliva off of my lips. "—I said, she wants your dick," I said blatantly.

A quiet chuckle came from him. "Tell me how you want my dick. Like this? Slow, sweet, and lazy." He pushed my thighs open as much as my body would allow him, his hard cock brushing against my already sensitive pussy. "Or..." His hand trailed up my chest until he reached my throat, and he squeezed my neck, sending my skin erupting in goosebumps. "Do you want your god?"

My chest caved as his grip slackened, and the moment it did, I shot up straight and grabbed him by the neck, pulling him flush to me. Our lips met in a reckless crash. I didn't give him time to think. There was only his primal response of lust as I yanked his hair, scratched his skin, and tightened my thighs around him.

I wasn't sure how he looked at me when I finally drew back, and I didn't care. "Punish me," I hissed. "Give me your godly wrath, *Eros*."

There was a brief second where all I felt was his hands on the outsides of my thighs, fingers extending wide, an intensity stretching between us where I knew he was calculating exactly how much of himself he was about to give me.

A huff of air hit my face, amusement in the salacious chuckle that left him.

"You're a fucking dream," he said in a rasp.

He yanked me off the desk and twisted me around, then shoved my front down onto the desk in such a fast motion that I became limp, my body completely at his mercy and whatever person I had drawn out of him. He slapped my ass so hard that I cried out.

"That's it," he said, yanking my left leg off the ground. "Bend your knee. Get that sexy thigh on the desk and sprawl this pussy out for me."

The inside of my thigh landed by my side, cold air hitting my wet sex. He moved my arm so that I was holding my leg up, and he spanked my ass again before shoving my face down onto the desk.

"Grab the edge of that desk, baby, and hold your leg wide," he said. "Don't let go even when you want to."

I heard the noise of his dropping pants, felt his cock beat against the now-sensitive spot on my cheek, and I whimpered into his jacket.

And when he slammed into me, I knew there was no going back. Goddamn, that fucking cock.

His dick filled me and filled me. Every thrust rougher than the last. His hand was on my face, smushing my cheek into the desk, his other atop mine on my thigh. My ass ached with every hit from his pelvis, the top of my right thigh bruising against the lip of the desk. I gripped the other edge. My scream muffled into his jacket, my hand numbing around the edge. He railed into me, fucking me dirty and unmercifully.

God, it was amazing.

I loved how he could go from sweet and giving to this... *animal*.

Fucking hell.

And it felt *so good* to scream.

I wondered what I looked like then—bent over my desk, scarf wrapped around my head, my legs spread wide while he fucked me so hard that I was already on the verge of coming.

I wanted to record just the noises of our bodies slapping together, the sounds of my pussy responding to his cock, his moans, and mine. Shit, to think how he groaned was all because of how I felt around him... that was enough to make me come.

"Gavin—shit, right there, *right there!*" I cried when he hit the right spot. "Don't stop." I began to wiggle and writhe, my body unsure of if it could take that pleasure.

"I won't, baby," he swore. "Gods, you feel good. *Chloe.*"

Saliva dribbled from my lips onto the desk. I couldn't close my mouth or move with his grip. He threaded his fingers in my hair and yanked my head, arching me and sending a pulse down my spine. I was stretched, my muscles on edge and ready to snap. That orgasm teetered on the tip of my body. I tried squeezing my thighs to keep from coming again, but it was useless.

He had me spread and begging, and fucking Eros... I had no choice but to let go of all restraint. My willpower was shot.

I surrendered.

"Fuck, baby, are you coming for me?" he asked.

"Yes." I screamed his name.

"Shit, you're so tight," he hissed. "Gods, Chloe—"

I couldn't hold it back. He lifted my leg off the desk and shoved my face down again, pushing my muscles past their breaking point, and he rode me through that orgasm. He fucked my throbbing cunt, the noises of our sweating bodies, our moans, and my squelching pussy sounding aloud in the quiet room. Tears fell from my eyes. I sobbed into his jacket. I couldn't breathe. It was so fucking much.

I never wanted it to end.

He was nearly on top of me as he pressed his weight into my head and jolted at my thigh, his hand bruising my skin and defiling my body. He cursed again, and I felt him come inside me. His body stilled, cock buried to the hilt as he released.

The pressure on my face lifted when his hand moved, and I could finally breathe again. He let my foot touch the floor— my leg a limp, numb mess of what had once been muscles and bone and flesh.

His arms wrapped around my thighs, and he collapsed atop me. I tried to steady my breath as his chest rose and fell against my back. We settled there, both too satiated to move. I still couldn't see, and with him, I didn't care if I ever did. I trusted him to guide me through the rest of our lives without the fear of becoming lost.

My skin tingled as he kissed down my spine, one vertebra at a time. He slowly pulled from inside me and cupped my body, tugging me up and around, so our chests were once more flush. I held tight to his waist, his wet cock against my abdomen. I couldn't stand upright on my own. Not yet, at least. I felt him unraveling the scarf around my head. The light hit my eyes. I had to blink at the brightness around us, though a smile slipped on my lips when my eyes landed on his face.

His hair was a mess, his cheeks red, mouth still sagging. The gleam in his eyes made my heart melt. I reached up, trying to make his hair a little tidier but failing spectacularly. A crooked smirk lifted his mouth at my frustration, and he leaned forward, his nose brushing mine.

"Are you okay?" he asked.

"Ask me again later," I managed. "I can't really feel my limbs yet."

He chuckled softly. "I think I lost my mind a little," he whispered. "But you... gods, you draw it out of me."

I leaned in, my teeth raking his bottom lip. "I fucking love it," I breathed. "I love the way you love me."

He reached for my hair, attempting to straighten out where he'd disheveled it. "Are you ready to go meet your friends?" he asked.

"I'm not entirely sure how I'm going to walk or appear as though I haven't been railed over backward, but sure," I answered.

His smirk widened, and he kissed me softly before glancing around the room. "I'm sure they already know," he said. "Ezzie told me no office sex because of the cameras. Now, I'm going to have to kill the security guard."

"What—*Gavin!*" I grabbed his jacket off the desk and covered my chest.

He laughed outright this time, head swinging back. "I'm joking. I just wanted to see you sweat."

I grinned stupidly and shook my head, then shoved his side. "Ass."

But he swept me off the desk and into his arms, my feet off the floor, and he gazed at me with pure bliss in his eyes. "Will you smile like this for me every day?" he asked.

My hands pressed to his cheeks. "Every day."

Chapter Forty-Three

Gavin

I wanted to live in the absolute ecstasy of having Chloe back in my life—wholly in my life—peacefully, for all of eternity. However, with every phone call and text about her canceled wedding, I felt her fade, and I wasn't sure how to help her.

Lana and I tried to keep her occupied and help her continue living normally with work. I wasn't sure we realized how much it would affect her. It hurt me to see her like that, and I wracked my brain to figure out what I could do.

"She just needs time," Persephone said when she came to my office a week after Chloe left Tyler. "It's a breakup."

I sighed and sank back into my seat. "It's eating me," I admitted. "I feel like I'm not enough."

Her mouth twisted into a pout. "So cute," she cooed. "It's just a timing thing, Eros. She has to let herself feel happiness. And on the day her wedding was supposed to be, I'm sure she'll be a little more depressed. You just have to be there for her."

"Lana is taking her to the cliffs to jump in the ocean and then burn her dress," I said.

Persephone's eyes lit up at the mention of fire. "Do you think they'd let me join?"

I gave her a flat look. "And have you accidentally mention she's a long-lost goddess? No. I can't trust you arou yet. She'd never trust me again."

"Yes, how are you planning on bringing that up?"

My insides curled as I thought about it. "My mother has been calling me," I said, ignoring her previous question. "She keeps asking me to come home."

"Why don't you?"

"I'm going to see her at the retreat," I answered.

"Oh? So you are going? Are you bringing Chloe?"

"I have a plan," I said, picking up a pencil and twirling it between my fingers.

Persephone raised a brow. "You can't tell me any of it?"

"I'm keeping this one close," I said.

"Fine, fine," she sighed. "Hades isn't thrilled about going either."

"I'm surprised you're conning him into this. I can't imagine he's happy about a retreat with Zeus."

"I told him we can stay at the other end of the compound." She shrugged. "He just has to make one drink appearance. Though, he keeps saying he needs to work."

"Considering he's the only one of us with a job that he actually has to do, I'd say he's not lying," I replied.

"Now, you sound like him."

I chuckled quietly as my phone vibrated on the desk.

Do you think your friend Zayn is free on September 16th? Chloe asked.

I can ask. Why?

Lana needs a date for Ezzie and Raegan's wedding.

I didn't have the wedding on my calendar yet. *Do you need a date for yourself?*

I wondered if she smiled.

Ha-ha, she replied. *Will you go with me to their wedding on the 16th?*

I'll have to check my calendar. I'm very busy.

Gavin.

I chuckled, and Persephone cleared her throat. My gaze lifted to her. "Sorry. Wife," I said.

"I figured out that much by the stupid smile on your face," she replied.

I think I need a picture of you in the dress you're wearing before I say yes, I texted Chloe.

"I'll leave you alone with your little girlfriend," Persephone said as she stood. She made a disgusted face. "Girlfriend… that sounds lousy. I hope you plan on rectifying that soon."

"With getting her memories back or another wedding?" I asked.

"Both. You need to renew your vows," she said.

I stood, laying my phone face-down on the desk. "I'll work on it," I said, ushering her to the door. She turned into me as she paused, picked the lint off my shoulder, and stared at me with a subtle smile.

"You have her back." Her palm hit my face in a playful slap. "Now, wake her up."

On August 26th, I woke up in the dark to the noise of her in the shower. I knew she and Lana planned to drive up the coast, jump into the ocean in her wedding dress, and burn it. I had offered to drive them, which Lana had gladly approved since the pair planned to drink while they were out there.

Only it wasn't the sound of her in the shower that made me stare at the door. It was how, somehow, in that space, I felt her sadness.

I didn't ask if she was okay as I opened the door to the steaming shower. She was sitting on the bench, her head in her hands as the hot water rained on her from above. Fucking Styx. I hated seeing her like this. I knew it wasn't her mourning the wedding. She had little attachment to it. But years of her life… feeling as though it had been wasted, she continued to dwell on it.

She looked up as I opened the glass door and stepped inside the shower with her, although she didn't speak, and when I reached her, she stood and wrapped her arms around me. I hugged her close, closing my eyes and inhaling her sorrow, determined for her never to feel this way again.

Gods, it hurt.

"I just feel so stupid sometimes," she whispered. "Why did I think I ever needed to settle? Why did I think I needed someone else to hide behind when I'm perfectly fine at loving myself?"

I pulled back and tilted her chin back with my knuckle. "Societal pressure, most likely," I said, and her mouth flinched upward as she gazed at me. "It's annoying these days, though not nearly as bad as it used to be. Back then, if you weren't married off by fifteen, they thought you a hag."

She snorted, shaking her head as she tightened her arms around me.

"What?" I asked.

"I thought you were going to say something all broody and sweet. Like 'you're not stupid,' or 'we only accept the love that we think we deserve,' or I don't know… *anything* else?"

"Saying 'you're not stupid' is broody and sweet?" I asked.

Her expression flattened. "You know what I mean."

"I can quote romance novels if that's what you would prefer," I said.

A quiet chuckle left her, and she stood on her toes to kiss

me. "No," she finally decided. "No, you're perfect."

I kissed her a little longer then, letting the hot water beat on my back, relishing her taste and the smell of the vanilla rose shampoo she'd used already.

"Are you ready for today?" I asked when we'd parted.

"Yeah," she said. "I'm ready to put it all behind me, to start new," and her hands pressed on my chest, eyes lifting to mine. "To only remember life with you."

Lana was waiting for us when we finally emerged from the shower—after I devoured Chloe with morning praise, bending to my knees and holding her leg over my shoulder, lifting her against the wall and embedding my length inside her until neither of us could take it anymore.

"God, you two are loud," Lana said, grinning as she sipped her tea and checked her emails.

Chloe's gaze darted to me, and I winked at her in response, then took down two coffee mugs from the cabinet.

"After Ez and Raegan's wedding, you can tell us how loud Zayn is," Chloe said.

"I would've loved to have been physically introduced to him before the wedding," Lana said. "Although, texting with him has been fun."

Chloe glanced at me. "You gave him her number?"

I shook my head, pouring oat milk into both mugs. "He's the CFO of a major dating app that loves having fun more than anyone I know," I said. "I'm sure she didn't have to do much digging to find him."

Lana was smiling smugly behind her cup when Chloe looked at her. Her long, tightly curled hair was pulled atop her head behind a silk scarf this morning, as it had been nearly every morning for the last three weeks, though this was the brightest scarf I had seen on her thus far. She had taken her therapy appointments with patients online while there, usually sitting out on the balcony or in the private guest room if Chloe and I were home.

"Do you have any patients this morning?" Chloe asked Lana.

Lana gave her a look, and Chloe snickered softly, apparently remembering what day it was. I loved that the weight of today had slipped from her mind, even if it was only for a moment.

"Right. Well, what time do you want to leave then?" Chloe asked.

"Hour or so?" Lana replied. "How long do you think it will take us to get there," she asked me.

I handed Chloe her coffee. "A few hours," I said, glancing at my clock. "We should get moving soon."

The drive up the coast to where they wanted to go took three hours, which didn't include stopping at Chloe's storage locker for her dress.

Chloe and Lana sat in the back seat, the wind blowing their hair as Lana sang the words to every song on the radio. And while I thought Chloe might join in, she only smiled at Lana occasionally and hugged that dress to her chest like a safety blanket.

I let the pair do their thing once we arrived at the empty beach. Seeing Chloe in that wedding dress made every muscle within me come alive. She was stunning. The dress fit and accentuated her body in the best way. Our eyes met when she had it on, and she gave me a small smile before Lana tugged her arm and pulled her toward the crashing waves.

One step into that salty water and the dress was forever ruined.

Lana made sure to document the ruination with her phone, though I knew better than to think she would have posted the photos anywhere.

They lit it on fire an hour after in one of the fire pits the park had buried in the sand and watched as the thing practically melted away. Lana hugged her arms around her best friend as she let go of that past—of a person and a life that never deserved her.

And that night, I held Chloe a little tighter than I had in the weeks before. That hesitation that had lingered between us was finally gone. That part of her life was over, and this new one was just beginning.

I wish I had been happy with that. I should have been. I should have let it go. But every time I looked at her, I thought of all the years we had spent apart, of the centuries I'd spent without remembering that I'd once been married.

I needed to know what had happened, who had taken her. It was bound to drive me to the brink of insanity if I didn't.

We drove Lana to the airport two days later. She would have stayed, but she kept saying her cat would forget her if she stayed away much longer. We would be seeing her in a few weeks anyway, so she and Chloe's goodbye wasn't as hard as it would be after that.

Even still, by the way in which Chloe held her best friend, I wondered if she would ever be happy so far away from her.

"Do you want to grab anything from your storage locker?" I asked as we drove back to my condo.

"What do you mean?" Chloe asked.

"Clothes, photos, blankets… anything that might help you feel more at home at my place?"

Her lips twisted slightly, and I had to look twice at her smirking face. "What?" I asked.

"Gavin Erosin, are you asking me to move in with you?" she asked.

The gleam in her eyes was so cute.

"I can ask you to marry me again if you'd rather hear that first," I said.

She bit her lips together to keep from smiling, a blush

rising on her cheeks. "Ask me again," she said, and a lump formed in my throat. "Maybe not today. Maybe not tomorrow. But ask me."

I reached over and squeezed her knee. She pressed her hands atop mine, and I know I beamed at her more brightly than ever.

"What can I do right now to make you feel at home? Finally," I asked.

She leaned over the console and kissed my cheek. "You are my home," she said. "But a few photos around the place would also cheer me up. And my sunflower blanket."

I chuckled and made a U-turn. "Okay."

Chapter Forty-Four

Chloe

****Warning: the following chapter contains a story of domestic violence****

We arrived at the vineyard for Ezzie and Raegan's wedding weekend on the morning of the rehearsal dinner. We planned to drive up the night before, but once Lana's plane was delayed and Zayn decided he wanted to ride with us, Gavin ended up chartering a jet instead.

Ezzie and Raegan greeted us in the dirt parking lot with bottles of wine in each of their hands. Their families and many of their friends were already there, and the gathering was in full swing.

"So, what's on the agenda for tonight?" Lana asked once we'd all showered each other with greetings and hugs.

"Rae and I have a quick run-through for the ceremony tomorrow," Ezzie said. "They'll show us our marks, all of that. However, you all are free to do whatever you want. We'll have dinner once we're back, and then we have a live band and a few other things, including speeches."

"What's the other?" I asked.

"Ezzie hired fire dancers," Raegan said.

"My *father* hired fire dancers," Ezzie corrected. "He wanted to pay homage to our Samoan heritage. We aren't doing anything traditional, so I thought, why not?"

"Are they actual Samoan fire dancers?" I asked.

Ezzie's smile broadened. "They really are."

"Oh, I can't wait," Lana said, a gleam in her eyes.

"So, it's dinner, fire dancers, speeches, and then they've set up some fire pits in the courtyard for us to sit around while the musicians play," Raegan said. She grinned as she looked between all of us. "Let's have some fun."

It felt so fucking good to have someone on my arm who wanted to be there and enjoyed being around my friends. Someone who joined their shenanigans and didn't disappear on the phone or make excuses to get another drink. Even Zayn fitted in well with the group, and with as happy as I was surrounded by so much love, I, again, wondered what the fuck I had been thinking the last three years.

Everyone was wired and drinking, happy to have a few nights off work to let loose and commemorate the union. Ezzie and Raegan's families celebrated lavishly with dancing, games, and speeches that had us all nearly falling out of our seats laughing. It was a true joy being there, and I knew had I gone .through with my own wedding, it would have been nothing like it.

I found myself falling asleep in Gavin's arms as we sat around the fire pit—well after the dancers and the dinner when everyone was deciding whether they were ready for more or ready to turn in.

Gavin and I were the latter.

The sun had set long ago, and I was happy to return to our villa to relax and enjoy the mountain air.

I kissed both Ezzie and Raegan goodnight, noticing that they, too, were winding down. The only two that weren't were Zayn and Lana; however, I was dying to know how the pair hadn't snuck off into a coat closet and fucked yet. There was as much tension between them as there had been with Gavin and me that Valentine's night.

Gavin held my hand as we walked back, the sound of live music and laughter echoing in the background. There was a delight in his gaze when he looked at me, and I had to eye him when we were ascending the hill to our villa.

"What?"

He raised my hand to his lips. "Just looking at you," he said.

I had brought new lingerie for this occasion—but not the pink dinosaur suit, though I had brought it, too. It was so much fun, I couldn't resist.

This lingerie set was pink and black—an underbust corset with garters and a lace-up back, crotchless panties, heart pasties, and stockings. As Gavin took a shower, I slipped into it and checked myself out in the mirror. I didn't know why, but vacations always made me crave intimacy more than at home.

I was lying on the bed with my tablet when Gavin emerged from the bath. At first, he walked right past me to his suitcase in the other room, but then I saw him walk backward out of the corner of my eye, brows narrowed as if he'd noticed the lace.

"Fuck me," he muttered under his breath.

But I ignored him.

Each step he took around my side of the bed made me want to squirm, look over the device, and meet his eyes. I wanted to know what he was thinking. What his plan was upon seeing the lingerie.

"So… what's new in monster erotica?" he asked, his voice hesitant as he sat on the bed by my bent knees.

My insides heated with anticipation, forcing my eyes to reread the same line repeatedly in my book. "How do you know I'm reading monster erotica?"

His hand trailed down my calf, squeezing the muscle slightly. "Lucky guess," he said. He picked my leg up and kissed the inside of my knee. "Minotaurs?"

I shifted. "A few."

"Fuck, are these crotchless?" he said, though I wasn't sure he was speaking directly to me.

I finally glanced over the screen toward him and had to bite my lips together at the hungry look in his eyes. He was touching my legs like it was his first time seeing them, staring at my panties and corset like he could eat them.

I made a mental note to purchase edible lingerie for Halloween and Valentine's.

"Mm… you can keep reading if you like." He kissed my hip in the small area between the corset and my underwear. "Let me take this in. Gods, you're fucking sexy," he muttered as he settled between my thighs. "Tell me about your book."

"Ah… it's about a princess who—" I swallowed as he clenched my ass, thumbs running beneath the garters. "— who has an arranged marriage to a foreign prince to bring together kingdoms. Shit—" I found my hips undulating against his rubbing my thighs and kissing my stomach. "And she… she is assigned a knight, who happens to be a minotaur, and she falls in love with both the human prince and the minotaur."

"So, who does she choose?" he asked.

"*Fuck*… She doesn't have to choose," I managed. "Why should she?"

"Isn't that what usually happens? She has to pick between the two lovers?"

"We don't have to choose anymore. She gets the human prince, the minotaur, and all the activities that… *shit*… come with it."

Gavin chuckled against my breast. "Is that what you want, baby? A threesome with a minotaur?"

I glanced up, unable to stifle my smile, and Gavin stopped sucking my skin. "I mean… do you know one?" I asked.

"I know several," he replied.

There was another pause, during which Gavin sat up and laughed.

"Listen, you laugh, but that sounds like a great anniversary present," I said, grinning widely. "I think *you* might enjoy that. Watching a mythical creature bend me over, claw marks on my back. Or maybe me on top grabbing his horns—"

"Should I leave you alone with your fantasy?" he teased.

I snickered, set the device on the bedside table, and reached for his adorable face. His smiling lips landed on mine, and he settled over me, his bare body lying between my bent legs.

"Do you think my fantasies and smutty books are ridiculous?" I asked.

He kissed me again. "I think they're part of who you are, and I love that you share it with me. Even if you're fantasizing about monster cock."

I snickered, and he kissed me once more.

"I love this lingerie," he said.

"I thought you might," I replied as he bit my neck. "But it's not meant for me to lie here while you touch me."

"No?" His teeth raked over my throat. "What is it meant for, then?"

I pushed on his chest and turned him onto his back, my legs hiking on either side of his hips. "I know how much you like seeing me in lingerie while I suck this big cock." I reached beneath me and began stroking his already hardening length.

He moved his hands to my hips, squeezing my ass to the point that I whimpered, and then he spanked me hard. I shifted until his cock was in front of my bare pussy, and I began to swirl my thumb on his tip, my other hand caressing him up and down.

"Fuck, baby," he hissed, smacking my ass and grabbing me with every stroke down his shaft.

I loved watching what I did to him. It was addicting—how much he wanted me, the way he looked at me. I couldn't get enough of it.

I moved my legs between his widened thighs, settling myself there and bending down.

"You know I love you like this," he said, his eyes moving to my ass wiggling in the air.

My nails scratched his pelvis, tracing over the unicorn on his hip. "I thought you might," I said before licking the tip of his cock. He groaned into the mattress, his eyes closing as I began working him down. His dick disappeared further and further into my mouth. God, he was so fucking hard. My mouth stretched to fit around him, saliva dribbling out of the corners.

"That's it, baby," he rasped. "Take my cock. Just like that. Fuck, Chloe—" His head pitched back onto the pillow, hands threading in my hair, and he pushed in to me.

His length hit the back of my throat, and he didn't stop. He nudged me down and down until I choked and gasped. Until all of him disappeared. Tears welled in my gaze. I tried collecting myself at the suffocation and gag, but only when he allowed me to come back up could I catch my breath. Fuck, I was drooling. His fingers massaged and scratched my scalp, sending chills down my spine.

"Do you enjoy choking on me?" he asked, and I hummed a greedy response. He chuckled softly. "I think that ass needs to be redder, baby. Before you go down on me again, I'll make sure it's so red that it aches. Does that make your pussy wet?"

Hell, yes, it did.

I groaned around him, picking up my pace and grasping

his balls. He inhaled sharply again as I straightened and pushed my breasts around his length, bobbing up and down.

"Do you want to come on my tits?" I asked him. "Or do you want me swallowing that dick?"

Serious debate rose in his eyes. He wiped one of my tears away with his thumb, then rolled that damp finger on my breast. I licked his slit as I moved down, making his throat bob in response.

"Keep doing that," he rasped. "And when I come, I want you to open wide. You're going to take every last drop of me."

My breasts enveloped his cock, and I shifted up and down, slowly at first, tasting him every time I descended. I could feel him straining to deny himself that release, saw the veins in his neck when he almost gasped.

"Are you coming for me?" I asked after my lips popped off his cock.

"Shit," he cursed, his eyes opening to look at me. I watched him again as I wrapped my mouth around him, my breasts still pushed up. My pace quickened.

"Fucking gods, *Chloe*."

I loved when he called my name like that.

He was on that edge, the underside of his cock taut. His knuckles were white on the sheets. Every muscle in his body went rigid—

He spilled over my breasts and on my awaiting tongue. I captured his dick with my lips, sucking and swallowing his cum as he overflowed. His groan hadn't stopped. He was still coming down from that euphoria, his back resting on the mattress as though he could sink into it if he allowed himself.

I kissed his hip, the trail of his hair down his pelvis, his abs, to his chest, and his hands finally landed back on my hips when I crawled over his waist again.

"Mm…" he moaned when I enclosed my lips upon his

throat. *"Fuck,* baby." He spanked my ass twice as I sat on his stomach.

A daze rested in his gaze as he lifted his hand toward my face. His thumb brushed the corner of my lip, wiping the cum away that dared to dribble free. I ran my tongue over my mouth, swallowing those last salty drops.

Gavin threaded his hand behind my head and pulled me down to his lips, our tongues sweeping and tasting every trace of him that remained. He grabbed my ass, pulled my flesh, and spanked me hard enough that I flinched. Again and again. Moans escaped me into his mouth as I ground against his abs, rubbing my clit there and losing myself in that contact.

"Fuck," he hissed. "Give me a minute, baby. You can use me for everything you need," he managed.

He reached for my breasts, both hands palming them harshly as I arched back. His thumbs swiped over the heart-shaped pasties on my nipples, fingers curling around my ribs.

I was so lost in the moment, so satisfied and ready to continue fucking him until the sun came up and we were forced to mingle with friends—

"Chloe?"

I realized that he was motionless beneath me, his hands hadn't moved, and his energy... he felt stiff. I opened my eyes, finding him staring at my left breast where his thumb lingered on my tattooed rib.

Shit.

His gaze was narrowed as he rubbed over the ink and the long scar I had tried to hide three years ago with the carefully placed design. A shadowed expression of what I could only decipher as rage stretched over his eyes.

His lashes lifted to mine. "What... What is this?"

"What? The tattoo?" I asked, playing dumb.

"No, this—"

A lump formed in my throat. "It's nothing," I said, leaning over to kiss his neck. "Let's get back to—"

But he wasn't having it.

"You have a scar," he said. "Why? It's bad. What happened?"

The concern in his tone made me sigh. "Well, that's over," I muttered, realizing he wouldn't let it go. I sat up, pressed on his chest, and rose off of him one leg at a time. "It's nothing. Just a scratch," I lied as I grabbed a robe from the bathroom.

Hurt rested in his gaze when I came back into the bedroom. He was sitting on the side, hands gripping the edge of the mattress.

"Why are you lying to me?" he asked softly.

I had to clench my teeth as my emotions swelled, and I folded my arms over my chest. "Because I don't want you to think there's anything you can do," I answered truthfully.

"Did someone hurt you?"

"Gavin—"

"Chloe, tell me who hurt you," he said, rising to his feet. "What happened? What—"

"Oh, god, Gavin. *Who do you think?*" I snapped.

I hadn't meant to. I hadn't meant to raise my voice or sneer. It was just...

"Shit," I whispered, my head in my hand. "I'm sorry. I don't mean to yell." I sat down on the bed and sighed. I couldn't *not* tell him. If we were to spend our lives together, I couldn't go on with one more secret, especially one this big.

"It's why I had to move apartments that year," I admitted. "The reason I deleted myself from everything."

Gavin sat down at my side, but he didn't speak. Instead, he simply held my hand as I told him about one of the scariest days of my life.

"I was home alone. Lana was supposed to be coming over,

so when someone knocked on the door, I didn't think anything of it, but it was Aidan. I tried to get him to leave. He pleaded with me. Told me he'd changed. He swore things would be different. God, he was so... *adamant*. Desperate, even. It even crossed my mind that he might be on drugs with how out of his mind he seemed. I tried to get him to leave. I told him I was done, I wasn't falling for his lies anymore. And he... he tried to force himself on me. We fought, and I fell into my coffee table and broke the glass top. One of the glass shards stabbed me, and for some reason, he just didn't stop. Not even with me bleeding on the floor and screaming."

I had to pause, tears rising in my eyes. Gavin squeezed my hand, and I knew I could work through it.

"Lana heard me screaming when she was coming off the elevator, saw him standing over me, and she hit him over the head with a wine bottle. He started to turn his wrath on her, but she grabbed a knife, and he ran out of there before he could do anymore. She called 9-1-1, and I spent the next week in the hospital. They said the shard just missed my heart, but despite that, they didn't know how I was still alive with the amount of blood I had lost."

"Did you go to the police?" he asked.

"I didn't want to," I admitted. "I didn't think there would be much they could do. Lana ended up telling them everything while I was asleep. They caught Aidan at his apartment the next day and charged him with assault. He spent a week in prison, but somehow, his charges were dropped. It's like they were erased. Everything. Even his mugshot. Lana had packed my apartment by the time I was out of the hospital. She had found me a new place and rented it under one of our other friends' names. She took care of everything. She even changed my phone number and deleted my app profiles. I had a friend I hired once I was settled to scour the internet for any other mentions or photos of me from friends in the past and deleted them, too. And then, the next month, I saw that Aidan was back on tour with his band."

"What's the band?" Gavin asked, and I could see the rage billowing in his eyes.

"I'm not telling you," I said firmly.

"Why?"

"Because there's no point in drudging up the past," I said. "Aidan is crazy, and he's famous now."

"Does he still go by Aidan?" Gavin asked, and I glowered at him.

"No, he doesn't," I affirmed. "And I'm not telling you his stage name."

"Chloe—"

"Gavin." And I said his name so finitely that he sounded like he was growling at me in response. I sighed heavily, shaking my head. "If we ever cross paths with him, feel free to pummel him into a pulp. But I'm not telling you his name for you to seek him out."

Gavin ran his hands through his hair, teeth set, and finally, he let out a slow breath.

"Fine," he agreed, though his voice remained on edge. "Fine. But if we ever see him, I don't care who he is, Chloe. He's fucking dead."

Chapter Forty-Five

Gavin

I didn't sleep.

I lay there, staring at the ceiling as Chloe rested against my chest. Her ex was already on my list of beings to take care of, but now he had moved up, tied with the god that had taken her away from me. I felt like I was so close to pinning it down, like going to that retreat would be the final nail I needed to support the theory I'd been working on.

Even if I really didn't want to go.

I liked the bubble we were living in, and it was nice not worrying that someone might try and tear us apart yet.

Zayn met me outside at sunrise, shirt absent and only wearing his pajama joggers. I sighed as I sat on the opposite end of the beige lounging couch, and we cheers'd the air with our coffee mugs. I noticed his unruly hair, the hickey on his pectoral muscle, and a lazy smirk making its way to my lips.

"Take it you had a fun night," I said, looking at the purple sunrise.

"Understatement of the year," Zayn said. "She is… *wild.*"

I almost choked on my coffee. "That's a mild way of putting it," I managed. "Whenever you propose, though, make sure you suggest her moving here. I think Chloe misses her."

Zayn adjusted himself. "You might see less of me at the

office. I'll be chartering that plane from yesterday to take me across the country for booty calls. Fucking hell," he muttered with a shake of his head. "Where's she been hiding?"

I smiled against my mug as Zayn cursed and told me about Lana's wild ways. When Chloe emerged from inside, he had just gotten to the part where she'd put honey on his dick.

"She stole that trick from me," Chloe said, settling on my knee. "But I'm glad you enjoyed it," she winked.

Her hair was wet, her makeup absent, and she was wearing loose black shorts and a tank beneath a plaid flannel shirt. Our eyes met as she leaned her elbow on my shoulder. Unspoken words rang between us, both thinking of the night before, of her confession.

We had barely spoken after.

"I love you," she mouthed in silence.

"I love you." I kissed her, my heart strumming in response to the softened way her tongue swept against mine. Her hand rested on my cheek, nails scratching the scruff on my jaw.

A smile slipped onto her lips when we parted, prompting me to kiss her jaw and slide the hand that wasn't visible to Zayn beneath her shorts. A quiet giggle left her as she shoved me.

"We'll be gone most of the day," she announced, ignoring my hand on her ass. "You two will need to fend for yourselves until about four, then make your way to the big oak tree under which they're getting married. The ceremony is at 4:30, but we'll meet you there around 4:15ish, I think. They may not have an official wedding party, but they offered hair and makeup, so we took them up on it."

"Looks like it's me and you," Zayn said, raising his cup to me again. "What kind of trouble do you think we can get in?"

"I have some trouble for you," Lana said as she joined us. She barely glanced at Chloe and me before straddling Zayn's lap and kissing him hard, her hands spread wide on his cheeks. Zayn dropped his coffee mug, which rolled into the bushes as he grasped her hips and pulled her closer.

"So, are you hungry?" Chloe asked me, her eyes wide as she tried to ignore their public display.

I grabbed her ass again. "Please."

The pair were gone an hour later, both rushing out the door, insisting that they were in too much of a rush to show off their dresses.

Zayn looked at me, his hands on his hips as the door closed behind the girls.

"Want to go get drunk after a nap?" he asked.

I scoffed. "Sure."

Zayn and I headed to the ceremony site after attending every wine-tasting and event the vineyard had on its agenda that day.

The space was filled with flowers and boho decor that blended in with the landscape, so much so that it appeared as though it had always been there. Zayn and I snagged two seats toward the back among a few other friends we'd met that morning.

Are you and Zayn at the ceremony? Chloe texted ten minutes before it was set to start.

Sitting at the back, I replied.

Okay. We'll be up there in a few minutes. Lana took extra time deciding which lingerie to wear beneath her dress.

I scoffed. *I wondered why Zayn had been staring at his phone half the morning.*

Lol yes. See you in a few.

I didn't reply, but I angled myself so that I could see her when the pair finally made it up the steps.

We didn't have to wait long. The violinist began playing, and a few minutes after they started, I found myself staring at the most stunning creature alive. Fucking Styx, if my mother had seen Chloe right then, she might have tried to kill her herself.

Her emerald green dress had one long sleeve, and the diagonal neckline swept over her left side. It cinched the middle at her waist and hugged slightly on the tops of her hips before flowing straight down, a high slit on the right side. The nude pumps she wore made her legs look longer. Her hair had subtle waves, falling over her shoulder softly.

Her eyes brightened when she spotted me, and I stood, unable to stay seated with the restlessness in my bones.

A slight blush rose on her cheeks when she made her way over to me.

"You do clean up nicely," she said upon reaching me.

I tilted her head back with my knuckle and kissed her. Her lip drew behind her teeth when we parted, and I had to take a step back from her, holding out her arms to take her in completely.

"You look…" A low whistle escaped me, and she did a twirl under my hand.

"It's too much, isn't it?" she asked. "I told Lana it was."

"No, it's… holy fuck," was all I could manage. "It's making me want to skip this ceremony and haul you into the closest private space I can find, hold your arms around your back with this tie, and fuck you until you can't breathe."

Her brows raised. "Explicit," she bantered.

"Serious," I said.

She beamed, a licentious daze in her eyes, and she reached up to my tie to straighten it. "After dinner and speeches.

When we can disappear, and no one will notice," she said.

"Fuck, you're making me wait that long?" I asked.

"Worth it to see you squirm all night," she smirked.

I pulled her closer, one hand squeezing on her waist, the other beneath her hair so I could discreetly grasp her throat. She gasped softly, a quiet moan sounding from her, and I felt goosebumps rise on her skin.

"Minx."

My palms itched to touch her during the ceremony and cocktail hour. I wanted to appreciate how beautiful the day was, but it took everything in me not to stare at her.

And she fucking knew it.

Her hand had sat too high on the inside of my thigh through the ceremony. Her cheeks had pulled a little too taut around the straw in her drink during cocktail hour, and she'd taken too long to suck the olives off a toothpick when we snacked at the pickle bar.

However, she didn't let it distract her from having fun with her friends. I was a sidebar to her fun time, and I didn't care. I loved that she was completely herself and hadn't felt any need to hide. She was wholly Chloe, and I had never loved her more.

By the time the dinner had been served, the brides had been announced, the speeches had been given, and my face hurt from smiling and laughing. Chloe and I had already danced a couple of times to the band's music, spinning her in circles as she laughed and smiled.

I hadn't been to such a joyous wedding in decades. But Ezzie, Raegan, and their extravagant families were the epitome of happiness and union.

The band was taking down their set when the dance floor officially opened to the DJ playing nineties and early 2000s hip-hop and pop music, making many guests rush to the floor, where Chloe and Lana became the center. They knew every lyric as though they had rehearsed them several times.

During one of the group line dance songs, Chloe took my hand and dragged me down the hall to a random storage closet.

It took me less than a minute to press her against the shelves, haul her dress up, and sink inside of her. I held my hand over her mouth, moving in and out of her rapidly and drawing out every bit of desire that had ramped up between us all night. Fuck, she was soaking, so fucking tight and ready, as if she'd been thinking about this moment for as long as I had.

I moved my hand from her mouth and wrapped it around her throat, making her whimper, her lip flinching like she wanted to smile. Only my mouth caught hers, and I kissed her breathlessly. She grabbed the shelf edges, her end nearing, and I repeatedly slammed inside her.

When she came, she came with a squeal that I was sure people heard on the dance floor. I didn't care. The look on her face was enough to make me forget about all of them. She was irresistible, the only thing I had needed in my life since the moment we'd met.

There was one more thing I had to do to secure it.

"Marry me," I managed as we stilled, my cock still buried inside her.

Chloe's eyes narrowed, and I saw her breath hitch, jaw clenching with her swallow. "Are you serious?" she asked. She slipped off me, her feet hitting the floor, but she hadn't looked away from my eyes. "Are you sure it isn't just the joy of the wedding we're at getting to your head?"

"I was serious weeks ago," I managed. "I love you, and I don't want to wander around for years in some teetering relationship stage when I already know I want to spend my life with you—when, I think, you want to spend yours with me, too. Because 'girlfriend' is too weak of a word for what I feel for you, and fiancé is an in-between that we're well past. But wife… Wife might come close. Wife. Soulmate. Eternal partner. I just want you forever."

She stared at me, and I waited for the rejection. I waited for her to tell me I was crazy, that I was rushing things, and that she'd barely left her last relationship.

Except tears glistened in her eyes, and she took my face in her hands.

"Yes," she breathed.

My heart dropped. I finally exhaled, my lips meeting hers. "Yes?" I asked, needing to hear her say it again.

"*Yes.*"

We didn't come out of that closet and announce the news to the world. We held it close, knowing the rest of the night that we were something more than what the rest of the room thought us to be. I would have ran to the officiant right then and had her marry us if that was what Chloe wanted. However, I knew where she wanted to go, and maybe after the retreat, I would take her. I would give her exactly what she wanted.

So, for the remainder of the evening, we danced.

She stayed on the floor even when I left her, dancing with her friends to a slew of songs that I couldn't help but laugh at. Every time a slow song came on, or she took a moment to have a drink, her smile seemed a little brighter, her eyes a little softer.

And I fucking prayed I could hang onto that when I told her the truth.

Chapter Forty-Six

Chloe

It was the first of October when Gavin took me to the opening day of the local autumn fair. And while it might not have been the crisp autumn day we were hoping for, it was still that perfect date that he'd promised me—including the thorough fucking between the trailers and the cotton candy he ate off of me when we got home.

Home.

That word had a new meaning.

Fuck, I was so in love, it was disgusting—somehow, even more than I had been just weeks before.

As we lay on the couch that night, watching reruns of our favorite show, I noticed how much more attention he'd been paying to his phone since we had gotten out of the shower, almost sighing in annoyance at the distraction when it lit up.

"Who is it?" I asked when he nearly tossed it onto the table beside him.

"My mother and Persephone. Say the word, and I'll turn it off," he added.

"You sound like you want me to tell you that," I replied.

"I might," he said, and I smiled.

"What do they want?" I asked.

"Ah… mostly just to know if we're going to that retreat in a few weeks. Though, my mother wants me to go home before that." He ran a hand through his hair and then slumped his head back, lolling his face toward me. "Save me."

"What exactly would you like?" I asked, almost chuckling at his frustration. "I didn't think you wanted to go to that retreat anyway."

"Yes, but you want to go," he said.

"I mean… of course, I would love to go to some extravagant oasis in the middle of the desert held together by magic and meet gods and goddesses I've only ever read stories about while also watching you squirm at their questions since, apparently, you haven't been to one of these in years." I blinked twice at his taut lips, fighting my own amusement. "Did I miss anything?"

"I think you covered it," he replied.

"Although, you know, you still haven't offered me proof of your own godliness, so for all I know, I'm just going to meet a bunch of actors. It's a pretty elaborate scheme, but I've heard of worse."

He ogled at me, the challenge rising in his gaze. "You want to meet your god?" he asked.

I knelt on the couch, eager for his plans. "Yes."

"You realize there is no going back," he said, leaning over his knees. "Once I show you, you're in. Forever."

I held up my hand and wiggled the finger with the wedding ring he had presented me with at the carnival—two rough golden bands, one with five embedded natural amethysts, the other with a vine-like etching around a raw diamond. It was dainty and perfectly rugged around the edges.

I loved it.

"I'm already in forever," I swore.

A smirk lifted the corner of his lip, and he stood, holding out his hand. "Come on."

He led me up the last flight of stairs in the building that opened to the roof. We had been up there a few times to gaze at the stars. Someone had affixed a small raised-bed garden with bulb lights strung across the patio.

"Why are we up here?" I asked as he took me to the edge of the roof.

He turned into me, body flush to mine, and I reveled at the look in his gaze.

"Stare only at my eyes," he said, cupping my face. "Only there, and don't look away."

"Whatever you say," I replied, grinning broadly with amusement.

"I love how you look at me with that smile," he said softly. He was so fucking cute, his smile widening at mine. He pulled my arms around his waist, his own tightening on my hip and my cheek.

"Hang tight, baby."

I almost frowned. *Hang tight.* What did he—

I had to look twice at him when I went to respond. His skin was… *glowing.* Not like the sun, but a faint gleam, like his features were somehow highlighted against the dark night. Every crevice of his chiseled face looked somehow more godly than usual. His eyes were so luminescent green that I had to touch his face.

My fingers seemed to hover over his skin like the glow could wrap itself around my hands. I don't know why, but a lump formed in my throat. My heart began to ache. An emotion that I couldn't resist bubbled to the surface.

He was… so familiar. His appearance tugged on something in the back of my mind. A memory knocking on the door—no, *beating* on the door. Desperate to break free. It felt like a word on the tip of my tongue meant to drive me to madness.

Something moved behind him, and I stepped out of his

grasp.

Wings.

They weren't full wings of perfect white feathers, spread wide and glorious in the moonlight. No. They were an outline in the air, a shimmering whisper when he moved.

"This is just a portion of my true form," he said. "I'd hate to blind you with my complete self. Not until…"

His voice trailed, but I didn't care to ask what he meant. I wanted to tell him he was beautiful, that I didn't care if I went blind, so long as I got to truly see him before I did.

However, all I could think about was that feeling threading through my bones and becoming more profound with every passing second.

Gavin reached behind him, pulled a long golden arrow from thin air, and twirled it in his fingers. "I don't really need these anymore," he said. "Haven't used them in a long while. Still… the memories are fond."

My ears began to ring as nausea crept up my throat. I blinked profusely, to the point that he seemed to notice. His brows narrowed, and he reached out for my hand.

The moment his incandescent fingers laid atop mine, something shifted within me.

It was like a knot had broken free and set my limbs and heart loose from whatever restraint had been forced around them. I wobbled on my feet. A foreign yearning made its way to the surface from my subconsciousness, making me restless and insatiable for the man standing before me. I wasn't in my own body. It was as if my soul had removed itself, and I was looking at Gavin the way he was always meant to be.

"Whoa—" he grabbed my arm. "Chloe?"

I stared at him, my eyes wide. Unable to catch my breath. But I knew this version of him. I *knew* him. I knew him in the glow of candlelight. I knew him with his arms around me in the darkness. I knew him as every touch I'd felt on me in the middle of the night. I knew him as happiness and joy and pure desire.

I knew him as my…

I felt faint. I tripped over my feet, and as Gavin caught me, my face went numb.

"Gavin, what's… what's wrong with me?" I asked, thinking it had to be part of his magic. "Why does seeing you like this, why does it feel so…."

But I couldn't get the words out. I didn't know them. It was overwhelming. My chest began to ache as I was sure I had stopped breathing.

Gavin sat me down in a garden chair and knelt at my side. "What do you see?" he asked, no longer glowing. "Tell me."

I finally met his eyes again, jaw shaking as I resisted the strange emotion daring to surface. "All I know is that I feel you," I whispered. "I've *always* felt you. In every darkness. In every shadow. You've been there. And I don't know why that is."

His jaw set, lips pressing into a thin line as he caressed my cheek.

There was something he wasn't telling me.

"You know why, don't you?" I asked.

He swallowed. "I don't want to scare you," he said.

"Tell me," I begged.

I had to know. I had to understand why.

"Tell me what this feeling is," I said. "Why do I know you in that form? Why does it make me feel this way?"

"Chloe, please," he said.

"Tell me." I pulled away from him and stood, prompting him to also rise to his feet.

He threaded his hands behind his head, and I could see that reluctance in his gaze. It was something big. Something bigger than he wanted to admit.

"Gavin!"

"You're *her*," he blurted, rounding on me.

I could see the tears in his eyes as they also rose in mine. "I'm who?" I asked, emotion making my nostrils flare. "Who are you talking about?"

"You're her. You're Psyche," he said in an almost exasperated tone. "*My* Psyche. Goddess of the Soul. My *wife*."

His…

"What are you talking about?" I managed in a breathless voice, my heart pounding.

I had scoured every text about Eros that I could after that Valentine's Day party. No myth or reading said he had a wife, and there was no mention of a Psyche that I could think of.

Gavin reached for my elbow and gently pulled me into him. "You don't remember," he said. "And I barely do. Only I remember that feeling. I remember the things we had to go through to be together. You were the one fighting last time. But now, it's my turn, and I'm never letting you go."

"Gavin, what are you talking about? What fighting? What did we have to go through? I'm not… I'm not this girl. God, is that the only reason you love me? The only reason you came back for me? Because you think I'm her?"

"What—*no*," he said, fear in his eyes. "No. I fell in love with you that Valentine's night. I didn't remember even having a wife the first time I met you."

"Then what are we talking about?" I asked, exasperated with the conversation. "What… What is happening?"

His jaw set. "Will you sit down?"

The calm in his voice made me pause, causing me to second-guess whether he was bullshitting me.

"Please," he begged. "I'll tell you everything I know."

I hesitantly took his hand, and he sat across from me at the table.

"Gods, it was so long ago, and yet I remember the first

time my mother mentioned you," he began. "A mortal girl who men had begun worshipping as the most beautiful creature to walk the earth. They revered you and not the statues of her. So she sent me to take care of it—of you. But when I saw you, I couldn't. For the first time, I hesitated. I followed you in secret, falling in love with you every day. Until your family sought Apollo and the Oracle to find you a husband, and the Oracle responded that your husband was nothing more than a monster, and they should leave you in funeral clothes atop a hill."

My ears perked, stomach dropping.

The pilot…

Gavin reached across the table for my hands. "I was that monster, and you became my wife."

My heart was an erratic mess. I didn't remember any of what he claimed, though somehow… somehow, it didn't feel like a lie.

"Do you want me to go on?" he asked.

"God, there's more?" I asked.

His lips flinched like he might smile, and he kissed my knuckles. "The trials."

I clenched my teeth, a tear falling down my cheek. "Go on."

"My mother put you through trials after you didn't trust me—after I ran away like an idiot because you were curious about the man you had married in secret." His eyes softened apologetically. "You fought for me. You fought your way back to me through every trial she gave you, even going to the fucking Underworld for me. I was so stupid for thinking you would live out your days only knowing me only as a shadow."

"What happened?" I asked. "After the trials."

"Zeus gave you ambrosia to make you immortal, and we were officially wed."

I stared at him, numb with emotion. The story… it was—

"Gavin, you can't possibly think I'm her," I said. "I'm not immortal. I'm not—"

"The glass, your scar," he said, pointing to my rib. "You said it should have killed you."

"That doesn't make me immortal!"

"You see those things too," he interjected as he fell to one knee before me, desperation in his tone. "Those moments when you have flashes of memories that feel like another lifetime before. Do you… do you remember when you said you thought your soul was reaching out for mine?"

Of course, I remembered. I'd felt ridiculous saying it, but it had felt right.

"Gavin…"

"It's because it's true. It doesn't matter how long we're apart or how many lifetimes pass. We will always find each other."

I rose to my feet, pulling out of his grasp. My entire body burned with the story, with how he thought it was true.

"This is ridiculous," I managed. "Do you realize how ridiculous this all sounds?"

He pulled me by the wrist back into him, his hand landing on my cheek. "But you feel it," he said. "As crazy as it sounds, you know it's true."

"Then why don't I remember?" I asked, ready to burst into tears at the overwhelming feelings coursing through my bones.

"You were erased from memory," he said. "You were erased from the myths, from my memory, from our friends' memories after… to protect me after someone stole you from me."

"What do you mean someone stole me? What, like kidnapped?" I asked.

His jaw was taut, face red with sorrow. "Yes."

"But how? If I am immortal, what have I been doing these last centuries? Why now? How do I have memories of childhood, a family—"

"The same way that you were erased," he said.

I wanted to argue and tell him he was wrong. I wanted to tell him my family wasn't just a mirage, that I had been born to my mother and father, and that they were my blood.

And yet…

The way random strangers had begun smiling at me—the pilot, the baker, Hades, Persephone, and even Aphrodite. They all *knew* me.

Maybe…

God, I wanted to hide in a hole.

He reached for me, intending to pull me into his grasp, but I stepped out of his arms. I didn't know what to think or how to respond. It was *so much*. To be someone I didn't remember, who—as far as history went—never existed.

"Chloe?"

But I held up my hands, tears falling down my face now. "I need some time," I managed. "Please. Just… just give me a few minutes."

Chapter Forty-Seven

Gavin

I was such a fucking idiot.

Gods, the look on her face... the familiarity and then the absolute terror.

I watched her practically run back to the condo, and I did nothing. I couldn't move. I couldn't blink. My body was void of any feeling except fear. I wouldn't have blamed her if she had run. It was so much to take in—almost too much. To be told you were a lost goddess, that you were married, the *actual* soulmate to the person you'd fallen in love with.

It would send any person running for the hills.

I stayed on the roof until I couldn't take it any longer. I knew she needed that space, knew that she might even need days to come to terms with it.

If she even came to terms with it at all.

I fully expected her to pack up her things and leave me.

So. Fucking. *Stupid.*

The bedroom door was closed when I went back inside. I poured myself a drink and chugged it back, then went to stand outside the bedroom door. I didn't knock, even though I wanted to. I merely laid my forehead on the wood, pressed my hand against it, and closed my eyes.

I could hear her sniffing back tears, and I was desperate to know what she was thinking. I wanted to hold her and help her work through it. I wanted to answer every question she had. No one should have had to figure that out on their own.

I was a monster.

It was well past midnight before I saw her again.

I hadn't been able to rest and instead sat outside, knowing if I'd stayed indoors, I would stare at the bedroom door until I had lost my mind.

Her touch was soft on my shoulder as she emerged onto the balcony. My heart caved at it, and I reached up to take her hand in mine, kissing her knuckles as she sat on my lap.

Her eyes were swollen, cheeks puffy and red.

I had done this.

I had made her this upset.

"I'm sorry," I whispered. "I shouldn't have put all of that on you."

She swallowed as she stared at me, thumbs rubbing my knuckles. "I need you to be honest with me," she said.

"Always," I swore.

"When you met me, did you think I was her?"

"No. I didn't even remember having a wife at the time."

"Was the possibility that I was her... was that the only reason you wanted me after we found each other again?"

"No," I promised.

"Do you love me? Or do you love me because you think I'm her?"

My jaw hardened at the question. A tear dropped down her cheek, and I reached up to wipe it away.

"I love *you*," I whispered. "And I would love you whether you were her or not. I fell in love with you before I knew who you were, and it was important that you loved me before I told you about that connection." I took her hand in mine, my thumb rubbing over the ring. "If you ask me to give up trying to find out what happened to you, I will," I said. "Say the word, and I'll forget it. All I want is to be with you."

Chloe swallowed, sniffed back the tears threatening to fall, and stood. I watched her turn her back to me and stare out at the never-ending sky. Silence dwelled in the space, seconds ticking away slower than I'd ever felt them.

"No," she finally said.

I stood but said nothing as she wiped her face harshly and inhaled a deep breath, then pressed her hands to her hips. "No, we're going to that retreat," she said as our eyes met, her voice shaking. "We're going, and we're going to find out who did this. Because while I may not remember a damn thing, somehow, I feel it. I feel *you*. I feel the pain of losing you. I feel the joy of being with you. And I know I can't have made it all up in my head. So, we're going. And someone better have a good fucking explanation for why we just had to spend *lifetimes* apart."

I stepped up to her, heart aching painfully as I cupped her cheek. She was trembling, but there was truth in her eyes, and she leaned into my touch.

"We'll find them," I promised. "And they'll regret ever having looked at you."

Chapter Forty-Eight

Chloe

My nerves were shot as we drove through the night and into the Mojave Desert. Gavin had a location on the invitation —longitude and latitude only, and it said to arrive precisely at either sun up or sun down or else risk not being able to get in.

He held my hand through some of the ride, and I could tell he was as nervous as I was.

"If at any point you want to leave, use your word," he said. "I don't care if it's the middle of the night or at dinner. We'll leave."

Every breath that entered my lungs wasn't enough. I ended up yawning more times than I cared to admit, my body and mind short on oxygen as we continued driving. I kept looking toward the GPS on his screen, the minutes drawing longer and longer, or so it seemed.

Eventually, I fell asleep over the console, still holding Gavin's hand.

It was still dark when I felt the Jeep stop moving, and Gavin nudged me slightly.

"Are we there?" I asked, my hair stuck to my face.
His jaw was set as he stared out of the window. I followed his gaze, my stomach knotting upon seeing that we weren't the only car. I sat straighter, leaning toward the dash and squinting at the shadowed vehicles.

"Is that…" I stared at the car waiting in the dark purple light, a motorcycle's headlight shining nearby and illuminating it just enough to see. It was a Panther DeVille, the same car that had become famous during the Disney film.

"Yes," Gavin said as he put the Jeep in park. "I'll give you one guess as to who drives it."

His lips drew into a flat line, and we glanced at the woman standing with her arms crossed by the motorcycle.

Oh.

Well, that made sense.

Aphrodite had a scarf wrapped around her hair to block out the sand and dirt. She looked so… *her* in the white pantsuit she wore.

"Only she would wear that into the desert," Gavin muttered. "Come on. They'll swarm the car if we don't get out."

He was right. The others were beginning to stare our way. God, I was a wreck. I wanted to hide in the backseat and pretend I wasn't there. At first, it sounded like so much fun, but now that I knew the real reason for our attendance, I didn't know how to act.

Would I be the girl they remembered? Would they even know me? And if they did… would that help my memory?

I needed to vomit.

A cold sweat beaded on my forehead, and my hands were clammy as I crawled out of his car. Eyes peered through the darkness, including the eyes of Aphrodite and Ares. Ares revved up his bike as Gavin and I approached the front of the station wagon parked by Aphrodite's car.

"It's a family reunion," a familiar voice said as they exited the station wagon.

My gaze narrowed at the person. The moment his face came into view, things made sense.

Gavin's grip tightened on my hand. "I don't believe you've met him yet," he said, yawning at the last words. "This is Hermes."

I eyed Hermes's smirking face. "Oh, I know him," I said. "I think I want my money back now."

Hermes huffed amusedly and opened his mouth to speak, but whatever look rested on Gavin's face sent his smile faltering and words stammering.

"How exactly do you know him?" Gavin asked.

"He was the pilot of the plane Tyler chartered to the vineyards a few weeks back." I tilted my head. "We had a *nice* little conversation on the way back."

"Now, I don't think that warrants a refund—"

"Pay up," I said, extending my hand.

Hermes's mouth twisted, but he shelled out a wad of cash from his back pocket and started counting bills. He glanced at Gavin. "She's more demanding than I remember," he muttered.

"*You* tried to tell me who I was that day," I said. "He told me I looked like a girl he had once known," I said. "A girl who had been dropped off atop a mountain to wait for her husband."

Aphrodite turned in our direction. Ares shut off the bike.

"Ah, well, if we're getting technical about it—"

"Fucking Styx, Hermes," Ares muttered behind him.

"You remember?" Aphrodite asked me.

"Wait—"

"How much do you remember?" There was a look of panic on Aphrodite's face that I didn't understand. "What happened to you that day? Why did you leave him—"

"That's not what happened," Gavin said, trying to step in front of me.

"So, now *you* remember?" she snapped at her son.

A commotion began, voices talking over one another and

arguing. I took two steps back, realizing I had made a mistake by bringing it up amongst others.

Shit.

I felt someone come up beside me then, the smell of sweet pomegranates entering my nostrils, and I turned to find Persephone standing there eating the seeds out of a plastic cup. She was still in pink skull pajamas and fuzzy slippers, her pink hair twisted in a black scarf like Lana usually wore.

She offered me a few seeds and said, "Damn, it's early for this. What are we fighting about?" as she popped a few into her mouth.

I accepted the fruit. "I fucked up."

She snorted. "Welcome to the family again, Psyche," she bantered. "He said he told you?"

"He did."

"Do you believe him?"

I sighed heavily. "Maybe," I replied. "I'm hoping this weekend helps my memory."

"I'm surprised this display doesn't," she said, pointing to the arguing group.

Another woman came up on Persephone's side—a petite woman dressed in a hoop skirt and cat eyeglasses.

A woman that I recognized.

"Oh, you've met my mother, haven't you?" Persephone said. "Psy—wait, do you want to be called that or Chloe?"

I considered it. Since telling me about my past a few weeks back, Gavin had called me the name just to see how it made me feel. I honestly hadn't hated it. It didn't feel awkward or unnatural.

However, it was easier to stick with my usual name.

"Ah… let's stick with Chloe when we can," I said. "I'm still getting used to everything."

Persephone nodded. "Chloe, this is Demeter, my mother. Mom, Chloe."

Demeter, the baker I had met at the vineyards, gave me a familiar smile and a small wave, apparent that she was also still waking up.

"Where is your husband?" I asked Persephone.

"Coming tomorrow," she answered. "Mom is leaving in the morning. We can't have them in the same place for very long, so I try to spread the wealth that is me," she said with a wide smile.

I resisted smiling outright at her.

"Okay, I've had about enough of this." She handed me the cup of pomegranate and put two fingers in her mouth, an ear-splitting whistle sounding over the arguing.

Silence shuddered over the desert. Each of them stared at her, and Persephone slapped her leg.

"Can we at least wait until we've had drinks?" she asked them. "Where is D?"

"Already here," Aphrodite answered as she calmed herself. She turned her back on the others and looked at her watch, Ares's arm sliding around her shoulders.

Hermes settled on the front of his station wagon, crossing one ankle over the other as he took his phone out. Gavin sighed and pushed his hand through his hair, coming toward me.

"Are you sure you don't want to leave?" he asked as he stood before me.

Persephone nudged my side, smirked, and then strode over to Hermes, leaving Gavin and me alone. I smiled at Gavin.

"I didn't mean to cause a fight," I said. "I was halfway teasing him."

"You'll find it doesn't take much to start a fight with us," he said.

"It's that time," Hermes announced.

Gavin and I turned our attention to the awaiting sunrise, as did everyone else. Hermes looked at his watch and counted down the time.

"Three... Two..."

I had to blink. I thought perhaps it was a mirage, that the desert was playing a trick on me. But there, in the heat shimmer of the sun, rose an oasis.

An oasis of sprawling gardens and pools, of a palace and villas, seated a mile away in the middle of green grasses and trimmed hedges. My mouth nearly dropped at the scene.

"So dramatic," Aphrodite muttered with a roll of her eyes. She pushed off the front of her car, her gaze wandering back to the expansive garden estate, and then she gave an upward nod to Ares. "Let's go."

Ares revved up his motorcycle, and as Gavin and I jumped into the Jeep again, the God of War led our brigade through the wrought-iron gates.

Chapter Forty-Nine

Chloe

I don't know what I had expected when we drove down the lush driveway and came upon a grand fountain with a statue of who I could only assume was Zeus in the middle. I could practically hear Aphrodite rolling her eyes at it, and the thought made me snicker.

"What?" Gavin asked.

"Nothing," I said. "Just thinking about what your mother is more than likely saying about that statue."

"She'll probably knock it over by the end of the weekend," he replied.

"What—no, she...." But my voice trailed at the look on his face. "Oh, you're serious."

"She might trash the entire house," he said with a shrug. "It's a favorite pastime."

"Why, exactly, does she do this?" I asked.

"They have an ongoing feud." He switched hands on the wheel. "One day they're fine, the next they're not. Rumors flew around once about them having an affair, but I doubt it. It's honestly tiresome keeping up with it."

I smiled sideways at him. "You know, you like to play like you're always angry with your mother. But you love her. You love her schemes and her attitude and everything else that she is," I teased him.

Gavin sighed. "It's a hard relationship," he said.

"Why?"

"Because she once used me as more of a henchman than her son," he admitted. "I thought the world of her."

"What changed?"

"Ah… *you*," he answered, and I sank back into my seat. "When I married you, I was supposed to be getting rid of you. It was the first thing I did counter to what she asked, and it opened up a lot of old wounds. And, most recently, it's been tough with her again because of something else she's done."

"What did she do?"

He looked at me for a long moment. "She erased you," he finally said. "After you were stolen from me and I couldn't find you, she erased you from memory so I wouldn't be in pain."

My ears began to ring. "She's the reason I can't remember you?"

"I don't know about your memory," he said. "Your lost memory is different. I think it has to do with the person who kidnapped you. But everyone else… yeah."

The revelation gutted me. I swallowed and turned away, staring out of the window a moment as Gavin put the Jeep in park.

"Are you okay?" he asked softly.

"Not really," I replied. "But… I guess I understand it. I've seen you in pain, and I never want to see that on your face again. I can't imagine what that was like for her."

His lips twitched like he might smile, and he reached for my hand. "Every pair of eyes that sees you this weekend will start to remember you. Are you ready?"

"Do I have a choice?" I asked, nausea sweeping over me.

"You always have a choice," he swore.

I inhaled deeply and stared at the mansion before us, the

others leaving their cars and taking out bags. Gods and goddesses whom I'd seemingly once known so long ago. So familiar, and yet not.

"I can do this," I said, squeezing his hand. "For you. For *us*."

Someone knocked on my window.

Aphrodite.

"Eros, can you help Ares with my bags?" she asked loudly.

I snorted as I met Gavin's eyes. He huffed. "Yeah, give me a minute," he replied reluctantly.

She walked away, and I burst out laughing at the unwillingness on his face. "Oh, shit, that's adorable," I managed.

Gavin pinched my thigh, making me squeal, and I hurried out of the Jeep before he could wrestle me any further into that seat. I had barely gotten out before he was on me, his arm wrapping around my waist, his lips on mine to capture the laughter that had just escaped my mouth.

"Okay, okay," Persephone called out. "We know you're excited to have your wife back but save a little for the bedroom, oh *God of Lust*," she teased.

Gavin responded by flipping her off.

I rolled in the suitcase and small bag that we'd packed with both our clothes in it while he helped his mother bring in her many matching bags, catching up with Ares while Aphrodite hung back to walk with me.

"Chloe, I wanted to apologize," she said as we fell in step together.

"For what?" I asked, trying not to ogle too noticeably at the expansive foyer we were walking into. The whole architecture was audacious, rich, and generous in every way, and I felt so small in its vastness, even though it didn't seem to bother anyone else.

Gavin glanced back at me and smiled as I mouthed, *'holy*

shit!' to him.

"For basically wiping you from existence," Aphrodite said, and I remembered she had been talking to me.

"Oh. Oh, Gavin—or Eros—told me. I get it," I said. "I understand. I think we just want to know why it ever had to happen or who is responsible, rather."

Her lips pressed together thinly as she looked straight forward.

I almost stopped walking.

"Wait. Do you know?" I asked, wary of the look on her face.

"I wish I did," she said.

I didn't completely believe her, but as we turned the corner into the great room, I realized I didn't have time to argue.

Because the entire room had hushed, and everyone was staring at me.

Aphrodite left my side to join Hermes, who was already sitting at the bar where a man was pouring large glasses of wine. Gavin and Ares exchanged glances, and Gavin set down the bags before starting my way.

A man and woman stood by the excellent portrait painting across the room. Both tan and beautiful, the woman with onyx hair pulled into a high ponytail, her slender frame hidden behind a flowing white chemise dress. The man had black curly hair, a salt-and-pepper beard, and large, round eyes. I wasn't sure who they were, but their presence demanded attention, more so than any of the other gods and goddesses I'd met thus far.

Well. Except for Hades.

"Fucking me," the woman said, eyeing me up and down. "Is that... wait. Oh. *Oh, gods.*" She started blinking profusely, her hand swiping across her forehead as memory apparently washed through her, and she muttered under her breath in Greek, her accent coming through thick.

The man with the beard sat back in his chair like gravity had shoved him into it. His wide eyes traveled to the floor, his hand rubbing his forehead. "Shit," he mumbled before his gaze lifted accusingly toward Aphrodite.

"Aph…" he said expectantly.

"Oh, get over yourself, Zeus," Aphrodite hissed, rolling her eyes.

I grabbed Gavin's arm.

Zeus.

"What the fuck did you do this time?" Zeus snapped.

"I protected my son," she sneered. "She was gone. He was lost. Maybe you would understand that if you loved *any* of your children."

"He has too many for that kind of love," the first woman mumbled behind her goblet.

"If we start getting into Zeus's infidelities, we'll be here another century," Hermes muttered. "I know of a few that the rest of you don't."

"Hermes!" the woman snapped.

Nonetheless, Hermes just topped off his wine and held it up. "Cheers," he said with a grim smile. "Of course, we could get into how you treat your children as well, Hera."

The woman, who I realized was Hera, looked like she might throw her cup at Hermes's face.

I leaned closer to Gavin. "Are things always like this?" I asked quietly.

"Yes," he said bluntly. "Prepare yourself for the most horrible family reunion you've ever been to, then add in power complexes, never-ending wine because none of us can get truly drunk, narcissism, and a few dick contests, and you might come close to this weekend. Oh, and sometimes, Zeus likes to play murder mystery." His eyes met mine. "I apologize in advance."

I almost laughed. "I do enjoy a good murder mystery," I

said. "I'm kind of hoping he wants to play now."

Gavin ushered me toward Hera and Zeus, introducing me to them as Chloe, and Hera had tears in her eyes when she let me go. Zeus stood to give me a hug that caused my eyes to widen and Gavin to grind his teeth.

There were several other guests there, though Gavin didn't introduce me to everyone, and I was glad about it. I was having enough trouble remembering the big ones I had met.

However, none of them seemed to have a problem remembering me.

Every person who saw me had the same reaction—a flood of memories that made them almost double over. Some were worse than others, but they all greeted us with smiles.

It was the weirdest experience of my life.

To be remembered by everyone around you, yet know nothing about them. I wondered if this was what people with amnesia felt like when waking up after a coma. Granted, I supposed that was me now.

It was going to be a long fucking weekend.

Persephone and I lounged in the pool for some of the afternoon while Gavin entertained Zeus. He had so many questions about the dating app and what Gavin had been up to since he'd been to one retreat that Zeus had practically tackled him into staying inside and talking.

"Fuck, I'm glad you're here," Persephone said as we lounged on the shallow ramp, only half our bodies under the clear water. "It's been annoying the last few times. Arte and Hecate will be here tomorrow. You'll like them. They haven't been to the last few, either. Arte was helping out her brother there for a while. I don't know if he's coming or not."

"That's… Apollo, right?" I asked.

Persephone nodded. "The local celebrity. Thinks he's some great rockstar now," she said, rolling her eyes. "He used to be so humble and nice. One day, he just snapped. It was tragic, really."

"What happened?"

"Well, one thing that happened was your husband humiliating him with the whole Daphne situation." She shrugged. "He genuinely wasn't the same after that. I think that was why he chased that rockstar gig for so long. Sort of desperate to be a 'bad boy' like people thought of Eros as. Though, no man can come close to the reputation of a god responsible for sexual desire."

"What's the name of—"

"Chloe, sweetie, put this on," Aphrodite said as she emerged from the house, wearing a wide-brim hat and a sheer robe around her body that barely hid her red one-piece swimsuit.

She had another hat in her hand, and she walked all the way around the large pool with it extended from her arm. "I don't want you burned," she said as she reached us. "Your skin is too porcelain."

"Thank you…" I said, hesitantly taking it from her hands.

Persephone snickered behind her wine as Aphrodite settled into one of the lounge chairs on the opposite side of the pool from Demeter.

I kicked water at Persephone.

"At least she's not trying to drown you," she said. "I'll take overprotective mother-in-law over that."

"True," I agreed.

By the time the sun set, I was tipsy, as was every other person there. Dionysus kept the drinks flowing, especially

Aphrodite's.

I had texted Lana a few times and sent her some pictures of where I was. Even sent a selfie with Persephone, to which she replied with surprise and jealousy.

YOU BITCH!

Wait. So, he's not lying?!

Oh, there's quite a bit I have to catch you up on, I told her. I hadn't explained everything yet since I'd wanted to wait until this weekend was over. **I'll call you in the morning over coffee.**

Where's Ares?!

I laughed as I sent her a photo of Ares and Aphrodite lounging on the other side of the pool, and she replied, *Look at Mommy and Daddy.*

I was lying on one of the lounge chairs when Gavin finally made it out of Zeus's grasp. He practically dived atop me, his head burying against my stomach as he hugged my waist and sat on the end of the chair.

"Hi," he muttered on my skin.

I chuckled, running my hand through his hair. "Hi," I managed.

He sat his chin on my breasts to gaze at me for a second, then pulled back slightly to look at my tits. "Hello to you two, also," he said.

"Oh, fucking Styx, Eros," Persephone said as she stood from the chair beside me, having heard him. "I'll see you two at dinner."

I wasn't even sure I heard her with the way he was smiling at me. He leaned up and kissed me. Thoroughly. His tongue explored my mouth, and his hand grasped at my thigh. He was settled between my thighs, and the only thing keeping us from fucking right there was that several other people were staring at us.

His teeth tugged at my lip when he pulled back, and he

grinned outright. The sneaky look on his face made my brows narrow.

"What are you thinking about?" I asked. "You have a very suspicious look in your eyes."

"I was thinking that I don't know if I can wait until after dinner to show you what I packed," he replied.

My eyes went wide. "Why? What did you bring?"

"Just something fun," he said. He kissed me again, gave my ass a slap, and then practically jumped to his feet. "Dinner?"

"Starving," I replied.

Chapter Fifty

Chloe

I couldn't think straight as I brushed my hair that night, staring out at the night sky from the stone balcony in our room. Gavin had chosen one of the rooms in the mansion instead of one on the sprawling estate simply because he knew some of the more prominent gods would want their own space, and he didn't feel like causing an argument.

I didn't care. This one was so far from everyone that it felt like our own private wing.

I was still in shock that I had just spent the day surrounded by people who had known me in another life. It was starting to sink in more, and the more I accepted it, the more comfortable I was around everyone.

"Hey."

I turned slightly, finding Gavin leaning on one of the columns separating the bedroom from the outside balcony. No doors or glass windows separated the spaces, only audacious columns and long white sheer curtains that billowed in the slight breeze.

"Hey," I said, giving him a small smile.

He had gone downstairs to get a few things he said we needed for the night while I had showered.

"How are you holding up?" he asked.

"I'm…" I sighed, setting the hairbrush down on the small

table beside me. "I'm okay," I answered. "Yeah. I'm okay. Dinner was—"

"A shitshow." He pushed off the column and strode toward me, a crooked smile rising on his lips. "I warned you earlier."

"It was fun," I said, recalling the drama that had ensued.

"There will be more of us tomorrow. It's only going to get worse," Gavin said. He pushed my hair back, his palm landing on my cheek. "Have you felt anything else?" he asked.

"Nothing," I sighed.

"I'm sorry," he whispered with a slight shake of his head. "I thought this might help us both."

"It isn't over," I said. "However, it is frustrating when *you* have your memory—when all of you have it. Everyone knows me, and yet all I know is this familiar feeling. Do you know how maddening it is to have everyone around you remember your past when you don't know anything?"

His arms slipped around me. "You're cute when you're flustered."

I shoved him slightly, and he chuckled. "Shut up." I rubbed my hands up his muscular arms to his chest, feeling his heartbeat beneath my palms. Gavin leaned in, his forehead pressing to mine, hands squeezing on my waist.

"I don't know what I'll do when I find out what happened," he said. "So, I want to apologize now for the person I'll become once that happens—*if* that happens."

I pulled back slightly. "What do you mean?"

"Someone stole you from me. They took you, and I have wandered for centuries wondering why I felt a part of me was missing." His hand pressed to my cheek, and the pain in his eyes made my heart hurt. "I don't know the amount of rage I'll feel or if I'll be able to stop it. I don't want you to run."

"I'm not going anywhere," I said, reassuring him.

But his grip tightened as though if he held me close enough, no one could ever take me away again.

"I would tear this world apart if anyone tried to take you again," he said in a low rasp.

"You would drive this world mad with lust?" I asked, almost smiling.

"Lust. Power. Insatiable desire. Love is the most powerful emotion ever to exist," he replied. "It doesn't matter whether it's for a being, an object, or an idea, or if it's one's reaction in the absence of it… People lose their minds because of love, and I am no different."

There was an edge to the way he spoke, as though his magic dripped within those words, within that promise. He wasn't joking. He wasn't smiling. He was making a vow, one that could have made the earth beneath us tremble had he let his magic free.

It made me realize just how powerful he indeed was.

"You don't want to know the things I've done, the things I could do with that power," he said in a dark voice. "I said a long time ago that I was done taking things to that extreme, that I would only use it for pranks and mischievous deeds from then on. But I swear to you now, if someone dares to try and steal you again, I will use it in ways far worse than any mortal or god could ever imagine."

My heart stumbled. A thread of promise attached itself to those words, wrapping its way from my heart to his, securing that vow for all eternity.

I felt it in his touch. I heard it in his words.

"Have you ever used it on me?" I asked.

He wrapped his hand on my cheek, brows narrowing. "Why would you think that?"

"I don't," I assured him. "Just curious."

"Never," he swore. "And I never will. I wanted you to love me of your own choices, to choose me because you wanted to, not because of an arrow or because of some predestined thing. I want you."

"You have me," I whispered. "And they'll have to kill me if they want to change that."

His lips met mine in a deep, claiming kiss that worked its way into my soul. His hands wrapped beneath my jaw, that touch making chills erupt on my skin, and I swore a faint golden glow surrounded both of our bodies.

I dropped my robe, exposing my naked body to the chilled air, and his arm slipped around my waist. He pulled, gripped, and kneaded my flesh, his erection growing between us. Every swipe of our tongues increased our cravings. I wanted to consume him wholly, bury myself within his bones somehow. I clawed his neck, his cheeks, and his body, not caring if I ever breathed again so long as I was with him.

Gavin released my lips with a biting tug, his forehead touching mine as we caught our breath.

"Get on the bed and pose that beautiful ass in the air for me," he whispered. "I have something I've wanted to use on it a while now."

I inhaled sharply, my heart skipping in anticipation. He kissed me one more time before smacking my ass so loudly that the sound echoed out into the gardens. I winced delightedly with the sting and resisted the skip in my step as I made my way toward the bed.

I fell on it face-first with a plop, bending my knees and leaving my feet in the air as I watched him go to the carry-on bag we'd packed.

I had my phone in my hand, checking where Lana had messaged me again when he crawled onto the bed and straddled his knees over my thighs. Biting my lips, I hit the camera button, and Gavin lay atop me, his chin on my shoulder so I could snap the selfie, along with a few more of him kissing my cheek and my shoulder. I couldn't help myself from smiling and giggling with every snap.

I tossed the phone onto the floor when I felt his hand between my thighs.

He groaned approvingly at my wetness, lips pressing to my shoulder and down my spine. I loved being like this in front of him—face down, molded into the mattress, and entirely in his grasp—perfect for whatever devotion to my body that he had planned.

He had laid something on the bed at my side, and my eyes narrowed when I saw the three candlesticks, a lighter, and a large tray, which I supposed was to sit the lit candle on.

"What is that?" I asked, eyeing the candlesticks.

"Wax, baby," he said.

My thighs squeezed, heart skipped. He huffed amusedly at what I assumed was whatever look was on my face and kissed my cheek.

"Relax," he whispered before moving my hair off my back. "Let me please the goddess of my dreams. This will help get the wax off of you later."

When he touched my back, I realized there was massage oil on his hands, and I melted into the mattress as he began massaging my skin, working that oil into me, taking extra care on the sides of my breasts and ass. Moans left me with every stroke of his hands until I was completely relaxed and saw him reach for the candle.

"If it's too hot, let me know," he said before lighting the end of it.

I flinched as that first dribble of hot wax splashed on my hip and then groaned into the mattress as the stinging sensation erupted chills over my flesh. My arms stretched out in front of me, my cheek hitting the pillow. God, that was amazing. Another drip hit me, this time at the base of my spine, and I sucked in a too-shallow breath.

"Is it too much?" he asked.

"Fuck no," I moaned. "More."

His palm hit my ass with the next dribble, and I heard him chuckle softly. "So greedy," he muttered. "Lift that ass for me, baby. Let me see this wax drip off those gorgeous curves."

I obeyed, only lifting my hips, my knees bending wide beneath me so that I was stretched out for him. He cursed under his breath, thumb swiping over my clit like he couldn't resist touching me.

The next splatter of wax rolled down the curvature of my ass, and Gavin spanked the opposite cheek.

Another whimpering groan left me and muffled into the sheet. My eyes closed, and I surrendered to whatever he wanted. I was his toy to play with as he pleased.

I saw him bending behind me, and I melted as his warm tongue licked my drenching pussy.

A low groan emitted from him. He held my ass steady, letting the wax dribble one splash after another on my sensitive skin as he licked and teased me. I spread my legs wider and arched my back, settling into his pleasure.

"Fuck yes," I moaned. "Right there."

"You like this wax, baby?" he asked.

"Mm… yes," I replied as two fingers found my entrance.

"Your ass looks amazing right now," he said, fingers curling inside me. "I could fucking eat you."

I moved my hips greedily toward him. "All yours," I nearly whimpered.

His laughter was deep as he dripped more wax on my skin and then flipped me over a few minutes later. I was met with his lips on mine, his stiff cock brushing my entrance as I lifted my hips to guide him inside.

But he pulled back, one hand landing on my stomach. "I'm not done with you yet, baby," he said as he picked up the candlestick again.

I cursed as the heat almost blistered my tits, rolling down the curves, settling between them—hotter than it had been on my back.

I sat up and pushed Gavin down onto his back, almost sending the candles to the floor, though he just laughed as I straddled over him.

I rubbed some oil on my hands and rubbed it into his chest.

"Careful, baby," he said when I lifted the lit candle.

I let the purple color dribble between his pecs, making him almost gasp. He gripped my hips, slapped my ass, and then moved his thumb between my widened thighs, the pad working over my clit. My shoulders limped with that touch, so much more intense with how sensitive my skin was.

"Bring that cunt right here," he said, sticking his tongue out. "Let me taste how wet you are from that pain."

I blew the candles out and stared at him. "I don't think I've ever done that before," I admitted. "Sitting on someone's face, I mean."

A crooked smile lifted the right corner of his mouth, and he took my hand, his lips pressing to my knuckles. "Then the word 'euphoria' is about to get an entirely new meaning," he swore. "Come up here and grab that headboard, baby. Don't make me handcuff you to it."

I almost smiled, the thought of hovering over his face making my clit throb. "Are you sure?" I asked, already knowing the answer. "These are a lot." I gave my thighs a teasing slap and squeezed the tops, and his tongue darted across his lips.

"*Fuck*. You know what that does to me. I love the way your body moves," he hissed under his breath. He reached my chin and gave it a tug, tilting my head down so that I was looking directly into his eyes. "I've had millennia's to think about all the ways I'd prefer to die. You are the most beautiful creature to ever walk this earth, and you're *mine*. So, when I say I want you to sit on my face, I mean suffocation by that pretty pussy of yours is a demise I welcome with open arms. Let me ruin you."

"You've already ruined me," I admitted breathlessly.

A quiet scoff left him, the rumble of that noise embedding within my bones. He grasped my ass and pushed forward, making me move up on my knees, and I slowly ascended his body, grabbing the headboard hesitantly. When I was hovering over his face, his nose nuzzled against my inner thigh, the word "*fuck,*" escaping him in a desperate whisper.

"Feel free to pretend the headboard is the horns of a minotaur since you love that fantasy so much," he said, and I bit my lips together to keep from laughing.

"You're okay with me fantasizing about a great beast while you're tongue-fucking me?" I asked.

"You're on my face. You bear my name. I'm not worried about a little smutty fantasy taking you away from me," he said. "Get comfortable, baby. I don't intend to make your first sitting experience a quick one." His lips pressed to my clit, and my knees weakened, arms somehow already heavy as they rested atop the headboard. Gavin's arms slipped around the undersides of my thighs, his hands pressing down on the tops, and he forced me lower. I shifted until my legs weren't burning, and I felt him smile against my pussy.

"Such a good girl."

Every stroke and suck of his tongue on my clit made me almost forget I was sitting on his face. He teased me to the point of languish surrender, and I held that headboard with both hands, my forehead lying atop my knuckles as I fought each orgasm.

Shit. I was weak. Spent. Every noise I made grew louder and louder, to the point that I forgot we were in a mansion surrounded by other gods and goddesses who undoubtedly could hear us.

I supposed the God of Lust had a reputation to keep up.

My teeth imprinted on the board as I screamed into it, his tongue lashing inside me, mouth sucking on my clit to the point that I began to shake. Oh, god, this torture, this absolute wrecking pleasure. I could still feel the sting from the wax all over my body, heightening his tease.

My body reached—*reached*—with the desperation in my listless muscles. I couldn't breathe, couldn't think. And when I came, my entire body shuddered, my thighs trying to squeeze together, pushing on his head. Gavin didn't seem to care. He grabbed me under my arms and threw me onto my back. I didn't have time to catch my breath before his cock slid into me, and I lifted my hips to give him more room.

My orgasm hadn't even finished, and I was already on the precipice of another.

"Look at me, baby," he said.

My eyes opened to his beautiful face, his mouth still wet from my pussy, his eyes such a dark shade of green that they were almost black. That slight glow emitted around him—around *us*, and I reached to his cheeks to pull him down to my lips. He pulled my thigh into his hand, opening me up as he sank deeper.

"Gods, I could fuck you all night," he groaned, his forehead against mine. "You feel so fucking good. Shit, you're perfect."

Every word was a desperate groan. His pace quickened, somehow his cock deeper, more filling. Our bodies met in every undulation. Both of us trembling as our orgasms rose. I couldn't take it anymore, couldn't hold back as my pussy tightened, *tightened* around him. My head was falling off the end of the bed, my chest arching, neck exposed.

I came around his cock and shouted his name—his real name, though I didn't realize I was saying it until it came rolling off my tongue. I felt his cock throb inside me and heard him groan into my neck as if saying his proper name at my end had called to his desperate soul.

His release followed mine, his groan echoing into the night air. He collapsed atop me, and I allowed my head to loll off the bed, my muscles too tired to move.

Gavin kissed my chest, my collar, and my neck, and as he pulled from inside me, he shifted me so that I was back on the bed. His smile met me when I opened my eyes.

"I didn't know you were falling," he said, and it didn't sound like an apology.

"I don't care," I said. "You felt too damn good inside me to care."

"You're addicting," he whispered. "Everything about you makes me want to consume you whole."

I laughed softly. "That's how I feel too."

He kissed me, and I lifted my left hand to his cheek after, my ring staring back at me. "When do I get to marry you?" I asked. "In this lifetime."

"Whenever you want," he said. "Say the word, and I'll get the jet. Or, rather, I'll hire Hermes."

"What if we didn't go home?" I asked. "What if we went straight to Greece after this and got married?"

"Is that what you want?"

"Lana would kill me, but she'd get over it." I pressed my other hand to his cheek. "I want to call you my husband, and I want to remember it."

He kissed me long and tender again, then pushed my hair back. "I am the luckiest idiot alive," he whispered. "Roll over, baby," he said with a chin jerk. "I want to see the lovely little pattern the wax left behind on your skin. Maybe I spelled my name right."

"You wrote your name on my skin?" I asked, almost laughing.

"Just on one ass cheek."

Chapter Fifty-One

Chloe

I woke still sore in all the best places. I could still feel the sting of the heat on my skin, feel his cum inside me from all the times we'd fucked overnight.

Once hadn't been enough. Not here. Not in this place.

He'd even fucked me over the banister and let gravity take my torso over the railing, my hair flailing in the wind.

I wondered how many gods had seen that display.

My body still smelled like him when I made my way downstairs before sunrise, intent on sitting in the garden in peace and having time to myself before the rest of them woke up, as well as calling Lana.

At least the coffee was already out, and I was familiar with the espresso machine.

I took my steaming mug into the gardens, bare feet warm against the cool stucco ground. It was still pitch black outside except for the stars and a few fire torches scattered around the expanse.

I sat my mug down on one of the tables and stretched my arms over my head, pulling and tugging on those muscles, cracking my spine and neck with deep exhales.

Something made me wonder if Aphrodite led yoga classes in her spare time.

I made a mental note to ask her.

"I thought I was the only one of us who enjoyed a quiet morning," a gruff, accented voice said behind me.

I jumped, thankful I had already set my coffee down, and found Hades staring back at me in the amber light from one of the torches.

He was leaning back in one of the cushy wicker chairs, a rich red and black satin robe wrapped around him, showing off the space between his pectorals and the top of his muscled stomach. Hades wasn't ripped or defined with minimal body fat. Hades was a *man*—rough like Ares, with a thick neck and muscles that you could also cuddle against and not feel as if you were lying on a washboard.

Though, I did love Gavin's washboard. It was fun to lick and watch contract when I played with his cock.

Hades was puffing on a cigar, the red and orange fire igniting when he drew a smoke. He looked over me coolly, and I couldn't tell if it was a disapproving gaze or just his regular look.

"Hades," I managed, clutching my chest. "I didn't realize you were here. Wait. How did you—"

"I'm Hades, love," he said. "I don't wait."

I almost smiled.

He moved his chin to the seat next to him, and I hesitantly sat beside the God of the Underworld. Absolute power radiated off of him, so much that every breath I tried to take came up short, and I cleared my throat just to continue living.

"How are you finding things?" he asked.

"A little weird," I admitted. "Three weeks ago, I almost thought Gavin was being untruthful about being a god."

What looked to be a smirk rose on his lips. "I should have removed the glamour from Cerberus that day. It would have helped."

God, that day seemed like a lifetime ago.

My being engaged to another man felt like a lifetime ago.

"You're just like you were back then," he said, and my ears perked up. No one had talked about the 'me' whom they'd known, other than Hermes vaguely mentioning it.

"Curious. Mildly cautious," Hades continued. "The first time you came to the Underworld, I thought, this girl is fearless." He puffed again on his cigar. "Here you were, a mere mortal girl, performing tasks for one of the most ruthless women I knew, all for the love of her son."

"Do you know how to get my memory back?" I asked, hoping he might.

"You'll need to find who took you first," he replied.

"Do you know?"

He shook his head as he blew out an 'O' of smoke. "I only know how upset my wife was that day," he answered. "Some of your lapses could be because of the trauma of what happened, not just because Aph attempted to protect her son. I think you've pulled so far away from that memory because of the pain that you've locked it away from yourself."

I stared into my cup of coffee and considered his theory. Maybe he was right. Perhaps I had stuffed it away in some chamber, never to be thought of again.

An audible sigh left him, one that made me glance his way. "That'll be the rest of the calvary," he said with an upward nod to the headlights in the distance—more gods waiting on the sun to rise so that they could also enter. He lifted his coffee mug to me and pushed out of his chair, groaning as he did. He cracked his neck once, then padded off toward the opposite side of the pool where I knew the villa was that Persephone had chosen for them.

"Let yourself breathe, Chloe," he called back. "You'll find it."

My phone lit up before I could give his suggestion a second thought. A picture of Lana and me from the wedding came on the display, making me smile as I hit the green button to answer.

"Good morning, gorgeous," she said, smiling widely. "Fuck me. Is it still dark?"

"Barely purple," I said, looking out at the skyline. "Guess who I just had a conversation with?"

"Zeus?" she asked, and I think she thought she was teasing me.

"Hades, actually," I answered.

She sputtered up her tea. "Like Hades, God of the Underworld, Hades."

I sipped my coffee. "He's hot, too."

"Oh, fuck me," she said, throwing her hands in the air. "I hate you."

I laughed. "God, I have so much to tell you," I said.

"So, spill."

"I think this all requires us to be face-to-face. Maybe I'll come to see you."

"You better," she said.

I stood and turned the camera around so she could see the sprawling gardens and pool. "This is… insane, to say the least."

As the sun rose, I walked around and talked to her in the garden. Six cars were coming up the drive this morning, and my stomach tightened with the anticipation of who it might be.

I showed her all the statues and flowers and told her some of the drama that had gone on the day before. I had just started up the steps to the back entrance of the mansion when I saw the newcomers.

Thank fuck, there was another staircase outside that I could use.

"Who all is there now?" Lana asked.

I squinted at the two women setting their things down in

the foyer. "I genuinely have no idea," I said. "I think I might head upstairs and wait for Gavin before any of these people see me. I—"

Words caught in my throat. The blonde woman who had just sat her luggage down had pushed her sunglasses atop her head. Her loosely curly hair was frizzy and untamed. She was wearing a leather coat over a band tee—a *Scorcher* band tee. The band that...

I *knew* her.

My stomach dropped. "Shit," I muttered, nearly tripping down the steps.

"What's up?"

"Brielle," I said, though I barely heard myself. "That's fucking Brielle."

Blood evacuated from my insides. I was a walking corpse; what was once a thriving heart was now a hollow shell thudding violently in my ringing ears.

"Brielle... isn't that—"

"Aidan's twin sister," I managed as my chest collapsed.

No.

No. No. No—

Tears swelled in my eyes. Fear jolted me to my bones. I couldn't breathe.

"Babe, calm down," Lana said, trying to catch my attention. "Are you sure it's her?"

My eyes scanned the foyer, praying. Praying, *praying* that he wasn't there. Praying that I was wrong, that I was still laying in the bed beside Gavin.

Wake up.

Wake up.

Wake up.

But as I opened my eyes, my nightmare had come true.

Tears clouded my eyes and streamed down my face.

The man standing in the doorway was the one who had

crawled under my skin and embedded himself in the darkest parts of my soul. Everything in me switched to flight mode.

Blonde curly hair. Dark eyes. Perfect facial structure that he fucking knew. Wearing a matching leather jacket to his sister's, a white tee, and ripped black pants.

"Fuck."

"Babe--"

"He's here," I hissed, bile rising in my throat. "He's here. He's *fucking* here."

"*Who?!*"

"Aidan."

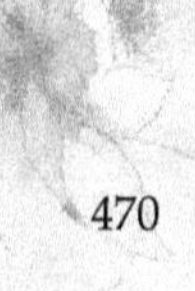

Chapter Fifty-Two

Chloe

I nearly fell on my face as I bolted up the staircase—almost running over Hera in the process. Only I didn't care. I couldn't see from the tears in my eyes as well as the panicked heartbeat throbbing in my ears.

Aidan was… he was a *god?*

Gavin was pulling on a shirt when I ran into the room.

"Hey—"

I started throwing all my things into the suitcase, ignoring his concern. My breath still hadn't caught up with me. I was lightheaded, dizzy, ready to pass out at any moment—

"Whoa, Chloe." Gavin grasped my elbows and pulled me into him. I fought him, squirming to get free, but his hands wrapped around my wrists, and he forced me to look at him.

"Chloe. *Chloe!*"

"Arrow," I said exasperatedly. "Arrow. Arrow. Arrow!"

Tears fell from my eyes. I was in such a panic that I barely heard his response.

"Wait, what happened?" Terror lined his own voice. I was spiraling, unable to straighten out the words in my head. "Chloe, talk to me!"

"It's fucking *Aidan.*" My entire body shook. "He's here."

"What do you mean he's here? Why would your ex—"

Gavin's panic turned to pure, unadulterated rage. The

world went silent as if whatever had clicked in Gavin's mind ruled over every domain.

"Tell me his band name."

The slow, threatening way Gavin spoke soothed me slightly. Somewhere deep inside of me, I had heard that voice before, and it was all I could do to talk myself out of that panic.

"Chloe, tell me his band name," he said, and his finite tone was so dark that I swore a cloud covered the sun.

My teeth chattered as I answered in a breathless whisper, "Scorcher."

Gavin looked like he might break apart the earth right then and there.

And he stormed away from me before I could stop him.

"No, wait! Gavin!"

I ran, considering sliding down the banister to try and get in front of him. But he was taking the steps two at a time, his strides long and harsh.

"Gavin!"

My shouts fell on deaf ears. Persephone was striding up the walkway by the pool, lazily yawning, but I called Gavin's name again and saw her perk up. Her eyes darted from me to Gavin, to the people below, and her pace picked up.

As if she, too, had figured it out.

The noise of cheerful greetings and hugs filled my ears. Everyone was exchanging niceties. *Everyone* was in the room.

I reached the bottom of the stairs just in time to see Gavin push through the throng of people to Aidan and punch him in the face.

Brielle and the other girl screamed. Hera nearly tripped, trying to back away. Gavin went in to punch Aidan again. Zeus grabbed Gavin and yanked him back, yelling that he wouldn't start a fight in his house. Persephone and I ran, but she pulled me back before I could interfere, her arms wrapping securely around my chest.

"Eros!" I shouted.

"You fucking bastard!" Gavin was pulling, yanking, spiraling. Power billowed out from his body as he fought Zeus's grip.

"—the fuck, you clobbering idiot," Aidan said, grabbing his bleeding nose. "What the shit was that—"

"It was you, wasn't it?!" Gavin nearly screamed. "You fucking took her, you cowardly little shit."

Aidan did a double-take upon seeing me, and the wildness in his eyes turned to mirth.

"Oh, my gods," the other girl said, her voice as shocked as everyone else's. "Is that…"

Silence fell upon the room.

Gavin stopped struggling. His chest heaved as he tried to catch his breath. He tore his arms out of Zeus's grasp as Ares ran up to his other side.

"What's going on?" Ares asked.

"Ask him," Gavin sneered, eyes never leaving Aidan. "Ask him how he *kidnapped my wife*. Ask him how he kept her hidden all these years. Ask him how he woke her up just to give her new memories and abuse her—how he tried to *murder* her after she found the strength to run away."

"Fucking Styx," someone muttered.

"Oh, my gods…."

"Apollo," Zeus said expectantly, sinking his head in his hand.

Aidan was… *Apollo?!*

"Tell me you didn't," Zeus continued.

Aidan—*Apollo* hadn't stopped staring at me. There was a crooked sneer on his lips, his dark eyes downcast, chin dipped. I knew that look. I had seen it too many times—that smug glint, terrifying and arousing all at once. I had once worshipped that look, had tried to pull it out of him in every way I could.

He dabbed at the blood coming from his nose, the sound of his boot on the floor breaking the silence when he stepped forward. "Hey, sweetheart," he said to me. "I wondered where you'd run off to."

"Don't you fucking talk to her," Gavin snapped, and Ares grabbed his arm.

Apollo's eyes moved to Gavin, and his smirk somehow widened. "It hurts, doesn't it?" Apollo asked in a deep, rolling rasp. "To watch something you love disappear."

I wanted to take Gavin's hand, to tell him I was there with him. I could see him shaking as he tried to hold back from beating Apollo to a pulp.

Brielle—no, *Artemis* was standing with her hand over her mouth. I squinted at her, feeling her betrayal in my knotted stomach.

We had been friends, or so I had thought.

"Did you know?" I asked her.

Her jaw tightened, regret filling her glistening eyes. "I'm sorry," she whispered.

"You knew?" Persephone asked disbelievingly.

"I didn't know until he started dating her," Artemis argued. "I didn't know what he had done. I didn't know he had hurt her!"

"Why?" Hera demanded. "Why would you do this?" she asked Apollo.

"I wanted to damage something he loved," Apollo said, his voice remaining calm. "So deep that she'd never be able to love anyone again. So deep that she would reject him just as he made Daphne reject me."

"It looks like you failed," I snapped, barely holding myself back.

Apollo's gaze moved from me to Gavin, and he appeared as though he might laugh. "Gods, I wish you could remember how fucking pathetic you looked after I took her that day," Apollo mocked. "You should have known not to bring her to Delphi. You should have known that I would seek revenge after what you did."

"Daphne would never have touched you anyway," Gavin sneered.

Apollo scoffed. "Yeah, but you made sure of that, didn't you?" He glanced at me. "Lucky your little bride was there to compensate for all those lost moments." He winked my way, and bile lurched into my throat.

Gavin flinched, but Ares was there to keep him steady.

"She made the most perfect little screams in those early days," Apollo continued, his voice such a sinister taunt that my skin began to crawl. "And she would have continued had I not grown so tired of her whining. *Eros, Eros, Eros.* She begged for you, sobbing every night, praying you would find her, and then during the day, she'd spit and scream and refuse to eat. So, I went to the Underworld, where your stupid friend handed over the same box of sleep she'd once given to Psyche for Aphrodite."

Persephone froze behind me. "I didn't… I didn't know…."

A maniacal noise sounded from Apollo when he saw her crestfallen face. "All of you. So *stupid.* So easily manipulated —"

The earth rumbled beneath our feet.

"Careful, boy," came Hades's drawl behind us.

Everyone looked his way, finding Hades leaning casually against one of the columns. Power seeped from the look in his eyes, the quake of the earth a mere warning of what he might do if Apollo insulted his wife again.

And yet, despite his threat, Apollo kept going.

"—none of you had any idea what was happening thanks to Aphrodite's memory botch."

He moved directly in front of Gavin, hands stuffed in his

pockets. "And do you know what your little wife did when I finally woke her?"

Gavin had stopped breathing.

"She fucked me," Apollo said bluntly. "She sucked my cock, and she worshiped me because I was the only real thing she knew. Everything else was fiction, and she was so desperate to fill the void you left behind that she turned into a foolish feeble mortal, ready for me at any moment to bend and break as I wanted her to. And fucking Styx, did she wilt."

"Chloe…"

My name hissed from Gavin's lips in an expectant tone, like he was asking permission.

"I heard you had to beg to get her back this time," he continued, smirking at Gavin. "I heard you sank to your pathetic knees and pleaded for her to love you again. Let me guess what held her back… Fear that you reminded her of me."

"Chloe."

Gavin repeated my name again, and my heart thumped wildly in my ears.

"I made sure when you found her again that she wouldn't be the same person you'd loved before. She'd be broken. Beaten down. A scared little whore that feared anything real. Because I knew you would fall head over fucking heels in love with her as you'd done last time. And I wanted you to know how it felt for the love of your life to run. To flee. To bolt away so fearful of you that they turned into something you didn't recognize—"

"*Chloe.*"

At that moment, I was signing Apollo's death warrant—if such a thing even existed. But with everything that had just been revealed— his stealing me, wiping me from existence, taking me away from my husband, and trying to crush and break and maim my soul to the point that I was unrecognizable and weak…

Tears fell down my cheeks, and Gavin looked at me over his shoulder.

My chin made a minuscule dip.

"—I wanted you to know what it felt like to love someone so much that you drove them away. And I hoped it killed her."

A glow suddenly erupted around Gavin's figure, and not even Ares could hold the god back from vengeance.

Gavin lunged at Apollo. Apollo tried to unleash himself, to rise off the ground and out of Gavin's grasp before he could grab him, but wrath ensued and consumed the room.

Gavin clawed and struck Apollo with his strength, fighting against the beams of sun that Apollo shot down.

Apollo was quick.

I screamed as beams struck Gavin's skin. I started to run toward him, but Persephone held me back. Aphrodite held me back. Artemis began to launch forward to help, but Zeus hauled her away. Other gods and goddesses shouted and screamed as the fight ruined the room and swallowed our world.

"Eros!" Ares shouted.

But Gavin ignored him. They were matched, strike for strike. Gavin yelled and groaned through the pain of Apollo's blasts as he grabbed Apollo's feet, and in one swoop, he wrenched the god down and threw him onto his back.

No wings erupted from Gavin's back.

No arrows pulled from the sky.

There was only his strength. Only the weight of his rage. Only the wrath of a god thought to be nothing more than an impudent, lovesick boy.

He released himself and began to pummel the god once thought to be good and beautiful into something unrecognizable.

Every punch of Gavin's fist made me scream. I could feel his fury. Persephone and Aphrodite held me tight each time I started to run for him again. Apollo's face crunched, broke, and split. He scratched Gavin's chest and legs. Shredded his clothing and emitted streams of light over and over that ripped Gavin's flesh.

The pain only fueled Gavin. Finally, his punches became more precise. Gavin's hand wrapped around Apollo's throat, pulling his chest off the ground.

"From this day until your last, I make this vow—"

The incandescent glow grew brighter along Gavin's skin. Thunder rumbled overhead. The room began to ring as if a bell had chimed in the far distance. The floor cracked. A fine mist hovered in the air as if waiting for instruction.

And that golden shimmer of grand wings appeared at his back.

"You will *never* know love," he hissed.

Apollo spat blood in Gavin's face, and Gavin slammed him into the ground again. Apollo's head bounced on the stucco floor, and his body limped.

The sun went dark.

"You will *never* know affection."

Power dripped from his words, the mist in the air thickening as it extended out of the room.

"You will *never* feel desire."

Gavin punched Apollo again, and the god's head jerked to either side with every rotating strike.

"Every person who ever loved you will look at you with disgust."

Again.

"You will be ridiculed, despised, and completely alone—"

The mist spread thinner and moved to the clouds. Darkness swallowed the earth.

"—Bound to wander this world the rest of eternity in

solitude and despair."

Gavin paused, his chest heaving with those breaths, fists bruised and bloody. And he bent down to Apollo's ear.

"And if you ever so much as think of Psyche again, I'll find you. I'll tie blocks to your feet and sink you to the bottom of the ocean, where you'll live an eternity gasping for breath. And you'll beg your petty father for the *mercy* of mortality."

With the last of his vow, lightning struck outside, sealing that promise with the power of Zeus himself.

I should have flinched like the rest of the room, should have been bothered by how the earth bent to his vow and how the sun had disappeared behind the mist filling every vacant space. But all I saw was my husband, sitting on his knees and staring at what he'd just done—for *me*.

"Eros…"

Zeus's voice was soft, the only noise in the stilled room. Everyone seemed to be holding their breath as Gavin rose to his feet, his entire body covered in Apollo's blood, in his own blood. And Apollo…

Apollo lay unrecognizable and unconscious on the floor. His face was beaten and broken to the point that I could see bone and tissue.

"What did you do?" Hera screeched

Gavin opened and closed his fist, still staring at Apollo. Rage, unlike anything I'd ever seen, burned in his glowing eyes.

"I became the monster he wanted me to be."

The tone in his voice made me want to weep. Tears continued down my face as I tried to squirm free, but Persephone and Aphrodite's grips on me were so tight that I knew they had left bruises on my skin.

Gavin's gaze met mine. My chest caved. An audible whimper escaped me, and I finally wrenched free of their clutches. The other gods surrounded Apollo in shock as

Gavin moved my way.

I threw myself into his arms, my body becoming sticky with blood when he caught me. I didn't care.

He was okay. Hurt, but okay, and I…

A sob choked in my throat as I pulled back and pressed my palms to his now-scarred cheeks. He held me tight, his body trembling.

"I told you I wasn't the knight," he whispered.

His forehead pressed to mine, and as the room descended into chaos around us, all I saw, all I felt, was him.

"Fucking Styx, will someone get him out of here?" Hera sneered.

Artemis's wails filled the room as she sobbed over her brother, begging Zeus to help him. Hera had grabbed another glass of wine, as had Aphrodite and Hermes. Persephone ran past us and hurdled into Hades's arms, who was still leaning just as casually against that pillar as he had been before the fight.

I barely noticed.

"Are you okay?" he asked.

"No," I answered. "Are you? You're hurt—"

"I'll heal," he swore. He wiped my face, eyes glistening as a rough smile flickered on his bleeding lips. "You never have to be afraid again," he said. "You're free."

A tremendous burden had been lifted from both mine and Gavin's shoulders. I felt like I could truly breathe.

There was something different in Gavin's gaze. I held his face, memorizing the lines and the way he stared at me. But something else…

I wavered on my feet, blinking profusely as I tried to gather my wits.

"Chloe?" Gavin's hand tightened on my face, my waist. "Chloe!"

"I just need…." My eyes were heavy. I couldn't stay

upright. My knees weakened—

The last thing I saw was Gavin's face before I collapsed into darkness.

Chapter Fifty-Three

Chloe

I woke in a room that wasn't at the retreat.

I was in Gavin's bed, back in California, staring at the silver ceiling fan above my head.

Fucking Styx, did my head hurt.

I wiped my face with my hands, pressing the heels of my palms hard into my eyes. Gods, I was so sore, so stiff… Why was I back home? How long had it been since the retreat?

Suddenly a dizzying feeling washed over me, and I was thrown down the rabbit hole of my past life.

Everything flooded my mind and body. It was such an overwhelming wave of emotion that I jerked upright and launched myself into the bathroom, vomiting all over the floor before I could reach the toilet.

And it didn't stop.

Wave after wave hit me. My head throbbed. Visions of life and loss poured through me. I was drowning, over and over, my head being forced beneath the surface until I was on the edge of breathlessness and then yanked back up, where I gasped for air and stability.

With every new vision, it was like a part of me fell into place.

Someone shouted for me in the distance. I scrambled to come back to him. To Gavin. To my husband. To Eros. I could see him sleeping as the wind snatched me off the ground, as a smirking Apollo met me with ropes and gags. A cage surrounded me that I tried to break free from. Screaming. Crying. Shouting at my captor.

"Chloe!"

I knew that voice. It filled my heart with warmth. His smile settled my throbbing heart in a vision behind my eyes.

My husband leaned against a table in the middle of a crowded room, smiling at me just as he always had—my husband who I hadn't recognized at the time.

"There you are...."

Candy hearts and stiff drinks.

"Sweet girl, I'm not your hero."

A Jeep and the snow. Pizza and a balcony.

"I think I could see myself getting lost again just to have you."

I struggled against the memories, pushing through them as he shouted my name.

"It's the way I'll never stop looking for you."

He was close. So close that I could feel his arms around me.

"I swear to you now, if someone dares to try and steal you again, I will use it in ways far worse than any mortal or god could ever imagine."

"Chloe!"

I was lying in the shower, the warm water pouring over my face. Strong arms surrounded me and held me close. I tightened my grasp on him, and he looked up, his beautiful green eyes meeting mine."

"Eros," I whispered.

I could see him more clearly than I ever had. All of him. Not just the man I had most recently fallen in love with but everything we had gone through. All of it into one beautiful person that I never wanted to part from.

A glisten rose in his gaze, and he pressed a wide hand to my cheek. "Hey, sweet girl," he whispered.

I kissed him, and when I did, my body burst with more sensation than I'd ever experienced. I felt him in my fingers, my toes, the pit of my stomach, and the hair on my head. I felt him everywhere, all at once.

When he pulled back, his forehead relaxed against mine, and for a moment, we savored how complete we were.

I noticed a large wound on his arm as we stayed there, another burn across his chest, smaller ones on his face and dotted along his flesh, and the memory of the fight filled me. I swiped my thumb over the one on his cheek.

"Are you okay?" I asked.

"Just a few scratches," he promised.

"And Apollo?"

Gavin's jaw set, the same darkness that had been present in his gaze upon realizing Apollo was my ex settled there again. His hands tightened around my own, and he kissed each of my knuckles. "Unfortunately, I can't kill him," he said. "So I had to do things that… Things that I might regret one day. But for now, you're safe, and you're here, and that's all I care about."

I held his hand to my face, watched his throat bob with his swallow. "What?" I asked.

"Zeus said your memories would trickle in over time. And the ones that weren't real would fade," he said.

I began to ache at the mention. *My family…*

"None of it was real?" I asked.

"The childhood you remember in this century was a fabrication," he said. "Everything before meeting Apollo, or Aidan, was made up. Memories given to you and your family for his ruse. Your childhood was as real to them as it was to you."

A sadness settled in me. "Will they forget me?"

He took my hand and kissed my knuckles. "We can talk to Zeus and find a way for them to continue remembering you, use glamour when we see them so that they see you growing older as they are."

"I'd like that," I said, thinking of the father I'd known in this life. I wasn't ready to let him go or forget him. Those memories had molded me, no matter the hardships that had come with them. I wanted to thank the god responsible for seeing what I had gone through and giving me a life worth remembering.

His thumb brushed my cheek, the warm shower continuing to pour over us. "I was scared I had lost you again," he whispered. "The fear on your face when you said Apollo's name..."

I remembered it. I remembered the terror swimming through my bones upon seeing Aidan, upon realizing who he was. I still felt it, but one look at Gavin, and I knew I never had to feel that fear again.

His lips landed on my forehead, my cheek, and my jaw, and then he pulled back to look at me. "It doesn't matter how many times they try to keep us apart. We will always find each other," he said as he took my hands. "I will always find you."

My heart skipped. I could almost see our souls entwining, the faint glow trickling over his skin and mine.

"And I will always fight for you," I whispered.

Epilogue

Gavin

An eastern breeze brushed through my hair as I stood at the edge of the mountain cliff. The sun was setting, cascading an amber glow upon the high tops.

I shifted nervously in my suit. My hands were clammy, and it was all I could do to not fidget or stretch my fingers in and out. A singular wedding band sat in my pocket, waiting to be slipped onto her finger.

Just Chloe and I—and Lana, who had had herself ordained just for this occasion, insisting that there was no way her best friend was getting married without her being a part of it.

Even if it was technically a vow renewal.

I turned my back as Lana saw Chloe coming our way. Ares had volunteered to carry her up so that she wouldn't have to hike the entire mountain in her dress.

My body continued to ache, knuckles still bruised from the fight.

I think I had lost my mind that day.

I only remembered pieces of it, mainly the smell of Apollo's blood and my own burning flesh.

And the horrified look on Chloe's face when she'd uttered that fateful word.

Arrow.

I heard Lana sniff at my side, and I crossed my hands in

front of me.

"How does she look?" I asked.

"Fucking stunning," she managed.

I started to turn, but Lana pushed my face forward.

"Nope, not yet," she said.

I sighed as I continued staring forward, my heart skipping every time Lana made any noise.

It was another two minutes before I felt a hand on my shoulder.

I stilled, every hair standing on my neck, and I slowly pivoted around.

Fucking Styx.

If I hadn't already fallen to my knees for her, I would have. I would have groveled before her and begged her to be mine.

Gods, she was…

If there was a word beyond stunning, beyond beauty, that was what she was. Her eyes were bright, her lips a subtle pink, her hair straight and perfectly in place, and a bouquet of sunflowers and red poppies in her hands.

And wearing a beautiful, soft black dress that had my mouth dry.

A faint blush rose on her cheeks as I rubbed my hands over my face, sure she was a mirage before me.

"What do you think?" she asked.

I had to take another step back and bend down over my knees, in complete disbelief that this was the woman I got to spend the rest of my life with—the rest of *eternity* with. Gods, my chest ached. Tears stung my eyes, and I pinched the bridge of my nose for a brief second as Chloe and Lana snickered.

"*Fuck*," I managed as I tried to collect myself. "You look…" I scrambled for the right words to describe her. "I think my mother would throw you off this cliff in a jealous spat," I managed. "If you weren't a goddess already, I'd have to have you declared one. Gods, Chloe, you're... You're breathtaking. "

She brushed the scar on my cheek, her smile softening. "So are you," she whispered.

I cupped my hand on her cheek, my body, heart, and mind stammering before her. "How lucky am I," I whispered, "to get to love you every day."

Lana cleared her throat, and Chloe handed her the bouquet. There was a book in Lana's hands that she opened up as Chloe and I joined hands. Nerves threaded my stomach as the sun cascaded on Chloe's face.

She was mine, and I was hers.

Wholly. Completely.

Finally.

Lana began to read off a story as she smiled between us. *Our* story. The poetic story of Eros and Psyche and the love that conquered eternity. It had appeared after the retreat, taking up space across the globe as though it had always been present.

However, there was one part of that story that would never be told, and we were okay with that.

My Psyche.

My Chloe.

My *wife*.

And this time, it was truly forever.

Acknowledgments

First and foremost, I need to thank my sister and mom, because without them, this book would NEVER have been finished. Thank you for being so amazing and supportive, and for grabbing my little dude when I needed a few days to focus and crank this story out!

A HUGE thank you to Alexis and Leighann for always being such amazing beta readers, and for always pointing me in the right direction with my stories. I cannot begin to tell you how much I appreciate you both.

To Kay, thanks for letting me throw emotional scenes between these two at you with absolutely no warning, and for supporting me during the emotional rollercoaster that this last year has been.

To Angie… THANK YOU for always being a rockstar and helping me with all that you do. You are everything, and I hope you know how much I appreciate how hard you work and how amazing you are.

To every person that shared, promoted, or even just told a friend about Sweet Girl, thank you. You all have pushed my career in a trajectory I only ever dreamed about. I couldn't have done this without you, and I hope this sequel lived up to everything you dreamed of.

Telling Gavin and Chloe's story was therapeutic, especially

Chloe's side. It showed me the gaps in my own life and helped me realize some things about myself that I hadn't come to terms with. I only hoped it helped some of you, too. Chloe's journey means so much to me. And for everyone confused about that dedication, if you go back and read it now, it'll make a little more sense.

I just want to say thank you to all of you.

My readers are everything to me, and I want to continue delivering stories like this to all of you, so thank you all for being so patient and supportive.

I never say never, so I can't tell you this is the last time you'll see Gavin and Chloe. I think we have a lot more 'exploring' to do, don't you?

Until next time, stay beautiful, ravens.

National Domestic Violence Hotline
1-800-799-SAFE (7233)
Text "START" to 88788

Other Works by Jack Whitney

Now Available:

Dead Moons Rising
Book One in the Honest Scrolls Series

Flames of Promise
Book Two in the Honest Scrolls Series

The Gathering
An Honest Scrolls Novella

Sweet Girl
Book One (Novella) in the Sweet Girl Duet

Finding You
Book Two (Novel) in the Sweet Girl Duet

Ballad of Nightmares
Book one in the Nightmares Duology

Anyone And You
An autumn erotica novella

Break The Glass
A Halloween erotica Novella

About The Author

Jack Whitney is an adult dark fantasy and romance author out of North Carolina, US.
You can usually find her playing in dark and strange worlds. Her characters are always in charge.
She is fueled by coffee, whiskey, and shadow daydreams. If you're reading her books, they probably came with a warning label.

Welcome to the Nightmare of Ravens.

Jack also feels very weird about writing bios because she's not sure what you want to know.
She is almost always stalking social media and procrastinating, so if you would like to find her to ask more questions, please feel free.
@Jack.Whitney.Writer